# LISHKA

## JAIMA LINDELL

# LISHKA

### JAIMA LINDELL

This is a work of fiction. Names, characters, places, and incidents are either the product of the author's imagination or are used fictitiously. Any resemblance to actual persons, living or dead, business establishments, events, or locales is entirely coincidental.
Published in the United States of America, Bellingham, Washington, by Jaima Lindell.
jaimalindell.com
Instagram @jaimalindell_author

Copyright © Jaima Lindell, 2024. All rights reserved.
No parts of this publication may be reproduced, distributed, or transmitted in any form or by any means, or stored in a database or retrieval system, without the prior consent and permission of the author, except as permitted by U.S. copyright law.
The scanning, uploading, and distribution of this book via the Internet or via any other means without the permission of the publisher is illegal and punishable by law. Please purchase only authorized electronic editions. Thank you for your support of author rights.

Hardcover edition: ISBN 979-8-9888714-1-5
Paperback Edition: ISBN 979-8-9888714-0-8
Digital Edition: ISBN 979-8-9888714-2-2
Printed in the United States of America
Library of Congress Control Number: 2023949928
First Edition

Cover and interior designed by Rena Violet (Covers by Violet)

Cover Photography © Kevin Hense

Map by Jaima Lindell, enhanced by Rena Violet

Edited by Killian A Thatcher, Cami Krema, and Jill Bailin

For Kendra

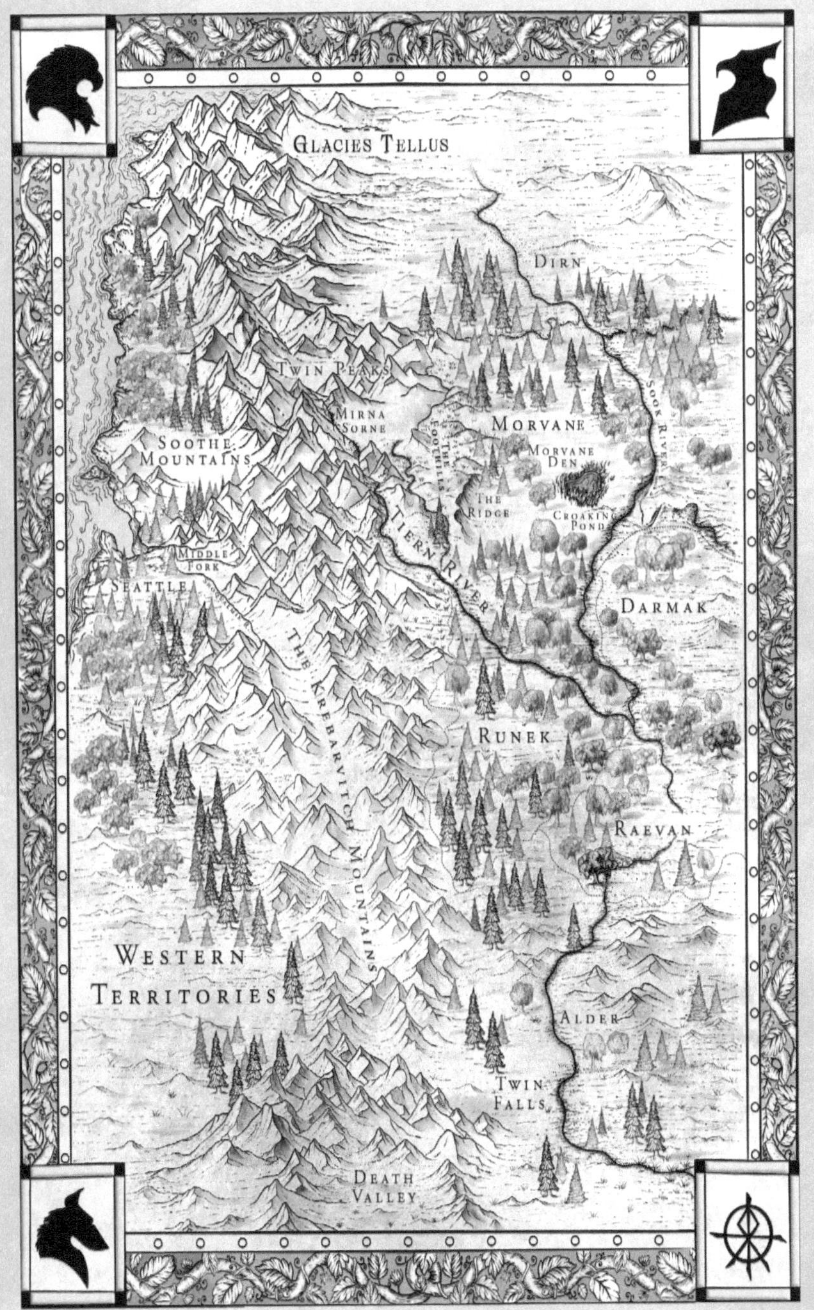

GLACIES TELLUS
DIRN
TWIN PEAKS
MIRNA SORNE
MORVANE
MORVANE DEN
SOOTHE MOUNTAINS
THE FOOTHILLS
THE RIDGE
CROAKING POND
SOOK RIVER
TIERN RIVER
MIDDLE FORK
SEATTLE
DARMAK
THE KREBARVITCH MOUNTAINS
RUNEK
RAEVAN
WESTERN TERRITORIES
ALDER
TWIN FALLS
DEATH VALLEY

# Contents

## PART III: Wielder

*The Finder will find the way*

*The Bearer will draw the blade*

*The Wielder will wield it*

*And break the world.*

PART I

OLD SEATTLE

C H A P T E R   1

# THE COVEN

RAIN POURED DOWN IN heavy drops to drench the already sodden city. In all directions for miles around, oppressive gray clouds hung low in the sky, pierced by narrow city skyscrapers. A strip of clubs and bars stretched below the thickest rainfall, neon signs humming in their dingy windows. Near the end of the row, tucked between its taller, flashier neighbors, a dark club pulsed. Music vibrated the peeling walls so that the building became not just a husk of wood, nails, and brick, but a living thing with its own pounding heartbeat.

Inside, an assortment of beings had crammed into every corner. Those on the fringes melted into the shadows to form one amorphous shape. The flashing lights in the mob's center illuminated sweaty bodies that writhed to the jarring rhythm, while strange symbols drawn on arms and backs glistened. A bar spanned the far side of the room where cushioned booths lined the walls, allowing those on the outskirts to observe those who danced.

Positioned in a shadowed corner, a young woman scanned the faces around her. She wore all black, matching the others in the club. Yet unlike the delicate clothes of the dancers, her garb served another purpose. A thick, laced top doubled as a protective vest, set over a long-sleeved shirt paired with fitted pants that allowed for easy movement. She crossed her arms in a casual stance, while her heavy knee-high boots designed for tougher terrain hid a spelled dagger. Her dark hair hung unbound to trail down her back, and she flicked a strand away from her pale face. A strange mark graced her forehead, visible only to those who knew how to see it: a circle dissected into quadrants, with a diamond shape overlaid in the upper half.

Her eyes searched the crowd.

He had been there the night before, distinguishable amongst the others. *Midnight* did not attract just any humans. Only a select few found their way to the club of shadows without invitation—mostly addicts, chasing either a high from Northern drugs rampant at *Midnight*, or else the thrill of proximity to death. The man she sought fit neither profile. Instead, he had sat at the bar and searched the unfamiliar crowd, his demeanor expectant as though he waited for someone. No one had approached him all night.

Lishka scanned the room once more. Still no sign of the strange human, although she did identify Darrak lurking in the far corner of the bar. The club possessed a motley collection of patrons. Their supernatural auras tangled with magikal drugs to form a chaotic and overwhelming blend. Yet despite the sensory overload, Lishka could not mistake Darrak's scent. She'd recognize *that* aura anywhere.

Sensing Lishka's attention, Darrak looked up to match her gaze for a provocative second before shifting focus, hooded eyes gleaming beneath reddish-brown hair too long for current fashion. Lishka followed his pointed stare to the middle of the dance mob. As expected, she saw Darrak's mate, Syral, divide the dancers to approach her Maker with a young woman in tow.

The woman, or girl, Lishka realized, followed Syral obediently, her expression dreamy. Her mousy hair had been teased into loose curls and her cheeks still had a youthful roundness. Lishka frowned.

*Way too young to be at* Midnight.

Letting the girl inside violated the Human-Prey Rights Code. This Coven law protected unwilling and vulnerable humans, including those too young to know the weight of their choice. Her frown deepened and she tensed, hesitating between intervening or ignoring the violation. Lishka had no jurisdiction at *Midnight*, and yet this bothered her in a deep and intimate way. As if sensing her conflict, the slightest hint of a smile twitched at the corner of Darrak's mouth.

Syral twisted back to the girl, opening her gray eyes wide to weave her spell. Her long slim body moved gracefully, and her gold hair drifted about her as though she walked underwater. As Syral led the girl closer, Darrak leaned forward in anticipation of Syral's touch.

The girl, now completely under Syral's compulsion, nearly collapsed across Darrak's lap. Syral coiled herself up next to them, entwining herself around the girl's limbs. Lishka noted the telling scars on the girl's bare arms and neck. She had been to *Midnight* before.

Darrak met Lishka's glare, the challenge veiled but

clear. He stroked the girl's hair, then tightened his grip and yanked her head back to expose her neck. Syral's tresses shone in the strobe light as she leaned over. A moment later, the rich tangy scent of life cut across the thick musk.

The energy in the club flipped, from an indulgent haze to full alert. Shadowed creatures focused on the vulnerable life, appetites responding to the blood in the air. Hungry eyes shifted to the dancing mob, where many legal volunteers lingered in hope of such attention. Others slipped out into the cover of night. Lishka ignored her own primal urge to feed and looked away, disgusted at the satisfaction she caught in Darrak's eyes. She should not have risen to his bait.

The twitchiness of the group around her itched its way under Lishka's skin. Her body, on edge from the lingering smell of blood, hummed with suppressed energy. The sensation of cool air and the dark forest flooded her mind; she longed for the scent of trees, the smooth caress of wind, and the solitude of a night outside the club. At once, Lishka grew tired of *Midnight* and those like her. Perhaps she would leave and search for the human another night. She took a step out into the crowd, and then, *something*. The slight twinge of a new energy tapped at her senses, though the scent smelled oddly familiar. She stopped and gave the room one last visual sweep.

The dancers parted as if choreographed to reveal the human man. He sat at the far end of the bar, facing out toward the crowd, with no drink or other drugs about him. Lishka examined him further and, despite the distance, saw no visible marks on his skin. *Strange.* She considered this. He did not drink, and it appeared that he did not intend to offer himself to the creatures of *Midnight*. Lishka felt an odd sense of reassurance. He must not be one of the piteous creatures addicted to her kind's attention. *Yet if he did not come to* Midnight *to indulge, what did he come for?* Lishka straightened, now intent on further investigation. To get closer to him, she had to cross in front of the bar. Before he could catch her staring, she melted into the fringes of the mob, using the dancers to maintain a barrier between them.

At first glance, the man did not appear to be anything other than normal. Wavy light brown hair hung slightly too long, grazing the tops of his ears. His thick eyebrows shadowed warm eyes that studied the activity around him with open interest. Rolled-back plaid sleeves exposed sun-kissed skin that couldn't be anything other than human, still holding onto the summer warmth from over two months ago.

He looked decent enough, for a human. Yet for all his outward normalcy, Lishka still detected a peculiarity about him. Using her sixth sense, she reached out with her own power to test his aura, the energy field that surrounded every living being. A charged sensation snapped against her mind, and her nerves vibrated as if she'd hit a live wire. In an instant she pivoted from exploration to defense.

The man did not move, nor did he give any indication that he'd felt her touch. The sensation quieted, the charge now a dull pulse. Lishka relaxed the slightest amount, though she maintained a guard against hostile response. Again, she reached out to probe the edges of this man's aura. Where normally she would have felt the warm, soft yield of humanity, in its stead a foreign energy flared bright in reaction to her cold touch. Lishka had never encountered a full-blooded human with such electricity.

Without warning, he turned to look straight at her. At that exact moment, the mob again changed its movement, shifting once more to reveal her face to him. Soft brown eyes met cool violet. Lishka stood perfectly still as only her kind could do, with not even a heartbeat to indicate life, while the mob flowed around her. Beneath his gaze burned a fire, and an energy so fiercely alive, she almost felt embarrassed to have missed it before. The man did not balk at the intensity of her stare but instead reciprocated her scrutiny, his aura practically glowing in the air about him.

With the shock of his boldness, Lishka became aware of her kind around them. In this place, danger lurked in every shadow. So far, no one else appeared to notice the man's oddity. She started to look away from him, feigning disinterest to avoid drawing unwanted attention. At the last second, she hesitated, curiosity weighing against caution. The man stood. Lishka changed direction, turning her face and body away from him to recede back into the club. *Midnight* held too many interested parties, too many of her kind. She would not risk a public confrontation with the stranger, not when any one of them might notice both her interest and his difference. The dancers enveloped her, and she drifted into them, her body caught by their collective rhythm.

On the outside, Lishka appeared immersed in the revelry. Anyone who observed her connection with the stranger would, she hoped, view it as a passing inspection, leading to Lishka's disinterest in her potential prey. Inwardly, she assessed the power in the club. She became aware of another's attention; someone else had indeed noticed her surveillance of the human, despite her quick detachment.

At the risk of piquing undesirable interest, Lishka slid her gaze over to the opposite wall. To the casual observer, Syral and the young girl she coveted had Darrak fully engaged. Lishka knew him better. Though he appeared relaxed, his shoulders and legs tensed. He focused too much on the actions in his lap, a sinister smile pasted on his lips as if to conceal his awareness of Lishka and where she placed her attention.

The man, she saw, had resumed his post at the bar, though he now scanned where she had disappeared into the fray. A brief battle warred inside her, until finally caution won over her desire to investigate. Darrak's attention felt fleeting, so far. If Lishka stayed to formally stake her claim on the man, Darrak might decide to become involved. He might watch her and notify others of her movements. Lishka needed to discover this human's purpose in their part of the city, and to do so she would have to remain inconspicuous.

Lishka slid through the mob toward the front door. A mostly human woman gyrated across her path, her skin covered in dark green marks. She teetered unseeing, high on a hallucination from the powder that had been used to draw symbols across her bare arms and upper chest. Annoyed, Lishka reached inside herself for the dark power, drawing the energy up and out to repel the woman. Even through her drug-induced fog, the woman experienced the power's cold touch as an unwelcome slap of reality. It reached her core, and she pushed back into the crowd to seek refuge from the source. Others quickly followed suit, dancing out of Lishka's way as she propelled her influence farther out around her. She allowed herself a small, satisfied smile.

A tall shadow materialized at her side. With reluctance, Lishka shifted her attention to Kristoph, head of the Coven's main security team. His appearance could only mean one thing.

"We have a problem." He tipped his head toward an exit at the far corner of the room, opposite from the strange man, Darrak, and Syral. Without waiting for her reaction, he strode toward the door. Lishka followed him with reluctance. Unlike her, Kristoph did not need magik to part the dense crowd. The dancers instinctively recoiled from the pair, responding to his severe authority. At the exit, he paused to face her with a familiar expression of anger, frustration, and grudging acceptance.

"What?" she asked.

"Nigel."

Lishka bared her teeth. She could already picture the scene that lay waiting past the door. *Goddess curse that stupid fool.* He would expose them all, against strict High Coven Order.

"He's taken too much. *Again.*" Kristoph opened the door to the cool, wet night, and gestured out to the back street. His black hair had been plaited to lie down the center of his back and did not shift even in the sudden gust that blew through the door. "We've hidden the girl in the alley, but she needs medical attention. Human medical attention. I've already called ahead to the hospital, so they're prepared with the doctor and alibi." He looked back at her pointedly.

"Why do I have to take her?" Lishka asked.

"Because you are a Keeper and this is your duty, as

much as ours. We are taking Nigel back to the Coven to be dealt with." He watched her for a moment, waiting for her agreement. Lishka unenthusiastically motioned him to continue through to the outside. Arguing with him would achieve nothing. She certainly did not want the alternative: dealing with an angry, blood-fueled Nigel, who'd just had his prey ripped away.

Outside the rain still poured, flowing into drainage grates that exhaled a constant steam. Lishka paused for a moment in the sudden stillness, droplets wetting her hair and face, the white noise soothing her raw senses. The city sounded quiet compared to the pounding in the club, though she could still feel the bass vibrations seeping through the ground. She glanced up at the dense clouds overhead. *Typical Seattle weather.*

Without looking back, Kristoph walked down the street and around the corner of the neighboring building. Lishka hurried to follow him.

Turning the corner, she grimaced at the scene before her. Deep, unnatural gouges marred the already pockmarked asphalt. The smell of fresh blood lingered below the scent of water and garbage, the enticing fragrance mixing with city rot. Lishka spotted the source in several dark splatters along the ground and the brick wall. Across the alley, a dumpster lay on its side, with the plastic lid half detached. Takeout containers and napkins sprawled out from its gaping mouth.

"Second time this month," Kristoph stated. "This is getting out of control. I've warned the Council already about Nigel, but they are reluctant to put firm strictures on his behavior. They view such constraints as 'unreasonably limiting the inherent nature of the species.'" He shook his head in open disgust at the Council's lack of policing.

Across the alley, six Keepers gathered around a single form. Together, Kristoph and Lishka walked over to present a united front. The others parted to let them through to the figure wrapped in strands of black magik that manifested as ropes. Nigel sat with his back against the wall, head tilted upward. Upon their approach, he opened his eyes and a slow smile spread across his pale face.

"Kristoph. Lishka." Sharp extended teeth glinted against lips crusted with blood. Rusty flecks broke off as he spoke. Lishka kept her face still, hiding her distaste behind a cool exterior. Nigel rested his head back against the wall, assessing her through slit eyes.

"Oh, come now, Lishka. Don't look at me like that." He pushed away from the wall and leaned closer to her. She stayed still, coldly returning his gaze. Darrak had gotten a rise from her. Nigel would not.

"You know you want the same thing," he whispered, still smiling. "You can hear the blood, feel it coursing, pumping through their veins. *Thump. Thump. Thump.*" He tapped his finger against the pavement with every thump, a soft sound unexpectedly loud in the alley. "You crave them, Lishka, just like the rest of us. Sinking teeth into their flesh and tasting their life, draining it from them. You cannot deny it." He leaned back against the wall, judging her reaction. "You are just like me. I simply choose to have fun with it. I do not hide, cowering in the dark, scared of my Maker—"

"That's enough." Kristoph's voice cut through. Lishka broke her stare and glanced up at him, surprised at the anger threading his words. She felt no need to tell him what he already knew, that the presence of a Northern drug lingered in Nigel's veins. Nigel closed his eyes, simulating submission.

Lishka took a step toward Nigel, her fingers already tracing the symbols to generate the magikal holding threads. His casual posture did not fool any of them. She heard the bite beneath his words, sensed the combination of drug- and blood-induced rage still flowing through him. Suddenly he lunged forward. The black ropes shimmered with power around his torso, cutting into flesh even as he strained against them. His eyes blazed red and the tendons in his neck bulged with the effort to break the magik. Lishka thrust out her hand, palm toward him, ready with the spell she had woven. At once the power rose to an apex within her, dark and twisting. She focused on the shape of the symbols, using them to direct the wild magik into purpose, now bound through the structure of the symbols to her will.

Kristoph leapt forward. In an instant, two Keepers jumped to his side and wrenched on the ropes, adding their own power to the threads and strengthening the binding spell. The force slammed Nigel against the wall and the sharp crack of his head against brick resounded through the alley. Momentarily subdued, he slumped down, coated in a thin layer of brick dust. Lishka let her hand drop, the power falling from her lips unbound to dissipate in the night air.

Nigel's eyes fluttered as he worked to recover from the spell. "Why should we hide?" he asked, his words bitter. "The humans are ours for the taking, they live to serve us, the superior race. In Zaral's Covens, we are allowed much more luxury, the freedom to live as we are, to take—"

"You are not in Zaral's Coven," Kristoph warned. "You are in the Coven of Zachriel. And as long as you are here, you will abide by his rule."

Nigel smirked. "For now," he said, closing his eyes once more. Kristoph's deft hands retraced a few of the marks, strengthening Nigel's binding. Lishka stood by his side, always on the alert. Her fingers twitched in a subtle mirror of Kristoph's gestures. Again, she drew the symbols of her own defensive spell, crafting the image of them in her mind to complete the final binding of magik.

"Lishka," Kristoph said, threatening to distract her.

She ignored him. Almost on instinct, she pinched her index finger and thumb to bring together the final line in the final symbol, to complete the spell.

"Lishka," Kristoph's voice insisted, breaking through her concentration. The symbols dissolved. Her movement stopped and reluctantly she let the spell go once more.

"Where's the girl?" She didn't take her eyes off Nigel.

Kristoph nodded at the entrance of the alley. Lishka pulled her gaze away and turned to walk toward the hybrid car parallel-parked on the main street. Once there, she paused to peer through the back passenger window. Inside, curled up along the leather seats, a slender form lay wrapped up in a woolen blanket. The cloth had absorbed most of the blood.

"I see you already volunteered my car." Lishka avoided looking directly at the stains spreading across the wool.

"Better get going. It will soon be dawn," Kristoph replied.

She followed Kristoph's gaze to the sky above them and sensed approaching daylight. The rain fell heavier and Lishka stepped around to slide into the driver's seat.

Without wasting any more time, she started the ignition and released the emergency brake, pressing her foot to the gas pedal. In a spray of water, the car slid forward down the narrow street.

Behind her, Kristoph's team flipped the dumpster upright while the rain washed the last traces of blood from the pavement.

BRIGHT LIGHTS ILLUMINATED the emergency entrance to Harborview Medical Hospital. Lishka pulled right up to the glass doors and honked the horn. She could hear the faint beating of the girl's heart pumping what little blood she had left through her body. This girl must be strong; she wanted to live.

Lishka suppressed the bloodlust threatening to rise within her and honked the horn again. A flurry of medical staff burst out of the glass doors, rushing a gurney to the car. They wrenched the door open and reached in with gloved hands, their voices calm but hurried.

"Careful," one murmured.

"Gently," said another.

Lishka kept her eyes forward, hands on the wheel, ready to drive away once they removed the girl. A shadow fell and someone tapped on the glass. She pressed the button to lower her window an inch, and gazed up into the doctor's face. His badge read "Dr. Steven."

"Ma'am, we need you to come in and answer some questions about what happened to the girl." Dr. Steven bent to peer through the narrow crack in the window, glasses already fogging from the rain. Lishka stared at him. The silence stretched beyond a normal response time. Dr. Steven blinked rapidly several times.

"The police will want to—"

"Kristoph has already provided an explanation for her injury," Lishka said.

"Well, yes, but we cannot just admit her like this," the doctor stammered, flustered at first by the interruption, then growing confident in his insistence. "The police will need information, who brought her." His desire to follow the rules displaced both his unease and his natural instincts warning him to obey.

"I trust you to handle it." Lishka allowed the bite to enter her words. Her fangs protruded the barest amount, and she let her stare grow even colder. Dr. Steven sensed the change in the air and blinked several times more as though he could break the intensity of Lishka's glower. He took a step back from the car.

"Right. Yes, of course," he said, all initial confidence gone. Lishka broke eye contact and raised the window. While the doctor had been busy speaking, his team had moved the girl from the back of the car to the medical gurney.

"Secure!" At the medic's call, they raced in unison back to the doors, rolling their patient between them. Lishka watched them leave in the sudden silence. She let herself briefly care whether the girl would live.

THE EASTERN SKY was aglow with orange- and yellow-streaked clouds when Lishka approached the stately iron gates surrounding the stone mansion and its outbuildings. The bars creaked open to grant her entry, her car recognized by the operator. She sped up to one of the side garages managed by the trusted human valet service. Though humans most often avoided her kind's area of the city, large sums of money drew some to work for the Coven. Fear also ensured their silence.

The mansion glowered gray in the early light. Lishka left the keys in the parked car's ignition and strode across the concrete to a nondescript side door. Once inside, an unfurnished hallway led from the garage to the main building. Lights mounted in elaborate iron sconces unnecessarily illuminated her way.

The passage remained quiet, as most of the building's inhabitants had already secured themselves against the coming daylight. Despite the stillness, Lishka perceived the tension in the air that had been present for months. A growing divide in the Coven's leadership created an unspoken pressure to choose a side, although officially, no lines had been drawn.

Ahead, the hallway opened into a grand, lightly furnished entrance room. Several black chairs and couches sat scattered along the walls, intended for waiting or study. Delicate in design, they added to the ornate minimalism of the Coven aesthetic. A decadent staircase, its iron rails matching the hall sconces, wound sinuously up from the center of the room. Thick dark curtains hung heavily across the tall windows that arched along the front of the house. To her left Lishka saw the door guards, familiar figures encased from head to heavy boot in black livery. They stood stationed at the main Coven entrance at all times, more a display of opulence than an indicator of anticipated threat.

Open hallways across the foyer led to conference rooms meant for nightly business, while the floors underground housed the library, armory, training arenas, and a large dome for the Council gatherings. Deeper still, at the lowest level, rested the sleeping quarters reserved for the Coven's oldest members, as well as guest rooms for any ancient visitors who needed the most protection from daylight. The Coven lay structured around the unavoidable truth of their kind: as one grew older and more powerful, the weaker they became against daylight.

Lishka stepped out of the side hallway and strode across the marble floor. On the far side of the foyer just beyond the stairs, a couple engaged in deep conversation. She glanced at them as she approached the staircase, before dropping her gaze to respect their privacy. Lishka recognized one of the two as her former mentor Mordan, his bold features unmistakable even in the shadow. A prominent nose swooped down between carved cheekbones to loom over thin lips, which right now drew even thinner with tension. Though he had been older for his time when turned, just shy of forty, his lean, hardened frame carried plenty of vigor. Mordan possessed the body of a man who had lived a soldier's life, skilled or else lucky enough to escape without any debilitating injury. His normally kempt hair now lay carelessly tousled, and as his gray eyes found her, Lishka saw the disturbance there.

The Lady Raseska stood regally beside him. Unlike Mordan, she offered a perfect picture of composure. Her ebony hair sat bound atop her head, crowning her unreadable expression. The silver and purple robes she wore denoted her high status as a member of the Coven Council. Mordan too wore his ceremonial robes, which matched Lady Raseska's in both color and style. Lishka noted the noise emanating from the deeper recesses of the hallway that housed the center stair to the lower levels. The Council must have just adjourned.

The two paused at Lishka's approach. Mordan nodded toward Lishka to acknowledge her presence. Lishka bowed her head to her superiors and continued on to climb the stairs to the upper levels. Only when she reached the second floor did they resume their frantic whispering, just low enough to be out of her keen hearing.

She managed to make it to the third floor without encountering anyone else. Scaling the last stair, she turned right down the hallway lined with heavy wooden doors. The wall between every third door bore a sconce similar to those on the ground floor. They each carried a magikal flame that illuminated the hall in evenly spaced shafts of light.

Lishka slowed her pace to think. Mordan had looked worn. In all their past time together, she'd never seen him so disheveled. She had not caught a clear word of his conversation due to their caution, which she found disturbing. The Council convened with increasing frequency. *What consumed their attention?*

Sudden footsteps sounded from down the hall. She started and, sensing the aura, mentally kicked herself for not paying more attention to the air around her. Now too close, the man spotted her, his eyes lighting up. Lishka had nowhere in the empty hallway to hide, her own room still several doors down and out of reach. She stopped and braced herself for the inevitable confrontation.

The man mockingly bowed his head.

"Sieth." Lishka spoke first, acknowledging him. The shadows that fell between the hall lighting stretched before him, elongating his angular frame. Almost all color had been leached from his body. Washed-out eyes studied her from beneath hair so blond that it appeared white. Even face to face, Lishka could barely see his eyebrows and lashes, which gave her the impression of a lidless snake.

"Lee-shkah," he murmured back, emphasizing each syllable of her name. His voice crept out dry and raspy, the sound of an adder's skin sliding across withered brown grass. "You are out late. I wonder what you have been up to." The words lilted over bared fangs.

Lishka weighed her response. She didn't owe him an explanation, yet offering no information at all would only encourage him.

"*Midnight*," she answered.

Sieth tilted his head at the defiance in her voice and he studied her carefully. "By yourself?" he asked.

She held silent.

He leaned toward her and sniffed. "You smell like…" He raised his pale eyebrows theatrically. "What have you been up to?"

Lishka resisted the urge to recoil from him.

"Nigel got carried away. I had to clean up his mess," she said, her tone intended to stifle further questions.

Sieth shifted back an inch to assess her, his face now cold and expressionless.

"There are rumors that members of the Coven are traveling north. Members loyal to Zachriel."

Lishka hesitated, taken aback by the abrupt turn in conversation. "There is always business going on. What difference does it make if they belong to Zachriel or Zaral?" Her words came as a light challenge, daring Sieth to acknowledge the unspoken tension between their leaders.

Sieth stood still as he considered her response. Lishka had no choice but to wait, unless she wanted to forcefully shove past him to reach her door. A long moment passed. Finally, Sieth seemed to come to his own conclusion and shifted, moving to walk past her. She kept her eyes forward and stood her ground, though her skin crawled to have him at her back. He brushed against her arm as he passed.

"Just remember who commands your loyalty," he whispered against her ear. She barely suppressed a shudder. The marked place at the nape of her neck flared, sending sharp sensations across her spine. She twisted away from him and walked toward her door with purpose.

"Oh, and Lishka." Sieth turned halfway to look back at her. A coldness spread over his face, sharpening the thin smile. "Nigel's girl you brought to the hospital…"

Lishka paused.

"She's dead."

# CHAPTER 2

# A FORGOTTEN MEMORY

DARK SAILS AT HALF-MAST rose from the shifting reflection of the night harbor. The wind that blew steadily had diminished and now only a slight breeze rustled the canvas. Stillness crept across the water's surface, broken by soft waves nudging against ship bellies.

Onshore, a wooden boardwalk outlined the water's edge. Twenty figures stood silhouetted against the bank, evenly distributed around a central dock free of moored ships. Together on the dock, Kristoph and Lishka watched the open ocean past the mouth of the harbor, waiting for the expected arrival. Lishka drew her long black coat tighter around her and adjusted her stance. Kristoph's eyes flicked to her, then back out to the water.

"Any minute. They said twelve."

Lishka shifted her weight again in acknowledgement. Moonlight shaped shadows on the docks, amplifying the crispness of the night. A soft scuttling drifted around the bins and wooden boxes stashed along the boardwalk. *Most likely a rat.* She detected no human or other noteworthy presence nearby. The docks remained abandoned at this hour, save for their greeting party.

Lishka reached down to the shielded blade strapped against her thigh, her fingertips drawing unnecessary security from the sword's worn pommel. Like the Coven guards, Lishka's own soldier role had become a relic, a leftover from more volatile days. No shipment had been commandeered in the centuries that she had been a Keeper, not since the early days of the Seattle Coven. Her hand dropped from her blade. Almost unconsciously, she reached up to brush the black brand at the nape of her neck. Despite the lack of threat in the harbor, she couldn't shake her unease.

"Incoming!" A Keeper called out from a short distance to the left, drawing attention to the open water. A tall mast manifested from the dark, its white sails presenting as ghostly clouds. The ship's upper wooden flanks gleamed against the water's reflection. Lishka knew that harder metals made up the underbelly, melded in its construction with symbols for swiftness and strength. Beneath the hull the engine rumbled, a modern addition that helped to shorten the month-long journey from the far south down to a mere week. The ship glided into the harbor, slowing as the sails lowered. Kristoph's unit shifted forward, preparing to transfer the ship's cargo to the Coven vehicles behind them on the boardwalk. Lishka resumed her guard stance, hand on pommel, and hung back with Kristoph.

The ship moved up against the wide dock and thick ropes tumbled from above. Swarthy sea men shimmied down to knot the ropes around posts, securing the ship. At a gesture from Kristoph, his Keepers moved forward to receive the cargo. The ship's crew dropped a plank from the lower deck to the dock and began to unload large coolers, stacking them for Kristoph's team to count and carry to their vans.

At the top of the ship a tall, lean man appeared. His limbs stretched out to an almost impossible length compared to his narrow torso, giving him a skeletal silhouette. Slick black hair twisted away from his face into an intricate braid that dangled down the mottled furs of his luxurious trader's coat. The man strode down the plank and passed through the staging of cargo, ignoring the activity as his subordinates moved wordlessly to let him through. Kristoph stepped out front to take charge of the transaction.

"Kristoph." The man's voice rolled out smoothly in greeting, belying the cold eyes and power beneath.

"Welcome, Fesca." Kristoph dipped his head in acknowledgement, displaying both hands with upturned palms as a sign of friendship.

Fesca drew his lips back over rows of small, pointed teeth in an unsettling semblance of what he must have considered a smile, his dark eyes appearing perpetually dilated. Those teeth revealed him to be other than human, though not like Lishka and Kristoph. Lishka watched the blood merchant, her fingers dancing over her blade.

"The shipment is as agreed upon. Seventy coolers total. Fresh." Fesca lingered over the last word, flicking his tongue out to tap his sharp teeth.

"From willing donors?" Kristoph asked.

Fesca smiled. "Of course. Generated from blood

banks owned by the Covens, though most of the donors are unaware. They think they donate to hospitals." His smile widened as his eyes darted from Kristoph to Lishka. Kristoph looked to those inspecting the product. One of his team caught his eye and nodded slightly. Fesca pretended not to notice; he had learned to be discreet during his long career as a blood trader.

Kristoph withdrew papers from inside his protective vest. "The payment as discussed." Kristoph held the papers out to Fesca. "These papers certify the product transferred, and that the blood produced is what the Coven ordered. Present these to the Controller for your money and credit. You are expected."

Fesca licked his lips as he took the notes. His long fingers stroked the parchment before tucking it back into his coat.

"You know, we can offer other…services. Why, down in the South are such delicacies—"

"We don't deal in human flesh," Kristoph interrupted.

"Other Covens are not so moral." Fesca smirked.

"Zachriel's Coven does not deal in the slave trade," Kristoph repeated.

Fesca nodded to Kristoph, a slow, laborious movement to overstate his respect. "Very well. Should you change your mind, you know how to contact me. As always, it is an extreme pleasure doing business." The smooth tones oozed like a rancid honey, hanging onto the air even after he had finished speaking. Fesca spun about and strode back to the ship, his body supple beneath the long coat as if his bones did not joint in the same place as humans'. Lishka watched him go, her eyes following every movement as he returned to the upper deck.

"You disapprove?" Kristoph asked. "You know this is necessary to survive in modern times, if we want to live alongside humans."

"I know." Briefly her mind darted back to the night before, to the girl bloodied in her back seat. "It's just, creatures like that." She gestured to where Fesca had disappeared into the dark.

Kristoph shrugged. "Business is business. All we can do is conduct clean deals and hope the other Covens will do the same." He moved across the dock to where the team collected the last of the coolers. Lishka stayed behind for a moment, studying the movement of the crew still aboard the ship. Magik stirred in several of them, a dark energy similar to her own. Some had acquired their power through temporary drugs, procured through clubs like *Midnight*. When spent, these stimulants left behind a terrible addiction to supersede all other desires. A select few had been born with the power that drew them into the supernatural world, as Lishka had been when human. Fesca's crew were the dregs of mankind, desperate to follow a blood merchant.

Lishka knew that her kind needed the blood banks to survive. Without their sustenance, far more humans would die to maintain their existence and slake their lust. Still, creatures like Fesca churned her stomach.

The final coolers being loaded into the vans released her from witness duty. From above, the helmsman called to take in the lines. There came a flurry of activity as Fesca's ship made to set sail once more. Fesca would not keep his ship in Seattle's harbor, out in the open. He would have a secret port further down the coast, to tuck in and weigh anchor so that he could return to the Coven for final payment. His crew would get the taste of land, alcohol, and who knew what else.

Waves from Fesca's vessel sloshed against the barnacled pillars, echoing in the space beneath the planks. Across the boardwalk, the sharp sound of a car door slamming shut concluded the transaction. The air stilled, the harbor quieted but for moored ships creaking on gentle waves. Despite the calm, Lishka hesitated. Her senses tingled with heightened awareness as if someone, or something, watched her. Darkness seeped up between the cracks of the wood to entwine murky tendrils around her ankles. The shadows thickened to become almost tangible. Lishka tried to take a step forward and her leg moved sluggishly, as if in a dream, half-stuck in the fog.

Without warning, a sharp prickle snaked across the nape of her neck. Lishka raised her hand again to press on her brand and stretched all of her senses to probe the harbor. The feeling of eyes intensified. Nothing. Only the fading sounds of vans pulling away from the boardwalk. No sinister being lurked in the shadows, besides herself and the others who had come to supervise.

At once, the feeling of being watched vanished. The inky tendrils about her legs became only harbor mist, damp and salty. Lishka surveyed the dock once more, unconvinced. With the release of the fog, a restless energy spilled down her shoulders, flowing through her at a rapid pace. The desire to feed grew, only adding to her edginess. With one last glance across the water, she crossed the wharf to her car waiting at the edge of the boardwalk.

Tires screamed as she peeled away from the curb and sped through the city, going well over a hundred miles an hour. She navigated the narrow one-way streets through

Seattle's center with ease, driving northeast toward the Great Lake. Lishka knew the city well, having been there at its beginning. Mordan had brought her to the Coven near the northern boundary centuries ago. Then, the trees had already been standing for thousands of years and the humans lived in balance with their world. Lishka had watched the settlers from the Old Country arrive, lured by the richness of the land and the dense timber. She witnessed the lumber town grow from a few shabby buildings into the large industrial port of today. The city's development, combined with proximity to the North, brought a multitude of supernatural beings to its core. Mordan had been sent there with Lishka for that very reason.

*I can smell the fey in you.*

Lishka shoved down the unwanted memory. The harbor always evoked feelings from when she first arrived on the Western Coast, regardless of the time that had passed since. She remembered the feel of the foreign earth beneath her heels, the excitement to explore a new land. She had almost felt free from her past, but for the brand that tethered her—a constant reminder of ownership.

Just before the strip that housed *Midnight,* a shift in the air signified the boundary change as Lishka entered Old Seattle. Along the streets, neon signs succumbed to darkened storefronts, and older stone replaced brick. Full, healthy trees became more numerous than buildings as Lishka drew closer to the water. The pavement transitioned to dirt, sloping down to a massive lake. Lishka drove up to the embankment's edge before shutting off the ignition and stepping outside.

Tall trees blocked out the city lights so that the only

illumination came from the stars and moon above. The lake reached out to the far horizon, its surface tranquil for the moment. Though she could see nothing but water from the shore, Lishka imagined the land that stretched beyond. A small island rose in the lake's center, connected to Seattle by floating bridges. Further east on the mainland, an uninterrupted forested expanse rolled to the craggy Krebarvitch Mountains, which crossed the country from north to south.

Lishka lifted her face to the moonlight and inhaled. Embedded in the breeze, coupled with the smells of cedar, mud, and water, drifted a warm, human scent. She froze. Instantly her nerves tightened, her entire being yearning for the human. She inhaled once more. The faintest shuffle of footsteps scraped against the earth, miles away on the southern shore.

Within seconds she calculated her next move. Lishka could not remember the last time she fed from the source, and her body ached for warm blood. The Coven allowed those proven trustworthy to hunt, with certain stipulations, though the Council often looked the other way at indiscretions. Lishka did not normally take advantage of this privilege. Tonight, with prevalent unease undermining her normal restraint, the deep hunger dominated. The shuffle sounded again, triggering her instinct.

With the full force of a predator, Lishka sped toward the noise. Her mind shrank to a single desire: the need for living blood. She crossed the distance in only minutes, earth and grass unspoiled beneath her step.

The scent grew stronger, and she slowed to move with stealth. Instincts pulling her to feed, she had parked much closer to the University District than intended. Ahead, the trees broke to expose a paved road that led to a small local park. She spotted her prey across the grounds, a dark masculine figure walking the circular path around the lawn. A thin trail of smoke from his cigarette rose into the night air.

Lishka crouched against the tree line, checking the area for others. No one else appeared to be in the vicinity. Silently, she crept along the trees, keeping in line with the shadows. The man paced the section of path parallel to the trees, looking at his feet as he puffed on his cigarette. He had on only a light flannel jacket despite the cool air, and jeans frayed at the knees. Lishka inched closer, then emerged from the shadows to slink toward him. The man kept his eyes on the ground, muttering to himself. Every once in a while, he flicked the ash from his cigarette angrily, as if having an internal debate. She straightened, now walking across the mowed lawn in long, deliberate strides. The faint whiff of alcohol clung to the air around him, mixed with tobacco. Her desire propelled her onward and when he finally looked up, she stood only a yard away.

"Oh, hello." The man flicked another spot of ash that drifted lazily down to the ground.

Lishka darted forward to grab his face in her hands. On instinct, he jerked back. She held him tight, keeping his face before hers. He opened his mouth as if to yell, even as terror replaced confusion. Wide eyes met hers and his entire body seized to lock him in place. Any intended noise dried up in his throat. Lishka dilated her pupils, pulling him under her influence. His eyes dilated in response and began to dull from the hypnosis. Beneath the flannel, his racing heartbeat slowed.

While he swayed in her grip, Lishka projected a numbing fog into his mind. The haze would erase all memory of this moment and keep him from feeling any pain. As the fog took effect, his body released, and he sagged. Lishka wrapped one arm around him and pushed off his hood. She tipped his head to one side, exposing his jugular vein. The vein pulsed with the slow heartbeat, entrancing her. She leaned forward, engulfed in his stale, human scent. The predator inside her rose. Fangs punctured skin, and she tasted the sweet, dark release of life.

Immediately, the black craving surged, and Lishka clutched the man to her. He emitted a soft grunt, but Lishka barely registered the noise. The life drained from him and poured into her, feeding both the power and the darkness at her core. Her veins hummed with the energy of his blood, her nerves tingled. The man's heartbeat began to increase, signaling the body's attempt to pump what little remained of the man's blood through his veins. Deep in her mind, Lishka realized she was approaching the point of taking too much blood. If she did not stop, the man would not recover. But she didn't want to stop. She shook her head and held him tighter. A moan escaped his lips.

Unwanted memory surfaced of that first killing. Her Maker's words flooded her mind, almost as though he stood beside her.

*I can smell the fey in you…I will make you mine. Feed, Lishka. Take her life for your own.*

Anger disrupted the hunger and Lishka wrenched her head up.

*No!*

She shoved the man from her, and he dropped heavily to the ground, legs crumpling beneath him. She stepped back several paces, fighting down the bloodlust. The copper smell hung thick in the air, and even now, she could see the crimson gleaming from his neck. She edged forward.

*No!*

She forced herself still. At once, the strange man from *Midnight* came to her mind. Again, his eyes found her through the crowd. The electric current sparked, emitting a charged warmth that permeated the bloodlust and pulled her away from the dark. Lishka closed her eyes at the ruined man before her. Instead, she focused on the rustle of leaves high above them. A coolness wafting off the water disrupted the heavy scent of blood lingering in the air. With the warmth of the memory, her body relaxed, the urge to feed lessening as she processed the fresh blood. When Lishka opened her eyes, she felt herself again.

She examined the man at her feet. He matched the stranger at *Midnight* in both age and build; with his flannel jacket, it could almost be him. A jolt ran through her and Lishka knelt beside him, her desire now sedated. His eyes remained closed, sunk within gaunt cheeks above a thin line of stubble. She reached out with two fingers to tip his head toward her. Guilt stabbed her at the sight of the wound on his neck. With tenderness, she pressed her fingers to his skin and traced symbols for healing. Even as she did so, Lishka drew power from a small rift in the Veil, the invisible barrier that separated the world's magik and energy from the physical realm. The mage's mark on her forehead helped to channel the energy through her body and into the symbols, and she stole a bit for herself. A comforting tingle, not altogether different from the memory of the stranger, warmed her core.

The flesh knitted together until no trace of the wound showed, except for the stains on his shirt. Lishka checked his pulse and felt relieved. He still had enough life to wake up on his own. A nasty headache would be his only indication that something had occurred, with no memory of her or the attack to justify it.

His limbs drooped as she lifted him up with ease. Gently, Lishka carried him to the sole car in the parking lot. Finding the car unlocked, she placed him inside. The interior smelled of him, a combination of his musky human scent and stale cigarettes. She arranged his open beer cans so that he would simply assume he'd drunk too much and fallen asleep.

Satisfied that he would be safe, Lishka stepped away and bolted into the trees. The force of her feeding caught up to her and she ran without restraint. *How stupid, to be so reckless.* She'd almost killed him.

Her feet took her to the northern edge of the lake, where the forest flowed uninterrupted by civilization. She had never been so close to killing her prey, at least not since her earlier days. Lishka slowed to a stop before the water. Without consciously realizing it, she held her hand to the brand at her neck, as if suppressing the mark could also suppress the memories of her first violent years.

The lake stretched before her, dark, calm, and unmarred by mankind. Lishka began to relax. Small tremors of energy vibrated in the breeze that blew from the north. Glacies Tellus, the northern ice land, remained wild to most humans. The lands that lay northeast beyond

Seattle grew increasingly sparse of human settlement. She moved closer to the water, the toes of her boots wetted by the lapping waves.

The image came to her of another lake in another country, centuries ago. She remembered the first tendrils of sunrise glinting over the water in those last precious moments when she had still been human. With that memory, the final words that had fallen on her mortal ears echoed through her mind.

*I can smell the fey in you. You may prove useful to me, if you can assure me of your loyalty.*

Lishka's fingers still covered the strange black symbol that graced her neck, the constant reminder of ownership. She had been only nineteen when she met the one who had ended her mortal life. He had come to her in the pre-hours of dawn, to the place where she often sat alone on the lakeshore. She had always found solace in the waters, as if somehow there she would discover the answers to her origin.

That answer never came, the only sign of her fey lineage reflected in the violet of her eyes. At no more than three years of age, Lishka had been dropped on the doorstep of a clan that worshipped the Mother Goddess. Her few early memories consisted of those devoted to the service of the Goddess, their teachings of the earth, and the harmony they found in daily life. That was before Christianity had spread like wildfire, wiping out the old religions.

Staring out over the dark water, she found herself humming a faint tune. She recognized it as a song one of the priestesses had sung to her as a young child:

*There is danger in the dark, my child,*
*Lurking in the night.*
*But pray to Mother Goddess,*
*And she'll bathe you in her light.*

*She'll wrap her arms around you,*
*She'll keep you safe and warm.*
*Till the Morning glow shines down on you,*
*To keep you safe from harm.*

Praying to the Goddess had not saved Lishka, and now *she* had become the danger to fear in the dark.

The shadows around the lake lengthened as the moon set, and the dense spaces beneath the trees grew even darker. The balsamic scent of cedar wafted through the night air. Lishka could almost see the lake of her past overlaid on the water before her, nestled amongst wide open hills covered in low grasses rather than forest. How different she had been, too, a young mortal woman standing on a wide pebbled shore. She recoiled from the comparison to herself now, her lips still carrying the stain of blood.

Lishka had not dwelled on her loss of humanity since her first years of being turned over a millennium ago. She wondered at her own feelings, at the cause for resurrecting mostly forgotten memories. With that thought, her mind again returned to the stranger at *Midnight*, and the electric charge that had passed between them. Lishka shoved away all memories of her past to distract herself with the puzzle of this human. His appearance at *Midnight* remained a mystery. The uninitiated human did wander in occasionally, but they never stayed long and rarely visited a second time. Very few humans ventured into Old Seattle by chance, though none could say exactly what dissuaded them from crossing the border.

He had looked right at her, as if deliberately seeking her out amongst the crowd. No human had ever resisted her influence before, or had blocked her access to their mind. That alone must be significant, though judging from his reaction, he knew not what he did. Despite wanting to dismiss him as inferior, Lishka could not deny her feelings of intrigue. As a Keeper of the city, she possessed the skill to investigate and answer the questions around him and his strange power.

Yet Lishka knew that her attention brought danger. An open investigation could attract the curiosity of others. The image of Nigel's girl bleeding in the back seat again filled her mind. Still, Lishka couldn't shake the feeling that *he* had singled *her* out. A disturbing notion, and one she must pursue.

Across the water, massed clouds reflected moonlight on their undersides. A gray haze had drifted over the lake, bringing a damp chill that lay unnoticed on her exposed face. The northern breeze smelled of snow and wafted sensuously through the branches above. Leaves shivered in response, mirroring the rippling water that stretched out to the far shore, now cloaked in low-lying mist.

# CHAPTER 3

# DOMINICK

WITH NO SHIPMENTS TO receive and no transactions to guard, the following night left Lishka free to do as she pleased. She returned to *Midnight*, isolating herself in the back corner as before, to observe. She surveyed the room expectantly to no avail. The man had not returned to *Midnight*, though there lingered the possibility that he had visited the previous night, while she had stayed away.

Lishka watched her kind, mixed in among the humans and nearly humans. Deep inside her the urge to join them rose, a desire to relinquish her tight control and indulge in the blackest cravings. That, and her near-accident in the park the night before, worried her. A weight pressed on her, that she might not be able to control herself next time. Lishka needed to remind herself of the feel of humanity. To do so, she would have to immerse herself in their part of the city.

Pioneer Square sat deeper within Seattle near the coast

of the Sound: human territory. Though her kind often used the harbor at night to receive needed shipments, the port bustled during the day, busy with traders and merchants unloading their cargoes of exotic spices and coffee beans procured from down south. Past the harbor, Pike Place Market sprawled along the city's coastline. Daylight would illuminate a market filled with rows of bright booths. Here the craftspeople sold their homemade goods, clothing, and colorful flower bouquets. The fish vendors fancied themselves the main attraction as they shouted orders and tossed the day's catch to each other across the constant crowd of spectators.

At night the market would be shut, and the docks largely abandoned. But not Pioneer Square. Full of bars and restaurants, this was the place humans gathered at night. Lishka drove more slowly through the one-way streets, approaching the row of bars one street up from the market. Humans gathered in groups on the sidewalk, smoking and laughing. They wrapped their arms around lightly clothed bodies to keep warm in the damp sea air.

She found parking in an alley and climbed a steep hill up to the main street. Behind her, the water stretched toward a distant mountain range hidden at this time of night. The peninsula marked the last landmass before the vastness of the open ocean. Lishka welcomed the sensation of the damp, salty mist on her bare arms. Her kind did not fear the cold as it could not hurt them, and so she enjoyed the heightened sensation against her skin as a reminder of living.

Enough humans loitered on the sidewalks, and entered and left restaurants, to make the city feel lively but not overcrowded. Lishka had entered that restless hour when evening dinner changed over to night festivities. A man walked toward her, an elegant black trench coat covering his equally refined navy blue suit. As he passed, he did not step away from the invisible boundary Lishka projected around her, but instead leaned inward so that he almost brushed her shoulder. Even as she continued walking, he paused and turned to watch her.

She knew what drew his attention. Her kind possessed an alluring power, the ability to transfix prey. Some humans found themselves pulled by this force even when Lishka did not compel them. Those wiser, less influenced by power, perceived that same allure and withdrew. Lishka ignored them all. She had no interest in hunting or otherwise engaging with the humans. Being in their presence, observing their interactions, would satisfy her objective.

Across the street, another presence made himself known. Lishka made eye contact with him and recognized a fellow Coven member, though she could not place him in their hierarchy. Based on the lack of a mage's mark upon his forehead, she concluded that he could be a lesser mage, or a junior guardsman. A scantily clad girl tucked herself under his arm, halfway draped across him in her eagerness to be close. Catching Lishka's eye, he nodded respectfully. She dipped her head in proper etiquette and walked on, feeling his interest return to his quarry.

Two blocks down, the attractive tourist bars faded into grungy establishments that refused any attempt to lure patrons. A nondescript dive squatted at the end of the block, alongside one of the city's last remaining hookah bars. Only a few people stood outside the shabby door smoking cigarettes, keeping their eyes on the pavement as she passed. These people lived on the fringes of society and knew to avoid the attention of creatures like her.

Lishka stopped at the dive bar. The place felt familiar somehow, though she knew she had never been there before. Surprising, as she thought she had investigated every nook of Seattle. The way the building sat firmly settled into the lot implied it had been there for quite a long time. No name graced the front door, and little attempt had been made to patch the broken sidewalk leading to the entrance. The building lacked windows that would allow peering inside, instead forcing a commitment to enter blind. Almost mirroring *Midnight*, this type of establishment did not seek out newcomers. Instead, locals and word of mouth must guarantee patronage.

Lishka opened the solid wood door to enter a dimly lit corridor. A large man slouched on a stool, waiting to card patrons, performing double duty as a bouncer in case of unruly behavior. He barely spared her a glance before returning to his phone and she walked by unhindered into the small bar. Despite the quiet exterior, inside the dive buzzed with tradesmen decompressing after the day's work. Many leaned against the wood bar that stood centered on the back wall, which had the name *Emmett's* stamped across the front in faded green. The position of the bar forced customers to weave through the patron seating and pool tables to reach their alcohol. An older tune played in the background, a stark contrast to the harsh music that pulsed through *Midnight*.

Lishka surveyed the room. The far corner of the bar offered the best vantage point, presenting a full view of both the room and entrance. She slid through the tables to claim a barstool, turning her body away from the counter to watch the clientele.

The bartender, a young willowy man with dark hair and a thin beard, leaned over to catch her attention. He had a small, glittering gem in one earlobe, and he flashed her an equally shining smile.

"Get you anything to drink?" he asked.

"No, thank you." Lishka barely acknowledged him and continued to scan the people before her. A familiar scent lingered in the air, triggering a memory she couldn't place.

"We have some great options here." The bartender rested his forearms on the bartop, clasping his hands before him. His shoulders hunched up as he pushed himself forward, settling in. "We have the usual beer on draft, but I could also make you a nice cocktail. How about a mojito?" He added a flourish on the end of the word, drawing out the second syllable. "Do you like mint? Some bartenders overdo the mint, but I've found the perfect ratio to give you just the right taste."

Lishka turned to him, irritation overriding her desire to surveil the humans. The bartender beamed at her sudden attention, assuming he had captured her interest and earned a customer.

"Or maybe you prefer something harder." He eyed her up and down. "Whiskey on the rocks? We offer the same selection you might find anywhere else, and at half the price." He winked at her, convinced he had her enamored.

Lishka didn't move, not even to blink. The bartender gazed into her eyes, his smile still plastered across his face. The two of them stayed frozen for one long moment. Then the man's smile began to lose its glow, locked in place without any warmth behind it.

"No. Thank you." Lishka broke the silence at last, enunciating each clipped word. The man couldn't help himself; he opened his mouth to push once more, no doubt another drink suggestion. Lishka tensed the barest amount, the cold wafting off her skin. He shivered. Straightening back up, he visibly shook himself and huffed to cover up his reaction. In an awkward movement, he shifted his focus to the customers waiting a few seats down, all charisma sucked from his face. Already, they barked orders at him.

Lishka sighed. Those humans disturbed her most. So naive and sweet, the bartender foolishly allowed ego to overpower any instinct for caution. He would get himself into trouble, and she hoped he never found his way to *Midnight*.

In front of her, at the table to her left, a gaggle of young women laughed over various cocktails. Silky tops revealed bare shoulders, while layers of makeup and styled hair put them out of place among the grubbier patrons.

"Oh girl!" the woman boasting the most makeup called out, her high voice cutting through the mumble of conversation. "Oh no, you never said that!" She let out a laugh for emphasis. While her friends tittered, she glanced over at the bartender, hoping to catch his eye. Her feminine laughter converted into an overcompensating cackle when she failed, though she garnered herself a few sullen looks from the locals near her.

Lishka looked past the group into the darker corners. She had sensed no others like her since the main street, yet the conversation with Sieth only a few nights prior had shaken her. He had known of her involvement in handling Nigel, mere hours after she had taken responsibility for

Nigel's victim. She couldn't be sure that even now one of his spies did not watch her.

The crowd at the bar grew, invading her space despite the coldness she emanated. Lishka debated using her power to repel them but didn't want to emphasize her status as an outsider. Already they must notice her difference. A man dropped into the stool next to her. Lishka ignored him as the warm, earthy scent drifted across her yet again. The newcomer watched her, pulling her focus. Irritated, she abandoned her analysis of the scent and turned toward him.

"Hello," said the man from *Midnight*, eyes locking with her own. Lishka went completely still. She kept her shock hidden, her face a cold slab of marble. In contrast, emotions played with a dangerous lack of restraint across the man's face. Wide eyes and raised eyebrows showed his surprise, as if he too couldn't quite believe she sat before him. Lishka returned his stare, and they sized each other up. He didn't say anything further, and instead seemed almost reluctant to speak again. He sat close enough that she saw the thump of his heartbeat in his arterial vein.

The pulse in his neck reminded her that he was just a mortal. Lishka possessed the ability to manipulate him into giving her answers he might not know he had. Though she didn't enjoy this skill, she could make the interrogation painless so that he would never even know what she sought. This time, she would increase her power to override any resistance. Inwardly, she reached out to feel the Veil. Her mind slipped through one of its cracks with the ease of long practice, to draw upon the magik that lived behind. Her mage's mark gathered the power and she willed the force to flow from her to this human, willed it to draw him in. Delicately she let the power dance through her eyes, sliding its way through to penetrate his mind and bring him under her control.

A hard wall met her touch, rejecting the intrusion. Her mind reeled back from the jarring stop as if a door had slammed in her face. The man twitched and his face tightened, becoming guarded as he noticed the change.

"What're you do—" he started to ask, confusion now splashing across his features.

"Be quiet," Lishka snapped, harsher than intended. She stared at him, as if she could pry the answers from his mind. No human had ever been able to resist the power beyond the Veil. He continued to gaze back at her, curiosity overcoming fear. Despite her inability to influence him, she could feel a strange connection, a bridge between the two of them. The electric charge about him drew her closer, and she suspected her presence had the same magnetic effect on him. Lishka used his unfaltering eye contact to penetrate as deep within his being as she could. Walls met her touch, same as before, as though he subconsciously protected himself.

A sharp sensation snaked across the back of her neck. She shrugged it off. The twinge flared persistently and then at once burned through her Maker's brand. Lishka abandoned her investigation to stand and scour the room. The memory of being watched on the docks pressed forcefully against her. *Maybe not a coincidence.*

Mirroring her movement, the man stood as well.

"What is it?" he asked. She meant to ignore him but, without thinking, shook her head in response. The opposing currents of people entering and leaving the bar made it difficult to see into the room's shadows. *Surely,*

He *was not there.*

Stretching out with her senses, Lishka detected nothing other than a warm human pulse. Even the brand on her neck had quieted. She turned toward the man with new focus, determined to discover more about him and how he resisted her influence. He must be some minor mage or witch linked to the Veil. Yet she detected no traces of magik in his being to indicate such ability.

Lishka captured the man's eyes once more, intending now to weave a spell of submission. In the space behind his shoulder, in the recesses of the crowd, soulless black eyes flickered. Adrenaline shot through her. The man shifted, his shoulder blocking her view. Lishka almost shoved him to the side, before checking herself. She didn't want to frighten him, not before she had her answers. Instead, she craned her head around him and again reached out to probe every crevice of the room. Still, she perceived no signs of creatures like her. But those eyes haunted her memories.

Mordan's voice echoed in her head from his lessons long ago: *The strongest can mask their auras.* Sudden alarm struck that she had been followed, that her pursuer would feel the odd connection between her and this man. Deep within her core surged a greater fear of who might stalk her now. She shuddered to think what *He* would make of the man's strange energy.

Abruptly she stepped away from the bar in the direction of the exit. A strong hand gripped her cool forearm.

"Wait." The man's voice resounded, low, melodic even, and surprisingly pleasing. Lishka hesitated, looking back at him.

"Where will you lead me?" His eyes bored into hers, searching for an answer that eluded him.

Lishka frowned, puzzled. She examined his face for some indication of what he might mean.

"What is your name?" she asked finally.

He released her arm, letting his own drop back to his side.

"Dominick."

# CHAPTER 4

# THE MISSING PROFESSOR

DOMINICK UNLOCKED THE DOOR and entered his tiny studio apartment. A lonely lamp in the far corner barely lit the interior, weak yellow light not quite penetrating the dusty corners of the room. Early daylight assisted, filtering in through the single window centered on the wall opposite the door. Through the glass, rows of tidy houseboats floated along the canal beneath a tranquil gray sky.

Dominick tossed his keys onto a scratched table by the door in a habitual gesture, not really processing the action. A mere five strides took him to the narrow bed shoved horizontally below the window. He flopped down onto the pile of tangled sheets and rested his head back against the wall.

She had been at *Emmett's*. Dominick had only stopped by for a quick drink and there she sat, a figure from dreams, amongst the regulars. She had been flesh and bone, undeniably real.

The first time he had spotted her at *Midnight*, that strange club full of shadows, it had been easy to second-guess whether she had really been there. He had only caught sight of her through the crowd of people, and from a distance. Now he knew for sure he had not imagined her. Deep down, Dominick felt the same odd connection he had in his sleep, knowing her to be the woman from his recurring dream. He had seen those strange eyes before, urging him to follow. *But where?*

The persistent dream had first led him to *Midnight*, a place he never would have considered visiting otherwise. Though he could not explain how, the building hummed just like the rocks he studied at North Pacific.

*And so did she.*

Dominick rolled over to the dresser that squatted a few paces from the foot of the bed. A small cluster of rocks lay upon a worn chemistry textbook, discarding dirt onto the beaten cover. He picked up one sample to turn it over in his hands. His fingers traced the familiar curves and the stone's glassy exterior glowed as if lit from within. Not just mineral or organic matter, the object contained something else. It emanated subtle waves of energy that vibrated the air and tingled his fingertips. The woman had felt the same way to him, as if she too contained a charged electricity.

Dominick sighed and tossed the rock back down, where it emitted a muted buzz with its companions. The woman had left the bar just after learning his name, with no further explanation or answer to his question. He didn't even get a chance to ask for her name in return. An urge to find her burned inside him. He had to know why she came to him in his sleep, how she had gotten into his head before he'd ever met her. Dominick had assumed that upon finding her, she would give him answers. Now he had only more questions.

A seagull cried outside, reminding him of the hour. Class wouldn't start until later that day, so he had a few hours to get some rest, at least. Though, at the moment, sleep seemed utterly unattainable. His mind whirled, replaying the scene from *Emmett's*. Dominick tried not to dwell on how it felt to have her beside him, so close but never touching. The woman didn't feel like anything he had encountered before, not in his normal life, or even at *Midnight*.

A weariness began to sink into his bones, regardless of racing thoughts. He slumped further into the mattress, letting his head slide lower so that he almost lay on the bed. Today he would be working with Professor McQuarry to test out one of their theories on the rocks. The test demanded operating all lab equipment with the utmost precision. Dominick would need to be alert and focused, without any distractions. He pushed himself off the bed to shed his clothes, hoping sleep would come easily and clear his mind. As he began to discard his clothing, he reached into his pocket to remove his wallet, mind already running through the test steps. He froze, fingers pushing against the empty fabric walls.

His wallet was gone.

LISHKA FLICKED THE smooth leather over in her hands. She sat on the edge of her bed, bare feet tucked up underneath her. Outside, light streaked the dawn sky. She forced herself to ignore the urge to rest and quelled the irritation that still lingered within her.

She had entered the Coven distracted by her interaction with Dominick, and found Syral, Darrak, and Sieth together, waiting on the couches by the main staircase. Had she sensed them prior, she would have taken the narrow corridor used by the cleaning staff. As it was, she'd come too close to slip by unnoticed.

"Missed you at *Midnight*," Darrak drawled. He lounged across the couch, his half-lidded eyes implying only partial attention. Lishka knew him better than that. As much as he tried to hide it, she sensed the cold, calculating mind beneath the relaxed exterior.

*He's searching for information.*

"I was there," Lishka replied.

Darrak studied her. "But only for a moment. Where did you go, leaving so soon when the night was still fresh?" His voice was deceptively light.

From beside him, Syral flashed an evil sneer in support of her mate. She sat with effortless elegance, the silky folds of her skirt parting to reveal long legs. A sharp noise erupted from where she tapped her stiletto heel against the marble floor.

"You know how Lishka is, Darrak," Syral barked. "Likes to be with the humans, pretend she's one of them." She released a harsh laugh.

Darrak frowned and rose in one fluid motion to approach her. He purposely stood too close, looming over her, forcing Lishka to either turn her head upwards or else stare at his chest in a clear sign of submission. Ever the exhibitionist, he leaned forward in an exaggerated move to sniff her, eyes closing dramatically as he inhaled.

"I can smell them on you," Darrak sighed, savoring the scent, before opening his eyes to look down on her. "Better be careful, Lishka. We are superior to them. You should only be getting so close to feed." He shifted to whisper into her ear. "I don't know what you're doing but have care. Play if you want, but you're one of us. You belong with your own." Lishka stepped back out of his reach. Darrak's eyes lit up, the small smile curving up the corner of his mouth.

Lishka kept her words calm and even. "What I do is no business of yours. Or anyone else's. I report to my *superiors* only." Her eyes flicked to Sieth. Sieth sat more poised than Darrak had been, with his legs crossed and one arm draped over the chair's armrest. He observed the interaction with some interest, a thin smile splitting his narrow face.

"Superiors?" Syral's voice twisted from her, drawing Lishka's attention. "You should show respect. You should know who your true superiors are," she spat. "Those much more worthy of the direct bloodline, the gift you have never deserved."

All humor, all cool control stripped away from Darrak's face to leave raw jealousy. Lishka almost took a step back at the fierce hatred but stilled herself to watch him instead. Syral, sitting behind him, could not see his expression.

"You should never have been chosen," Syral continued. "Not when there are other so much more worthy candidates." She threw her long hair back over her shoulder, a bangle on her wrist catching the magikal light from the sconces. "I will never understand it." She looked to Darrak, as if seeking his approval. The malicious disdain faltered as she noticed Darrak's stance. The muscles all the way up his back corded with forced restraint, and the line of his jaw twitched. Lishka stood before him, not taking her eyes from his face. She wondered what he might do, as Syral called to attention his deepest, darkest insecurity.

Syral could not help herself. "Isn't that right, Darrak?" she pressed. "You are so much more worthy."

Lishka glanced at the mage's mark on Darrak's forehead, the mark that had only been placed there many years after Lishka had earned her own. To Darrak, it was another symbol of his despised inferiority.

"Oh, I think our Master is well aware," Sieth said finally, his voice flowing like ice water. "He knows who is loyal. And who must be brought back to obedience." He stared at Lishka, and a cold sensation washed over her. At that, Darrak's lip curled slightly, the hatred in his eyes mutating into delight.

Lishka turned her back to them, veiling her anger with deliberate steps up the stairs. As she ascended the staircase, all three pairs of eyes burned against her skin, assessing her every movement, watching for weakness.

Lishka kept her control clamped tight until she reached her private rooms. Even there, she refused to give in to the fear that Sieth's warning had evoked. Lishka had searched Sieth's face for some indication that his Master drew close. She couldn't be sure if Sieth meant to merely subjugate, ever his Master's loyal dog, or if his words threatened something more. She thought again of the inky shadows on the dock trapping her legs, the sharp pain flaring in her branded neck. Her brand burned only through her Maker's will, though he had not sought to remind her of ownership for centuries. The image of black eyes in the bar flashed; combined with the other signs, Lishka felt sure she had not imagined them. She knew of only one being who possessed such eyes.

Alone now with her privacy, Lishka pushed out all thoughts and fears to instead focus on the human, this Dominick. Gently, she unfolded the worn casing and lifted it to her face, sniffing the hide. The wallet bore the recognizable smell of leather, but beneath that lay Dominick's scent. Tucked into the small pockets, she found a driver's license, a debit card, a punch card for a cheap local restaurant with three of the ten holes punched out, and a university identification card. *Dominick Michaels, student number 0016789.* She reviewed the driver's license, which presented more information. The little picture showed no smile, though he had a kindness about his mouth and eyes. His eyes showed his humanity, with intelligence and warmth.

Lishka examined his face for a moment, and then moved to his birth date, mentally counting the years to arrive at twenty-four. The license had a midwestern address, obviously outdated. Stuck in the clear license holder, Lishka found the information she needed. Triumphant, she smiled as she pulled out the white paper card with a local address and contact number written in cramped handwriting. She recognized the location as somewhere near North Pacific University, along the water. The University District sat closer to the boundary of Old Seattle, but at a far enough distance for the students to feel moderately safe.

After committing the address to memory, Lishka tucked the cards back into their proper pockets. She folded the wallet and placed it on the nightstand, next to a decadent lamp. Then she lay back into the soft pillows to think. *He's a student, so he won't be home during the day.* Lishka considered the day of the week; when one had lived as long as she, every night melded into the next. Using the blood shipment from several days ago as a marker, she concluded that it was Tuesday. Taking into account standard lecture class times, Dominick would most likely be out between the hours of ten and two.

Lishka's restlessness hardened into determined resolution. Now she would get the chance to glean real information about Dominick. Invading his private space should reveal what she wanted to know: why he sought her out and how he possessed such unknown power. In daytime, no one from the Coven would be awake to follow her. Lishka hesitated for a moment as the early daylight dragged on her mind, pulling her to sleep. She shook herself, pushing against the sensation. It had been a cloudy night, which would blend into an overcast day. With adequate cover, she could withstand the light. She gazed up at the canopied fabric above her, not really seeing the pattern. During the day she would investigate him.

*And if I don't like what I find?* Lishka's eyes narrowed at the canopy. Then the night that followed would be for the hunt.

As PREDICTED, DARK clouds blanketed the morning when Lishka left the mansion. She slipped out of her suite and glided down the stairs to the main foyer. At the foot of the stairs, she paused to check the human guards posted at the Coven entrance. She could alter their memory and make them forget that she'd ever passed. Then again, only the strongest Master Mages possessed the ability to cast magik untainted by the caster's signature. To leave her magikal footprint on the guards might only raise more suspicion, and there should be no reason for them to be questioned in the first place.

*Unless Sieth or Darrak have grown more suspicious than they let on.* She shook off her misgivings, determined to follow through with her plan. Again, Dominick's gaze flitted through her mind. His words echoed in her ears.

*Where will you lead me?*

The need to find him intensified. There had been no time to figure out what his words meant, no time to question his visit to *Midnight.* She had lingered too long with him already and risked attracting attention. Once more, Lishka remembered the black eyes. A chill slithered down her spine, though she resisted the urge to give in to her suspicion. Doing so would only dissuade her from investigating Dominick.

She crossed the main entryway to pass through the connecting hallway that led to the Coven's garage. Fluorescent lighting hummed above rows of sleek cars varying in degree of luxury. Lishka strode over to her vehicle of choice, nodding to the gate operator in his security booth at the garage entrance. He barely acknowledged her, used to showing discretion when it came to his employers' movements. Cameras lined the booth, allowing him a complete view of the surrounding exterior, including both courtyards.

Lishka slid into the car and drew her coat's wide hood up over her head. Both the tinted windows and her heavy hood offered reasonable protection against the early light.

The car started up almost silently, and she drove out of the garage and the circular courtyard, pausing just long enough for the gate's iron bars to swing open before she passed through. As she cruised down the hill on which the mansion stood, Lishka gave silent thanks for the trees lining the street that hid her from both the light and any unwanted attention.

Moving closer into the heart of the city, the mist off the ocean began to dissipate, replaced by a manufactured haze from the industrial centers at the south end. Lishka drove southeast toward the rippling waters of Portage Bay and the university that sprawled along its northern bank. After a few narrow bends and twists, she soon found herself in a residential suburb closer to the east end of campus. Dominick's apartment lay nestled a block back from the man-made canal, angled to overlook the water. The row of shabby apartments stood in contrast to the gothic elegance of gargoyles and turrets that marked the main academic halls several blocks away.

Lishka pulled the car around the back of a narrow four-story building and parked discreetly in the corner of the lot. She readjusted her hood to cover her face and exited the car. Trees shadowed the parking spaces, and she used their shelter to safely traverse the lot. As she approached the entrance, the apartment's main door banged open to reveal a young college student. The woman balanced a thermos in one hand and a half-open backpack in the other, trying to stuff a book into her bag as she rushed to her car. Giving up, she tossed the book and bag into a small green Geo Metro before jumping in herself. Flimsy tires squealed against the asphalt in protest as she peeled out of the parking lot. Lishka turned back toward the building. In her hurry, the girl had left the door ajar. Lishka slid through, letting the door shut gently behind her.

She soon found that she needn't bother with caution. Stains on the walls, combined with the lack of locks on the main door and windows, indicated general neglect. The ground floor hallway stretched before her, dimly lit from overhead. Several of the bulbs had blown and had not been replaced. She sensed some small movements within a few of the apartments, the stirring of inhabitants getting ready for their day.

Dominick's address had included his apartment number, 305. Lishka scanned the visible part of the stairway to her right, and seeing no one, began to climb. At the third level, she exited into a hallway matching that on the ground floor. Doors lined the corridor, while a dirty window in the wall behind her faced the parking lot and neighboring laundromat. The faint sound of a dryer drifted up through the single pane, combining with other city noises to emit a dull static.

Dominick's apartment stood exactly midway down the hall. Lishka tested the doorknob by jiggling it in her hand. At least Dominick had some sense and had locked the door. Choosing to save his door from damage, she pressed her fingers against the crack between door and wall, right over the lock. She reached for the power beyond the Veil, borrowing a thin thread of magik to send it into the locking mechanism. A low click sounded as she turned the knob and pushed the door open.

At first glance, she found the space to be cramped and ill-lit. She crossed the threshold and closed the door behind her, relocking it from within. The smell of Dominick filled the room, overriding the building's subtle moldiness. She stood in a small entranceway, with a full view of the studio. To her left, an open door revealed his tiny bathroom with a cracked tub. At her right, an archway led into a compact kitchen, with a cut-out space over the sink and counter that allowed one to view the full room. Several dirty dishes lay in the sink, though the countertop had been wiped clean.

Four short steps brought her into the main living space. An unmade bed had been pushed horizontally against the far wall, the light from a single window revealing rumpled dark blue sheets. Against the wall opposite the foot of the bed stood a dresser that supported an archaic box television. She wouldn't have been at all surprised to see a rabbit-ears antenna atop the box, but instead, a connecting cord snaked around to plug into the peeling drywall. Next to the television, a haphazard stack of books and notebooks covered the dresser's surface, overflowing into an open drawer.

The dresser appeared to be the most promising source of information. Lishka pawed through the clutter, searching for anything useful that would give her answers to Dominick. The textbooks had been well-used, with battered spines that revealed glimpses of the inner cardboard casing. *Advanced Chemistry* lay on the top of the pile, a wide, heavy book and of little interest. She set it aside and picked up a thinner, glossy book with illustrations of minerals on the cover, some sort of identification guide. As she flipped through the pages, Lishka saw that some contained handwritten notes. She dropped the guide on top of the chemistry book and continued to rummage through the notebooks and papers, all filled with the same narrow handwriting as the address card in Dominick's wallet. A pulsing increased against her temples. Her fingers grazed the top of something hard and smooth amidst the papers. She grasped the object, its energy calling out to her from the pile, and picked it up.

A rock.

Lishka brought the rock to her face for closer inspection. It appeared to be made of a glassy material. *Not just a rock.* She held it to her ear. The thrumming did not produce a sound per se, but instead triggered her sixth sense. A faint yet recognizable energy stirred within. Somehow, the power beyond the Veil had been trapped inside this smooth exterior. She frowned, sensing it move within its prison. No human, least of all a student, should possess such an object. She had not heard of stone containing magik before, not without the intervention of a witch or one of her kind, and she sensed no signature upon it.

*Kiaban would know where it came from.*

Still holding the stone, Lishka sifted through the rest of the papers. Two more rocks shuffled into the light. The fact that the rocks lay so casually about the studio led her to believe Dominick must not know what he possessed. Lishka examined the other two, then pocketed the one she held and restacked the papers across the others. The mineral guide took on new meaning and she flipped through it once more, though none of his notes made any sense. *What is he up to?*

Lishka lingered over his notes, deliberating whether to also take the pages with her. The work could be related to the stones, though from what she had seen so far, the writing depicted standard lecture notes and included nothing insightful regarding the rocks. Lishka left the notebooks in place to focus on the other side of the dresser. Several framed pictures lay stacked amidst the clutter. She picked up the first. A middle-aged man and woman smiled at her from beside a lake that glimmered in late-day sunshine. The photo's torn edges were visible within the cheap frame. She set it aside. Below rested a more recent photograph that showcased a grinning Dominick. His smile stretched wide and genuine, crinkling the corners of his eyes. A woman stood beside him. With her brown eyes and long curly brown hair, Lishka guessed she must be a relative, perhaps Dominick's sister. Dominick had his arm thrown comfortably about her shoulders, with a carefreeness that Lishka had not seen in the man at the bar.

Lishka stared at the picture for a moment longer, intrigued by the familial warmth foreign to her. The noise of a door slamming shut brought her back to the present and she set the picture down. She peered out the window, avoiding the touch of daylight on her skin. Houseboats bobbed up and down in the canal, with no sign of any residents on the pavement directly below. The noise had come from inside. Floorboards creaked with hurried footsteps in the hall, and as Lishka focused on the sound, she heard more movement in the surrounding apartments. The morning activity of students with late-start classes or early-afternoon jobs had begun.

Lishka glanced back over the room, scanning for any other clue she might have missed. Nothing of interest stood out. She sat down on the edge of the bed, the springs firm through the thin mattress. A deep exhaustion rose from her core, that inner clock signaling her to seek shelter from the day. She took a deep breath to inhale Dominick's scent. The human musk mixed with a hint of summer sun had become all too familiar. Almost too comforting, the scent lulled her toward sleep. Lishka shook herself. She needed to return to the Coven before the instinct to sleep became too strong to drive.

A piece of gray on the night table caught her eye. Lishka might have missed it, had she not sat on the bed. The paper lay mostly buried beneath the black alarm clock, as if, unlike the rocks, it had been intentionally hidden. Lishka pinched the edge to pull out a heavily creased newspaper clipping. The article's title was MISSING PROFESSOR and went on to explain:

Professor Barry Coleman, age 43, disappeared last Thursday, September 27. His family reported him missing when he failed to return home from work that evening. The police are conducting an investigation into the disappearance but have not yet indicated any leads. Coleman was last seen leaving the North Pacific University Geology Laboratory by two students, whose names have not been released. According to witnesses, nothing seemed amiss. The students have been brought in for further questioning. Coleman's disappearance may be related to the murder of Professor Rene Miller, though no evidence has been announced to support this theory. Both Miller and Coleman were leading a new study on unique properties found in Northern minerals.

Lishka wondered if Dominick had been one of the students to last see the professor. Judging from both the books and rocks, he looked to be studying geology. He must have known the professor, to have kept the article. The rock hummed in her coat pocket, responding to her attention. *Properties found in Northern minerals.* Many of the Covens would not like humans investigating the magik beyond the Veil. Most still wished for secrecy, and the power that came with being invisible.

Despite her efforts to process this information and remain alert, her eyelids drooped. The bed tempted her to lie down, just for a moment. She forced herself up off the bed and walked over to the door. At the entrance, she paused. After a moment's thought, she withdrew the stolen wallet from her pocket and placed it on the small table by the door. She no longer had use for it, and she knew with certainty that Dominick would seek her out. If he didn't, she knew now where to find him.

First, he had come to *Midnight* with no clear invitation or motive. Then he showed an unusual power—a nonhuman energy within a human body. Now, she had found an artifact with the power beyond the Veil, so casually located in his apartment. Rather than find answers, she had only more questions.

Lishka knew where she must go next. These rocks presented a disturbing piece of the puzzle. There was one person in the Coven who might understand the stone, who might have answers to the mystery that appeared to be growing around Dominick.

# CHAPTER 5

# KIABAN'S THEORY

"WHAT IS IT?" LISHKA leaned across the smooth metal examiner's table, eyeing the object Kiaban held in his hands. They stood two floors below ground level in a room deep within the Coven armory. Thick stone walls surrounded them, cold but for the door on the wall opposite the lab's entrance, which emanated constant heat. Beyond this door stood Kiaban's forge and tools for crafting the beautiful swords that earned him his reputation as the best bladesmith in all nine Covens.

While she waited for his answer, Lishka's gaze drifted to the wall behind Kiaban, which boasted rows of leather-bound books, their spines cracking with age. Her fingers itched to open the books, to study Kiaban's spells and weapon designs, but she restrained herself out of respect. Kiaban alone could open these journals, unless he elected to bestow permission on another. She glanced around the familiar room. The only other furniture consisted of a wheeled metal cart beside the entrance door, which contained a pile of glinting weaponry. Unfinished steel blades glimmered with half-cast symbols for strength and the unmaking of magikal flesh.

From his workshop and the greater armory, Kiaban ran both the Department of Modern Technology and the Department of Old World Weaponry. These two institutions held the responsibility for creating, maintaining, and monitoring all equipment and weaponry used in the Coven.

Kiaban stood silent for a moment longer, turning over in his hands the rock Lishka had stolen from Dominick's apartment. Despite centuries of living without the touch of daylight, Kiaban's skin still retained its original darkness. Thick, intricate braids bound his heavy black hair, which had been gathered by a loose tie to trail down his back. His cheekbones bore faded concentric circles, tattoos representative of a long-dead culture.

"Where did you say you found it?" Kiaban asked, studying the object.

"Somewhere in the city." Lishka kept her tone casual, as if the location did not matter. Kiaban glanced up, eyebrows raised, before returning to his examination.

"Well?" Lishka prompted him.

"It's definitely a remnant of the power beyond the Veil trapped inside." Kiaban's words lilted with a slight accent that, same as his tattoos, could no longer be linked to a known origin except by those like Kiaban. "Odd that the power is contained within, as the rock has not been spelled to hold it," he added. "This vessel has formed naturally." Kiaban turned it about, his fingers searching for any fissures in the stone and finding none. The power remained whole and contained within the natural-made prison.

"It's like…" Kiaban paused, forming his hypothesis. "You know when lightning hits sand? The extreme heat melts the grains and when it cools it becomes glass." He scanned Lishka's face to check on her understanding, his ice blue eyes flashing with excitement.

"Yes," Lishka replied, beginning to see his theory develop.

"Well, it's the same with this. A small bit of energy beyond the Veil must have leaked through the Veil's cracks. These cracks increase in frequency and size farther north, as the Veil is thinner. In the South, such fractures are fewer and much more minute, making it difficult for our mages to draw out the power, though not impossible…" Kiaban trailed off, then roused himself. "The rock absorbed the energy and the potency instantly fused the particles together to create a seamless container, trapping the energy inside. Altogether, it makes the perfect vessel for preserving the power beyond the Veil."

He held the rock out to her and Lishka took it, examining the stone once more herself. The power pulsed inside, like the rock's little heartbeat.

Kiaban's expression grew serious.

"Now that I think of it, I have heard rumors of local scientists investigating a strange mineral up north. They say this mineral has unusual properties, including the ability to generate its own energy. I had thought it simply another one of their stories about the North, just exaggerated tales brought down from fur traders. Maybe there is truth to this one, after all." His frown intensified. "If it is true, and the evidence you're holding appears to point that way, then I fear what might happen should humans pursue the study."

*Dominick had the stone.* Trepidation nudged at the corners of Lishka's mind as she recalled the books on geology. The weight of Kiaban's words hung in the air as they both considered what humans could do with this discovery. Again, Lishka wondered whether Dominick knew what the stone contained. *Perhaps he knows more of our world than he let on.* A thought occurred to her.

"How would humans even sense the power, to study it in the first place?"

Kiaban considered her question. "The vessel appears to not only contain but also to concentrate the power. It feels like a rather low dose, but it's still much more potent than if the energy flowed naturally in the physical world."

His explanation aligned with Lishka's understanding that, once escaped into their physical world, the power beyond the Veil dispersed. Only symbols or witch magik controlled the power and kept it from dilution. *Or consumption by magikal appetites.* Lishka felt a twinge deep inside that yearned for the power beyond the Veil.

"The potency in this energy means that a human with any magikal sensitivity might be able to feel it. Perhaps, say, an undiscovered witch, one without a coven or mentor to guide them. They would have to be a weak witch, unable to detect the power beyond the Veil outside of the stones," Kiaban added, seeing Lishka about to argue this theory. "Though even some humans may possess magikal sensitivity without any further ability to draw upon it. If such a person fell into science instead, using physics and human law to rationalize the natural world, they could default to using technology to investigate." Kiaban gestured toward the stone in Lishka's hands. "Even in such a small vessel, the power is strong. If humans have discovered a method of detection, I have no doubt they will likewise find a way to harness the energy."

"How could they do so?" Lishka asked. She found it difficult to fathom humans using science to access the power, when technology and magik refused to mix except when crafted together by the most skilled artists—artists like Kiaban himself, who already possessed some of the power, by nature of his being. "Harness it? The only mortals who can utilize the power are witches."

"That is more or less true, though there are humans who exist with other lineage that grants them magikal ability." His eyes flicked to hers as if to call attention to her own other-than-human origins. "But humans are developing rapidly. They show an unrivaled curiosity coupled with an urge to control their world. I would not be surprised if they find a way to use science, and not magikal affinity, to utilize the power." Kiaban went quite still, as if deciding whether to continue.

"There are many factions who do not want to see humans discover the power beyond the Veil," he said, dropping his voice. On instinct, Lishka leaned closer, her senses automatically scanning the area outside Kiaban's lab for any eavesdroppers.

"Zaral and his followers have done much to prevent that from happening," Kiaban continued. "Of course, you know this."

An uncomfortable understanding passed between them. Lishka's mind flicked back to the newspaper clipping about Professor Coleman's disappearance. She had assumed Kiaban would know more about the study: as their weapons specialist, he should know of any human investigation into artifacts affiliated with the power beyond the Veil. *Unless it has been deliberately kept from him.*

"I could search the archives," Kiaban offered. "See if any reference has been made before."

"No," Lishka snapped, a little too quickly. Again, Kiaban's eyebrows shot up.

"I'm not sure what it is yet. I don't want to…" she said, hesitating, "draw too much attention." The archives kept a record of who viewed what content. While tempting, to utilize the records would certainly call attention to the rock, to Lishka, and to Kiaban, now that she had involved him. *And maybe to Dominick.*

"I'll keep an ear out and will let you know if I hear any information on the stone. In the meantime, until we know more, if I were you, I would keep that hidden." Kiaban gestured to the rock. "And…" he paused, careful to select the correct words, "I suggest staying away from wherever you obtained it, at least for the moment."

Lishka slipped the rock into the folds of her overcoat.

"Now, look what I have for you." Kiaban walked over to the metal table, where he drew a long, slender sword from the top of the pile. He held it up to show off the gleaming razor-sharp edge. Intricate symbols danced across the blade, revealing bold marks of precision and strength. Crafting the marks required hours of painstaking work, both physical and magikal, as even the slightest imperfection would corrupt their purpose. Kiaban noticed her appreciation.

"See here." He balanced the blade on both palms before her. Lishka examined it and saw a symbol she didn't recognize halfway down the blade. Within a half-circle, three matching lines formed a narrow broomtail, crossing each other two-thirds down their length. A small circle enclosed the intersection point. She leaned in closer to study it, noting the mark's relation to the others etched along the steel.

"What does it mean?" Lishka asked. The air in the lab relaxed as she and Kiaban assumed their designated roles, any consideration of conspiracy momentarily set aside.

"The lines encapsulate the three practices of balance: immortal life, immortal death, and mortal being. They are bound together by the circle at their intersection, the flowing of all energy that neither begins nor ends. But see, the outer circle is broken." Kiaban tilted the sword, catching the mark under the light so that the etching shone.

"For breaking," Lishka said, studying the glint in the metal.

"Yes. See above it, you have the marks for unmaking." Kiaban pointed to the symbols above the new mark. "And below, you have the marks to prevent the healing." He directed Lishka's gaze to the symbols below the broomtail. "This new master mark takes the meaning in both sets, unmaking and preventing healing, uniting it into the final purpose."

"It will harm any who draw on the power beyond the Veil," Lishka finished his explanation.

"Beyond just flesh, it will impair the magik inside, slowing any magikal being's ability to heal itself. Of course, to bring death the blow must still be fatal, but this mark will certainly cause more destruction than the average blade." He held the sword out to Lishka. Grasping the bound leather pommel, she tested the sword's balance.

Kiaban, ever the true artist, had not only engraved the marks to perfection, but had also given the blade the exact distributed weight to fit Lishka's strength and skill. He stepped back as she swung the sword, the steel acting as an extension of her arm. Kiaban smiled with pleasure to see his creation in its intended owner's hands.

"It's perfect," Lishka said, her words unnecessary as they both saw the skill in the blade, but knowing that Kiaban would appreciate the compliment. Kiaban beamed even wider and handed her the accompanying leather scabbard. Lishka gripped the scabbard, the sturdy leather smooth in her hands. She sensed Kiaban's dismissal and exited the lab to Kiaban's circular testing arena, separated from the rest of the armory by a stone archway that led to the greater hall.

In the middle of the test arena stood a narrow stone pedestal. Scorch marks splayed out from the pedestal and marred the smooth floor stones, evidence of Kiaban's spell-testing over the centuries. Behind her, Kiaban retreated into his lab to continue his work. Only the barely audible noise from the main armory's training floor disrupted the stillness. Lishka lifted the sword once more to admire the perfection in the symbols. A quiet focus settled over the arena. She swept the sword before her in an arc, enjoying the sensation of its sharp edge cutting through the air. Again, she whipped the sword through the air, moving faster and faster through her practice until the steel became a shining blur. Lishka tuned out everything else, shutting out all thoughts of Dominick, the stone, Sieth, and the political struggles within the Coven, fixating solely on the feel of the blade extending from her hand. Light tinged the eastern sky when she finally emerged into the upper levels of the mansion. The sheathed sword, now strapped at her side, conformed to her body as if it were another limb.

Despite the brief distraction of a new sword, Kiaban's words had sunk into Lishka's bones, permeating her being with an unshakeable chill. While delivered with Kiaban's natural gentleness, they came as a warning: *don't pursue the stones while interest remains high.* Lishka found it difficult to imagine the Great Covens spending resources to quell a local university study. Yet Kiaban had stated that Zaral and his followers had done much to prevent humans from discovering the power. The fact that Kiaban, a follower of Zachriel, knew nothing of the stones, spoke volumes concerning the divide between the two Great Covens. A shiver trickled down her shoulder blades at the thought that the relationship between the Great Covens had deteriorated to the point of requiring such secrecy from each other.

Lishka heeded the warning and avoided city nightlife for the next few days, in the hope that she could diffuse any further attention from Sieth and Darrak. Instead, she sought privacy in the armory's training arenas, forcing herself to stay clear of the library and the urge to research the stone. Despite the security of her private rooms and the Coven rule that none could enter without Lishka's permission, she kept the rock hidden in a spelled hole within the walls. If anyone touched the spell, she would know instantly.

In training, Lishka kept company with her fellow Keepers, who would rather practice combat techniques than talk of politics. She provided no opportunity for further ambush by Darrak and Sieth. Darrak had always been a thorn in her side, taking personal offense at Lishka's lack of enjoyment in her vampirism. But this time his behavior felt different, as if something else drove him. As Lishka parried her opponent's attack, half her mind kept returning to the confrontation in the foyer. Seeing Darrak with Sieth had been unusual, as they did not often travel in the same circles. Sieth's warning echoed through her mind, try as she might to dismiss his words. *He knows who is loyal. And who must be brought back to obedience.*

When training could not quiet her thoughts, Lishka returned to the lake. She darted between trees and beneath moonlight, her bare feet skimming the moist earth. Here she enjoyed her form the most. The forest gave her a cool, wild freedom. Only the natural presence of animals pulled at her awareness, leaving most of her mind free to drift and to seek comfort in the closeness of the magik just beyond the Veil. The magik always felt stronger with fewer humans around. As she ran, Lishka drew on the power to renew her energy and enhance her unnatural speed. A soft mist dampened her skin and she allowed herself to embrace the dark power within, alone out in the forest.

Movement rustled from between the trees, at odds with the melodic swaying of branches. Lishka slowed to listen. A moment later, a deer bounded across her path. It pivoted mid-bound to bolt in the opposite direction. She considered chasing it, tempted by the blood pounding hot and thick within its veins, the fear thumping in its heart.

Lishka lifted her face to the branches above her, watching the mist encircle the trees. This was not a night for hunting. Inhaling brought her the scent of cedar, maple, and damp earth. Beneath those smells lingered the tang of magik, sharp like metal. A longing for the magik blossomed from within her, a primal yearning for the deeper connection to the power beyond the Veil.

Lishka had not sought full immersion in the power beyond the Veil for months. To do so meant she must depart her physical body, leaving herself vulnerable. Yet her mind and soul ached for the tranquility that immersion brought, the sense of being one with the source of her supernatural power. Lishka reached out with her mind to search for a weak spot in the Veil. Weaving through the trees, she followed the pull of energy to a place where the Veil grew thinner, allowing the energy beyond to intersect with the physical plane.

She found herself on a small hill clear of trees and ferns, which overlooked the lake. Here a large rift split the Veil, wider than the normal hairline cracks from which she drew power to enhance her castings. The dewy grass brushed glistening droplets against her thighs as she sat and crossed her legs beneath her in a meditative position. A light wind caressed her skin, draping strands of long hair delicately across her face.

Lishka closed her eyes and shut out the physical world to turn inward. She focused on the core of energy within her being, gathering the force of her own essence. By sheer will she propelled her spirit through the rift in the Veil. The barrier provided resistance at first, before the energy drew her in with a welcoming strength.

The immediate sensation of the ancient power enveloped her, somehow both coolness and warmth radiating at the same time. A gray haze obscured all, with light shimmering intermittently within the mist. This place had no physical landmarks, nothing to indicate up or down. Lishka knew that she didn't really see the air around her, as in this place she had no eyes to see; rather, she had become spirit, absorbing her surroundings with her sixth sense. The force engulfed her, flowing past, around, and through her being all at once. Her own essence had become a part of the power, and the power pulled at the edges of her self-awareness, urging her to give in and become one.

Lishka resisted. She envisioned the edges of her being to establish the boundaries of herself. At this resistance, the pull on her spirit subsided. With careful control, Lishka relaxed to float within the mist's current, releasing her tight grip on the physical plane. As she let go, the power nipped at her edges, blurring the lines where she ended and the energy began.

Despite the urge to become a part of the Source, Lishka kept a small piece of her own essence separate. She locked it away in the back of her mind, using the mage's mark on her forehead to bind it in place. This secret part formed the tether to her physical body. She still felt her body from a distance, sitting upright in the seated position. Without the binding, the power would have consumed everything that made her Lishka, turning her body to an empty husk. Mordan had told her stories, years ago, of vampires who could not resist the allure beyond the Veil. Some sought to gain more strength, and instead, the energy swallowed them. Others, she had heard, simply lost the taste for immortal life and so gave themselves willingly to the mist, choosing to let their consciousness dissolve into the original Source.

This, Lishka could understand. The temptation

to fade into the mist beyond the Veil pulled at her. Yet always she remained strong, able to resist the final release.

Lishka could not guess how many hours, or even days, she drifted. Time operated differently on the other side of the Veil. Years might pass there, while only a few minutes would elapse where her body sat waiting. After an indefinite amount of time, a sharp twinge from deep inside her core awakened her, warning that she must return to the physical world or risk weakening the tether. Lishka ignored the twinge. The power rippled against her spirit, drawing her further into the depths. All worldly desire faded so that only the impulse to join the power remained. For one second, Lishka considered letting go to dissolve into the mist.

A sharp pain tore at her essence. She convulsed, the boundaries of her spirit sharpening even as the power forced her back. Lishka exerted her will, further defining what made her Lishka, to separate herself from the energy. She reached out for the rift, using her mage's mark to pull strength into the symbol. Her spirit met with the slightest resistance, before at last bursting back into the physical world.

Lishka opened her eyes, which radiated a deep violet. Her hair and skin crackled with energy. She looked down at her arms, shaken from the pain beyond the Veil. The power had never rejected her before, had never caused pain. A subtle glow lit her skin from within.

Electricity rippled through her flesh, charging her blood, her veins. Despite her centuries of tapping into the power, she still felt a heady giddiness from full immersion beyond the Veil. The power racing through her lessened her concern at its rejection. For a moment she enjoyed the distracting sensation; then, foreboding darkened the edges of her pleasure.

*What might humans do with such power?* The stone held the smallest amount, and yet opened the door to the possibility of humans discovering what lay beyond the Veil. Destructive, impulsive, and too short-lived to feel the full weight of their actions, this power in the hands of humankind would be catastrophic. Lishka needed to learn more about the study, what they had found in this Northern rock.

Even as she considered the study's potential impact, Lishka shied away from reporting the stones to her superiors. If, as Kiaban suspected, Zaral's faction already knew of the stones, then revealing the study could put both of them, and Dominick, at risk. The thought of placing Dominick in harm's way caused a surprising twist in her stomach.

*Tomorrow.* Tomorrow she would confront Dominick and make him tell her everything. She would discover the secret of Dominick and of the stones. Then she would make him forget the study of the rocks, the power within them, and that he'd ever thought to seek her attention.

# CHAPTER 6

# THE ARMORY

THICK RIVULETS OF RAIN streaked down the tall windows flanking the Coven's entrance, their heavy curtains drawn back to reveal the dark and gloom outside. It had been raining since morning. The drizzle that dampened Lishka's return the previous evening had evolved into a steady downpour as the day progressed, casting a quiet pall over the Coven.

Lishka descended the winding center staircase, an unwelcome uncertainty hampering her steps. She paused at the foot of the stairs. Her determination from the night before had worn off upon returning to the Coven. In the forest, exhilarated by the influx of power, it had been easy to decide to seek out Dominick. Back in the Coven, with a new understanding of the potential implications of the study, the risk surrounding Lishka's interest in Dominick again rose to the forefront. The sense of disquiet persisted, hampering her thoughts, until Lishka found herself not at her car as intended, but instead, on the lower level facing the armory.

Great oak doors, more than two stories high and twenty feet wide, recognized Lishka and creaked open to allow entry. She stepped across the threshold, her skin tingling with the armory's welcome. An expanse of hallway stretched before her. Massive stone walls soared into an arched ceiling adorned with various banners accumulated over the centuries. Pillars on either side of the main walkway formed pointed arches, adding extra support to the ceiling. At each pillar's base stood antiquated suits of armor, dating from the late-seventeenth century all the way back to the early fifteenth. To Lishka's right, doors led to specialized rooms containing various types of weaponry originating from long before Lishka's birth to the present day. Lishka relished the mixed scents of leather and metal that drifted from these rooms.

Ahead in the armory's center rose three circular platforms, used predominantly by Kristoph's team for hand-to-hand combat. As Lishka passed the only occupied arena, she recognized two of Kristoph's Keepers practicing. Just beyond the platforms, the sound of gunfire echoed against the stone to her left, despite the closed door. Lishka did not often go to the ranges, preferring intimate steel to the more modern metal guns.

She continued down the hallway, coming upon no one else, until she arrived at the end of the hall and the open arch leading to Kiaban's testing center and workshop. As she crossed below the arch, a second warmth brushed against her skin. This time Kiaban's spell guarded the entrance, containing any errant spellwork within, as well as keeping unwelcome visitors out. Centered in the open arena, the stone pedestal boasted one of Kiaban's leather-bound books. The book lay open to reveal inky scrawls of symbols and definitions. Lishka hesitated, intrigued. Across the floor she saw Kiaban in his lab, fixated on an intricate webbing of spells that he intended to set upon the ax before him.

Sensing her presence, he looked up. He bowed his head to her, then made pointed eye contact to indicate the book open before her. Lishka dipped her head to him in greeting and, accepting his invitation, bent over the pages. She studied the map of the symbols and noted their relation to each other. *A fire spell.* Not a normal fire, this appeared to be a new casting, designed to produce a flame so hot that it would destroy almost any earthly substance. At Kiaban's encouragement, she shut out everything else save for the learning of the spell, fingers twitching with the practice of tracing the symbols even as she drew them into her mind.

The spell took five attempts before Lishka achieved success, as the symbols had to be perfectly drawn with the right amount of intent to create the desired effect. Lishka stood holding the flaming ball that burned dark violet, almost black at its edges. The flames flicked out across her fingers as light without accompanying heat. Kiaban had taken care to weave in the symbols to prevent harming the creator. Lishka stared into the flames, mesmerized by their dancing movement. The symbols had perfectly converted the energy into a destructive fire, urging her to fulfill its purpose by setting the flames upon a target.

A shift in the air signaled that another had entered Kiaban's arena. Lishka recognized the familiar presence.

"A new one." Kristoph had stopped on his way to

Kiaban's lab to study the fire she held. His eyebrows raised in appreciation at the skill and complexity of the casting.

"Yes," Lishka answered. "From Kiaban's book." Kristoph examined the castings and accompanying descriptions scrawled across the pages before them. Much of Kiaban's work benefited Kristoph's Keepers, his spells and weapons constructed to maintain order in the city. Lishka's own rank within the Keepers afforded her unrestricted access to the armory and most of its weapons, save for the oldest relics stored in the deepest catacombs.

Kristoph stepped away from the pedestal and Lishka to cross the arena to Kiaban's lab, his back perfectly straight, his strides long and even. Lishka watched his movement, letting the fire twist beyond her hands to her wrists. The tendrils coiled around her arms like ropes, building momentum and strength for the moment they would be used to attack.

Kiaban straightened up from his work as Kristoph entered his workspace. He had finished laying the spellwork and now he hefted the ax, holding it out to Kristoph for inspection in a mirror image of presenting Lishka with her sword several nights ago. Like Lishka, Kristoph examined the steel, his fingers tracing the sharp edge.

Lishka returned her attention to Kiaban's spell. The fire had spread up her arms, and she found with satisfaction that it did no damage to her clothes. At the flames' creation, the fire had burned dark purple. Now the flames deepened to a lighter shade of violet. Lishka narrowed her eyes in concentration. The essence of the energy had morphed. It became a fire of renewal, the natural burn required to inspire new growth, and no longer the destructive weapon Lishka had begun with. She focused on the burn, trying to assess where the mutation had occurred. It did not come from Kiaban's spell. Somehow, Lishka had altered its meaning.

"You've changed it," Kiaban said. Lishka started, having been so intent on the spell that she did not notice Kiaban and Kristoph approaching. She relaxed her focus to let the fire recede back to her palms. "No, leave it," Kiaban instructed. He faced her from the opposite side of the pedestal, studying the flame twisting in her hands. Lishka stared into the fluctuating waves of the violet ball.

"I'm not sure how," she admitted. "I must have altered one of the symbols."

"I don't think that is the cause," Kiaban said. "You created the initial spell, so the symbols remained intact. The symbols are drawing on a different power to manifest the flame. They must have pulled on an energy separate from your vampiric self. That shift in the power source changed the purpose, not the construction, of the symbols." Both Kiaban's and Kristoph's focus switched from the flames to examining Lishka herself. At once she became acutely aware of the color of her eyes, which she just realized matched the fire she now held.

"May I?" Kiaban held out his right palm with the flicking of a symbol to protect his skin. With a steadiness of hand, Lishka passed the ball over, Kiaban's own spell working to take ownership of the flame. As she severed the connection, the fire intensified back to dark violet. The energy balanced in a tight sphere, bound by Kiaban's castings. "Interesting," Kiaban murmured, leaning over the spell and pulling his book toward him. The sphere began to ebb as, one by one, Kiaban deconstructed the formula to study Lishka's magik.

Kristoph watched him for a moment, then turned to walk back to the main armory. After a few steps he paused.

"Lishka," Kristoph said, interrupting the quiet inspection. Lishka pulled her eyes from the sphere. Kiaban would lose himself for hours to his work and indeed no longer paid any attention to either Lishka or Kristoph. She turned to follow Kristoph, leaving Kiaban immersed in his work.

"I have information for you," Kristoph said, as they walked out into the main armory hall.

"What is it?" Lishka inquired.

"I've just come from Nigel's hearing with the Council." Kristoph nodded to the two Keepers in the center arena, who had paused their training momentarily to acknowledge his passing with a quick bow.

"The full Council met to rule?" Lishka asked, surprised. The unsanctioned killing of humans did break Coven law, yet this violation normally did not merit a full Council hearing. Kristoph shook his head.

"No, a partial Council. Only three members, majority in favor of Nigel's bloodline," he clarified. "They called me to testify regarding his actions."

"And?"

"One year of desolation."

Kristoph slowed to a stop. They had reached the armory's arched double door. Castings preventing entry ran around the edge of the doorway, carved deep into the stone. The doors inched open to let them exit the armory. Before them stretched a wide circular foyer to match the Coven entrance several floors above on ground level. Across the room, the center stairway rose to the upper levels. Another ornate set of doors stood near the staircase, marking the entrance to the archives. The open archway in the wall behind and to the right of the stairs led to the even deeper levels of the House.

Kristoph paused outside the armory entrance, surveying those before them. Several Coven members occupied the foyer, either concluding business or else convening for their nightly duties. Three wore the black boots and protective vests of the Keepers, and must have come from the armory just before Kristoph and Lishka did. The tallest, a broad man with a thick black beard, held up a curved dagger to show the other two. Lishka eyed the blade until a flash of pale hair drew her attention from Kiaban's workmanship. She focused on the two figures standing across the room, before a smaller side hallway entrance. *Sieth.*

He stood with his back to them, deep in conversation with Lord Sootha, a member of Zaral's faction and of the Coven Council. Lord Sootha's sallow face appeared even more gaunt in the shadows of the hallway, his mouth set in a narrow line. Sieth gestured in a short quick movement as if emphasizing his words. His shoulders lifted with tension as he hunched forward, making himself smaller out of respect for Lord Sootha's shorter stature.

"Was *he* at Nigel's hearing?" Lishka asked, nodding across the room. She heard the disdain in her voice.

Kristoph followed her gaze. "Lord Sootha was present as a representative of Zaral's faction, along with Lord Aragnus," he said.

*But not Mordan.*

As a partial council, two members from Zaral's bloodline would have been allowed to judge one of their own. Mordan ranked higher than Lord Aragnus, so he should have merited the second seat.

Yet Lishka could easily see why they wouldn't want to call on Mordan to represent that faction, despite the direct link to Zaral. Mordan would push for a harsher sentence than simply disallowing blood and company for one year. An uncomfortable sentence for one as bloodthirsty as Nigel, but a year would pass in no time. Lishka doubted it would be enough to control him. Nigel would barely be showing any signs of desolation by the end of his sentence.

Lishka watched Sieth and Lord Sootha. They kept their voices low, but she caught one word: *stone*. A shot of adrenaline raced through her before she forced herself still. In that moment, Lord Sootha glanced past Sieth's shoulder and recognized Lishka and Kristoph. His drawn face did not change expression and his narrow lips remained pursed shut as he met Lishka's gaze. At once, Sieth straightened and slid around Lord Sootha to disappear into the dark recesses of the hall. Lord Sootha walked smoothly forward as if Sieth had never been there at all. He veered to the back archway, taking the staircase to the final lower level where the Coven's oldest relics lay secured in the cold, dark earth.

"What is it?" Kristoph asked, picking up Lishka's change in mood despite her recovered control. Lishka forced herself back to her conversation with Kristoph, though she ached to follow Sieth. *Stone* could only mean one thing.

"I don't understand why they sentenced Nigel so lightly," she responded, as if her tension had been in reaction to the ruling.

"Yes," Kristoph agreed. "It does ill-fit the crime."

Lishka knew he would say no more. Kristoph remained careful in how much he said about the government of their kind, although she sensed his growing frustration. Nigel had only been the most recent example of Zaral's faction pushing the boundaries of law and receiving minimal punishment.

Kristoph took a step in the direction of the staircase. Lishka remained in place, and he looked back at her, in question.

"I'm going back to the armory," she explained. "Kiaban may have more answers regarding the new spell."

"Very well. I was going to request your support on a sweep of the city, but I'll recruit Cain instead." Kristoph tilted his head toward the black-bearded man holding the dagger aloft at the base of the staircase. "He looks well-equipped for Keeper duty. Fesca's crew only just left port last night after a several-days' reprieve from the sea. While we have not heard or seen any unrest, I want to be sure they respected the rules of the city during their stay."

Without waiting for her response, Kristoph parted from Lishka's side to stride across the foyer. He dipped his head toward Cain as he passed. Cain sheathed his blade and bowed in one fluid motion, not requiring verbal direction. They had all learned Kristoph's gestures during their years of service under his leadership.

Cain and the other two Keepers followed Kristoph up the staircase, their steps almost silent. Lishka waited a moment for them to reach the upper level. She found herself alone in the foyer. All need for caution removed, Lishka darted across to where Sieth had disappeared. No sign of him could be seen down the dark corridor. She hesitated, weighing her next steps.

*The stones had been kept even from Kiaban.* The

disturbing pit in her stomach grew as her thoughts circled. Lord Sootha sat on the Coven Council and belonged to the upper echelons of their society. *How deep does the silencing of the study go?* Lishka remembered Kiaban's words: *There are many who do not want to see humans discovering the power beyond the Veil.*

Already two professors had been murdered, likely more whom Lishka had not yet uncovered. She highly doubted that Professor Barry Coleman had simply disappeared. The unsanctioned murder of humans directly violated Coven law. As this Coven belonged to Zachriel, his Council Members would have to approve the ruling, with any resulting action to be carried out by Kristoph's team. No word had spread to the Keepers, that Lishka knew of. Even if she could explain Kiaban's ignorance, Lord Sootha appeared too secretive to allow her to believe that Zachriel's followers knew of the study.

*What had Dominick stumbled into?*

Lishka had not intended to seek out Dominick, with Sieth and Darrak displaying such interest in her, yet that single word uttered by Sieth struck her to her core. She could not permit them to find Dominick before she had a chance to get answers. Lishka hesitated between inaction and action, then finally made the move to scale the stairs to the upper levels, where she headed for the garage. She would warn Dominick; she must ensure that he stop his research on the stones and thus remove any potential interest Sieth may have.

After all, even a human such as he, one who possessed the ability to resist influence, could be compelled to obey—with the right amount of force.

# CHAPTER 7

# AN UNDESIRABLE MEETING

LISHKA DOUBTED THAT DOMINICK would return to *Midnight,* now that she had revealed she knew how to find him. A quick check of his apartment complex showed he had not been home since morning, the scent of him hours old. That left one more place.

No one lingered outside *Emmett's* that night. The downpour discouraged even the most resilient from standing out in the open. Lishka paused after she crossed the threshold, smelling the wood, stale tobacco, and alcohol embedded in the walls of the dive. She reached out with all senses to survey the interior of the bar and detected no signs of Sieth. Only the aura of warm, mortal flesh permeated the air. Reassured for the moment, she entered the main room.

The bar's empty exterior proved to be no indicator of its popularity. Every seat between Lishka and the bar had been claimed by locals, unwinding after a long workweek.

Pitchers of beer adorned many of the scratched surfaces. All three pool tables hosted groups of people competing for money and bragging rights. Behind the bar, two bartenders moved in a fluid dance, constantly working to service those hovering for drinks. Lishka recognized the man who had attempted to take her order earlier that week, his gem earring still glittering to match the smile he flashed for better tips. This time a slim, older woman partnered him, working with a diligent focus and at twice his pace.

A familiar scent struck her. Lishka almost smiled, despite the potential danger. She peered through the crowd, following the earthy musk at the far-left side of the bar. An odd spark rushed through her body at the sight of him.

*Dominick.*

DOMINICK SAT AT the bar, staring at his barely touched beer. Droplets of condensation ran down the bottle, gathering around the base. A wet ring spread outward on the already stained wood of the bartop. He picked up the bottle to take a sip, using the alcohol to help dull his racing thoughts.

He had not even wanted to drink tonight. He would have much preferred to go home and sleep off the frustrating work from the week. Three tests later and he found himself nowhere closer to understanding the origin of the stone's energy. Professor McQuarry seemed ready to terminate the study, with the founder still missing and no leads on finding him. Dominick tried not to linger on the disappearance of the two professors spearheading the research, even with the third found dead.

Dominick took a longer swig from the bottle. A weariness sank into his temples and lower back, tempting him to give up and go home. Yet something kept him rooted to the barstool. He knew that if he went home, he would not find the deep, energy-restoring sleep he so desperately needed. Instead, he would dream of *her*. Dominick couldn't explain the drive that seemed to come from every molecule in his being, urging him to find and follow her somewhere. It had increased from a distant itch to almost overwhelming sensation, consuming his thoughts except for when he worked on the stones. The irrational fixation had driven him to *Emmett's*. He had half expected to see her there, waiting for him.

Dominick rotated on the stool to look out across the room. He saw only the usual crowd. He swiveled back, giving himself something to do by spinning a cardboard coaster stamped with *Emmett's*.

A cold tingle snaked down his back. Dominick paused. The last time he'd felt that chill had been in this very place. The hair on his forearms raised, and he turned around again.

"You must come with me," Lishka commanded. Dominick stared up at her from his perch on the barstool. A cardboard coaster dropped from his hands to slap the floor. He didn't seem to notice. Instead, his eyes lingered on the dark hair that trailed down her back, much longer than the in-fashion bobs. Her heavy boots and hooded overcoat, with an intricate embroidery just visible on the black fabric, stood markedly out from the more casual clothes in the bar.

Dominick pulled out the stool next to him, inviting her to sit. When he saw she did not intend to move, he slid off his seat to fully face her. Despite his height advantage, Lishka felt the imbalance of power as her own strength emanated about them. Dominick examined her, taking time to assess each feature as if comparing her to memory.

"Who are you?" he asked at once. "What's your name?"

Lishka paused. A name held power. Once she had given it, he would be able to tell others of her. *But he willingly trusted me with his.*

"Lishka," she answered.

"Leesh-kah," Dominick repeated, exploring the sound of her name. He continued to study her, boldly meeting her stare. His eyes lingered on her own and Lishka wondered what he must think of the unique color.

Lishka broke their gaze and glanced around them. She needed to remove Dominick from the crowd, take him somewhere she could ask him questions and not worry about the answers being overheard.

"Why were you in my apartment?" Dominick asked, interrupting her surveillance. He sounded more curious than upset. Lishka remembered the wallet she had left behind in a moment of impulse.

"I needed to know who you were." She pushed away any guilt that she had invaded his personal space. "Why did you enter *Midnight* uninvited?"

Dominick frowned. "Uninvited? I came there for you."

Lishka focused her full attention on Dominick. She remembered his question from their first meeting in the same bar: *Where will you lead me?*

"Why?" she asked.

Dominick hesitated, clearly reluctant to tell her the truth. Lishka did not have the time to earn his confidence. If he could not readily answer, then she must force it. She dilated her eyes and leaned closer. A thin wave of her cold power drifted out to Dominick, and she projected her will toward him, seeking to weave the influence that would bend him to her will, and open his secrets to her.

A wall met her influence, the same as before. Within Dominick his power rose, blocking any attempt to compel him. His frown deepened to alarm as he observed the change in her eyes. Where the haze of compulsion would obscure her vampirism, Lishka's failure to influence revealed her true nature to Dominick. Even in the dim lighting of the bar, she would not look human. He started to pull away.

A shove against her back disrupted the moment. The sweet scent of liquor filled the air and Lishka turned to face the confused man behind her. His blurred eyes blinked at her, and he opened his mouth to issue a boozy apology. Lishka did not notice. Behind the man, through the crowd and tables, Sieth stood in the doorway. Before she could evade his gaze, his eyes alighted on both her and Dominick. A predatory gleam slithered across his face. Adrenaline rose within Lishka, fueling her movement. In less than a second, she scoped the emergency exits and deemed them too far for her to escape with Dominick unnoticed. Sieth wove his way through the crowd toward them, the people peeling away from his path. Lishka whirled back to Dominick, where he watched her warily, unsure of what he had seen in her face and blindly unaware of the impending danger.

"Say nothing," she instructed. Sieth's power strengthened behind her, flexing like muscles stretching after a day's confinement and charging the air. Dominick opened his mouth to protest when his gaze shifted to look over the top of her head.

"So this is where you've been running off to." Sieth's voice scratched across her skin. Lishka put her back to Dominick, planting herself firmly between him and Sieth.

No amount of alcohol could blind humans to Sieth's otherness and the danger he presented. An empty circle surrounded them, as the bar-goers instinctively kept clear. Sieth's appearance alone made him stand out in stark contrast to the humans at *Emmett's*. His hair shone so bright that it almost became white, with pale irises to match, barely distinguishable from the whites of his eyes. The power that flowed from him chilled the air, creeping into the flesh of those nearby. His mouth cut a sharp line across his face, mutating into a satisfied smile at the sight of Lishka, widening as he looked past her to Dominick.

*The snake eyeing the mouse.* Lishka squared her shoulders. She suppressed the urge to draw the spelled dagger hidden in her boot.

"I have not been running anywhere, Sieth," she said, to draw his attention back to herself and away from Dominick. "I have nothing to hide."

"Oh, don't you?" Sieth challenged, though he kept his voice light. He dipped his head back to Lishka.

*A game, then.* Lishka refused to rise to his bait. Her hands remained at her sides, her left palm close to reach for the dagger should she need it.

Again, Sieth's eyes flicked from her to Dominick. "And who is this? Your new pet?"

Dominick tensed behind her. Surprisingly, his heartbeat remained steady despite the increasing warmth in his blood. He did not feel afraid of Sieth. Not yet.

Sieth's cold eyes drifted over Dominick, observing the worn flannel over a rumpled shirt, the faded jeans.

"Perhaps he has no vocation of his own, other than to trail after you," Sieth mused, threading contempt into his tone. "Perhaps he is just another one of the pathetic junkies, consumed by desire and too weak to rise from the floor of their superiors."

"Junkie?" Dominick broke his silence. Sieth's eyebrows shot up at the sudden interjection. "What are you talking about?"

Sieth sneered. "Your kind, ever so addicted to ours. Always trying to find something more than your ordinary lives. Always trying to feel alive by chasing death. And yet, you yourselves are also so addictive." His last words slowed as if he began to weave the melodic hypnotism, though Lishka felt no power influencing Dominick.

"I have no idea what you mean," Dominick said bluntly. "I don't know anything about any addiction, or chasing death, as you put it. I go to North Pacific. I'm a student there."

A chill entered Lishka at Dominick's admission that he attended the university. Even as she watched Sieth, a glimmer of malice sparked behind his eyes.

"And what do you study?" Sieth asked, his words a little too sharp to be casual conversation. All disdainful superiority had disappeared from Sieth's face. He stood still, tense, a predator who had caught the scent of his prey, in harsh contrast to the comfortable movement of the humans further down the bar.

Dominick did not answer right away. He too saw the change in Sieth. Lishka stayed in her place, resisting the urge to press herself back against Dominick, to stop him from telling Sieth the truth. Sieth might be able to overlook Dominick's student status, but not his area of study.

"Well," Sieth prompted, dragging out the word.

"Geology," Dominick answered. The word dropped among them, a stone in the water.

"Really," Sieth replied. "How interesting." His eyes flickered red.

Dominick twitched. His heart pounded loud in Lishka's ears, his increasing pulse unmistakable to her and to Sieth. Lishka's predatory instinct rose in reaction to the adrenaline beginning to lace through Dominick's blood.

"Well," Sieth said at once. "I won't keep you from your fun, Lishka." He smiled down at her, his pale eyes flat. "Besides," he added, niceties vanished, "I have my own business to attend to." He stepped back and merged into the crowd. His power clung to the air like a bad smell, even after Lishka felt him exit the building.

Dominick stared into the space that Sieth had occupied. Warmth crept back around them, and little by little people started inching in to fill the void. Lishka assessed the situation. She could leave Dominick here, amongst his own kind. Already her attention had put him in danger; Sieth must have followed her, and it had been sheer coincidence that he'd found Dominick, someone affiliated with the stones. Lishka had no idea how Sieth would have connected her to the stones, otherwise.

*Unless Kiaban had told him.*

Even as the thought crossed her mind, Lishka pushed it away with guilt. Kiaban would never betray her trust, especially to Sieth. At this moment, Sieth's motives did not matter. The most sensible decision would be to leave Dominick, to not exacerbate the situation by giving him any more of her attention. That would have been an option, had Dominick not told Sieth of his relationship with the North Pacific geology department. Sieth now had more reason to investigate Dominick, separate from his need to know Lishka's every action. If she left Dominick here, Sieth could easily find him again, and this time without her to protect him.

"Dominick," Lishka said.

Dominick roused himself and looked down at her. "Who the hell was that?" Anger and uneasiness roughened his voice.

"We must go." She couldn't answer his questions, not out in the open.

"Go where?" Dominick asked, his words heated with frustration.

"Your apartment," Lishka answered, making a split decision. Dominick's apartment would be private and hopefully still secret from Sieth. *Unless he has already learned that Dominick knew of the stones before entering* Emmett's. Lishka shook away the voice of warning. She had little choice, doubting Dominick would agree to go with her anywhere unfamiliar, after Sieth's display.

"My apartment?" Dominick questioned. "Wait." He grabbed Lishka's arm even as she turned to lead the way to the exit.

The warmth from his hand seeped through her sleeve.

Lishka stopped and turned her attention back to him.

"Not here." Her voice came out low and firm. Dominick let her go, his hand dropping back to his side as he took in her hard expression. She pivoted on her heel to cross the floor, aware of each person in the bar. No one showed interest beyond getting out of her way. Dominick hurried after her, his movement less graceful than Lishka's as he pushed through the crowd. Upon exiting the building, Lishka conducted a quick visual sweep of the parking lot and road to ensure no one lay in wait. She sensed no others of her kind and crossed the street to her parked car. Dominick quickened his pace to keep up.

"My car," he said, regaining his confidence.

"Leave it," she replied. "You can come back for it, in daylight." Dominick opened his mouth to protest, then closed it. Instead, he opened the passenger door with just a bit too much force and slid inside. Lishka ignored him. She had larger concerns than Dominick's feelings of powerlessness.

Sieth had discovered Dominick. Lishka could not tell if Sieth had sensed the power in Dominick, had realized Dominick's resistance to his compulsion. Regardless, Dominick had made himself suspect by revealing his university major. Lishka twisted the car out onto the pitted streets. *If Sieth was responsible for killing the professors, he could come for Dominick.* She had to find a way to get Dominick out of the city, away from the stones and from the Coven.

Lishka flew through the streets, adrenaline from the interaction with Sieth manifesting in the reckless driving of someone who could not easily be killed. Dominick, preoccupied with gripping the safety handle as the car swerved around turns at breakneck speed, remained silent but for the odd grunt when he braced himself against the door. It took them only ten minutes to reach his apartment block. Lishka swung around to the back lot, guiding the car into one of the many open parking spaces. In the sudden stillness, she heard Dominick's heartbeat thumping in his chest. Salty blood rose in his veins, his heat warming the car's interior. Lishka's predator instinct quickened again.

Dominick took a deep breath and peeled his fingers from the upper handle. He glanced at Lishka, waiting for her next move. Lishka stared through the windshield to the concrete wall before them, considering her next steps. She had not detected any malicious presence on the road.

"You'll need wards." Her voice rang harsh in the small confines of the car. "To conceal and protect you. Though anything I can do won't withstand a serious hunt," she added, more to herself, "the wards may help to keep your location unnoticed, at least until we can get you out of the city."

"Get me out of the city." Dominick repeated each word with care, as he processed her statements. "Why do I need to leave the city?"

She opened the door.

"Lishka."

She paused at the sound of her name on his lips, spoken so casually by a human.

"It's not safe yet," she said, and exited the car to approach his apartment building, leaving Dominick little choice but to follow.

C H A P T E R   8

# BOREAL'S STUDY

LISHKA CONTINUED TO LEAD until they reached Dominick's apartment door. Only then did she move aside to allow Dominick access to his lock. Dominick stepped around her and pulled out his key. Lishka could have easily broken or spelled the door open but restrained herself. So far, Dominick had been compliant with her demands despite receiving little explanation from her. To make him afraid of her could stop him from providing the answers she sought. No need to remind him how little protection a locked door provided.

As Dominick turned the key, Lishka inched back to peer out the window at the end of the hall. She saw nothing unusual. Still, uneasiness gnawed at her and she followed Dominick into his studio. As the door shut behind them, Dominick moved into the main living area to give her some room to enter the small space. He faced her, opening his mouth to speak.

"Just be quiet a moment," Lishka said, cutting him off. "I have to be sure no one followed you." She listened to the noises outside, searching for any indication that they had been found. Thankfully, Dominick stayed silent. No unusual sounds came from the parking lot or stairway, and she could not feel any other supernatural presence. She still had time to offer Dominick some protection.

Lishka flicked her hands through the air, outlining the diamond-shaped marks for concealment. First she marked the door and then the window, muttering the symbol names under her breath for additional power. With the final symbol cast, the marks formed a linked net, flashing as the spell took hold, and then fading to almost invisibility. Lishka faced Dominick. He had observed her every movement, absorbing each flick of the wrist, the ripple of her hair as she swept her hand across her body to cast the last symbol. Even under Darrak's and Sieth's scrutiny, she had not felt so seen.

"Who are you?" she asked, breaking the weighted silence. "Why did you come to *Midnight*?"

Dominick held up a hand as if to stop her questions. "Wait," he said, his voice low and surprisingly steady. "Who is following me? What did you just do?"

Lishka studied him, a little disappointed. He asked exactly what she might expect from an ordinary human. "You're asking the wrong questions," she said. Dominick crossed his arms and his forearms tensed beneath the thin jacket. "Not *who*," she explained. "Why."

"Alright. Why, then? Why would someone be so interested in me?"

"What are you doing with the stones?" Lishka did not have the time to be coy, and sensed bluntness would work better than tricks. Dominick frowned at the seemingly abrupt subject change.

"The stones? What has that got to do with anything?" His eyes flicked over to where Lishka had tucked the rocks back amongst his books.

"That is why they look for you," she answered.

Dominick tilted his head and raised his eyebrows to peer at her. "The Boreal Stones?" Doubt raised his voice an octave.

"Is that what they're called?" Lishka asked.

Dominick nodded. "After the professor who discovered them," he clarified. "But I don't understand, why would someone follow me for the stones? They are special, but don't have market value. At least, none that's been established yet anyway. The study is only in its infant stages. We don't know enough."

Lishka watched him for any signs that he lied, but he appeared to be telling the truth. She detected no deceit in his eyes, no hesitation in his voice. "What is the study about?"

Dominick's eyes narrowed. She had just told him that people sought him for the stones. "You can read about it online," he said. "Anyone can, it's no secret."

"Show me," Lishka commanded.

Dominick pulled out his phone and began pressing the touch screen. "Hang on," he murmured. "The internet is slow."

"The Northerly blows strong," Lishka observed.

"What does the Northerly have to do with the internet?" Dominick glanced up at her, his eyebrows pinched together. "The winds are not high enough to cause signal disruption."

"Never mind." She did not want to confuse him further by explaining that when the winds blew from the North, they carried small particles of the power beyond the Veil with them, which affected human technology. A Seattle native would know the effects of the Northerly, if not the reasons for them, but she remembered that Dominick did not come from the city. "What did you find?"

Dominick shook his head. "Nothing. That's odd. I swear the study had a short article published, although that was many months ago that I last checked. But I can't imagine the university would have taken it down, even if it is not of much interest to the sponsors. We could barely keep our funding as it was, even before—" He stopped himself.

Lishka snatched the phone from his hand and crumpled it in her own.

"Hey," Dominick exclaimed. "What are you doing?" His eyes widened as he processed the strength it took to crush the phone.

"They might be able to find you through your search. I never should have asked you to look it up." Lishka flipped through the options in her mind, trying to decide what to do next. *Kiaban was right.* Zaral's faction suppressed the study. She had not quite believed they would go to such lengths.

"I still don't understand. Why would someone remove the publication?" Dominick asked, pulling her attention back to him. A flash of understanding lit behind his eyes for just a second before vanishing, but Lishka still caught it.

"Tell me about the study. Tell me what the report would have explained," she said again. She needed to learn more, to understand why Zaral might be so interested. *To better protect Dominick.* The thought skirted through her mind and she quickly shook it off, quelling alarm at the idea that she desired to protect a human. "And I will try to answer your question."

"Alright," Dominick said with finality, as if they had struck an agreement. "The stones have a unique vibration, an energy within them. Fern Boreal, a professor of geology at North Pacific, discovered them on an expedition to the North, where he intended to study glacier movement. He brought them back and found they contain an energy unlike any currently known." He stopped.

"And?" Lishka pressed.

Dominick shifted his weight, a small movement but enough to show his unease. "And he developed an instrument," he admitted. "The Boreameter. It measures the frequency of the energy's vibration. It can detect the precise amount of power contained within the stone."

Kiaban's warning resounded in Lishka's ears, almost drowning out Dominick's voice. Humans had discovered the power beyond the Veil. They had an instrument of technology that not only worked around the power, but detected it.

"Who else knows of the Boreameter?" Lishka asked. "Was anything about the instrument published?"

Dominick again shook his head.

"No. The university posted only a brief announcement when Boreal's research partner got permission to use the labs. We haven't gotten far enough to publish any of the research, and it's all under Boreal's name anyway. He left the study not long ago, vanished actually, and no one has any contact info that we know of." Dominick's face grew more serious. "At least the Chancellor has allowed us to continue Professor Boreal's work while they search for him. Only myself, the dean of the geology department, and a handful of professors are aware that the Boreameter exists, until North Pacific can get the patent. To be honest, I shouldn't even be telling you now."

*A handful of professors.* Even as he spoke the words, Lishka watched Dominick's face darken.

"Wait—do you think?" He leaned across the bed, one knee sinking into the soft mattress as he pulled out the clipping from his bedside table. He stood and handed the familiar article to Lishka. She barely spared it a glance.

"The person you think is following me—" Dominick gestured toward the paper. "Are they responsible for this?"

"Yes," Lishka said. She knew his next question, knew that now she must hold up her end of the deal. Yet, she hesitated. Dominick had barely scraped the truth in his investigation of the stones. Lishka's revelation would change his world forever, and not for the good.

"Tell me," Dominick insisted, as if sensing her reluctance. He took a step forward. "Who was that man in the bar?"

"Sieth," Lishka answered, her voice flat. She could almost hear Dominick's next question, the one he didn't want to ask: *What* was that man in the bar? She had watched Dominick observe Sieth's eyes flash red, and even the dullest human would sense Sieth's power.

"Here," she said, to spare him having to ask the question. From the folds of her coat she withdrew the rock she had stolen.

"I wondered where that had gone." Dominick stared at the stone, momentarily distracted. She held it out and he took it, his warm fingers just barely grazing her cold hand.

"There is a power in it," Lishka acknowledged. "It is a power that flows through this world, though not as readily as it used to."

Dominick shifted his attention away from the rock to study her.

"That vibration in the air, which grows stronger when the Northerly blows," Lishka continued. "That tingle down your spine that feels like electricity but isn't, it's somehow older, earthier." Without meaning to, Lishka's voice took on a lilting, musical tone, intent on lulling Dominick into a trance. Dominick nodded as she spoke, aligning her words to his own experience. She pulled back. Her vampire nature had risen to hypnotize her prey. The shocked face of the man at the park only days before momentarily appeared over Dominick's curious features.

"That's magik," she said, her voice hard. Dominick blinked. Disappointment dropped across his face.

"Magik?" Incredulousness saturated the word, and Dominick could not keep the judgment from his expression.

"For lack of a better term," Lishka qualified, "yes. There are many different types of energy in this world. This power is by far the oldest. What do you think people used to call electricity before they knew what it was? Magik is what humans use to name that which they do not yet understand."

"I suppose that's true." Dominick crossed one arm over the other. "So it's an energy without a name yet."

"Magik," Lishka reiterated, with the tiniest bit of irritation. "Some people can perceive the energy, as you feel it in the air."

"And in the stone," Dominick added. He still had the rock in his left hand, and he uncrossed his arms to hold it before him, examining it with new interest.

"You can sense the stone?" Lishka asked.

Dominick glanced at her, hearing the edge in her voice. "Yes. Boreal could too," he added quickly.

"Most humans cannot," Lishka explained. "Only a select few with a special affinity can detect it and out of those, fewer still can harness the power, control it, make it do things."

"Like the symbols on the windows?" Dominick asked.

"You can see those?" Lishka couldn't help herself and took a step closer to Dominick, as if being near could help her better understand him. She had felt that Dominick was not a witch. *But if he can see the symbols, what is he?*

"They are faint," Dominick admitted. "But there is a soft glow to them. I've never seen anything like them."

"You have a power all your own," Lishka murmured, more to herself than to Dominick. "It sits within you, warm like a small sun. Surely you have felt it." Dominick gazed down at her, both of them frozen in place and only inches from each other. Lishka shook herself and moved away to put distance between them.

"You said someone followed. You have yet to explain who Sieth is," Dominick said. He would not be shaken from the full truth. Lishka brought herself back to the danger.

"You're not human, are you?" Dominick's words fell from his lips, and he looked as surprised as Lishka.

"Not anymore," Lishka answered.

"What are you?" Dominick asked. Lishka calculated how truthful to be. She had been alarmingly open with this human, the words rolling off her tongue too easily. She had not spoken so freely since she could remember. Dominick had an ease about him, a warmth nonexistent within the Coven that she found hard to resist.

"I am a vampire."

Dominick stood frozen, the rock still clutched in one hand. Doubt, the desire to laugh her off, and finally the beginning traces of fear all chased each other across his face, each vying for the upper hand. He settled on doubt.

"A vampire," he repeated, as if saying the word himself would make it less ridiculous. As he stared at Lishka, she knew he saw her otherness. Her skin glowed white even in the ill-lit room, and her violet eyes, now shadowed, emanated a cold power that threatened to trap his own gaze. Lishka blinked to make herself appear more human.

"Yes," she replied. "At least close to the human myth in that we live for a very long time and rely on the blood of others to maintain that life."

Dominick stared at her.

"The Latin word *Lamia* perhaps draws closer to the truth, as it means both vampire and witch," Lishka continued. "We are able to tap into the same power as that contained within the rock, to produce the types of spells like the wards I put upon your windows."

In an interesting role reversal, Dominick had not blinked since she uttered the word *vampire*. "What do you want with me?" he asked.

"They want to stop you," Lishka said. "Sieth, the man you saw at the bar, is a vampire, a powerful one. He serves one of the strongest, one who does not want humans discovering the power in the stone. He works to destroy the study."

Dominick dropped to the bed in one heavy motion, as if his legs had suddenly gone out from under him. He leaned his elbows on his knees and peered up at Lishka. The lower angle made him appear much younger, and much more vulnerable.

"So you are telling me that one of the oldest… vampires," he struggled over the word *vampire*, "is against the study of the Boreal Stones and wants to stop it?"

Lishka nodded.

"And to do that, he'll—what? Hurt me?" Dominick's eyes flicked to the newspaper clipping that lay beside him on the bed. Lishka held still. Dominick's eyebrows shot up higher. "Kill me?"

Lishka remained quiet, watching him.

"Jesus Christ." Dominick leaned forward and put his head in his hands, his fingers twisting through the brown waves.

"The wards will help to hide you," Lishka volunteered after several silent minutes. "At least until I know what to do with you."

"The wards?" Dominick asked, not moving his head from his hands.

"The symbols on the windows," Lishka clarified. "They will conceal you. As long as you stay in the apartment, none can find you." *So long as they don't already know where to look.* She did not add that, for Dominick's benefit. Anyone who investigated the apartment would sense Lishka's presence in the spell. Though she had greater power and skill than many of her kind, Lishka was not a Master Mage. She could not cast spells without leaving a trace amount of her own aura.

"I told him I studied geology," Dominick said, his words muffled by his forearms. He looked up, his hair tousled from where his hands had been. "Sieth. I told him. Do you think he suspects?"

"Probably," Lishka said. "I'm not sure. As you are a student and not a leading professor, it is possible he will not pursue the matter further. You must stop all work on the study."

At this, Dominick stood.

"Stop the study?" He stared at Lishka. Heat from his chest warmed the air between them. "How can I stop studying the stones? This discovery could be monumental. Think of it, sustainable energy."

As he spoke, Lishka began to shake her head. What Dominick professed was exactly what Zaral would do anything to stop.

"You must," she said. "If you want to live."

"Why do you care?" Dominick's voice rose in frustration. "Why are you interested in the stones?"

"You sought me out," Lishka reminded him. "You asked me where I would lead you. What did you mean by that?"

Dominick looked almost embarrassed.

"Ah, yes. I didn't mean to—that sorta just fell out."

Lishka waited.

"It sounds ridiculous now, but," Dominick paused, matching her stare, "I dreamed of you," he said, his voice barely above a whisper. "You told me to follow you. This dream, it was more real than any dream I've ever had before. I can't explain it, but somehow, I knew that you were real, that you existed. In my dream, I saw you at *Midnight*. That's how I knew where to find you, although when I saw you, I—" he paused, "I couldn't believe you were actually there, that you were real."

"How is that possible?" Lishka asked.

Dominick shook his head and shrugged at the same time. "I have no idea." He sounded exhausted.

Lishka had pushed him too far. Still, she had to know more.

"Was it a spell?" Dominick asked, before she could pry further. "Did you, I don't know, send the dream somehow? Can vampires do that? Get into people's heads?" His voice grew angry at the suspected violation.

"No," Lishka said. "Some can send visions, but that requires an immensely strong connection between the two people, either blood bond or a deeper emotional and physical attachment." Even Mordan, her mentor and of her same bloodline, had never sent her a vision before. She could not imagine having accidentally sent one to Dominick. Lishka had not known of Dominick until he first appeared at *Midnight*, and she certainly had not sent him any messages while he slept.

"So why would I dream of you before I'd ever met you?" Dominick asked.

"I don't know," Lishka answered. But she intended to find out.

"Vampires are real," Dominick stated, as if trying to convince himself of his new reality. "Magik is real." He looked at her. "You are real," he said again, with a tone of surprise.

Lishka sensed the warm core pulsing within him. Unless he was a very skilled liar, Dominick did not know of his strange power.

"I must go. The hour grows late." She had gotten the answers she required, at least for the moment. It was unlikely Dominick would be able to tell her more.

"Wait." Dominick moved forward as if he might stop her. "Will you come back?"

Lishka did not answer. She knew that her attention would be dangerous for him. She could not be sure that she had not been trailed to his apartment, despite her diligence in checking for predators. Instead, she looked down at the rock lying where he had dropped it on the bed.

"You cannot be compelled." Lishka met his eyes to hammer her words home. "So, you must be warned. The Boreal Study is dangerous, Dominick. Those who desire it forgotten are more so. They will kill you if you pursue it."

Dominick's face grew hard with stubbornness.

"You are foolish if you think there is no danger in the dark," Lishka whispered. She pulled away from him. "I have to go. Don't go out at night, don't show that to anyone." She gestured toward the stone. "Anyone who sees it may work for the Coven and betray you." Lishka moved to the door. This time, Dominick let her go. A strange sense of guilt crept over her. She had pulled back the curtain to reveal a world that in all probability wanted him dead. Now she left him with only her wards as protection against monsters. She had no choice. Her presence in the apartment increased the chances that he would be found.

Lishka glanced back at him. Dominick watched her, still standing in the same place, his hair rumpled from where he had mussed it. She hardened her gaze all the more and placed as much intensity and warning into her voice as she could summon.

"And don't," she said, her words cutting through the air, "come looking for me."

# CHAPTER 9

# THE MAKING

A DAMP STILLNESS HUNG OVER the university in the late hours of the night. Sturdy gothic buildings loomed over the uneven brick that covered much of the campus in pathways and circular courtyards. High above, ever watchful gargoyles perched on the rooftops, their vantage point affording them full view of the grounds. Moonlight trickled through the clouds to dance upon the stony heads, the shadows shifting on their carved features creating the illusion of life.

Three hours remained till sunrise. Lishka had lingered outside Dominick's apartment for over an hour, until the quiet satisfied her concern that they might have been followed. Now, she maneuvered her car through the one-way roads that crisscrossed the sprawling campus. The late hour had stripped the streets of their usual night crowds, and the university slipped into a peaceful slumber.

*Midnight*, on the contrary, vibrated. Lishka approached the club, trying to detect any sign of Sieth.

He did not often go to *Midnight*, deeming the teeming crowd of addicted humans beneath him. Yet Darrak did, and Darrak reported directly to Sieth. Darrak had seen Lishka with Dominick there, much as he tried to feign disinterest. Even as she entered, Darrak shot her a fleeting glance from his usual booth, soon turning his attention back to the young vampire curled up along his side. Black wavy hair framed her narrow face, and as she observed the crowds, a smug smile curved the corners of her scarlet lips. She sat on the side of her hip and tucked lean, bare legs up beside her to better press herself against Darrak. Her smile converted to a laugh as he whispered something into the curve of her neck, while her sharp heels dug gouges into the leather seat.

Nothing would come of it. Darrak and Syral had been together for centuries, and allowed each other room to stray, although Syral's famous jealousy meant that freedom only flexed so far.

Lishka peered into the other shadowed corners as she wove her way through the crowd to the back bar. She neither saw nor sensed Sieth in the vicinity. For the first time, she wished for him to be close by, to monitor his actions.

She slid onto a stool at the corner of the bar, separate from the rest of the patrons. From the opposite side of the counter, the bartender caught her eye. James dipped his head in greeting. Lishka returned the gesture, inviting him over. He slid a drink toward the human before him, then approached, scanning along the bar to ensure all customers remained satisfied.

A tall, broad man with thick, gray-streaked hair drawn back tidily into a low knot, James could have been a raider on a Viking ship. Lishka could not recall his exact history, though they had spoken many times over the past few centuries, more recently at *Midnight*. As the club's owner, James could often be found tending his bar. He rested large forearms against the counter, joining Lishka to assess the crowd.

"Tense out there," he commented, a light accent lilting over fangs half-buried in thick facial hair. At first glance, the crowd appeared as usual. Those uninterested in socializing or else engaging in other activities lingered in the shadowed booths, while others joined the dancing in the center. Yet, on closer observation, Lishka could pick out the two factions separating into distinct groups. Where once they intermingled freely, now she saw many in Zaral's faction avoiding those in Zachriel's.

"It does seem to have worsened lately," Lishka agreed. "What have you heard?" They talked in low voices, the loud music hiding their conversation from sharp hearing.

"Not too much. Everyone is careful right now. There are rumors of odd gatherings up north, though no one seems to really know why, or to what purpose." James leaned in closer. "The beings of the Old World stir." A glimmer of delight glinted behind his eyes. "I've heard tales of travelers stumbling onto creatures that haven't been seen in centuries. Even the wolves grow restless within their territory. It's becoming harder for the mages to manage them."

Lishka too had heard these rumors as whispers in the hall, gossip trickling down from reports by those who traveled north to treaty with the wolves.

"Humans don't seem to be doing much better," James continued. "They move toward another war. But then, they always want to fight about something. Land, oil, weapons…" James trailed off.

"Chaos is the way of this world." Lishka's words rang with the truth of one who had lived a hundred lifetimes.

A call from the far end of the bar caught James' ear and he straightened, already turning to heed the order. Lishka continued to watch those before her and thought of Dominick. She had to get him out of the city before Sieth or the others showed any more interest. *But how?* She could not be sure of her ability to compel Dominick. Already he had resisted her influence twice. Lishka also had the sneaking suspicion that Dominick would not leave the city simply because she told him to. He had seemed too excited by the rocks to abandon his study, even knowing the potential danger.

A cold barb grazed her skin, prickling her flesh. Lishka surveyed the crowd for the source, recognizing the usual patrons and ignoring Darrak's attempts to catch her eye from his corner. Her gaze shifted to the club's entrance. Light from the mounted exit sign illuminated bright hair and Sieth peeled away from the doorway. He stared at her and ran his tongue over sharp teeth. Even at a distance, Lishka could make out the thick red substance that outlined his lips and clung to the edges of his long canines. A wave of earthy musk permeated the air.

*Dominick.* Lishka stood before realizing it. Her vision narrowed to only Sieth. His lips mutated into a wide slash of a smile, seemingly taking forever as time stopped. Then, before she could blink, he whisked around to disappear through the exit.

Lishka twitched, losing a half-second. She launched herself forward to shove through the dance floor, not caring that she pushed humans or her own kind to the side, inciting several irritated looks and a few snarls. Nor did she care that Sieth baited her, that he so obviously wanted her to follow. The musk lingered, driving her into the night.

Cold air slapped her face at the club's exit. Lishka paused to look both ways, all senses straining for Sieth. Inwardly, she cursed herself for leaving Dominick alone. The stillness outside helped her to refocus and plot next steps. Sieth had no doubt harmed Dominick. She shied away from the thought that he had killed him. *But what if Sieth has taken him?*

A glimpse of pale hair flashed again to her right, this time caught in the beam of a streetlight. Anger flooded her, dispelling any logic, and she ran after Sieth into the shadowed alleyway.

As she turned the brick corner, she slowed once more. A damp haze crept up the brick walls to clog the narrow corridor and obscure her sight. Not even the normal city sounds of traffic or rodents rustling in the garbage disturbed the air. Ignoring the tingling along her spine, Lishka inched deeper into the enclosed space.

At once, she grew frustrated with Sieth's games. Sieth might be her superior, but the same laws that governed Nigel, that governed her, also bound him. Sieth could not harm a human without Council approval, certainly not one that she had already claimed.

"Sieth!" she commanded. "Sieth, show yourself!" The heavy air absorbed her words. In the silence that followed, a light scuttling revealed that not all small creatures had abandoned the alley.

A faint call twisted from deeper in the alley, disturbing the oppressive fog. Lishka stopped moving and strained her senses to see beyond. The shadows shifted with intention to reveal Sieth leaning against the left wall, much closer than Lishka realized. He stared at her, eyes wide with a greedy hunger. Unease churned in her stomach, and adrenaline began to spike even as Lishka realized the unnaturalness of the haze that moved to envelop them. The noise intensified as if fed by her burgeoning fear, weighting the air to suffocate her senses. The prickling along Lishka's spine blossomed into a full-fledged burning. Too late, she realized that the voice did not belong to Sieth.

*"Lishka."* Her name rolled out of the darkness. A whisper at first, the sound grew to cocoon her body and mind, clamping her in place. *"My Lishka."* The voice boomed inside her, filling her head, consuming that which made her Lishka. An iciness seeped into her bones, freezing her veins as it ran down her arms and legs to bind her. In a weak attempt, Lishka summoned her inner strength to stop its progression, but the power flowed through her body too fast and too strong. She had been caught and could only stand now, and wait.

The shadows before her contorted and solidified into a singular shape. A head formed, then a torso, arms and legs. At last, a tall man emerged from the inky mist. Flat black irises caught Lishka's eyes and held them. They stared out from a pale face with features as sharp and hard as if etched from stone. Corded muscle ran up his arms, defined beneath his expensive suit.

Lishka's brand burned. The creature who had placed it there strode toward her.

"Zaral." Lishka's lips cracked as she uttered her Maker's name. Behind Zaral, Sieth remained in place, his eyes fixed on them both. No longer smiling, he leaned forward as if hungering for the electricity emanating from his Maker.

"I have heard some troubling things about you, my Lishka." Zaral's voice slipped out smooth, each word enunciated with calculated precision. "Have you forgotten who you belong to?"

At the words *belong to,* a strange energy blossomed from deep inside her. Warmth grew from her core, vibrant and alive, heating the ice in her veins. Lishka flexed her hands, seeking to disrupt Zaral's influence. Zaral laughed, the sound harsh and sharp, scraping her nerves raw.

"Now Lishka," he said, batting down her power as if it were nothing. "Your tainted fey magik did not save you before. It will not help you now." He studied her. His long black hair hung straight to either side of his face, silhouetting his eyes into hollowed pits. Lishka wanted to move, to flee, but her blood ran cold once more, no longer warmed by what Zaral called her fey magik. What strength she had could not match his ancient force. Zaral continued forward with deliberate steps to stop before her, forcing Lishka to tilt her head upward as she remained captured in his gaze. He raised his hand to cup her jaw, his touch hard and cold. Lishka's veins thrummed as he called her blood, his own blood, back to him.

"I think you have forgotten," Zaral murmured. "Perhaps I will remind you." He leaned forward and at once Lishka comprehended his intention. She tried to wrench her head away, desperation animating her frozen limbs. Zaral's grip, seemingly light at first, held her tight.

His face drew closer. The shadows extended his shape until he filled her entire vision, and her lips parted in response to his influence. Then his lips met hers.

A jarring, crackling force rushed through Zaral's mouth and into Lishka's. No longer of ice, Zaral's power flared white-hot, searing through her limbs and exploding in her chest. She jerked in his grip, her atoms vibrating against both the physical and magikal holds that bound her in place.

Memories of the night Zaral made her erupted. The blistering heat that tore into her neck, the brand Zaral had marked upon her human skin, just before he turned her, to ensure it remained etched on her body forever. The burn had throbbed with pain unlike any other, until a sharper agony replaced the flesh wound, carved by Zaral's blood pouring through her veins, tearing into her soul. That night his unbearable power threatened to strip the very skin from her body.

Now Zaral consumed her once again. He burned and ripped into every piece of her. All that made her Lishka peeled away, until a puppet remained, filled with *Him*.

After what seemed an eternity, though mere moments later, Zaral shifted. His force lessened and the fire receded from her body and mind to become a dull throb at the back of her temples. Little by little, her nerves tingled as she regained command of her body. The throbbing faded altogether, leaving behind the echo of a horrible memory. Zaral drew back, though he still gripped her chin in his hand.

Lishka's limbs sagged under her own control once more and her eyes dropped to Zaral's chest. The acrid smell of burnt hair filled her nostrils. The scalding heat from the brand on her neck had flared so bright that it singed her hair. Avoiding her Maker's eyes, Lishka looked beyond Zaral to Sieth. A cool smile slithered across Sieth's face, satisfaction oozing from him at the display of his Master's total dominance. Fierce hatred filled her at the sight of the ever-obedient shadow to their Maker. The blood around Sieth's lips flaked into cracked lines and adrenaline burst through her like a spark.

Zaral released her. Lishka fell to the ground, not yet recovered enough to catch herself. *Dominick.* The thought of him sent warm tingles through her cold limbs. She put her palms down against the asphalt and, with great effort, shoved herself to her knees. Zaral stood over her, his black eyes empty of emotion. Instinctively she twitched, expecting him to lash back out, but he did not move.

Lishka scrambled up, finally finding her feet. The ground heaved as she backed away from Zaral and Sieth, who stood as a pair, watching her. Only at the entrance to the alley, when she felt sure Zaral would allow her to leave, did she finally turn her back on him to face away from the darkness.

"We were always going to find him, Lishka," Sieth's voice called out at once from somewhere behind her. "You just made it quicker."

The fog carried his words, infused with Zaral's presence. Her head pounded and her vision became blurry. For one moment she stumbled, surrounded by gray. Then she lunged out onto the open street. Clean rain fell from the night sky, washing away the dank fog. The cool air cleared her senses and she half ran, half limped, to her car. She hauled herself into the front seat, slamming the door shut. In the quiet interior, the absence of both Sieth and Zaral allowed her to reclaim herself.

*Zaral. Here, in Seattle.* Her mind swirled with the revelation. Lishka had not felt Zaral's presence for centuries, not since Mordan had adopted her as his student. *But you did,* a small voice at the back of her mind whispered. *You sensed him at the docks. You saw his black eyes at* Emmett's.

The memory of *Emmett's* drove Dominick painfully to the forefront of her mind. Lishka shoved the car into drive and wrenched it away from the curb to race southeast toward the University District, putting more distance between herself and Zaral. She relied on the hope that Sieth had not taken Dominick. Sieth must not have left *Emmett's* as she thought. He must have bided his time, hiding like a snake in the grass, waiting for Dominick to be alone and defenseless. Her protective wards would have been useless if Sieth had seen where Dominick lived. Lishka pressed her foot down on the pedal, notching her speed well over 120 miles an hour. The car jerked with her barely controlled movement, as her limbs still shook from Zaral's power.

Mordan's teaching rose from memory, his voice a rush of cool strength that calmed the fervor of her mind. *The fear you feel, the hunger for blood, put that aside. Those are not affecting you now. Let your mind and body still.* Lishka tried to suppress the fear from Zaral's control. He had released her, this time. Even as she applied Mordan's teachings, the thought crept into the back of her mind: *Did Mordan know of Zaral's arrival?* Mordan had an even stronger connection to Zaral, and yet he had given her no indication that Zaral had arrived. Zaral would not have hidden in the shadows had he wanted Zachriel's Coven to know of his presence in the city.

Lishka shoved all thoughts of Zaral away. *Dominick must be alive.* She needed to know what his connection to her meant. The image rose of him standing in his apartment examining the rock, his eyes full of passion for the unknown.

Dominick's apartment building stood quiet and dark. Nothing looked different from earlier in the night, yet dread slowed Lishka's steps as she crept up to the outer door. She nudged it open, and the soft creak disrupted the stillness of the dim hallway. Silence greeted her: not that of a peaceful sleeping residence, but rather an ominous quiet that shrouded the building. Lishka moved to the foot of the stairs, assessing the human life in the apartments about her. Sleeping unconsciousness tickled the edges of her awareness, slow heartbeats identifying apartment inhabitants who lay tucked behind locked doors. The lack of human activity gave her hope as all appeared undisturbed.

At the top of the first flight of stairs, the smell struck. The scents of iron and salt lay heavy in the stairway, churning her hunger. Abandoning caution, she took the stairs three at a time, racing up the final two flights to Dominick's studio.

In the dark corridor, the door to apartment 305 hung an inch ajar. Lishka stopped before the doorway to assess. Human warmth permeated the apartment, and the shallow pulse of fading life. With a light touch she nudged the door open, the fear of what lay beyond sharpening her senses.

A thread of moonlight drifted through the uncovered window to illuminate the scene before her. The bed sat at an awkward angle from the wall as if it had been dragged, the bedding ripped off to fall into a heap on the ground. Torn textbook pages lay strewn across the floor, a blanket of mineral images and geological terms, and narrow handwritten notes in the margins. Lishka's wards dangled in broken shards before the window, the magik disintegrating back into raw energy that lingered in the stale air. Lishka barely noticed the damage to the room, focusing instead on the source of the smell.

Dark glistening crimson pooled in the living space before her, seeping between the floorboards and clotting the air. Lishka followed the liquid trail to the crumpled shape that lay in the space between the bed and wall.

*Dominick.*

She darted into the studio, all caution forgotten, and pushed the bed over to kneel beside him. He lay on his left side toward the wall, his right arm twisted at an unnatural angle across his face. Lishka lifted his arm to place it alongside his body, taking care not to adjust his position more than she had to, even as she ignored the grating of bone. That injury could wait. She needed to find the source of the bleeding. She rotated Dominick onto his back and a gurgle emitted from his throat. His chest lay open in ribbons, flannel sticking to deep slashes. Even more horrific, a gaping wound at his neck bubbled blood, choking his airway. The fact that he'd lain on his side had prevented him from suffocating before loss of blood could have claimed his life.

Lishka pressed her hands against his neck to staunch the blood flow. Her mind ran through how to treat his injuries, though the growing reality of the situation impressed itself upon her. Dominick had lost too much blood and not even her limited healing abilities could save him. He had but seconds left. Lishka released the pressure on his neck. She felt the urge to bend down, to put her mouth to the wound and feed. Instead, she focused on the soft curl in his hair, the curve of his lips now ghostly pale. Lishka had not been able to uncover why he'd seen her in his dreams, what it meant that she'd told him to follow. Now she would never know.

Lishka bent closer, until her face hovered barely an inch from his, and paused. Ever so slightly, she turned to bring her ear close to his lips. *Was that a quiet whisper of breath?* She reached out with her senses, and at the same time pressed her fingers to his wrist. A weak pulse still beat in his veins. Lishka hesitated. That unique energy flickered inside him, struggling to hold him there. Dominick fought to stay. He would lose the battle, that she knew for certain, unless…she had one option she could give him. Adrenaline flooded her body at the thought.

In all her long life, Lishka had never turned a human. To turn someone meant to strip away their humanity and replace it with something old and profane. It also required an immense amount of magik and skill. One misstep could result in monstrous consequences, sometimes killing both the victim and Maker. Even with successful Makings, the curse of the damned passed onto another soul. How could she inflict this curse on another life?

Dominick's energy flared in one last pulse, then dimmed. Only the smallest thread tethered him to this world. A grim resolution took hold of her.

"Forgive me," Lishka whispered. "It is the only way. Forgive me." Dominick had lost so much blood already but needed to lose more still. His life had to flow through her veins in order to seal the bond. Gathering her strength and focus, Lishka closed the gap between them and pressed her lips to the wound at his neck.

Dominick's blood thrummed with vitality, though he himself weakened. Lishka's eyes flew open in surprise. She consumed at a rapid pace, enough to feel him flow through her veins, connecting her to him. Energy stirred in Dominick. She drank deep and with control, unlike her feeding by the lake only days before. Her purpose focused her on the one task that mattered: to save Dominick. Dominick's heartbeat sped up, trying to pump the small amount of blood left in him through his body. Then it slowed. Then it stopped.

Lishka pulled back, instinct urging her to begin the transition. She bit savagely into her wrist and pressed the open gash to Dominick's mouth. He lay still, eyes closed and unmoving. She pressed harder, forcing her blood through his lips, willing him to accept it.

Suddenly the link took hold. A bridge formed between Dominick's blood in Lishka, and hers now in him. Dominick's eyes fluttered and she felt a tug on her wrist as he siphoned her blood into him, using her life to revitalize his own.

The bond intensified to become almost tangible in the thick air. Dominick's heartbeat quickened, now pumping her blood through his veins. The pull at her wrist sharpened. Already he grew much stronger. Suddenly Dominick twisted. He reached up to grip Lishka's wrist to his mouth. Lishka jerked at the sudden movement but kept her wrist in place. She had felt worse pain in her lifetime. Spots began to flicker at the edges of her vision as her blood left her body. Still, Dominick drew more, now digging his teeth into her flesh in his desire to feed. Lishka tried to sit back, stabilizing herself by pushing her other hand against the floor. The room started to grow blurry around her. *That's enough.* She made to retract her arm, but Dominick held fast, lifting up off the floor with her movement. His eyes opened and shone red, as if Lishka's blood had completely filled him up. He no longer looked like Dominick; no humanity existed in his face. She had created a monster.

Lishka wrenched back her arm and finally broke free. She used her legs to shove herself away from him, sliding on the floor still sticky with Dominick's blood.

Dominick fell back. His red eyes stared at the ceiling, unseeing, while his body processed the new blood. His chest rose and fell in frantic movement, his heart thumping too fast. A low groan escaped his lips. At once his body arched in an impossible bridge as his boots scrabbled against the floor, and his eyes rolled back into his head. The convulsion shook his body and every nerve, every atom, seized in response to Lishka's foreign blood. He threw his arms out to each side, his hands stiffening into claws, as if in rigor mortis. Another seizure pulsed through his body. He strained against the confines of his physical form, which now mutated into a vessel that could contain the new lifeforce.

Without thinking, Lishka inched toward him, instinctively reaching out in sympathy. Her body tightened with the memory of her transition. She could almost feel Dominick's soul tear apart, as one life left to be replaced with another. Smothered by her dark gift, his own strange energy no longer beamed inside him. Lishka curled her wounded right arm beneath her, the gash in her wrist halfway healed, though slower than normal with her loss of blood. With her left hand, she reached out to grasp Dominick's wrist.

A surge of electricity exploded out from Dominick and shot through his arm into her. Lishka gasped. Once more, a heat rushed through Lishka's limbs, though not malevolent as Zaral's had been. A spark flared within the blackness that welled up from Dominick, growing in intensity to fill her vision with white. Lishka blinked, unsure whether the fire blazed within her mind or had become physical, consuming the studio. At once, the room disintegrated, the furniture, walls, and even the floor disappearing into the white electricity that swirled about them. Lishka clenched her hand around Dominick's, reassured that he still existed in the space with her.

The barrier to the Veil broke. Lishka dropped with Dominick into the current. No longer the soothing, invigorating flow of the power beyond the Veil, the magik churned in rapids. The power hammered through Lishka, punching away any remaining boundary of herself. She tried to assert her will to repel it, to stop the absorption. This force would break her apart. The current burned down her arm and flowed into Dominick, coursing between the two of them in an infinite loop. She latched onto him as the sole physical anchor in the vortex. Though she could not see him, somehow she knew Dominick shone, lit from the flames within him. A searing pain tore her throat, and Lishka realized that she screamed, yet no sound escaped her. She would disintegrate in this power, along with Dominick. It would swallow them both, to scatter their atoms like dust.

At once the fire extinguished into pure darkness. Lishka no longer drowned in the current beyond the Veil. She shifted, and a hard surface pressed into her hips. *Hips.* Her body once more encased her, the pressure of the physical world pushing her into solid form. She opened her eyes and the darkness eased into normal late-night shadows. The shape of Dominick's dresser came into focus.

Lishka's fingers twitched, now empty. She raised her head just enough to see Dominick before her on his back. His chest lay still and free of injury, and a coldness flowed through his body. He lived, now in another form. A faint warmth tickled her senses, and Lishka recognized it as Dominick's own lifeforce. It had survived somehow. Lishka almost smiled at the thought. The room swirled once more, and she gave way to unconsciousness.

# CHAPTER 10

# THE COUNCIL
# AND THE MAGE'S MARK

THE MOON ROSE JUST OVER three-quarters full. Soft mist floated down to dew the leaves and grass on the Coven grounds. In the distance echoed the faint hooting of an owl that lived in the woods beside the Great Lake. The hoot wafted through the air, not quite absorbed by the damp fog. Hidden in their burrows, woodland mice and voles trembled.

Lishka paced the length of her suite for the hundredth time that night. She found herself alone, as the servants who painstakingly dressed and prepared her had left hours ago. Her long sky-blue robe swept the floor, rustling with each step. Made of a heavy embroidered material, symbols of the Coven, the Veil, and of her kind adorned the cloth.

Lishka tried to ignore the restrictive movement of the gown about her legs. She had never cared for the decorative wear of the Coven elite, and now the forced finery only added to her agitation. The high collar offered one saving grace: the stiff fabric wrapped about her neck, inadvertently hiding the black brand. Lishka alone bore the mark of Zaral. She had been cursed with the forever mark of ownership, though many in Zaral's faction considered this a gift. Yet her attempt to cover the most obvious sign of her bloodline was futile. Despite her endeavors over the centuries to remain unseen in the shadows, she had not managed to escape the attention of those who followed her Maker: Sieth, Darrak, and now those on the Coven Council.

*There will be no hiding now.*

Lishka tried not to think of the encounter in the alley. She had no desire to remember the taste of Zaral.

*But Zaral may yet be at the Coven,* the creeping inner voice whispered. Lishka did not sense him nearby, which meant little to nothing. Zaral could easily conceal himself from Lishka, and those more powerful than she. In the privacy of her suite, she shuddered. *What might he do, once he finds out about Dominick?*

*Dominick.* She mulled his fate again, her mind circling to match her feet. The Keepers had taken him away and locked him up somewhere within the Coven. She thought of him as she had last seen him truly alive: uninjured, standing in his apartment and watching her leave. Guilt filled her mouth with bile.

A full night ago, Lishka awoke from unconsciousness to familiar hands lifting her off the floor. The cool night air had sharpened her senses and she found herself half-carried, half-struggling to walk across the parking lot, Kristoph's reassuring presence helping her to focus. He had lifted her inside a black van belonging to the Coven, before sliding the door shut with the finality of the lock clicking into place. Part of his team remained behind to clean up the mess. Lishka had sensed Dominick close by for a moment before she lost track of his presence. He must be somewhere in the House, warded and hidden from her.

An abrupt knock came at the front door. Lishka stiffened, then walked across the room to stand ready at the entranceway. The door swung open, and a Council Guard entered. His black livery made his position evident, the uniform much the same as the rest of the Coven Guard, though finer with embroidered marks of power and control to signify his elevated status.

The guard beckoned with his hand for her to follow. Gathering her strength, Lishka strode after him, exuding an air of calm control to hide her growing trepidation. She followed him down the staircase, ignoring the stares of those who loitered in the lobby. They must have heard what she had done. The focused attention burned like flames on her skin, reinforcing the consequences of her actions.

At the foyer, the guard led her to the right wing to continue their descent. *To the Council Dome.* A coldness spread through Lishka's flesh. The Dome existed for Council meetings and trials of the severest crimes. *Like turning a human without permission.* Though this must have been done before, she had never heard of such a case. She doubted Zaral's representatives would sentence her as easily as they did Nigel. He had only killed a human, after all. Her transgression would be seen as much worse.

Upon reaching the lower level, Lishka followed the guard down the hall until they stopped before a pair of impressive stone doors. The tops of the doors curved in an arch, carved with images depicting the Coven's history. The Coven crest adorned the doors themselves: a double-headed bird of prey, the left head an eagle to represent Zachriel, and the right a hawk representing Zaral, perched on the scales of balance to show the equal unity between the two Great Covens. Along the border, marks for strength and power enhanced the crest. She noted the symbols illustrating death, unity, and balance, designed to demonstrate the supposed harmony between the two brothers, yet favoring Zachriel as this Coven belonged to him.

Recent marks for security had been surreptitiously placed in the corners of the doorway. With representatives from both Zaral and Zachriel in each of the Covens, there should be no need for security within the Coven itself.

"Wait here." The guard ducked through a small side door camouflaged in the wall.

Lishka stood still, staring at the doors before her. She must retain her composure. *But would they ask of Zaral? And if they ask, dare I tell the truth?* Even worse, could Zaral now be here, on the Council, to preside over her judgment? His authority would be ultimate as no one, not even those of Zachriel's bloodline, would dare to oppose him.

Thinking of Zaral only quickened her nerves, so instead Lishka distracted herself, taking the opportunity to reach out with her senses. Still she detected no hint of Dominick. He had to be close, perhaps in the deep recesses of the Coven, hidden away from the outer world. Doubt crept into her mind. She had thought she would be able to feel Dominick, but it seemed as though their connection grew weaker than when he had been human.

*Unless he did not live.* She forced the thought back. Surely, they wouldn't kill him, not now that he was one of them.

The massive doors creaked open, summoning her to court. Lishka steadied herself and stepped across the threshold.

Before her stretched a great room with a high, domed ceiling that boasted more detailed images of the symbols on the front door. Significant scenes from the Coven's history spanned the curve of the ceiling. Lishka took them in with a quick glance. The oldest image depicted the first establishment of the Seattle Coven thousands of years ago, the most recent of the nine. Beside it, the signing of the treaty between the Coven and the wolves who lived in the North. More recent scenes showed the arrival of humans from the Old Country, and how the Coven helped them to build the city. The far corner held a smaller, cruder image of mountains, highlighting two peaks that cradled a lake. Lishka had never seen this scene before. It lay tucked to the side, almost as an afterthought in the artist's rendering of their history.

Being underground meant no chance of natural light. Instead, bright flames in iron sconces lined the walls, illuminating the room's center. A closer look revealed the flames to be not of fire, but thousands of glowing symbols for light. The symbols flowed in constant movement around each other to emit a blaze far brighter than any natural flame.

Across the room there stood a dais and upon it sat seven ornate chairs, set behind a narrow stone table. Behind the table sat the Coven Council, facing her in a uniform wall of elaborate silver and purple robes, the colors honoring their highest rank within the Coven.

Each Council Member fixated on her, the intensity of their gazes tangible even at the distance. Lishka had spent the entirety of her time at the Coven avoiding the attention of its rulers, with the exception of her mentor, Mordan. Mordan sat with Zaral's faction at one end of the table. His familiar face did nothing to calm Lishka's nerves. Something odd about his position made her pause, until she realized what struck her: Mordan must have fallen out of favor to be seated last. She noted this for later consideration. Regardless of his status, Mordan would not be able to help her, not now.

Lishka looked for the Voice of the Council and found Lord Dorwan in the middle seat, the oldest and possibly the strongest of the Council Members. Lady Raseska, next in age and strength, sat at Lord Dorwan's left. Though Lady Raseska regarded Lishka with a neutral expression, Lishka remembered the Lady's hushed whispering with Mordan in the hall just days earlier. Beside her sat Lord Barik. His white hair glistened beneath the light castings and old age sagged the skin along his jawline. He stared at Lishka with a disdainful air of disinterest, as one might assess a hound that had worn out its use. Finally at the end of Zachriel's line, Lord Cutler shifted to lean forward. His beard, shaped in fashion from the Middle Ages, betrayed the era of his origin, more recent than the others.

Lishka assessed Zaral's Council, stopping herself from lingering on Mordan at the edge of the table. She would only draw attention to their connection. She had not considered how her actions might reflect on Mordan and cringed at the thought that she could be the reason for his fall from favor.

Instead, she focused to his left, where Lord Aragnus sat. Of them all, he displayed the most emotion. Anger rolled across his face in waves. Wiry and hook-nosed, Lord Aragnus had supposedly descended from a place not too far from Lady Raseska's origin in ancient Egypt, although he had been turned many centuries later. Lishka glanced to Lord Aragnus' left and met Lord Sootha's flat eyes. Adrenaline flicked through her. Lord Sootha merely watched her impassively from his seat as the most senior member of Zaral's faction in the Seattle Coven, his wispy hair unable to attain the elegance of that of the other Council Members.

*Lord Sootha knew of the study.* Lishka ensured her face did not betray her. She had last seen Lord Sootha with Sieth, only the previous night, mere hours before the attack on Dominick. They must have spoken of the rocks, and of the study. Lord Sootha had always been a faithful and trusted follower. If Sieth knew of Zaral's presence in the city, so must Lord Sootha.

The guard motioned her toward the center of the room, where a circle drawn with symbols of truth had been engraved into the stone floor. Lishka approached the circle, leaving the guard to shut the doors. As she crossed its border, the spell tingled. She stopped at the epicenter and lifted her face toward the Council.

Lord Dorwan spoke first. "I will be the Voice of Zachriel, leader of the Western Coven." His voice echoed throughout the room, surrounding her. "We convene this night to establish judgment for the crimes committed by Lishka, lineage of Zaral, who is hence charged with turning a human without the consent of the Coven. A charge to which she is found guilty."

No question lingered of her innocence. Lord Dorwan looked down upon her with hard eyes. "Not since the two Great Covens were first brought into being by Zachriel and Zaral has there been a Making without the full consent of said Covens. You have broken the oldest covenant." His words rang out, puncturing the stillness of the room. "Why?"

The question hung in the air.

The Council Members all leaned forward, waiting for an answer. Lishka thought to explain the situation with Zaral and Sieth, and glanced at Mordan. He watched her with the same stern curiosity as the others. Only the centuries spent with him told her of the subtle shift in his expression, the small sign of warning in his eyes. She paused.

"I had marked the human as mine," she said instead. "I had shown him attention before others. By Coven law, no vampire could touch him without explicit Council permission. He possessed fatal injuries. In marking him, I was responsible for him." Lishka waited to see if Lord Sootha would challenge her, as he had clearly given permission for the attack on Dominick. Lord Sootha remained silent, only watching Lishka and giving away nothing of his own thoughts. The other Council Members sat back, disappointed at the weak excuse.

Lady Raseska studied her. "Why did you not simply bring him to a hospital?"

Lishka faced her. "He was too injured for that, my Lady. He would not have survived."

"The welfare of humans is not our concern," sneered Lord Aragnus. "Are you saying that you value this human's life above the laws of your Coven?"

Seven pairs of eyes bored into Lishka's body and mind. The tingle of the truth circle shivered across her spine.

"I acted on instinct, my Lord," Lishka said, as evenly as she could under their suspicious stares. "His body had been badly ravaged. I was afraid that the wounds might mean possible exposure, or at the very least, cause problems for the Coven." She felt enough truth in that to pacify the marks she stood upon.

Lord Dorwan peered down at her. "There were the markings of another upon his body." He paused, obviously meaning for Lishka to address his statement. Lishka had to answer, and quickly. Yet accusing Sieth would only spur further investigation, and that would lead to both Zaral and the Boreal Study. She weighed how to answer.

"Yes, my Lord," she acknowledged. "I believe my interest in the human attracted hostile attention from another member of the Coven." She kept her gaze forward, though Lord Sootha's presence pressed at the edge of her vision. Still, he made no sound.

"Be that as it may, that is no excuse for your actions," stated Lady Raseska. "The attack itself is a minor violation. Clearly your attachment to this human muddled your reason, resulting in such a reckless and foolish mistake."

Lishka pushed down the immediate rise of shame and defensiveness at Lady Raseska's accusation. Though insulting, Lady Raseska had skillfully explained away Lishka's actions without triggering the truth spell and closed off any opening to question Lishka further on her motives.

"I understand," Lishka replied, biting her tongue.

"And what of the mage's mark?" exploded Lord

Aragnus, unable to contain himself. "Not only did she turn a human, but she cast upon him the symbol of power. She gave one unworthy the ability to draw upon that source and channel the energy. A right that must be earned." He spat out the words and glowered at Mordan, as if Mordan, not Lishka, had cast the mark.

*The mage's mark.* The revelation hit her, temporarily abolishing her careful control. She had given Dominick the mage's mark.

"That's impossible," Lishka blurted. Silence greeted her inappropriate outburst. Lishka searched their faces for a sign that Lord Aragnus spoke false. She could not have given Dominick the mark. Such casting took enormous skill, with both involved requiring a strong, developed bond. Her own mark had been cast by Mordan, centuries after Zaral had first made her.

Her skin tingled, remembering the white-hot sensation that had surged from her into Dominick. The Veil had dissolved, and she had been swept up in the raw energy of the power beyond. At once, she recognized the truth.

"The mark was cast," confirmed Lord Cutler. He leaned back in his chair and stroked his pointed beard as he spoke. "You must have more power than you think." He looked down at her, not with anger but curiosity, as if studying a puzzle to be solved. His casual posture betrayed his upbringing as a street urchin, quite unlike the rest of the Council. They had been plucked from privilege, their elevated human status alluring to Zaral and Zachriel. Lord Cutler knew how to live in the dirt and stay alive on his wits alone.

"The casting is unacceptable," hissed Lord Aragnus. "To give a newborn this ability is a gross dereliction of duty—"

"*All* of Lishka's actions have been considered." Lord Dorwan's voice echoed throughout the chamber. "And all have had the chance to speak their verdict. The Council has decided your fate."

Lishka looked up at his cold face and braced herself.

"We cannot undo what has been done," he began. "Yet we cannot allow one so new and inexperienced to possess a live mark. He would be a danger to himself and others. Dominick's mark will be bound, until he has proven himself worthy to bear it. And—" he paused. Lishka held herself perfectly still, though her mind skipped at the mention of Dominick. *He lived.*

"To make sure that such a thing does not happen again, your mark will be bound as well, until you prove yourself worthy to bear it once more."

Lord Dorwan's words punched through Lishka. She had prepared herself for imprisonment, a sentence much longer than Nigel's. She had even entertained the thought that she might be put to death. Instead, they meant to restrict her from the power beyond the Veil, to strip her of her magik and her strength. She would be raw and weak. *Prey.*

"No!" Lord Aragnus pounded his fist on the table this time, the crack echoing about the room. In unison, Lady Raseska, Lord Barik, Lord Sootha, and Lord Dorwan turned to watch him, their stoic expressions unchanged, though Lord Cutler failed to suppress the smallest eye roll.

"The covenant must not be broken. The mage's mark must not be cast without full consent from the Council."

Lord Aragnus shifted to glare at Mordan beside him. "Is this to be allowed, Mordan?" Spittle flew from his mouth.

"Enough." Lord Dorwan held up a hand. "You have spoken already and the time for debate has passed. Lishka's mark will be bound, and with it, the core of her power. That is the judgment upon which we all agreed."

Lord Aragnus sat back fuming. Lishka searched the Council for any weakness in their resolution. Mordan had not moved since Lord Aragnus' outburst. He watched her with steadfast eyes and offered her no refuge. The judgment upon her could not be avoided.

The Council Members stood as one. Despite her centuries of control, Lishka twitched. Her instincts pushed her to react, to defend herself. She clamped down and forced herself to stand still. The Council Members began to draw the power through minute cracks in the Veil and the air crackled around them. The energy streamed into their bodies to gather in the mage's marks upon their own foreheads. Then they directed the force into Lord Dorwan.

In an instant, he left the table and stood before her. His robes billowed around him to cast deep shadows on the floor. He placed his hands on either side of her face, and he stared at the mark upon her forehead.

A burning sensation sank into her forehead and traveled into her core. Lishka reflexively tried to jerk away, but Lord Dorwan held her tight, a jarring parallel to her encounter with Zaral. All her senses screamed in resistance. The fire raced along her veins through her arms and legs to explode in her chest. Then it dissipated. Lishka had one brief moment of respite and almost wondered if the binding had been completed.

A roaring pressure began to build in her chest. The rush of rapid water flooded her ears and drowned out any external noise. Gray mist twisted about Lord Dorwan until he disappeared and the pressure on her face from his hands released.

Lishka had once more gone beyond the Veil. The desire to consume the power rose, stronger even than the urge for blood. She reached out, seeking to use her mage's mark to draw the power in, to channel it through her body where it would fill her with strength. Instead, the energy slipped through her grasp. Lishka tried again. The power floated around and through her but became intangible the second she tried to hold it. She could exist within it, but she could not absorb it into herself.

As quickly as it had arisen, the gray dissipated. Hard stone floor pushed against her feet and pressure gripped her skull. Lishka tensed at the abrupt re-entry to her physical body. The air around her felt thin, the space in the Dome cavernous compared to the dense mist.

Lord Dorwan dropped his hands from her face. Lishka returned his stare, though she barely registered the smooth lines of his face. A dull throbbing pounded between her temples and her mouth tasted of ash. She ignored the uncomfortable sensations to focus on the growing emptiness inside her.

She could not feel beyond the Veil.

Where before the power flowed alongside her, there now stood a void. Lishka's magikal senses strained to find a connection to the power. A numbing cold spread into her forehead, as if the flesh around the mage's mark had also died. She barely suppressed a shudder. It would not do her well to show weakness.

"It is done," Lord Dorwan declared. Behind him on the dais, Lady Raseska nodded toward the far-left wall. A guard moved to Lishka's side. Her mind had gone blank and so she turned to him out of habit. He took her just above the elbow and guided them across the wide floor to exit the chamber. Lishka could only put one foot before the other. She walked steadily, her body still strong, though a vital part of her had been taken.

Lishka regained her composure once they reached the door. She pushed down the horror at the emptiness inside her. When she was alone, she could explore the void in the relative safety of her suite. She had survived the trial. Now she would have to wait and see what her new status meant, as one bereft of the mage's mark.

The guard led her into a waiting room that opened to the main hall. Without a word or gesture, he turned to retreat into the Dome. Lishka continued forward, her only goal to move as quickly and inconspicuously as possible to the upper levels. She must not draw too much attention. Though the others did not yet know the verdict pronounced upon her, many would detect the difference in her aura. Lishka found herself defenseless, a mouse in a nest of adders.

As if summoned by her thoughts, Sieth appeared to block her way. He stood rigid before her, his fury palpable, though he kept himself restrained. He must have known that Dominick lived, now under the protection of their kind. Satisfaction penetrated her shock—that she had thwarted his plan.

"It doesn't matter," Sieth hissed. "*His* will was done in the end. Your human will be kept quiet just as effectively now that he is bound by our laws. The secrets of the

North still lie with us."

At once, Lishka could only see Sieth sneering behind Zaral, a sudden recall of that horrific night. She glowered at him with cold hatred. He opened his mouth to say more but at that moment, Mordan appeared at her side.

"Know your loyalties," Sieth whispered, and straightened.

"Lishka." Mordan's cool voice flowed over her raw nerves. "You must come with me. Lady Raseska wishes to see you in her chambers." He glanced at Sieth and Sieth stepped back from them both. Lishka nodded in acknowledgment. Still Sieth lingered, though Mordan had dismissed him. Sieth grew emboldened by his Master, to disobey Mordan so openly.

Mordan ignored him and turned to lead down the hallway. Lishka followed, relieved at the excuse to escape Sieth, though his stare bored into her back. The brand on her neck tightened as if to punctuate his words. *Know your loyalties.*

Lishka and Mordan passed fewer Coven members as they moved into the deeper levels of the mansion. Lishka burned to ask Mordan questions. Again, she wondered whether he knew of Zaral's presence, or of the Boreal Study. She could not guess what he now thought of her, after she had turned a human without permission. Lishka had not considered consulting Mordan on Dominick or confiding in him her discovery of the Boreal Stones. Since they had arrived at Seattle over three centuries ago, Mordan had grown more distant, and had been sent away for years at a time. Lishka had not questioned him on his activities or sought to remain close. She wondered whether that had been a mistake. Mordan did not seem angry with her, but he offered no more information as to why she had been summoned.

In the quiet moment, Lishka again instinctively grasped for the power behind the Veil. A distant echo met her touch and she almost stopped in surprise. Pushing a little harder, Lishka detected the faint presence of the ancient power, just out of reach, but there. She still had an affinity for the magik. Perhaps with practice, she could regain some of the connection that had been weakened by the binding of the mark.

Mordan stopped before a heavy door marked with powerful symbols mirroring those of the Coven Council's. He touched his own mage's mark, then held his hand up to where a symbol lay carved in place of a doorknob. The symbol glowed momentarily, then faded.

"Enter," a woman's voice uttered, resounding from behind the oak. Mordan pushed the door open. He gestured Lishka forward and, with caution, she entered the room.

# CHAPTER 11

# A JOURNEY EAST

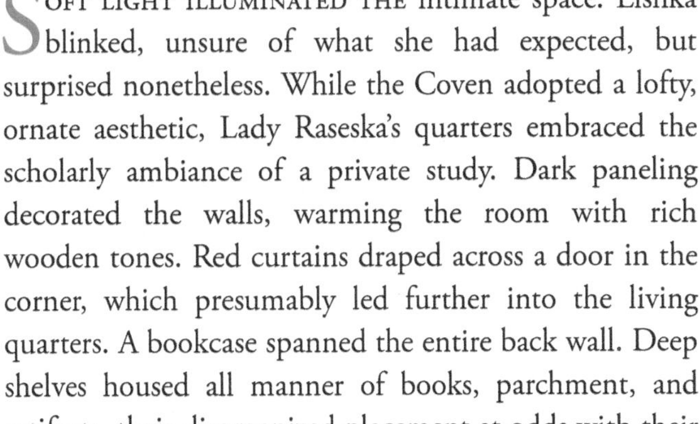

SOFT LIGHT ILLUMINATED THE intimate space. Lishka blinked, unsure of what she had expected, but surprised nonetheless. While the Coven adopted a lofty, ornate aesthetic, Lady Raseska's quarters embraced the scholarly ambiance of a private study. Dark paneling decorated the walls, warming the room with rich wooden tones. Red curtains draped across a door in the corner, which presumably led further into the living quarters. A bookcase spanned the entire back wall. Deep shelves housed all manner of books, parchment, and artifacts, their disorganized placement at odds with their immaculately composed owner. The air held the faint hint of an unknown spice, evoking a faraway desert.

Lishka took only seconds to absorb the room before focusing in on the center, where three figures clustered around a low table. She dipped her head in respect to Lady Raseska, who sat poised on a high-backed chair farthest across the room. At Lady Raseska's left, Lord Dorwan ignored Lishka's entry to stare into the stone fireplace built into the wall before him. An unnatural fire swirled, made of the same symbols that had lit the sconces in the Council Dome. The flames twisted and danced, emitting a glow that produced no heat.

On the opposite side of Lady Raseska, nearest to the fire, lounged Lord Cutler. He alone had discarded his ceremonial robes for a fitted jacket and trousers, and he raised his eyebrows at Lishka's entry. The hint of an amused smile plucked at the corner of his mouth. Beside him, another vacant chair sat expectantly. A tree had been carved to run up the wooden back. Leaves flowed along the top rim, while twisting roots crept down to form the legs.

Lady Raseska gestured toward this chair, and the silky folds of her robe slid back to expose a golden-brown arm. Lishka hesitated, the power among the group palpable, then stepped forward to take her allotted place. Mordan made his way to the remaining empty seat at Lady Raseska's side to settle himself between her and Lord Cutler.

"We appreciate you coming so quickly," Lady Raseska said, as if Lishka had been offered the choice. "There are important matters that must be discussed."

Lord Dorwan's attention shifted from the fire to Lishka, no less intimidating here than he had been as the Voice of the Council. Lishka ignored his steady gaze to instead face Lady Raseska, who appeared to lead this small gathering. A gathering of only Zachriel's Council Members, she noted, save for Mordan.

"As you know," continued Lady Raseska, "Trouble brews between the two Great Covens. The divide between Zachriel and Zaral has grown for centuries. Soon, we fear, this tension will come to a head." She regarded each Council Member and her somber eyes landed back on Lishka. "It is no secret, the lack of love you have for your Maker. But are you still loyal?"

Lishka almost flinched at the words and stole a glance at Mordan. Mordan gazed back with his familiar gentle expression that betrayed none of the thoughts beneath. Lishka couldn't help again noticing that this intimate room held several of Zachriel's most powerful and loyal followers. Mordan did not look ill at ease among them.

"He is my Master," she acknowledged, though the word *Master* threatened to choke her. "What choice do I have but to follow him?" Her brand twitched against her neck, and she repressed the memories of Zaral's power burning through her veins.

Lishka tried to avoid looking at Mordan then, but he leaned forward to draw her focus. He hunched over with his elbows on his knees, his hands clasped in the air between them. "The bond between Maker and child is usually very strong, though it can be broken," Mordan said gently, as if sensing her pain. "That is one of Zaral's oversights. The bond must be strengthened in the first years by mentoring, through training in our ways." Deeper meaning ran beneath his words.

"I doubt Zaral knows how deep your hatred goes," Lady Raseska commented. Lishka held Lady Raseska's gaze, burying her surprise at how much the Council Member had observed despite her attempts to remain unnoticed these past centuries.

"Mordan has vouched for you," Lady Raseska stated at once, disrupting her own train of thought. "But we must have your word that you will not repeat anything uttered here. To anyone."

Once more, Lishka found herself the sole subject beneath the watchful gaze of those strongest in her Coven. She had the immediate urge to retreat, to escape from the claustrophobic room and their attention. Lady Raseska demanded fidelity; she saw that with harsh clarity. Lishka wanted no part of the Council's secrets. She also did not see that she had much choice. They had revealed themselves as united in some plot that excluded Zaral's faction—she would not leave this room without relinquishing her loyalty to them.

"I will not speak of anything said within this room," Lishka agreed after several seconds. The binding of her words settled upon her and the tension in the air lessened by a millionth of a degree. Against her back, a truth spell that had been carved into the chair made itself known with a kindly tickle.

"Turning a human is a sacred process, and has not been performed for centuries," Lady Raseska said, though her words did not hold the accusatory tone Lord Dorwan's had, a mere hour before. "In your hearing, you had stated that you performed the Making on instinct, to protect the Coven. You could have easily let the human die, and called Kristoph's team to help cover the incident, as he has so often done before. Why, then, did you choose to break one of our oldest laws, knowing the consequences of your actions?"

The question hung in the air: why had she really turned Dominick? As Lishka looked about the group, she knew that her previous answer would not satisfy them.

"I'm not entirely sure, my Lady." Again, the symbols tingled as they welcomed her honesty. "I had met him only a few times before, and yet…" She hesitated, unsure how to explain herself. The truth would sound foolish to this group of powerful leaders. The spell urged her on, as if sensing her indecision. "Dominick first sought me out at *Midnight.* He said that he dreamt of me. I sensed a unique power inside him, unlike any human or other creature I had met before. Somehow, I knew how to find him again, in the human part of the city. He asked me where I would lead him." The last words dropped from her lips as if compelled. She had not meant to divulge Dominick's words, which somehow felt intimate and meant only for the two of them.

Lady Raseska's lips tightened, and Mordan straightened the slightest amount as if on alert, placing his hands on his knees.

"What did he mean? Lead him where?" Mordan asked.

"I don't know," Lishka replied. She thought she might as well confess to them everything; perhaps they could solve the riddle of Dominick. "The dream told him to find me at *Midnight,* but I sensed no premonition about him, or any other magikal ability. I didn't get any more answers."

"Did you tell anyone else of this?" The beginnings of a frown marred Lady Raseska's otherwise flawless complexion. Lishka shook her head.

"Not of the dream. But there is more. I think Dominick may have been conducting research for a study at the university. When I investigated his living quarters,

I found three rocks that contained power from beyond the Veil. The humans have somehow discovered the force contained in these vessels and are studying them." Lishka stopped, not knowing how to tell them of the murders surrounding the study without revealing what Zaral meant to keep secret. But they needed to know why Sieth had attacked Dominick. "I found a newspaper clipping in Dominick's apartment. The leading professors on this study have been found dead or have disappeared."

"The Boreal Study," Lord Dorwan interjected, his voice deep. "The university research that Zaral seeks to hide."

"You know of it?" Lishka turned to him, surprise overriding formal respect. Lord Dorwan ignored her to resume his stern stare into the fire. *Of course the Council is aware of the study.* Rather than reassuring her, that revelation was disquieting. The Council knew and still the murders continued. Lishka scanned the faces around her, searching for any sign that one of them could have sanctioned the murders alongside Lord Sootha.

"Zaral has made it known to a select few of his followers that humans are to be prevented from rediscovering the power beyond the Veil, at all costs," Mordan explained.

*Mordan must be one of those chosen few.* Her stomach twisted. Even worse than the Council being complicit was the knowledge that Mordan had betrayed Zaral's confidence.

"I showed Kiaban," Lishka admitted, all too aware that she had placed her confidence in Kiaban, and not Mordan. "I wasn't sure what they were."

"Can Kiaban be trusted to be discreet?" Lady Raseska asked Mordan. Lishka's suspicions had been correct: the knowledge had not passed beyond the Council to those like Kiaban and Kristoph.

"Kiaban will not reveal anything unless directly asked," Mordan answered. "Though Zaral's faction has acted to stop this research, it would not take a lot of investigation to realize that the study exists and is surrounded by suspicious deaths. I suspect that while Zaral does not wish the study to become common knowledge, even within the Covens, he knows that many would agree that the stones should be kept from humans, at any cost.

"Permission to kill a human can only come from a Council Member," Mordan continued, directing his assertion this time at Lord Dorwan, "and as this is Zachriel's Coven, such authorization should be aligned on by those in this very room. Lord Sootha must be sanctioning these killings we've heard of to discourage the research. Lord Aragnus would not be so tactful, and I did not give the order."

"Lord Sootha knows," Lishka confirmed. "I saw him on the armory level with Sieth, the night of the attack on Dominick. They acted secretive, disbanding when they saw me there with Kristoph. Later that night, Sieth tried to kill Dominick for his involvement with the stones— and as a message to me."

"Sieth?" Lord Cutler spoke for the first time from deep within his chair. "I thought I smelled him."

Lishka noted his words: smelled him. *Lord Cutler must have investigated the attack himself.*

"Lord Sootha has grown quickly in Zaral's favor," Lord Cutler added, directing his comment to Mordan. He rested the tip of his boot against the table, his heavy footwear similar to Lishka's own Keeper's garb. An ache struck her, a longing for the comfort of her soldier's clothing. Lord Cutler caught her observation and winked.

"He must be charged with terminating the study," agreed Mordan. "That does indeed explain the attack on Dominick, if, as Lishka said, Sieth became aware of his association." Mordan looked to Lishka. "But what do you mean, as a 'message' to you?"

Lishka paused. She had been reluctant to reveal Zaral's presence in front of his followers at her hearing. Now considering everything else that she had disclosed, Lishka did not see how she could avoid telling the Council Members the full truth.

"Zaral—" She hesitated once more at uttering her Maker's name and then plunged forward, the truth symbols urging her on. "Zaral came to me, here, in Seattle. He meant to ensure my allegiance. Sieth stood with him." She rejected the feeling of Zaral forcing her to submit.

Silence greeted her revelation.

"Zaral? Here in Seattle?" Disbelief hung from Lord Dorwan's words. He sat up even straighter and his fingers gripped the lionheads on the front of his armrests. "Impossible. We would have sensed him."

"Zaral has long possessed a deep connection to Lishka," said Mordan.

"Yet you have felt nothing. Why would he not have come to you?" Lady Raseska asked Mordan. She turned back to Lishka. "Are you sure?"

"Yes," Lishka said, her voice flat.

"Is it possible he suspects—" Lady Raseska stopped at a glance from Mordan. Lishka observed the exchange; in a brief moment, Mordan's eyes met hers and she sensed that something within him had changed. "And you?" Lady Raseska's voice broke their connection. "You have not heard of anything?"

Lord Cutler shook his head. "My sources have detected not even a rumor, my Lady. Although—" he tilted his head and looked to Lishka, "Sieth and his followers have been unusually attentive, have they not?"

"They have, my Lord," she acknowledged, keeping her surprise from showing, though she suspected Lord Cutler saw through the facade. Considering her status as a simple Keeper, the Council Members had noticed much about her daily interactions.

"That could be a sign," Lord Cutler suggested. "Not that they wouldn't have reason to keep one like you close." He flashed a charming smile, and his teeth gleamed white against his dark beard.

"What was Zaral doing here?" Lord Dorwan interrupted.

"I don't know," Lishka answered. "I think I sensed him, maybe even days before he revealed himself. He appeared the night that Sieth attacked Dominick. Sieth followed me when I sought Dominick and confronted him. Dominick told Sieth he was a student majoring in geology. Sieth must have deduced that he was involved in the study, possibly because I had shown interest in him." Lishka couldn't help admitting her own guilt, that she had drawn them to Dominick in the first place.

"Perhaps," Lady Raseska acknowledged. "Though it seems a weak link, that Sieth would suspect him simply because of his major, and closeness to you, unless, as you said, the attack in part was a message. Was there anything else about this human that might have piqued Sieth's suspicions?"

"He could sense the power in the stones," Lishka admitted. "He told me he could feel the energy, though I didn't have time to find out why. He did not appear to be a witch or have other supernatural blood."

Lady Raseska frowned. "How is this possible if he is not a witch? Are you sure he was only human?"

Lishka shook her head. "He felt human, though he had a unique energy inside of him. I'm not sure where it came from. But he told me they had created an instrument that could detect the energy, regardless of magikal affinity. The Boreameter."

The room went still.

"Ah. Now that would explain Zaral's sudden interest," Lord Cutler observed, his voice soft.

Lord Dorwan remained quiet, once more studying the fire. He showed neither surprise nor any other reaction to Lishka's confession of the Boreameter. Lishka wondered if he'd already been aware of its existence. *Had they already known of Dominick?*

"Zaral has always tried to keep humans from the North," Mordan added. "He believes if they discover the secrets hidden there, humans will remember the existence of our kind and band together to destroy us."

"Do humans really have such power?" Lishka asked, momentarily distracted from Lord Dorwan's lack of reaction. She couldn't imagine humans summoning the power to fight the Covens, regardless of their destructive technology. Other than witches, and those rare souls who had fey blood, humans did not possess the ability to draw on the Veil.

"Possibly," said Lord Cutler. "It is not a chance Zaral would risk, especially not when he can gain power with their ignorance." He had dropped his flirtation and his words held disdain. "As long as they fight amongst themselves, Zaral can continue his rise to power."

Lady Raseska shot Lord Cutler a pointed look and he stopped speaking. At once, the mood in the room changed. Tension crept back into the air and though none of them breathed, it seemed as though they collectively held their breath. Lady Raseska leaned forward and, without thinking, Lishka mirrored her.

"What I am about to tell you must not leave this room." Lady Raseska repeated the bond from before. She spoke in a low voice, despite the fact that the walls surrounding them had wards of secrecy and silence. Her eyes bored into Lishka's, and Lishka found herself nodding beneath the weight of Lady Raseska's authority, stronger than any truth spell.

"Zaral has ambitions greater than simply sharing control of our kind with Zachriel. His plan has progressed further than we knew." Lady Raseska's words fell upon the group with an air of familiarity, while Lishka frowned at the vague statement. Next to her, Lord Cutler shifted in his seat, reaching up to again stroke his pointed beard.

"Zaral does not seek to rule over humankind alone," Lady Raseska continued. "He plots to seize control of both Great Covens and lead this world into the depths of chaos."

Lishka sat quite still. *So, the rumors are true. The brothers are no longer united.*

"Already Zaral whispers in the ears of the human leaders," growled Lord Dorwan. "War is brewing.

Humans have always warred with one another, but this time their aggression feels different, more strategic. Their technology grows, as does their potential for mass destruction. And Zaral…there are rumors of pacts being made. He begins to force allegiances, although so far all is done in the shadows."

Each Council Member turned to stare at Lishka, in unison. Even Lord Cutler dropped all sense of amusement.

*Forcing allegiances.* Lishka remembered Zaral's words in the alley. *Have you forgotten who you belong to? Perhaps I will remind you.*

Lishka knew she must speak, though her mind reeled. She did not want to know of this coming war. A desperation flooded her. Lishka yearned to flee the room, to forget about the Boreal Study and Coven politics, and to return to life as a simple Keeper. Instead, she chose her words carefully. "I had heard that there was trouble between our leaders. Of course, most know that. But surely, Zaral would not move against Zachriel? His own brother?" Her blasphemy clanged in her ears.

"The time is almost upon us where the two must meet on the field," answered Lady Raseska. "Zachriel hopes to avoid bloodshed, though he prepares his allies for the possibility of war. Sides will have to be chosen, loyalties pledged." Lady Raseska studied her, and Lishka blinked first.

"Will it come to war?" Lishka asked, wanting to deny Lady Raseska's assertion, and what it would mean for the Covens.

"We believe so." Lady Raseska maintained her focus on Lishka, as though assessing Lishka's response. "Zaral will not submit to Zachriel's authority, and we cannot let

Zaral assume full power. Not now, when humans have obtained such abilities to destroy."

"But what about Zachriel?" Lishka insisted. "Where is he, and why does he not stop Zaral now?" Surely Zachriel held the power to subjugate his brother, to maintain the balance in the Covens, as it had been for thousands of years.

"Zachriel has a different goal," Lord Cutler said cryptically.

"As do you, Lishka," Lady Raseska broke in. "We have a mission for you."

"A mission?" Lishka barely registered Lady Raseska's words.

She had no desire to become a pawn in the conflict between the two brothers. Lady Raseska sensed her reluctance.

"Your violation provides us a unique opportunity to utilize your skills." Lady Raseska kept her voice low, and yet her words commanded the room. "For a long time you have hidden here, in the Coven of Zachriel. Now it is time for you to assist him. You will journey to the realm of the fey, high in the Krebarvitch Mountains. There you will seek out the Fey Queen and ask for her support, should it come to open war."

"We will need all the help we can get," muttered Lord Cutler.

"The fey," Lishka repeated. For all her long life, the fey had been little more than myth, the only proof of them in the color of her eyes and the meager inheritance of a strange yet largely useless power.

"The heritage you possess is stronger than you think," Mordan said. "Your fey blood makes it possible for you, and you alone, to enter their realm. Zaral knew this when he chose you. It was no accident that you were placed here, in Seattle, so close to the Northern wilderness and the fey."

Lishka considered Mordan with this new perspective. He had brought her to Seattle centuries ago. Mordan had invited her, Lishka assumed out of kindness, when he accepted the position as Zaral's third Council Member in Zachriel's Coven. Yet now she wondered at his motives. Perhaps it had been a mistake to keep herself ignorant of the agendas of those around her. For the first time in years, Lishka wished to seek Mordan's counsel, to lean on him for guidance as she once had.

"If you succeed in your mission," said Lady Raseska, "your mark will be unbound."

Lishka sat up straighter. The ability to push beyond the Veil and channel the energy, bend it to her will, could be hers again. The promise of it was enough to make her do anything. Then realization dawned.

"You mean I must venture into the mountains without the use of the mage's mark?"

Lady Raseska nodded. "You retain your magikal ability, even without the mark to properly guide it. And you have the power of the fey. Diluted as it is, this will mature as you rely on that power more now that your mage's mark is bound. You will need all your fey magik to enter their realm, and even then, you may not possess enough."

"So, I travel to the realm alone," Lishka said, for the moment overlooking Lady Raseska's suggestion of possible failure. Sitting surrounded by Zachriel's Council and Mordan, she found it difficult to imagine herself in the vast wilderness of the Northern mountains, far from both humans and her own kind.

"Well, not alone," Mordan paused. "Dominick will travel with you."

"Dominick?" Lishka repeated. Her earlier relief at learning Dominick had survived dissipated. "He is newly turned. He belongs here, at the Coven, to learn our ways."

"You turned him, intentionally or not," accused Lord Dorwan. "He must indeed be taught our ways, and you must teach him. You will show him how to survive in his new form. That is your responsibility as his Maker."

Lishka stopped her protest at the set expression on Lord Dorwan's face. She glanced down at his hands, the same hands that had gripped her face and channeled the power that bound her mark.

"Dominick will learn well, I think." Mordan disrupted the moment, and any further chance for Lishka to make her case against bringing Dominick into the mountains. "He has his own power within him, as you have sensed. You must train him how to be one of us. He possesses the mage's mark, bound though it is. He must be taught to safely access the power beyond the Veil, how to draw the energy. You must teach him to hunt."

Lishka balked at that thought. New vampires had notorious hunger and lack of control. She had already made Dominick a monster. She couldn't make him a killer as well.

"I think you might be glad to have him with you, in the end," Mordan added, his voice gentle.

Lishka stifled any protest. She would not change their minds, though she doubted that she would be grateful for Dominick at any point. Traveling to the realm of the fey would be challenging enough. Doing so with a newly turned vampire became quite another ordeal entirely.

Mordan leaned toward her. "There may be something more to this Dominick. Zaral coming to Seattle, Sieth's attacks, even Dominick's ability to sense the Veil, these are not just coincidence. You are his Maker, and you must strengthen the bond." His hands lay open before him in supplication, willing her to mentor Dominick.

Lishka looked down at her own pale hands. Her guilt once more crept up from the dark place she had pushed it to. She did not desire to be alone with Dominick, to face him and what he'd become out in the wild. Yet Lishka knew even without Mordan's urging that she could not leave him at the Coven, alone and at the mercy of those like Sieth. Even Mordan would not be able to fully protect Dominick from Sieth and Lord Sootha, and Lishka could not be sure he would choose to, given what they had revealed tonight. Dominick's fate had become tied with her own.

Then, too, and her guilt flared even more, was the promise of the mage's mark. The absence clawed at her gut, itched under her skin, and left her vulnerable. Once she completed their mission, her power would be returned to her. Lishka raised her head and met Mordan's eyes.

"How will I find the realm of the fey?" she asked.

Mordan sat back satisfied. At a nod from Lady Raseska, Lord Cutler stood and walked to the bookcase behind her chair. Books filled most of the shelves, their spines cracked and dirty from centuries of use. Sprinkled among the books sat several artifacts that pulsed with entombed ancient magik. They ranged from stones to sculptures to animal bones, and some looked suspiciously like fossilized human remains. Lishka remembered that Lady Raseska had been a prominent witch as a human, many millennia ago.

Lord Cutler stopped at a neat pile of rolled parchment. His fingers danced across the scrolls, before drawing a roll from the top of the stack. He spread it out across the table and the group leaned in to study the ink.

The map detailed the Krebarvitch mountain range, which crossed the full paper from south to north. A thin line depicted the Snoqualmie River, which flowed from the north in parallel to the mountains, before splitting into three forks almost directly east from Seattle: the North Fork, the South Fork, and the Middle Fork.

"You will follow the main roads east out of the city," explained Lord Cutler as he traced her route. "From there, continue northeast and follow the Middle Fork. Go as far as your truck will take you. You will enter the mountains by foot and travel north, up into the high peaks."

The small ink drawings of the mountain range looked so harmless on paper, although the impending winter would make the mountains treacherous.

"How far north?" Lishka asked.

Lord Cutler moved his hand closer to the border of Glacies Tellus, located within the mountain range. "Here." He pointed to Mirna Sorne, a lake cupped between two mountain peaks, which was the origin of the great Tiern River. "You will find the entrance between the Twin Peaks."

Lishka concentrated on the markings on the map to commit them to memory, as she would not take any proof of her mission with her. In all her years at the Coven, she had not left the western coastline. Rumors echoed in her ears from stories overheard at *Midnight*, of the wild men who made their own civilization deep in the forests, and of the strange creatures that preyed upon them in the dark. The Twin Peaks evoked familiarity and Lishka paused on the etchings. She had seen this before. *The Council Dome.* The image had been roughly carved at the corner of the ceiling, the oldest of all the depictions of their history. Lishka suppressed a chill that ran the length of her spine.

"You cannot trust memory alone," cautioned Lady Raseska, interrupting Lishka's study. "Your fey blood must guide you. If the fey allow you to find them, that is."

"They will," said Mordan, and his words held no doubt of Lishka's ability.

"Has Dominick been told of the journey?" Lishka asked.

"He knows that you go to the mountains to request help from the fey," answered Lord Dorwan. "I do not think he fully understood what the fey are. He is in the initial shock of transition."

Lishka drew her eyes away from the parchment. "Does he know about Zaral and Zachriel?"

"He knows enough," Lord Dorwan replied. "He will follow you."

"Be ready in an hour's time," Lady Raseska instructed. Lishka snapped her head up.

"Already you have been noticed by Zaral's followers. Dominick's Making has drawn considerable attention," Lord Cutler explained, almost sounding impressed at the commotion Lishka had caused. "We must move quickly to ensure that you are able to sneak away." He flashed a conspiratorial smile. "We will put word out that you have retreated to confinement, to hide your shame."

They planned to use her humiliation to hide their true intent. She could not help a moment of anger mixed with regret, that her careful effort to build her place as a respected Keeper over the past three centuries had been demolished in a single night.

"It's getting close to dawn," Lishka said instead, her one last attempt to put off the inevitable. She tried to process all that she'd been charged with in such a short amount of time: first the binding, then the knowledge of the coming war, now this assignment.

"Therefore, not many will be about," concluded Lady Raseska.

"It's the perfect time to depart unnoticed," added Lord Cutler, once more amused.

Lishka stared down at the small line marking her path, which crossed to the east and up through the mountain pass. Soon she would be there in the wild, journeying toward the unknown, to prepare for a battle that so far consisted of only whispers.

DAWN HAD ALMOST fallen upon them when Lishka departed the Coven that had housed her for three hundred years. Lady Raseska and Mordan stood shadowed at the entrance, and Lishka permitted herself a moment to study the mansion. Its stone walls loomed above them, unchanged from when she had first arrived, though the sides now boasted more ivy that crept across the windows. Light had barely begun to hit the uppermost turrets, its presence signaling that most inhabitants would be securely tucked away in their places of rest. No one would be there to observe her leave.

Behind her, an old, nondescript truck sat parked in the drive. Dominick slumped against the passenger window, staring out across the Coven grounds. A mere shell of his former self, he barely acknowledged her. Only time would tell who he had now become.

For comfort, Lishka gripped her new blade, secure in its scabbard. Once more in her Keeper's standard-issue boots and hooded coat, she almost felt like herself again, though the emptiness from the mage's mark lingered at the edges of her mind. Dominick's own weaponry had been packed into the cab. Lishka would need to train him to use the sword properly.

Lady Raseska held her clasped hands against the smooth silk of her gown. "Remember, much depends on your ability to convey Zachriel's message to the fey," she said, her voice soft yet firm. "We will need their alliance."

"Travel swiftly," said Mordan. The shadows from the Coven walls deepened the lines in his face, temporarily aging him though he would never grow old. "Be vigilant, watch for those that might follow or try to stop you. We will do all we can here to prevent you from being tracked."

Lishka nodded. Lady Raseska leaned forward to take Lishka's cold hands between her own. "Trust your instincts and you will not go astray."

"And trust in each other," Mordan added, looking from Lishka to the truck. Lishka had not been given a chance to talk to Mordan and obtain much-needed answers. Now she didn't know when she would see him again. She had no choice but to trust him and follow him as she always had, even through shifting allegiances.

Feeling simultaneously restless and reluctant to leave, Lishka bowed her head in respect to them both, then turned to the truck and Dominick. Once she left the Coven grounds, she would solidify her fealty to Zachriel. She climbed into the cab and tucked her sword into the back seat, alongside the blade meant for Dominick. She started the engine, which rumbled loudly in the pre-dawn night. Dominick remained facing the door window, unreactive to her presence in the cab. Lishka ignored him and maneuvered the truck out of the driveway and through the iron gates. She did not look back.

"SHE WILL BE weakened by the binding," Lady Raseska said after a moment's silence. "Unfortunate."

"Unavoidable," replied Mordan. Quiet settled over the driveway, and the mist that had been disturbed by the truck blanketed the gravel once again. "But perhaps not so unfortunate. The binding of her mark lessens the bond between her and Zaral. She will have to rely on the ability her fey blood brings her, a power that Zaral has no control over."

They watched where the truck had disappeared into the night as if they could still see Lishka and Dominick heading east. The heaviness of their obscurity spell hovered above them, ensuring that no enemy eyes watched. Finally, Lady Raseska turned toward Mordan.

"Do you think…" She hesitated for a moment as though choosing her words carefully. "Is it really possible that they, together, could be the ones spoken of?"

Mordan paused. "I've lived long enough to know too much stock cannot be put in vague prophecies and premonitions. Still, one thing is clear: they are both important to the outcome, one way or the other."

Lady Raseska sighed. "You never can give a straight answer."

Mordan smiled.

Lishka glanced over at her silent companion. Dominick pressed his forehead against the window's glass and stared at the passing landscape, his eyes unseeing. Lishka wondered what thoughts went through his head. In the distance, Mount Rainier loomed high into the southeastern sky unusually clear of clouds. Pink tinged its permanently snowy cap as the sun began to rise. Lishka faced forward again, eyes intent on the road ahead. Deep inside, an unexpected excitement squirmed at leaving the Coven for the greater wilderness beyond the city.

They moved east, across the floating bridges and into the densely forested mainland. In the distance, the Krebarvitch Mountains rose high above the trees, their peaks covered by freshly fallen snow.

# PART II

# EAST

# CHAPTER 12

# MIDDLE FORK

FULL SUNRISE FOUND LISHKA and Dominick traveling through Ravensdale, a small coal town nestled in the foothills of the Krebarvitch Mountains. With luck, dawn brought in more clouds as they neared the mountains. Weak light trickled through the tall fir trees that gave way to a post office, police station, church, and a cheerful red market. A patch of houses joined the storefronts to mark what could only be tenuously dubbed downtown. The crisp air that wafted through the cracked open window smelled of wood smoke.

They passed through in silence.

Lishka risked a glance at her stoic companion. Dominick had not moved in the hours since they had left the Coven. His now pale skin, no longer so sun-kissed, had taken on an ashy tinge. He would need to feed soon. Dominick's nostrils flared and he tensed, while his unfocused gaze sharpened on passing houses. Lishka recognized the scent. Humans stirred in the nearby homes and shops. Dominick closed his eyes, and his breath quickened as he inhaled their warm smell. Lishka pressed her foot down on the gas pedal, accelerating them out of the town. Before them, undeveloped hills swept up out of the valley in a blanket of dark evergreen. Soon, they would have to turn northeast toward Middle Fork, and the mountain pass.

Despite the rising sun, Lishka kept her foot to the gas and pulled her wide hood closer around her face. Mordan's warning rang in her ears. *Travel swiftly.* She must put as much distance between them and Seattle as possible, utilizing the daylight hours while the Coven slept. The heavily tinted windows on the truck helped to protect them from sunlight, and the thick cloud layer created an additional shield. While the full glare would cause her considerable pain, Dominick would fare better. Freshly turned, he would only experience discomfort in the light, equivalent to a harsh sunburn for a human.

They would have to stop that night. Lishka must teach Dominick to hunt. She suppressed a grimace, and her eyes again flicked to him. He had resumed staring out the window, his predator instinct replaced once more by the dull, dazed look in his eyes.

Left alone with her thoughts, Lishka replayed the secret conversation in Lady Raseska's rooms. Mordan was no longer loyal to Zaral. By accepting this mission, Lishka had likewise followed Mordan in forswearing her Maker for his rival brother. She tried not to dwell on the question she feared most. *What would happen should Zaral find out?*

The snow began to fall as they gained altitude. The daylight reached its apex, slowing the blood in Lishka's veins with drowsiness and urging her to slip into a coma-like sleep. Lishka resisted, instead turning the truck north to follow the lesser-used roads up toward the pass. The asphalt road transitioned to packed earth, and the ruts turned to muddy troughs from the wet snow. She shifted into four-wheel drive and pushed the truck on. Alongside the road, the firs and spruce grew more twisted, churning up from uneven earth and rock. Moss dripped from the evergreen branches. Every so often, a break in the trees revealed a glimpse of heavily forested hills and snowcapped peaks. Gray clouds rested over the jagged horizon and the white slopes glowed with now-fading light.

If Ravensdale could be considered a town, then Middle Fork stood as no more than an outpost at the edge of the Northern wilderness. The settlement sat squarely at the point where the mountain range split into two: the main ridge of the Krebarvitch Mountains that continued northward and the Soothe Mountains that diverged west, back to the coastline. Here the folk held onto outdated superstition and suspicion of strangers. The wind often blew from the North, bringing with it a perpetual metallic energy that hung in the air. This high in the Northern mountain range, the use of technology became nearly nonexistent. Horses remained the primary mode of transportation, though a few rusted trucks could be seen parked at various driveways. Their truck fit in well, as ground clearance became a necessity where summers passed quickly, while the winters held on too long, full of ice and deep snow.

The mountain road became Middle Fork's main street,

the lane only a touch wider and slightly better maintained than the side roads leading to other homesteads. Rough storefronts lined the road, complete with a small chapel that desperately needed new paint. At the end of the street, there hunkered a single weathered inn. The sharp-slanted roof kept heavy winter snow from breaking through, while the thick stone blocks of the lower walls trapped in heat. A sign hung off the iron rod over the door, too faded now to read.

Lishka pulled onto the unevenly graveled parking space near the entrance. A smaller, rougher building had been erected behind the inn. The musty smell of horse and hay indicated that it must be the stables.

She climbed out of the truck without a word to Dominick and stepped into the slush. She considered whether to bring him inside with her or leave him be. No humans lingered outside in the cold, though she smelled them in the buildings. The bloodlust could overpower him in such close proximity.

She walked around the car to assess him through the window. He met her eyes for the first time, and she tipped her head toward the inn. He unbuckled his unnecessary seatbelt and opened the door. He moved gingerly, as if he'd just recovered from a long illness. Lishka let him step out of the truck before speaking in a low whisper that only he could hear.

"We will stop here for the night." Lishka tried to hold Dominick's gaze and failed. He looked over her head, taking in the town. "Dominick, tonight you must hunt. You will need strength before we head north into the mountains," Lishka explained, as if to apologize for what she must now teach him. At this, Dominick focused back on her. His once open face remained closed to her, a foreign soul in a familiar body. Lishka pressed on. "We'll stay at the inn to help avoid suspicion. We can blend in with the trappers and other travelers."

Dominick shot her clothing a pointed glance, the first sign of his former human self. Lishka's rougher travel garb, while appropriate for the harsh conditions of the mountains, was a little too fine and clean to blend in with the mountain folk. Lishka ignored him, though a small hope blossomed that some semblance of Dominick remained after all.

"Do you think you can enter through the front door?" They both knew what she meant: could Dominick enter without giving way to the temptation of nearby humans. Again, he looked over her head at the inn. "Dominick?"

He turned his attention back to her, his brown eyes so dark they could almost be black. Lishka suppressed an impromptu shudder.

"Yes." The word came out clipped as his lips maneuvered around his new, longer canines.

"Good."

Lishka led the way to the inn. The soft crunch of gravel indicated that Dominick followed. If the worst happened and Dominick could not control himself, she could subdue him with magik. At this thought, Lishka became acutely aware of the dead place on her forehead. To cast such magik would require a lot of her energy, considering she no longer had her mark to both channel the power and control it. Already her reserves waned, the adrenaline from Lady Raseska's meeting having worn off during the drive through daylight. Better to conserve her strength.

The sun had begun its rapid descent behind clouds and the light drifted low between the trees, further cooling the outside air. As they crossed the threshold into the inn, a warm billow greeted them in drastic contrast to the cold. They had entered a small lounge, which smelled strongly of wood smoke from a fire blazing in the hearth against the far wall. To the left, Lishka spotted a bar and dining room adjoining the main lobby. She approached the narrow welcome counter, where the receptionist picked at her nails.

The young woman peered up at them from behind dirty bangs.

"One room?" Her voice drawled out in a bored tone, even as she took in their unusual clothing.

"Yes, just for the night." Sharing a room with Dominick would allow Lishka to keep a better eye on him. The receptionist fumbled below the desk for a key, while Lishka extracted the necessary payment according to the price advertised in a sign on the counter. Lishka put the money on the counter and reached for the key in the woman's outstretched hand. The woman didn't move, instead staring past Lishka to Dominick.

"Is he okay?"

Lishka turned around. Dominick's eyes had widened to large, black plates, his face drawn gaunt as all muscles tensed. His nostrils flared, consuming the scent of the woman, even as he tried to hold himself in control. Lishka spun to snatch the key from the woman's hand.

"He's fine." She shoved against Dominick, forcing him to the stairs. With belabored movement he turned and took the first step, then the next. His back filled the width of the narrow stair and blocked her view. Footsteps clunked above them, but luckily no one descended. Lishka stopped herself from giving him another push, eager to confine him in their room. She knew he had fed from blood bags before they left the Coven, per policy for the newly made. Still, she had never been with one so recently turned before, let alone while surrounded by so many humans. Dominick halted at the top of the stairs, and she almost collided with him. He peered down the hall lined with rooms.

"210," Lishka instructed, checking the number on the key.

Their room turned out to be conveniently located at the end of the hallway, sandwiched between a vacant room and an external exit. Lishka unlocked the door, her ears on alert in case anyone else entered the hall.

The simple room held a queen-sized bed, an armoire, a padded chair, and one small bathroom that contained a tub for bathing. Thick shabby curtains covered a window on the opposite wall, near the bed. Those would do well to block the potent morning light, though Lishka did not plan to spend much time in Middle Fork. Their hasty departure from the Coven had left her with an underlying sense of urgency, and she itched to move on.

Dominick edged into the room and sat down on the bed to face the window, his every muscle tense as if ready to jump through the glass. His jaw clenched and he kept his hands in fists on his knees. Lishka let the door shut behind her and lingered in the entranceway, watching him. He closed his eyes and inhaled as if to calm himself, his breath catching at the scent of humans.

A knock came from behind the door. Lishka snapped her head around. She had been so fixated on Dominick, she had not detected the presence in the hallway. She opened the door just a crack. The young woman from the front desk stood there, the bored expression on her face quickly turning to curiosity.

"I thought maybe he could use some food." The woman, closer to a teenage girl, gestured toward the trolley beside her, which boasted two trays heaped with roast potatoes and an unknown type of meat sparingly drizzled with a thin brown sauce. Lishka stared at her, all too aware of Dominick's attention at her back.

"He looked so pale," the girl added, her voice tapering off.

"Fine. Thank you." Lishka purposely kept her tone curt to invite no more questions. Behind her, Dominick rose from his perch on the bed.

The girl had clearly dressed herself up, her long bangs pinned back to present a heavily made-up face. She craned her neck, peeking around Lishka and into the room in an obvious attempt to catch sight of Dominick. As she did so, she held out the silverware, gripping the sharp end of the knife. A drop of blood welled at the tip of her finger.

"*Shit.*" She dropped the silverware onto the cart, scooping up one of the napkins to wrap around her finger. She glanced up to see the door closing. "Wait, don't you want your food?"

Lishka slammed the door shut on the stunned face of the girl whose eyes had grown noticeably wider as she stared over Lishka's shoulder.

The bed creaked and Lishka whirled around just in time to glimpse Dominick's face before he rammed into her with the full length of his body. She crashed against the door, where her head bounced off the hard wood. The door held sturdy despite its apparent age. Dominick's eyes dilated and his lips pulled back from sharp teeth in a snarl only inches from Lishka's face. He did not even register her presence; Lishka could have been just an extension of the door barring him from his prey.

She shoved him back enough to force her left arm between them. Her right hand reached out and gripped his throat. She continued her momentum to flip him about where she pinned him against the wall that separated their room from the next.

"Stop," she commanded.

Dominick fought against her, intent on the door and the human who stood beyond it. She could feel his desire lessening, but not enough yet for him to regain control.

"Dominick." She locked eyes with him. "Stop." Lishka let the word flow from her, smooth and hypnotic, weaving her own inherent influence into the tone.

Dominick twitched several times, then stilled. Recognition glimmered in his eyes as he refocused on Lishka. She retained her firm grip. The adrenaline still raced through his body, ready to fuel his enhanced strength.

A shadow crossed Dominick's face as hunger gave way to shame. At this, Lishka released her hold, one finger at a time. When Dominick showed no signs of aggression, she withdrew her arm and stepped away from him. His body slumped, and he stumbled back to the window where he sat on the floor between the wall and the bed.

Lishka mirrored his movement, sliding her back down the door into a seated position. Dominick did not move. Lishka's eyes drifted to the crack in the curtains above his head, where the evening light had almost faded.

"Get some rest," she said. Dominick glanced up at her. "In a few hours, we hunt."

He tucked his head down to rest his forehead on bent knees. Lishka grasped for the power beyond the Veil. Despite their proximity to the North, the barrier resisted her influence. Her lack of the mage's mark made itself known. Finally, she sluggishly managed to draw a small amount of the power into symbols. She flicked a few concealment signs with her fingers, sending the clumsy symbols to hang above the window and door as an extra precaution against curious eyes. Dominick twitched as the magik passed him. Lishka leaned her head back against the wood, closed her eyes, and waited.

THEY SLIPPED OUT of the inn close to midnight. Lishka opted for the window to avoid using the exit outside their door in case any late-night guests also took those stairs. Lithely, she slid through the frame, her movement clearly beyond human ability. She held her sheathed sword quiet along her thigh as she dropped down to the ground below. It would be careless to leave without some protection, especially now, with her access to the power beyond the Veil limited. Lishka's pathetic attempt at the protective castings further underscored her weakened ability. Despite Mordan's and Lady Raseska's stealth, there existed the possibility that she had been followed. Lishka doubted that Sieth would believe she had been shamed into hiding.

Dominick landed silently behind her, having easily made a graceful jump from window to ground. He glanced back up at the window above them, surprised. Before them, what moonlight trickled through the clouds reflected off patches of snow. Lishka crept forward, avoiding the snow that would give away their footprints. Behind her, Dominick moved in bursts. A restlessness surged through him, what she recognized as the desire for blood.

Lishka led them only a short way down the main road before identifying a shadowy side street that would better hide their passing. Tiny snowflakes trickled from the sky, dusting in white the evergreens that cast elongated shadows across the road. Dominick stumbled, caught himself, and stumbled again. Lishka stopped and turned to him. He looked around them, blinking rapidly. It took her a moment to realize the problem.

"Your senses are heightened," she whispered. "Your eyes can absorb more light than before. That, combined with the ability to see thermal energy, means you can see in the darkest places better than any human in daylight. We are, after all, nocturnal."

Dominick tilted his head to focus on the shadows between the branches.

"You'll get used to it." Lishka put him at her back to continue leading their way through the town. The snow created a muffled stillness, and not even a breeze added movement to the night.

Soon, Lishka realized her mistake in choosing such a small town for Dominick's first hunt. No nightlife existed to keep people out late, and the cold only added to the sense of abandonment. They would have to go into the woods to hunt animals instead. Yet the consciousness humans possessed meant their blood provided additional sustenance, an energy that would be needed for the journey into the mountains.

Then too, Dominick must learn how to take human blood without killing the host. Otherwise, he might find himself unable to stop when the time came and could drain someone dry.

Lishka paused in the shadow of a lean-to filled with firewood, and searched for any sign of movement in the surrounding streets. They had arrived at what appeared to be a logging yard and the trees alongside the road gave way to stacked logs. Dominick joined her, calm for the moment. They stood for a few minutes, the silence deepening with the night. The tang of otherworldly magik sharpened the air, faint but worrying.

Dominick shifted from foot to foot, the scraping of his boots breaking the silence. He had not yet adopted the aptitude for long stillness. Lishka understood this would take time but couldn't help her irritation. She needed to concentrate, and Dominick was proving a distraction.

Lishka inhaled once more. While the air contained the metallic scent of the essence beyond the Veil, it also held a primal musk unfamiliar to her. Beside her, the shuffling stopped. She broke her focus to glance at Dominick. His entire body had gone rigid and his eyes once more dilated to fill his irises. He lifted his head, closed his eyes, and inhaled so deeply, the air could have been blood. Then he opened his eyes. No longer soft brown, now red encircled his pupils. Lishka anchored her right foot behind her to brace herself.

He turned and bolted back the way they had come, tearing into the darkness. Lishka leapt after him. His boots pounded on the packed earth ahead of her, near silent to all but Lishka. The magik intensified. Lishka pushed herself to run faster; Dominick headed straight for the source of the unknown magik.

Ahead, the footsteps slowed. Lishka turned a corner to see Dominick approach an intersection that contained several dark storefronts. She slowed her pace, searching the road ahead for what had triggered him.

Dominick stopped and crouched forward. With careful, deliberate movement, Lishka positioned herself beside him. He didn't acknowledge Lishka's presence, his attention focused on the street stretching before them. The scent of human, mixed with the unfamiliar musk, wafted over them. She set her hand on Dominick's arm. His muscle tensed beneath her fingers, and he stared at her with shadowed eyes, finally registering awareness. Her grip tightened and she jerked her head to the left, indicating that they should duck out of sight. He looked out into the dark, then back at her, his muscles jumping beneath his skin. Finally, he nodded, and she led them under the cover of the buildings.

They dissolved themselves into the shadows, watching the street. Lishka kept her touch on Dominick's arm, ready to hold him back. Her senses stretched before her, and she knew a human drew closer to them. Dominick flexed his arm under her grip, his body practically vibrating with energy. He needed to feed. Despite the strange magik, this would be his best opportunity. A shuffling sounded ahead, much closer. Lishka glanced at Dominick.

The man at her side barely resembled the stranger she had first met, what seemed ages ago, at *Midnight*. Dominick's face glowed chalk pale, his eyes black pools surrounded by faint blue bruising. He inhaled, fixated on the form somewhere before them. The shadow of the predator hung across his face. Lishka shivered; she had done this.

She asserted her own power over Dominick's blood to pull his gaze down to hers. Reluctantly, he let himself be drawn, unable to resist the Maker's call. Lishka dipped her head to indicate that he should watch and emulate her. She reached down into her internal cold power and drew on her ability to command human attention. Instantly the aura around her changed to become soothing and welcoming, enticing to humans. Instinct drove Dominick to mirror her, Lishka's blood in his veins helping him to copy her action. He had already become so strong. She both saw and felt the air around him shift. His presence became irresistible. Satisfied, Lishka turned and stepped out into the middle of the road. Dominick followed her and together they walked out of the shadows and down the path, to the human approaching in the dark.

CHAPTER 13

# A WITCH AND A GHOUL

THE WOMAN SHAMBLED ACROSS the rutted dirt, her head bowed low to focus on her path. A hump rose from her back, either a deformity from birth or caused by hard living in the mountains. Long scraggly hair draped across her bony shoulders and her skirt's torn hem dragged in the slush. Yet despite her haggard appearance, Lishka sensed youth. She was not too much older than Lishka had last been when human. Though she appeared weak, the hint of a veiled power still clung to the woman's body.

Lishka and Dominick slunk toward her. Influence wafted from them to draw her in, and Lishka dimmed her own hypnotism so that Dominick could take the lead. The woman lifted her head. Her eyes, dull and glassy, sharpened as she spotted them. She began to shuffle toward them eagerly, unaffected by Dominick's influence that should have put her into a hypnotic state.

"Wait," she called out in a husky voice. Her eyes

flicked from Lishka to Dominick. "Wait," she said again, her voice softer. "There is no need."

Lishka finally recognized the aura.

"What do you want, witch?" Lishka asked. The woman pivoted to one side to reveal the source of the strange scent in the air. Dominick stiffened.

A demonic creature clung to the woman's back. The size of a four-year-old child, it had a bald head and bat-like leathery wings that it kept folded along its body. It gripped at the woman with two clawed arms and two strong legs, and its bald tail draped down to rub against her calves through the folds of her skirt. Hollowed pits took the place of eyes in its round head. Its mouth opened a few inches to reveal a hole filled with tiny, razor-sharp teeth. As it inhaled, it drew in the witch's energy.

Lishka looked at it with disgust. *A ghoul.* It lived off organic magik, making this witch the perfect host. *Strange to see a ghoul this low in the mountains.* The scent of the human settlement had most likely drawn it away from the higher crags of the mountain cliffs. When feeding, the creature became translucent and could only be seen in one's peripheral vision. Even then that vision must be supernatural; humans would not be aware of it at all.

The witch took another hopeful step forward. "I sensed you as soon as you arrived," she said.

Lishka tensed. She had not picked up the witch's presence in the town, nor the ghoul's. The witch paused, then stumbled closer, eyeing Dominick. So far, he had not moved from Lishka's side, though his hands clenched into fists. The ghoul had not yet reacted to their presence, intent only on stealing its host's energy.

"This demon came upon me in the night, catching

me unaware, or else I would have been able to keep it off. I was wondering…hoping…" The witch's voice trailed off as she gazed up at Lishka and Dominick. No fear shone in her eyes; the ghoul had already drained a large portion of her energy.

"Yes?" Lishka prompted.

"Well, if you were to rid me of this creature, I would be grateful. Extremely grateful," she finished. The woman proposed her blood in exchange for freeing her from the ghoul. Lishka glanced at Dominick. He had lost all interest in the ghoul, his eyes now fixed on the woman's pulse. She possessed a vital lifeforce, despite what the ghoul had already consumed. *This witch must have been powerful indeed.* Destroying the ghoul would be easy enough, and she doubted another opportunity for human blood would present itself tonight.

"We accept your deal," Lishka agreed. The woman grimaced, unable to manage a smile in her dejected state. She turned to put the ghoul's head closest to Lishka and Dominick. Lishka drew her blade, the symbols on it shining in the dark. Dominick took a step back to give her room. She gripped the blade tight, its keen edge slicing the air even as she brought it into position. The ghoul tightened its hold on the woman and stared with soulless eyes. Its round mouth gaped open, and it sucked in the witch's energy with great gulping inhalations, intending to drain her dry and use her lifeforce to flee. The witch sagged and ducked her head. Lishka whisked her blade up to bring it crashing down along the ghoul's body, carefully avoiding the witch's back.

Steel met leathery skin and the ghoul shrieked. Its cry filled the space, raking across Lishka's skin like sandpaper.

She again lifted her blade. The creature loosened its grasp on the woman and raised its damaged wings for balance, extending its reach. Out of habit, Lishka attempted to summon power through the mage's mark and found it uncontrollable. Instead of harnessing energy to project toward the ghoul, the magik slipped through her grasp like water. Seizing its moment, the ghoul swiped at her, knocking her off balance. The jagged edge of a claw scraped against her leather sleeve.

Lishka leapt back out of the ghoul's reach and regained her footing. A guttural growl rumbled to her left. She spared a quick glance to Dominick, who had dropped once more into a low crouch. Red glimmered in his eyes, and he inched a step closer. Realizing it was outmatched, the ghoul began to beat its wings frantically to escape into the air.

Lishka kept her momentum going, turning on her heel to face the ghoul once more. This time, she swung her blade high. As the ghoul lowered its wings on the downswing, it left its neck exposed. Lishka brought the steel down in a clean stroke and lopped off the head.

The beast's body teetered for a moment, then slid down the witch's back to the ground, the small round head rolling a few paces off the road. Upon hitting the earth, the body shriveled into a lifeless, crumpled heap. Lishka dropped her blade to her side. Her left hand flicked across the familiar symbols. She drew on her own inner reserves of strength instead of the power beyond the Veil. The body and head burst into a cleansing fire that erased all traces of the creature except for a few lingering ashes, which drifted out to blacken the nearby patches of snow.

The witch heaved a great sigh and with some effort

straightened her back. At her full height, she stood several inches taller than Lishka. She closed her eyes, relishing her newfound lightness. The lines on her face softened, and her cheeks grew plumper with color returning to her skin. Her hair, though still dirty, fell thicker about her shoulders.

The woman opened her eyes and pulled her hair back to expose her pale neck. At Lishka's side, Dominick froze. The fight with the ghoul had only raised his adrenaline, and he was fixated completely on the witch's carotid artery. His lips drew back to showcase his long canines and the shadows beneath his eyes deepened.

Lishka put her hand on his shoulder and squeezed. Not even her physical strength could pierce Dominick's lust for blood. Yet the Maker's authority could. She once more pushed against his mind to penetrate the haze.

"Use your influence," Lishka instructed. Dominick twitched at her words. He fought a war inside, the desire to feed combating the urge to listen to Lishka. Dominick closed the gap between himself and the woman, with Lishka close behind. The witch did not move, though her right hand, the one not holding back her hair, traced symbols that made the air hot. She prepared a spell, in case Lishka could not control Dominick.

With the forced restraint of someone fighting all natural instinct, Dominick raised his arm to wrap it around the witch's waist and bring her in close to him. The muscle along his jaw twitched, and he gripped her just a little too tightly. Her fingers flicked the edge of a symbol, and then she sagged in his arms as at last he caught her eyes. Her head lulled against his shoulder, and he leaned down, opened his mouth, and bit. She grunted at the sharp pain, which penetrated the clumsy hypnotism. The scent of blood filled the air. Dominick reached his other hand up to grip her neck. At this, Lishka took a step forward, but Dominick only drank and showed no increased aggression. The blood had not turned him into a monster.

After a few moments, Lishka determined Dominick had taken enough to replenish his energy without harming the witch.

"That's enough." Her sharp words cut through the hypnotism and should have triggered Dominick to stop. He ignored her. "Dominick." Lishka imbued his name with the command of the Maker's bond. Dominick withdrew, his lips lined in red, and released the witch. A sudden look of horror and awareness sank into his face, and he retreated several steps back from both the witch and Lishka.

The witch slumped in her stance and began to sway. She had already been weakened by the ghoul and would not be able to endure much more. Her eyes flicked to Lishka with the faint beginnings of fear, fear that Lishka would demand her part of the deal and would take too much. Lishka reached out to stroke the woman's hair, emanating warmth. The woman's eyes drooped once more, only in part from Lishka's affect. Lishka bent over her.

The woman's blood still held strength despite the ghoul, and Lishka required only a few sips to rejuvenate herself. She withdrew and licked the last few drops of blood away. The rich scent of blood hung in the air and Lishka inhaled, relishing the life bursting through her veins. They were lucky to have found this witch.

They escorted her to a small shop where the witch said

she could find shelter for the night. She did not live in the settlement; instead, she resided in a small hut farther west up the mountain ridge. Lishka saw no need to adjust her memory despite the opportunity to teach Dominick. The witch posed no threat, and Lishka did not want to waste any of the energy they had just consumed. She could not even be sure that such a spell would work. The organic magik in witches did not always react as expected to the death magik that the Covens possessed.

Before they left her, she gave them valuable advice regarding those who lived in the mountains.

"There are bandits that rove further north, not too far from here," the witch warned. "They are gathering in greater numbers as the winds grow stronger from the north." She shivered and wrapped her tattered shawl around her. The wound at her neck had already clotted. She glanced from Lishka to Dominick, then her gaze shifted beyond them, to the trees. "It seems things are becoming more and more barbaric."

"What kind of people are these bandits?" Lishka asked. "Will there be witches with them, those who could sense us pass?"

The witch shook her head. "I doubt it. They are wild men, certainly dangerous, but not to ones such as you." She nodded to both Lishka and Dominick. "However, if you do not wish to be seen, I suggest that you head northeast out of the Middle Fork, rather than directly north."

Lishka nodded. She had heard talk of the wild people who lived in the inner foothills and preyed on travelers. While she and Dominick could manage any humans, she wanted to avoid as many curious eyes as possible.

They returned to the inn just as light began to

pierce the night's shadows. Dominick followed Lishka obediently, subdued from the blood. Lishka stood on the ground while Dominick launched himself into the air. The new energy enabled him to reach the open window in a single leap, and he slid through into their room. Lishka followed suit, her boots making no noise against the wooden frame as she gripped the sill before ducking inside. Once in the room, Lishka drew the heavy curtains tight behind them. The fabric was no wall of stone, but it would suffice.

Dominick slumped into the padded chair and closed his eyes to shut himself off. Lishka let him be. The first hunt was always overwhelming, as it marked the final step in transitioning from human to vampire. At least he had not killed.

An unbidden memory splashed before her, of pleading brown eyes growing dull with death. Lishka shoved down the image and sat on the edge of the bed. She unbuckled her scabbard and lay it within easy reach, then lay down, turning away from Dominick. Heaviness stole across her and she willed herself to sleep. But sleep would not come. Instead, memories flooded through her.

*"Drink, Lishka," Zaral's voice commanded. She stared down at the girl, just on the cusp of adulthood, who crouched before her. Brown eyes locked onto hers and desperate hope shone in the girl's face. She leaned forward, recognizing Lishka as one of her own, as though Lishka could possibly help her. Lishka convulsed and her body arched toward the girl with hunger. The craving for blood filled her, nearly consuming her mind. Yet she couldn't quite make herself do it. Zaral knelt and the girl, paralyzed by fear, released a low whimper.*

*He reached out a pale hand to stroke back her hair. Immediately the girl relaxed, and her eyes glazed. She leaned into him, subdued. Lishka twitched, fighting her new instinct. Zaral looked up at her and, too fast for even her to follow, whipped a hand across the girl's exposed neck. Lishka inhaled the sweetness from the small droplets of blood that welled up.*

*That scent permeated her body and banished any remaining hesitation. Lishka fell upon the girl and her teeth sank into flesh. The thick liquid life oozed at first, then began to pour from the girl into Lishka.*

*The girl's heartbeat sped up, frantically beating what little blood she had left through her body. Still, Lishka drank. Memories not her own engulfed her: memories of family, warmth, and happiness, but also of sadness and hardship. Even as she drained the girl's life, Lishka couldn't stop. The girl flopped to the floor, now just a husk. Above, Zaral's black eyes watched them both.*

Lishka's hands clenched, her fingernails digging into her palms. The girl's life, the first she had taken, still burned in her veins despite the long centuries that had passed. She willed the memory away, though her blood ran hot with guilt and shame.

Dominick's presence filled the room and a feeling of calm stole over her. Her hands released as the memory receded back into the fog of her early years. Already he had slipped into day hibernation. Lishka focused her senses on him instead, and soon she too found respite in safe, dreamless sleep.

Dominick's consciousness tugged at Lishka, bidding her to wake despite the daylight. She sat up to peer about the room made dark by the covered window.

Dominick remained in the chair, his head tilted back against the wall to stare at the ceiling. Lishka slid off the bed to stand before him. Awareness drifted back into his expression, as though he came from far away.

"How do you feel?" she asked, her voice hushed in the peaceful stillness of the room. Dominick blinked and then lifted his head to face forward. He flexed his hands and rolled back his shoulders, as though taking inventory of his new body.

"I feel okay. The same, only…different." Dominick stared down at his hands as if he had never seen them before. In structure they had not changed; he still had the same calluses and small scar on his thumb from when he was human, though his skin was several shades paler. But the sunlit warmth had returned just a bit to his skin, coaxed back by the witch's blood. He opened and closed his fists, flexing his forearms. "I feel strong."

"Do you understand what happened?" Lishka asked. The blood had done as she expected: dampened the bloodlust and sharpened his mind.

"They told me I am a vampire." Despite all that he had experienced, Lishka still heard the doubt in his voice.

"That is true," Lishka said. "I will teach you what I know, help you to be what you are. But you must follow me now, and always obey."

At this, Dominick looked up, the beginnings of a

frown marring his otherwise smooth forehead. Lishka remembered his words, from what felt like long ago, though it had not been more than a week.

*Where will you lead me?*

THEY DEPARTED THE inn at midday, just as the sun reached its highest point behind the layer of solid gray clouds. The overcast sky eased their travel. With hoods drawn, they checked out of the inn and left Middle Fork. The snow had stopped falling, and patches of white clung to the damp earth at the sides of the road.

Overhead the trees leaned to interlace their thick boughs across the road, forming a canopy that protected the truck from the light filtering through the clouds. Only a few weak rays managed to wend their way down to the earth. Dominick stared out the window, and Lishka couldn't help observing him. She had never known one of her kind as human first, and had avoided new vampires as much as possible. Dominick had not become unrecognizable. True, his skin was paler, and a cold energy now emanated from him. Yet his demeanor remained gentle, and he had fought for control when the hunger threatened to overcome him. Lishka noted the shape of his lower lip, which now protruded ever so slightly over his longer canines. Dominick shifted, and she returned her gaze to the road.

"Where are we going?" His voice broke the silence of the cab.

"To the highest mountains," Lishka answered. "I must look for someone."

"The fey," Dominick said.

"Yes." *So he does remember.* Lord Dorwan had said that they told Dominick of the task at hand. Lishka had not been sure he would recall that conversation. Those first hours of the change often lay cloaked in a haze lifted only with fresh, human blood. Sometimes the first memories still remained veiled, even after the bloodlust had been satiated. She wondered if he remembered Sieth's attack, and what she had done to him. Lishka had not wanted to remind him that she had made him into this new form.

"What are they?" Dominick asked.

"The faeries, fair folk, made of mischief and light." Lishka's voice took on a lilting tone akin to one who recited an old rhyme. With a start, she recognized the words from her human past. "They are immortal creatures of life magik, and utterly at odds with what we are."

"Magik," Dominick repeated. His jaw tensed around the word and Lishka wondered if he also remembered their exchange, only two nights prior, when she had first told him that such a thing existed.

"Last night, that woman." Dominick swallowed. "I drank her blood."

"Yes," Lishka acknowledged. She didn't know what to say to help Dominick come to terms with his new state.

"I can't stop thinking about it. It's like I know I shouldn't want someone's blood. But it's all I can think about." Dominick shifted in his seat, the desire to feed satiated for the moment, but fresh still in memory.

"It will get better." Lishka kept her eyes on the road to avoid any look of horror once more on Dominick's face. "The cravings. You will always want the taste of fresh blood, but over time, you will learn to compartmentalize it." Though Dominick had controlled himself far better than she, in his first feeding.

"And what did I do to her last night? You told me to do—something—and I don't remember thinking, I just somehow knew what you meant. This sense of calm focus happened, and I connected with her. I don't even know how to explain it." The words flowed almost as a stream of consciousness, as if Dominick had been thinking them over and over again for the duration of the ride up the mountain road.

"You influenced her."

The front wheels hit a pothole and jerked them to the left. Lishka focused on steadying the truck. She did not want to tell Dominick of death magik, though she knew she must.

"We have an innate ability inside us to transfix our prey and calm them. It makes the…feeding much easier and less painful for the victim." Lishka instantly regretted her poor word choice.

"Oh." He went silent for a moment. "You called her a witch. What's a witch?"

"What do you mean?"

"What makes her a witch?" Dominick gripped the handle above the passenger window, as though physically anchoring himself would likewise ground his mind. "There are representations of witches across movies, books, all throughout history. Like, say, the classic Halloween version that portrays witches as old, with warts and pointed hats. They use cauldrons to make potions, and they cast spells and curses. But that woman was young. She tasted," he said, shuddering with both disgust and desire, "like the earth, I guess. But what makes her a witch? What does she do?"

"It's not so much what a witch does, it's more what a witch is," Lishka explained. "A witch is someone who feels a closer connection to a power that surrounds this world. You've felt it."

"What we found in the stones," Dominick remembered. "Like the symbols you put on my window."

"Yes." Lishka kept her response short, that he might not linger on that night, on what came after her introduction of magik. "Some say it is the Earth's spirit that's separated from the physical plane by what we call the Veil. Those same people claim the Veil is caused by humans. A long time ago, humans believed in the spirit, and their belief gave it power. But they turned their back on it. That disbelief created the Veil." The hours of silence and a sudden desire to provide Dominick with knowledge spurred her on, and her words filled the cab. "Most humans can't feel the Veil, or the power beyond it. Occasionally you get a human who's strongly connected, can harness it somewhat, channel it. Nothing like what we can do of course," she added, "and witch magik is of a different sort. But still, human witches can be powerful in their own right."

"What do they do with it?"

"Depends on the human." The truck lurched over a particularly deep rut, and this time Lishka navigated the front wheels to the side, to creep up the rocky trench while avoiding the softer earth on the shoulder. "Some don't do anything consciously, though their magikal affinity can manifest in heightened senses, unusual strength, longer life, with the ability to heal faster, and immunity from diseases. Those more ambitious use it to gain power in the world, control over others." The truck leveled out, only to dip once more into a deep pothole. The shocks groaned in protest.

"Mostly, though, it's an organic energy, used for earth magik," Lishka continued. "Growing things, keeping elements in balance, healing, influencing the weather."

Dominick sat back in his seat. *Earth spirits must be hard to swallow, for a scientist.*

"That's probably why the ghoul was so attracted to her," Lishka said as an afterthought, more to herself than to Dominick. "They like organic magik and hers was strong. They won't bother us." Water from the tree limbs dripped down on the roof of the truck, making tapping sounds above their heads.

"And the memories?" Dominick asked, his voice suddenly quiet. "Are they always like that? Do they always…do we always share them?"

Lishka held still, her hands gripping the steering wheel tightly. "Yes."

Dominick faced away to resume staring out the passenger window, dropping the cab once more into weighted silence. Lishka knew she should offer him reassurance, as Mordan had once offered her, but the guilt rose like bile in her throat, choking any words of comfort.

The snow started falling again in late afternoon. The road became narrower and the potholes more frequent. They jolted over small boulders that had been deposited by spring floods running down off the mountain. Lishka drove determinedly across, though the truck's protests grew louder. Finally, the rocks became too numerous, the ruts too deep, and the truck would go no farther.

Lishka managed to maneuver the truck off the road,

not that there was much of a road anymore. She banged the door open and stepped out onto the cold stones. Dominick followed, hesitating by the passenger door to scan the trees.

"Take your weapons," Lishka instructed. Dominick opened the door to retrieve the sword and scabbard lying on the back seat. He lifted them clumsily, banging the hilt against the open door as he wrested the weapon out of the truck. He held it up to examine the strap and buckle attached to the scabbard. Lishka opened her mouth to give him additional instruction, then quieted as he strapped the scabbard across his back, with the belt wrapping across his right shoulder and under his left armpit, the buckle at an angle across his chest. He positioned the sword satisfactorily, placing the hilt within easy reach just above his left shoulder, likely as one of the Coven Keepers had shown him. A dagger made by Kiaban went into the side of Dominick's boot, where it could be easily drawn if needed.

Lishka mimicked Dominick, tightening her own sheathed sword at her back and reaching down to pat the dagger strapped to her calf, inside her boot. Wearing their blades at their backs allowed for ease of travel by foot and freed their legs for climbing in the higher peaks.

The snow hadn't stuck in most places, leaving the earth bare. They stepped off the road into the dense underbrush of the evergreen forest. Ferns grew in abundance and fallen logs became nurseries for tree sprouts, luxurious mosses, and lichen. Lishka slipped between the old growth without a sound. Dominick followed alongside her, his strength enhanced with the witch's blood coursing through his body. Once or twice, he strayed from Lishka's side to travel at a distance, though he always remained within eyesight.

The ground began a gentle decline from where the road cut through the mountains, then abruptly dropped to the pebbled shore of a swift river. The water ran relatively shallow for autumn, gliding around exposed boulders dispersed across the riverbed. The far bank rose at a steeper incline. Instead of trees, thick brush covered the mountainside, interspersed with granite boulders. The valley extended on either side of the river for miles, while the edge of the mountain sloped in the distant east to reveal a dark expanse of sky. In that space the moon had risen, a bright orb that shined light down on the surrounding forest, making the river current glitter.

Lishka gathered her legs beneath her. In a burst of strength, she leapt across the river, touching down briefly on a large boulder in the middle of the water. She landed on the other side with barely an imprint in the soft riverbank, then turned to watch Dominick. He had already leapt the river and landed next to her without a sound. She turned forward again to lead them into the brush, where they began to climb.

Half an hour later they crested the top, only to be faced with more craggy peaks. Lishka stopped to study the mountains and get her bearings.

"We go there." She pointed to the far distant northeast. She could not see the Twin Peaks from the map but knew the direction from memory. A sensation began to awaken deep inside her core, a tingling that tugged her onward.

Dominick followed where she pointed, narrowing his eyes as if to help himself see beyond the visible peaks. They turned north to walk the ridge for several hours, following a natural trail of flattened rock and dirt. On the east side of the ridge stretched lower mountains with barely any snow, and beyond them the higher peaks rose, which remained white year-round. To the west of the ridge, smooth green hills petered out in the distance to flatter lands. Beyond the hills, on the far horizon, water glinted and tiny blurred shapes of skyscrapers stretched up from the blue. Seattle.

Lishka turned her back to the city to bound down the mountainside and into the lower valleys, where deciduous trees grew alongside the ever-present evergreens. They continued that way for several days, scaling and descending mountains, cutting between when possible, until gradually the ground rose, lifting them into the higher peaks. Always Lishka held the map from Lady Raseska's chambers in her mind. Lady Raseska had indeed been right: the tingling grew as they traveled farther north, guiding Lishka to their destination.

They moved whenever they could during the overcast days, and throughout the nights. The air grew crisper the farther they traveled, and clouds consistently shrouded the sky. There was no path beyond the odd animal trail, and these often veered sporadically and usually not in the right direction. Dominick grew used to his new night vision, learning how to see in the long shadows cast by faint moonlight. He followed Lishka diligently, though he kept quiet. Lishka set a pace that left little time for talk, as she focused on leading their way through the mountains.

About four days into their journey, Lishka became aware of a new pressure on her mind, separate from what pulled her north. She cut her gaze to the left and right.

Only mountains, alpine vegetation, and rock rose about them. Dominick strode alongside her, yet after an hour or so, she noticed a change in his gait as well. He began to walk more quietly, stepping with extra care. It was as though he was holding his breath, listening for something that neither Lishka nor Dominick could yet identify.

The unease at the back of her mind grew. Lishka quickened her pace, her steps matching Dominick's to become more deliberate as she contemplated what to do. He no longer veered off on his own path, instead keeping close to Lishka. Neither felt the need to voice the problem that had arisen, though their senses pounded the reality of the situation on them.

They were being followed.

# CHAPTER 14

# THE TRACKER

DOMINICK LIFTED HIS HEAD to sniff the wind that shifted wisps of golden-brown hair across his forehead.

"What should we do?" he asked. They had emerged from the forest to stop at the base of a wide boulder field. On either side of the field, the evergreen continued to spread up the nearest mountainside.

Lishka scanned the surrounding rock face and trees. She could detect neither visible nor audible signs of their tracker, though the scent indicated they followed not far behind. Something beyond skill aided the tracker's steps.

"I'm not sure. Killing them would give us away."

Beside her, Dominick tensed. Lishka did not like the thought of killing either, but she could not allow them to be tracked.

"It would be much better if they just disappeared," she half whispered.

"Do you think they followed us from Seattle?" Dominick asked, matching her low voice.

"Most likely. Someone must have seen us leave, despite our caution. Whatever their motives, we cannot allow them to track us." Lishka stretched out with her mind, seeking the warm pocket of life that would indicate human consciousness. She soon found the tracker many miles lower down the mountainside. At least a day's distance lay between them, even for a magikally enhanced human. She probed further to ascertain the state of their mind. A sharp coldness met her touch, and she drew back.

"They—he, I think—is suspicious." The coldness troubled her. It did not feel altogether human. "He can tell we've stopped. He's human, but a mage, a powerful one."

Dominick raised his eyebrows.

"Mages are much stronger than those who do not possess magikal abilities. They're quicker, and can heal faster," Lishka explained. "They can go days without eating or drinking by using the power beyond the Veil as sustenance. And a mage could sense us through that same power."

"So, in other words, they're not easy to shake," Dominick summed up. He stared across the rock into the distant scrubby hemlock, as though trying to detect the mage himself.

"We have to be careful," Lishka cautioned. The mage remained too far away to trigger Dominick's bloodlust, but any gusts of wind from that direction could bring his scent closer. "If he suspects we know of his existence, he'll send a message to whoever sent him." Alarm flitted through her, thinking of who might command the mage. "We can't let that happen," she said, more to herself.

"What then?" Dominick repeated.

"We need to get him off our trail, permanently. And we need to make it look accidental, to relieve us of any blame. I cannot use magik, or the trace will give us away." Lishka remembered the witch's warning. "I have an idea."

They turned their path due north, maintaining a consistent pace so as not to spark concern in their tracker. The lush evergreens gradually mutated into scraggly spears, more resistant to harsh weather. Their dropped needles coated the ground in a springy carpet that muffled any footsteps. Through the treetops, the glowing moon illuminated clear patches of night sky. The moonlight unfortunately assisted only the mage, as Lishka and Dominick had no need of light to see.

A stale musk filled Lishka's nose. She froze. Beside her, Dominick stopped to peer into the forest. She caught his eyes, and together they melted into the trees' shadows. They had caught the scent of nearby humans.

The trees helped to conceal their movement as Lishka took them around the edge of bandit territory. She slowed their pace to ensure the mage still followed them, his presence now a constant pulse against her mind. He maintained a careful distance, always a day's travel behind them.

Lishka led them closer to the mountain men than caution would dictate. She needed to make certain the mage would enter the territory. She had heard the tales of these men, rogues who chose the dangers of the mountains over society's rules. They made their own laws and held their own beliefs. And they were highly hostile to any uninvited intruders.

Many miles from the bandits' main camp, they almost walked into the first sentry.

The man had tucked himself into the nape of a wide maple tree. Decades of dirt caked his wiry beard and rough clothes made from animal hide, camouflaging him against the tree's bark. He stilled his breath to a barely audible exhale, in rhythm with the movement of the leaves high above him. Only Lishka's and Dominick's supernatural abilities enabled them to detect him in advance, and even so, Lishka had inadvertently brought them much closer to him than she cared for.

Though they gave nothing away, years of living in the forest trained the guard to sense when something changed. He looked up, gripped his archer's bow, and stared into the woods. The muscles of his arm flexed against the smooth curve of the bow, ready to notch a swift arrow. Lishka and Dominick stopped. The man had covered his scent well, but not well enough to hide it from them. Dominick's nostrils flared as he inhaled, making Lishka doubt her decision to bring him so close to humans. Her attention flicked to the man and back to Dominick, preparing herself to act should Dominick's control falter. After a long minute, Dominick shifted just a hair, settling into the same motionless stance as Lishka.

The sentry surveyed the woods for almost thirty minutes, his hand not leaving his bow. Finally, he relaxed back against the trunk and released his bow to hang loosely in his grip. Without a sound, Lishka stepped backward into the undergrowth, with Dominick close behind.

LIGHT HAD BROKEN through the trees and over the jagged ridgeline of the mountains that loomed above them when Lishka stopped for the day. They had traveled a good distance past bandit territory. Her energy waned, drowsiness threatening to drag her limbs down to the quiet earth. She could no longer sense the tracker near them. Either her plan had worked, or he had moved beyond her reach.

They found shelter in an enclosure formed by four granite boulders leaning on each other at the foot of the ridge. With the ascent into the alpine ridges, the mountainsides grew rockier, and another boulder field stretched across the evergreen valley. They ducked down to enter the small space and Dominick pulled a rock across the entrance to protect them from daylight.

Lishka settled down on the dry dirt and leaned her head back against the granite. Only a hint of moonlight trickled in through the cracks where the boulders intersected. She positioned her hood over her face, making sure that when the light turned to day, it would not touch her skin. Across from her, Dominick navigated the tight space to sit against the opposite wall, bending his knees so that his boots rested inches from hers. The hilt of his sword knocked against the rock and he fumbled into a position that would keep it from digging into his back. Lishka closed her eyes and prepared to enter the heavy daysleep.

"Lishka." Dominick's voice, though low, filled the enclosure.

Lishka opened her eyes.

"What happens, if the plan doesn't work?"

"We find another way to lose him. Find a route that he cannot cross and outrun him."

"What if he figures out we know he's following us? What will he do?" Dominick's words did not carry fear of the mage, only curiosity. He drew his legs up to afford Lishka more space, and rested his forearms on his knees, his hands dropping to hang in the air.

"I doubt he'll make it through the wild men's territory. You saw how well they know these forests."

Dominick nodded, a small movement restricted by the rock at his back.

"That arrow the man had—were we in any danger?"

"Human iron and steel cannot harm immortal flesh, beyond a brief moment of pain. It must be imbued with magik to do real damage. Though, it is possible his arrow was such a weapon," Lishka acquiesced. "They have a mountain magik of their own. Even if the mage does somehow make it through the territory, he'll maintain the distance. His purpose is likely to follow, not to engage. He won't want to risk his mission by revealing himself. It would be foolish."

"His mission," Dominick mused. "Who do you think sent him?"

"What did they tell you at the Coven? About our task?" Lishka countered. She searched Dominick's face for any indicator of what he had been told.

"Not much," Dominick admitted. "When I woke up, I was in a small stone room. It's hard to remember exactly, my head was killing me, and my mouth…my mouth was so dry. And the thirst…I think I knew, though, what had happened." His voice dropped as he remembered. Dominick had not told her about his awakening, and Lishka had not wanted to ask. She knew that the newly turned were kept in the lower levels of the House, secured away in stone cells.

"A man was there with me," Dominick continued. "At first, I was afraid, but he didn't seem dangerous. He looked worn-out, somehow. Tired. He said we shared the same blood."

*Mordan.*

"He told me that your—our—kind is split into two Great Covens. He said that those Covens used to be aligned, but now there is division. He spoke of you. I knew then that I could trust him. He said 'Lishka can help us gain support for the right side.' He told me to trust you. To follow you."

*Follow you.* Those words hung once more between them.

"Tension is building between the two Great Covens," Lishka acknowledged. "What he told you is true. They sent me to commune with the fey, in order to secure their allegiance." The task sounded ridiculous when spoken out loud, in a rough mountain hole far from the elegance of Lady Raseska's study. The fey had long ago receded from the human realm, to become only a remnant of an older forgotten world.

"Sieth is a part of the other side, isn't he?" Dominick said, startling her from her thoughts.

"Yes."

"Is he powerful in the Coven? Did he send the tracker?"

*He remembered Sieth's attack.* Lishka debated how much to tell Dominick of her history and of her relationship to Sieth. So far, Dominick did not appear to be afraid of his new life. She could not decide whether that boded well or ill for him.

"Sieth belongs to a very powerful vampire," she replied, choosing her words with care. "He's dangerous, not only due to his own power, but because of his Master's influence." Lishka didn't need to remind Dominick how dangerous Sieth was. Dominick was living proof of the lengths Sieth would go to in service of his Master. "The Coven's leaders represent both sides, and Sieth serves those who would oppose our mission. It's possible he, or one of them, sent the tracker. I cannot be sure."

"Lishka." Dominick paused. "I don't want us to kill that man."

"I don't either," Lishka admitted.

They sat in the moment, their agreement lingering in the air.

"Get some rest," she said, breaking the spell. "You'll need it for tomorrow." She turned her face away from him and closed her eyes. The steel of her sword lay reassuringly against her thigh, ready to be drawn should she need it. Dominick shuffled against the wall, unable to sleep just yet, and listened for any signs of danger around them.

"Goodnight, Lishka," he whispered into the dark.

She ignored him and forced herself to sleep.

A THIN CRACK of light flickered, then flashed, across the insides of her eyelids, before disappearing altogether.

Lishka awoke. Her eyes adjusted to the dark in nanoseconds. The shadows outlined Dominick across from her, where he sat with his legs still bent up in the narrow space. He watched their hovel's entrance, his body taut as he fought to maintain control.

The odor of humans permeated their hole. Lishka inhaled the musky scent and studied Dominick. He had shown great control around humans, yet his encounters had been out in the open air. In the confined space, the smell could become almost overwhelming for one so new.

Yet Dominick did not move. Instead of hunger, intelligence sharpened his gaze as he listened to the sounds beyond the rock barrier. Lishka relaxed the smallest amount. Satisfied with his control, she turned her attention to the voices just outside their hiding place.

"They should know better than to come up here," growled a masculine voice.

"Aye, well learnt that lesson, didn' he?" Another voice drawled, smooth as ice, and just as cold.

"Hmpf," a third snorted in agreement.

*Bandits.*

"That will teach them," the second voice continued, encouraged by the third. "They won't be coming around no more."

"That's not what concerns me," the growly voice interrupted. "What was a man like him doing up here in the first place?"

The men went silent, clearly considering those words.

"Send Kiernan to Middle Fork. See if he can find out anything." *The growly man must be their leader.* "There is a strange smell, I can't put my finger on it…" His voice trailed off.

Without a sound, Lishka's fingers found their way to the pommel of her sword.

"Should we send a runner east?" the smooth voice asked.

"Not yet. The packs keep to themselves more and more these days, especially with what's goin' on up North. We'll wait for Kiernan first." The leader's voice quieted, and footsteps vibrated the earth, fading as they moved off.

Lishka met Dominick's eyes. The plan had worked, though the bandits' conversation worried her almost more than the appearance of the tracker.

*With what's going on up North.* The bandit's words resounded in her mind. Lishka had been so focused on their mission and training Dominick, she had not stopped to speculate on what, even now, might be happening at the Seattle Coven, or within the others'. For the first time since she'd learned of the growing division between the two Great Covens, she considered the impact the civil war would have on the rest of the world. A foreboding chill crept along her spine to settle deep in her bones.

THE WEIGHT OF Dominick's hand on her shoulder stirred Lishka once more to wakefulness. Her senses told her night had not quite fallen, despite the darkness of their enclosure. Dominick pushed the boulder away from the entrance and crisp air flooded the space. Lishka grabbed her sword and rose to a crouch to scoot out into the dusk. She straightened and sheathed her sword at her back, taking stock of their surroundings. Fading sunlight ribboned the sky in orange, while the ridge behind them created a safe shadow across the rock field.

Lishka tested the breeze. "No scent of the tracker."

"No," replied Dominick. "The bandits have gone, too."

Lishka listened for a moment to confirm his assessment. "We'll double back and see if we can find anything."

Dominick knew what she meant—see if they could find the body. Despite Lishka's confidence in their combined ability to sense anyone nearby, she could not continue their mission without confirmation that they did so alone. It had taken them several days to sense their tracker in the first place, and the inhuman coldness she had detected in the mage still disturbed her.

They found him fourteen miles from the boulders that had sheltered them during daylight. His body lay face up in a small valley tucked between the hills. The strong scent of the bandits lingered, though now at least half a day old.

Lishka looked down upon the man who had tracked them. He didn't appear to be older than thirty, although one never knew for sure with mages. Dark curly hair trailed down to his neck where it met the stubble that swept across his jaw. A long traveler's coat half-covered a woolen winter shirt, and mud encased his worn boots.

Lishka leaned down to investigate his belt from

which dangled bags of herbs and various ingredients used for spells. He likely used these to track his quarry and communicate their whereabouts to his Master. Her eyes traveled up to his face, and she bent to sweep his hair from his forehead. Shock froze her fingers a millimeter from his skin.

"What?" Dominick bent to bring his face almost alongside hers.

"His forehead. Do you see this mark?" Lishka pushed the man's hair back to expose his face, careful to avoid touching his skin. A symbol lay upon the mage's forehead: a circle dissected into quadrants with a diamond overlaid in the bottom half. A perverse inversion of the mage's mark.

"What is it?" Dominick whispered. Even he could sense the wrongness of the mark.

"A tether," Lishka answered. "The mage's mark allows the wearer to channel the power beyond the Veil through the body and bend it to one's will. The inversion tethers the wearer to the one who placed it there. Instead of drawing on the power beyond the Veil, this mage sources his power from the one who linked to him, though at a cost."

"What's the cost?" Dominick asked, still staring down at the body before him.

"Only our kind bears the mage's mark. No other creatures possess the secret of the casting. It is forbidden to gift the mark to one not of our kind." Lishka stopped herself from glancing at Dominick's forehead. "The inversion can be given to a human, though it is rare and usually under the authority of the Coven Council. This mage is tethered to someone at the Coven, and he channels that energy through them. But he does not have immortality to protect him. While the force empowers him, it also burns away his own lifeforce."

"But he still looks so young," Dominick argued.

"The mark is newly cast," Lishka observed, noting the shininess of the symbol. "He would have had only months, maybe a year of life left, depending on the rate at which he drew the power through him." Her guilt at having led him to his death lessened at this realization. "It's rare for a human to possess this. It takes power and skill to place it there. A lot of power." She reached toward the man's forehead.

"What are you doing?" Dominick asked.

"I'm going to see who sent him," Lishka said. "This mark can act as a calling card. It will show me a small glimpse of the power being funneled through this man. Be quiet now so I can concentrate."

She placed her right index finger on the mark. A thick, black influence emanated from the mark, invisible to the naked eye. Its coldness coiled about her wrist and began to sink into her flesh. Lishka jerked her hand back to break the connection. Dominick caught her as she rocked back onto her heels and his hands gripped her upper arms, more out of reaction to her abrupt movement than to stabilize her. He let go as she righted herself.

"What was it?" Dominick asked, looking from Lishka to the dead man.

Lishka's veins ran cold, remembering the ice that had flooded her in the alley. She stared down at the mage. His Master's will still lingered about him.

"Zaral," she whispered.

"What?"

Lishka had expected the Master to be Sieth, or maybe Darrak. Sieth would have been dangerous enough. Yet the taste of Zaral's power filled her mouth with deadened ash. *Not months.* This man would have had only days, maybe a week, channeling even a modicum of Zaral's undiluted power. Lishka swallowed, unable to help the very human reaction. Fear of Zaral spread under her skin, threatening to overcome her senses and any logic.

"What's wrong?"

Warmth seeped into her back. Dominick had placed his hand on her left shoulder and his touch began to dispel some of the iciness in her blood. Lishka forced herself to consider the situation. Zaral rarely bothered with human minions to do his bidding. Though he had been in Seattle the night of Dominick's Making, Lishka found it hard to believe that he would stoop so low as to mark and send a tracker after them himself.

"I thought I felt…I will check again, to be sure." She knelt once more, reaching her hand out to the tracker. Her fingers twitched as she drew closer, and this time Dominick knelt with her, keeping his hand on her shoulder for added strength. She rested a light finger against the mark, barely touching the skin.

Once more, the inky blackness seeped from the mark. The surge of Zaral called to her blood, yet as Lishka fought past her primal fear, the power weakened. She did not sense Zaral himself, but the bloodline. This mage must have been linked to a direct descendant. The connection felt too strong to be Sieth, powerful and favored as he was. *Can it be Lord Sootha?*

She stood and Dominick dropped his hand to his side. "We have to go now. We must get as far away from this man as possible. It might already be too late." She strained to sense whether her touch had been noticed in the link between the mark and the Master. Only the void of the dead greeted her.

"Could you tell who sent him?" Dominick asked.

"It's not an exact trace, but it is of the other bloodline," Lishka confirmed. "Remember I told you there are two factions?"

Dominick nodded.

"One of the Coven's leaders must have sent him. I cannot tell if they have a tracking spell on him or not. If it is one of the Coven Council, and it likely is, then they are a Master Mage and I will not be able to detect the spell's origin. I dare not check for the spell in case the Master senses my touch on their magik. Even now, they may feel his death."

She deterred any further questions by turning away from Dominick. They must put distance between themselves and this tracker. Dominick studied the man for a moment longer before following her.

They traveled swiftly and soon passed the boulder field where they had waited out the day. Clouds shrouded the moon and the air hung still. As they climbed, the boulders became smaller and looser, till they scrambled over only thin sheets of rock. Dominick slowed to study them, and Lishka couldn't help the irritation that disrupted her fear. Finally, three-quarters up the mountain, rock gave way to stunted evergreen patches.

Closer to midnight they scaled the ridge. A wide view of sharp peaks stretched out before them, layering out to the far horizon. Lishka paused at the top to confirm her bearings, and Dominick stopped alongside her to take in the view. She closed her eyes momentarily and tried to block out the residual taste of Zaral's power in the bloodline. Sudden wind whipped along the exposed ridge and lashed her hair across her face. Lishka opened her eyes and inhaled an unnecessary breath, soaking in the crisp mountain air and using it to cleanse herself of fear.

As she focused on the distant peaks, she became aware of a tingling deep inside her. A warmth spread from her core, what she envisioned as a vibrant violet energy, and drew her attention to the north.

*Fey.* That was what Zaral had called it in the alley, when he so effortlessly swatted it away. Her fey magik. It flexed once more, only stronger, tugging her northward to where the Twin Peaks, and the entrance to the fey realm, must lie. The fey called to her blood.

With her sense of direction solidified, Lishka turned to lead the way northeast along the ridge. Dominick, as ever, followed close behind.

They ran through the night. The ridge spanned several miles before descending back into forested mountainside. They made camp as light began to filter through the trees. A dense stand of spruce offered adequate coverage and Lishka tucked herself in between two rough trunks, again using her hood for additional protection.

Dominick stood at the trees' edge, his head cocked to one side as though he listened to something far away that only he could hear. Finally, he seemed to deem whatever he heard benign. He entered the stand and sat down close enough to speak to Lishka, without touching. Lishka closed her eyes, but this time Dominick would not be put off.

"The mage," Dominick said. Lishka opened her eyes

to face him. "You said the mark on his forehead was an inversion of the mage's mark. Is that what this is?" He gestured to his own forehead. Half buried beneath strands of hair that had fallen to his eyebrows, the mage's mark lay bound and powerless.

"Yes. That is the mage's mark, the sign of our kind's power." Lishka couldn't help the bitterness in her words, and not for the first time did anger flare that Zachriel's Council would send her into the mountains so ill-protected.

"And the mark allows the person to channel the power beyond the Veil. What does that mean?" He waited for her to speak. Lishka had known his questions would start to come. Dominick could not be kept ignorant forever.

"It is a symbol that allows the bearer to channel energy. We have our own internal magik. Then there is the power beyond the Veil, the source of all energy." Lishka found herself reiterating her words from the night at his apartment, the night of his Making. "None but our kind bear the mark—it is a source of great power. The mark allows us to draw large amounts of that energy into our bodies. We then use symbols to help us shape the energy and bend it to our will."

"Like the symbols you put on my window," Dominick remembered.

"Yes, those were for your protection." *Little good they did you.* "But I must be careful. I am not a Master Mage. When I cast any kind of magik it leaves its own mark, like a scent. Those skilled can sense me in the residue left by my magik. It's why I could not cast a spell on the tracker to dissuade him from our trail. It would be a beacon to those who sent him."

"Why didn't you become one? A Master Mage." Dominick clasped his hands before him and sat back against the tree trunk. The pommel of his sword rested at the top of his shoulder, nestled against his left ear.

Lishka remembered Kiaban's words from long ago: *You have the skill, but not the will.* Lishka always had an affinity for magik but her desire to remain forgotten, out of sight, overrode any urge to pursue the higher learnings. To be a Master Mage, an elevated status almost equal to a Council Member, would be too public and draw too much attention.

She didn't know how to explain this to Dominick without also describing her history. A history that included Zaral.

"I became a Keeper instead," she answered. "Some Keepers ascend to Master Mage, but that often goes hand in hand with Coven leadership. Master Mages are called upon at a higher level to service the Covens."

"A Keeper?"

"They are the soldiers of the Coven. We patrol the city and ensure our kind are following the Coven's orders."

Dominick nodded; this was a familiar concept to him. "You said a name when you inspected the mage. Who is Zaral?"

Lishka flinched at Zaral's name falling so casually from Dominick's lips. "Zaral leads one of the Great Covens and is the originator of that bloodline."

"He is the first?" Dominick examined her face, as if to search for additional unspoken information.

Lishka shook her head. "No. His brother Zachriel is said to be the first of the species. The Seattle Coven belongs to Zachriel." Lishka did not volunteer more information and for several minutes Dominick sat silent. The air hung thick between them.

"Lishka," Dominick said at last, his voice thoughtful. "How old are they?"

She could not guess what Dominick suspected, and hesitated to confirm, or exceed, his suspicions. He had not yet had to come to terms with what immortality meant.

"Our kind lives for a long time, I suspect forever unless we are killed. They are old. Older, perhaps, than the human race."

Dominick swallowed, though he met her eyes steadily.

"Do not think of that now. Focus on the mission." Lishka kept her words soft to lessen their impact. Though Dominick had much to learn, and Mordan had tasked her to teach him, the tracker increased their urgency. "We must move more quickly. We must get to the fey before anyone else connected to Zaral discovers us. Get some rest. We'll leave as soon as possible, at dusk."

Lishka closed her eyes once more, this time effectively shutting off further conversation. A sense of imminent dread had begun to infiltrate her thoughts. At some point, she would have to tell Dominick what sharing her blood truly meant.

Instead of empty slumber, soulless black eyes filled her mind. They lingered at the edges of her consciousness, buried deep in her blood, inescapable even in the vast wilderness.

# THE KREBARVITCH MOUNTAINS

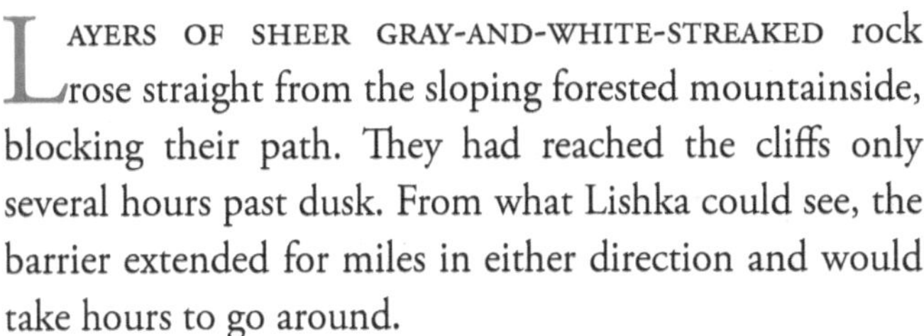

LAYERS OF SHEER GRAY-AND-WHITE-STREAKED rock rose straight from the sloping forested mountainside, blocking their path. They had reached the cliffs only several hours past dusk. From what Lishka could see, the barrier extended for miles in either direction and would take hours to go around.

"What now?" Dominick asked, craning his head back to stare up the cliffside. Lishka reached out a hand to the rock face, judging the surface. While it appeared to the naked eye as sheaths of smooth stone, her fingers sought out the narrow divots and cracks in the rock that would provide just enough purchase. She lifted her gaze to judge the quickest path up.

"Now we climb."

Hours later they reached the top of the cliff. To the west, higher mountain peaks rose in the dark, but directly before them the view opened to layers of ridges like the one they stood upon. Lishka stretched out with her senses but once more found nothing to cause alarm. The mountain beasts—birds, deer farther below, and once even a small herd of mountain goats—still remained the only other consciousness in the wild. Yet she could not shake her sense of urgency. A nagging fear clung to her that, somehow, Zaral knew of their task and even now pursued them through the mountains.

Overhead, the clouds parted to reveal a patch of black velvet sky and stars whose light set the granite aglow. A wind rushed up the ridge to stir Lishka's hair, bringing with it the smell of ice.

The next night brought rain. The air changed and dropped almost to freezing. So far, they had avoided the snow. Though the cold temperatures had no real effect on them, Lishka did not look forward to trudging through snow and ice. The hunger had begun to rise in Dominick, so when an elk herd passed nearby, they took advantage of the opportunity.

"It's different," Dominick said after they brought down a large bull. "No memories."

Lishka nodded. She preferred to hunt animals, despite the craving for human blood and the energy human life brought. Animals only transferred base instincts and sensory images, with the common desperate struggle to hold onto life at the very end. Lishka stroked the elk's fur and without thinking, murmured a prayer to the Goddess to take its spirit back into the earth. Dominick watched each movement from several steps away, affording her space. The elk's blood tinged his lips red.

Their route led them down into lower valleys, where

the basins housed squelching moss, sharp reeds, and hidden pools that threatened to soak their boots. Despite the lingering daylight, Lishka insisted on traveling at dusk, forcing them to hack their way through the soggy wetlands filled with persistent mosquitoes. The insects did not bite Dominick or Lishka, but that didn't stop them from swarming about their faces and eyes, annoying the pair with their incessant humming. The temptation to cast a spell and disperse them grew almost overwhelming; however, any casting would leave a footprint. The image of the tracker still hovered fresh in the back of Lishka's mind. She reminded herself of that once more as she swatted buzzing clouds away from her eyes and nose.

The mountains loomed in the distance as if taunting them.

The hours in the lower valleys seemed to drag on, despite the fact that Lishka and Dominick were no longer bound by time. Though they traveled fast at night and well into the dawn, resting only when the sun shone strongest in the height of day, the mountains remained obstinately on the horizon. After several nights slogging through the wetlands, they managed to get back on the upper slopes of the mountains. They had left Middle Fork less than two weeks ago, and yet it seemed they had been in the mountains for much longer.

A short outcrop provided shelter, the rock ceiling hemmed in by smooth dirt and brush. Lishka had chosen the western side of the mountain, and they would not see the brightest part of the day.

Lishka pulled her legs up to her chest and leaned against cool rock, settling on top of the outcrop. Dominick sat alongside her, dropping his legs to dangle over the edge, his scuffed boots hanging in the open air. He gazed out at the valley below.

"I've always liked the mountains," he said. "It's peaceful here. Every animal, every plant follows its own rules for survival. It all fits together harmoniously." He fell quiet in his own thoughts and together they watched the sky brighten.

"Do you think that whoever sent the mage will send more trackers?" Dominick asked after a few moments.

Lishka had not sensed anything to give them alarm, yet this thought had been plaguing her as well.

"I'm not sure. It will likely depend on how long it takes them to find him." She didn't need to clarify who "him" meant. "There is a chance we made sufficient distance to give us enough of a head start, if they do."

"Would we be able to sense them? You said before that a Council Member had sent the mage and that they can hide their spells."

"A Master Mage can hide the fact that they cast the spell, which makes it hard to trace the spell back to the originator. It's possible they could hide the spell itself, though all energy leaves its own mark. But they cannot hide a human from us. We would sense if there was another." Doubt squirmed in Lishka and she hoped that her words sounded more confident than she felt. She did not know the limits to Zaral's power. Should he choose to get directly involved, they would have little chance of escape.

"Is Sieth also one of them? Is he a Master Mage?" Dominick gripped the ledge, his fingers indenting the rock.

"No, Sieth serves the Council but he is not a Master

Mage. Although he is a skilled mage and does bear the mark." Lishka could almost see Dominick's thought process as he worked to fit together all the pieces of the Coven's governing body. "The Coven is led by nine Master Mages," she said in a sudden display of transparency. "They all bear the mage's mark, allowing them to harness the power beyond the Veil."

"Is that what you had me do before?" Dominick faced her, his attention pulled from the expansive view before them. "What you called influencing that woman, the witch, in Middle Fork. Does that come from using this mark?"

"No, the ability to influence humans is part of your own internal power. It is the force we possess within, that helps make us what we are." Lishka gestured to her own body to illustrate the point. "It allows us to entrance others, mostly on instinct."

Dominick frowned and chewed his lower lip, being careful of his sharp teeth.

"Okay," he said after a pause. "And what is that? Mind control?"

"Not quite." Lishka tried to remember how Mordan had explained it to her. Failing to recall his words, she suffered through her own less articulate description.

"There are two ways of influencing humans that come naturally to our kind. Compulsion is one—it relies on the subject already desiring what you are compelling them to do. You are encouraging something that already exists. There are different ways to manipulate or compel. For example, I wanted you to stay away from the stones," she admitted. Dominick's face tightened at the reminder. "You obviously had a strong desire to pursue the study.

I could have planted the idea, enforced by compulsion, that something you cared about was tied to the study to make you afraid to pursue it. It would be amplifying an existing feeling to obtain a desired behavior."

"And the other way?" Dominick asked.

"Hypnotism. That is putting someone into a trance and fixing them in a singular spot. This helps to reduce pain and damage. While the witch agreed to supply her blood, exerting some hypnotism helped her to feel no pain or fear. Hypnotism is used both to calm those willing and to subdue those…who are unwilling." Once more Lishka felt grateful that Dominick's first taste of fresh blood had been from a willing source. He would not always be so lucky.

"And you always hypnotize the…person?"

"Most do. Some don't," Lishka admitted, not wanting to lie to Dominick about the worst of their kind.

"Why don't they?" Dominick's reluctant tone indicated he knew the answer already.

"For the thrill of the hunt."

Dominick looked away from her, and the shadows cast from the rocks above contoured his face. If they had breath to utter, clouds would be puffing from their lips, but they didn't, so the air remained clear.

"I don't want to hurt anyone," Dominick said, his words quiet but determined.

"Maybe you won't have to," Lishka replied. She heard the lie in her voice. Immortal life was a long time to try to hold onto humanity. "And there are other kinds of magik, beyond the instinct to dominate prey. You cannot use the mage's mark. It is bound, like mine." The pain of the binding sharpened her words. "But I will teach you what I can. It is my duty, as your—"

She stopped.

Dominick studied her. "As my what?" he asked.

"As your Maker," Lishka finished, finally acknowledging her part in his death.

"And Zaral is yours." Dominick barely spoke above a whisper, and yet his words pounded in Lishka's ears.

"Yes." This time it was her turn to look away.

"What happened?" Dominick asked, his voice grown even quieter.

Lishka knew she owed him some explanation. She had killed him. He deserved to know how she had been made, where he now came from. After all, she had ensured that Zaral's blood flowed in him too.

Across the mountain range, she saw not snow and rock, but a vast sparkling lake in a sprawling green land, with rounded hills covered by mist in the early morning. The stone building that housed the Followers had rested on the lake's western edge. Relatively simple, the structure had only one livable level, not including the base cellar that lay below ground for storing grain and providing access to the underground spring.

Dominick waited.

"I was raised in a clan in ancient Europe," Lishka said at last. "They were Followers of the Goddess, mostly women who kept the Old Ways." She let her thoughts drift back over the centuries. She remembered the feel of the breeze, cold on her human face. The feel of the life in her, so short yet full of passion and peace. And then…

"I was only fourteen when he first came to the convent. Zaral."

Dominick did not move beside her, allowing her the space to speak, to remember.

"He was traveling then. He had already gained power and established the Covens, but every so often he liked to go off on his own. He always wanted to know the way humans thought and acted. The better to manipulate them. He was passing through our land when he stopped to hunt. That's when he caught my scent." She shook her head at the memory. "He sensed the fey in my blood." She glanced at Dominick and gestured to her eyes.

"He tried to take me then, but the clan had already seen him for what he was. They used their own power to keep him away. I'm surprised he let them hold him off, but he must have had his own plan." The Followers had been afraid, yet despite that fear, they possessed a strong determination to keep her safe. Their faces had grown hazy in Lishka's mind, across the lifetimes.

"He came back. He met me on the shores of the lake when the sun had almost disappeared below the hills. He was prepared this time, for the power in the Followers. He was able to reach through their protection. They didn't know he had returned. His will called me and drew me to him. I was nineteen then, a powerful priestess in my own right, but naive. He turned me that night and made me into what I am. He told me I might be of some use to him."

Zaral's eyes once more filled her vision, hard and unflinching as she lay crumpled at his feet, the burning fire of his blood pounding through her veins. His voice echoed through her head and bound her to his will.

"What happened, after?" Dominick's voice melted

away the sensation of her binding. Lishka thought back to the years after she left the Followers.

"I traveled with him for a while," she said, dredging up the memory. It had been such a short time, filled with things she didn't want to remember. "A few years, maybe more. No time at all in his long life. He took me with him, taught me how to hunt. But Zaral was never one to be bothered with lesser beings. He was too busy shaping his world. He gave me to Mordan."

"Mordan?"

"You met him," Lishka said. "It was Mordan who came to you when you first awoke. He became my mentor." She released a small smile at the thought. Her only good memories of those initial years were of the time she spent with Mordan. He had provided a cool respite against the burning thirst and horror at what Zaral had made her.

"What do you mean, your mentor?" Dominick interrupted her memories.

"One who teaches the ways of immortal life. Sometimes, a bond is formed, especially if the mentor is also the Maker, though not always. Mordan took responsibility for me. I traveled with him for centuries as he taught me how to be what I am. Eventually he brought me to Seattle." She shrugged as if to say the rest was history.

"What about your parents?" Dominick asked. "Did you have a family?"

"I was brought to the clan when I was a young child. I don't know who my parents were. I have no memories of them. The women there were the only family I knew. Until Mordan, anyway."

Dominick studied her, as if trying to envision her as she had been then, many centuries ago. Lishka had not considered the long years that passed. She had forgotten how brief mortal life flickered before burning out.

Dominick's human life still existed now, though he was no longer a part of it.

"Do you have family?" Lishka asked on impulse. She remembered the photo in Dominick's apartment, his arm thrown across a woman who shared his smile. The thought had not occurred to her until this moment that Dominick could have a family looking for him.

"I have a sister. We're not close anymore," Dominick said, confirming Lishka's suspicions. "My dad passed away seven years ago. Cancer. My mom a few years ago. She had early dementia mixed with some other issues, but she never really was the same after my dad. I haven't talked to my sister much since."

An image flashed through Lishka's mind: a man stood before her who shared Dominick's curly hair and warm eyes, though gray peppered his hair and short beard. He reached out a hand to grip her shoulder as he laughed at some joke. To grip Dominick's shoulder. Lishka shoved away the image, born from the blood she had taken from Dominick. *His memories.*

"I'm sorry." Her words sounded empty, and she hoped Dominick wouldn't notice.

"My life was at the university," Dominick said. "My friends, the professors, the study…" He trailed off as a thought occurred to him. "Won't they look for me? I mean, I'm still enrolled in the university, and my apartment is under lease."

"Kristoph will take care of it." Her words sounded unintentionally threatening. "He is in charge of the Coven's security, of the Keepers. He will make sure that all loose ends are tied up."

Dominick frowned. "This Kristoph. He is a good man?"

"He will do his duty to the Coven, as he is bound. But he will not go beyond to inflict unnecessary pain." She knew her words offered little comfort, but she could not bring herself to lie to Dominick.

"It is better if you don't think of your life before," Lishka offered. A strange desire to take away hurt from Dominick rose in her chest. "I am sorry, Dominick."

"Lishka." Dominick caught her eyes and held them. "This isn't the life I would have chosen, had there been more of a choice. But I am grateful to you for saving my life. I didn't want to die."

A warmth tingled through her body, which Lishka recognized as relief. Dominick had shown no sign of hostility toward her, yet to hear that he did not blame her for his death lifted some of the weight she carried. Even if she disagreed.

"Somehow I feel okay." Dominick released her gaze to look to the far horizon. The evergreens swept down the sides of the boulder field and up again to a ridge of bare rock. Patches of snow lay in the shadowed crevices and below them, the sound of water echoed from a narrow river. "I can't explain it. I've felt…off, ever since I dreamt about you. Restless. Like there was something I should be doing. I don't feel that way anymore. I feel like I'm where I'm supposed to be.

"Soon, we'll find the realm of the fey. I know that sounds crazy, but I also know it's true. It's close now. I can hear it, like a hum in my mind. I think I'm supposed to be here with you." Dominick curved up the corner of his lip in a wry smile and shot Lishka a quick glance as if to laugh at his own admittance. Yet she heard the seriousness of his words.

She tried to return his smile, knowing that it manifested as more of a grimace. She could not tell him that his words disturbed her, not after he'd trusted her enough to confide in her. Dominick should not be able to sense the realm of the fey. He had not given her reason to suspect that he could, until this moment. Again, she wondered what power he possessed that made him so different. Who had she brought with her, alone and beyond any vestige of civilization? Dominick's words echoed once more in her mind: *Where will you lead me?*

As if Dominick, not Lishka, had been tasked with the success of their mission.

*Or with something else.*

# CHAPTER 16

# A HIDDEN PATH

"REACH OUT WITH YOUR mind to the Veil that separates this world from the other. You should feel resistance. Can you feel it?"

Dominick frowned, concentrating hard on the air around them for the third time in as many minutes. *Too hard.*

They had stopped earlier than usual, at least several hours before light would strike the eastern sky. The sharp edge of a ridge rose high above, cradling them in its basin. From deep inside, instinct tugged Lishka north. The mountains drew her; somewhere amongst the peaks must lie the origins of the Tiern River and the entrance to the realm of the fey. Despite the pull, she forced herself to stop moving northward. Lishka had other duties besides finding the fey. As she had promised, Dominick must learn magik.

"Use your hands to guide you," she instructed,

remembering how Mordan had helped teach her in the first years. "As a human, you largely affected your world through physical touch. The transition from physical power to mental can be difficult at first. Try to feel the weak points in the Veil with your fingers. This can help to focus your mind."

Dominick obediently reached out his hands before him, and the muscles ran taut along his arms. He kept his eyes closed to better use his other senses.

"Don't force it." Her voice sounded sharp. Lishka took a mental breath and willed herself to have patience. She had grown used to the ease of the power. Dominick was not a bad student, only new. The lines in Dominick's face smoothed while he lowered his hands an inch. *Better.*

"Can you sense any weakness?" she asked.

Dominick shook his head in a small, slow movement while his focus remained elsewhere. His fingers twitched before him across the air, seeking out the rough edges that would alert him to cracks. The lines in his forehead deepened once more.

"You'll feel it," Lishka assured him.

Dominick barely heard her. The air around them seemed to loosen, the molecules moving away from each other to allow more space in between. Suddenly, Dominick shuddered as though he'd touched electricity, and Lishka smelled the sharp metallic of magik. Dominick opened his eyes. Golden fires shone in his pupils.

"That was amazing." A stunned smile jerked up the corners of his mouth. "I feel so, so—"

"Strong," Lishka finished. She ignored his delight in the power beyond the Veil. Dominick should not have been able to draw that amount of force with so little resistance, not without the mage's mark. He had touched the power beyond, and it had not tried to hold him. Lishka remembered her own first journey, the struggle to break through the barrier, the drag of the currents that threatened to carry her away into the mist. Her eyes drifted to the mage's mark dulled upon his forehead. It emitted no hint that the binding had broken.

Their closer proximity to the North could account for the ease with which Dominick had managed to pierce the weak point in the Veil. The barrier had indeed become thinner, affording Lishka easier access. *Still...*

"What is it?" Dominick's voice broke her train of thought. The fires in his eyes had already begun to dim as his body consumed the power.

"Nothing," Lishka replied. "Try again." Dominick obediently closed his eyes and lifted his hands.

"No," she said. He opened his eyes. "Try without your hands."

Dominick placed his hands on his knees. This time, he tilted his head downward. Once or twice his fingers twitched, though he kept them in place. Lishka's other sense detected the minute cracks in the Veil as effortlessly as she felt Dominick beside her, like a pressure on her mind. A part of her craved the taste of the power.

She knew when Dominick's spirit left his body to go beyond. His skin paled to almost translucent, and he froze to utter stillness. She settled to watch and wait, assuming his journey would be as effortless as before. At once, all spark inside him vanished. Where before he had retained a part of himself, now nothing existed within him to bring him back. Dominick had completely entered the realm of mist.

Lishka leaned forward without thinking and gripped his wrists. Her nails dug crescents into his flesh.

*"Dominick."* She uttered his name and her own magik carried it beyond the physical world and through the cracks in the Veil, searching for his spirit, calling him back. Fear nipped at her. She had let him go too deep. Without the mage's mark, he did not have the proper tether to anchor him, to guide him back.

The faint hint of life warmed her hands. Lishka brought herself closer to Dominick, as if by her presence she could will him back to his body. The warmth increased. Little by little, the feel of Dominick grew stronger. Color returned to his body. Though still pale, he practically looked rosy compared to what he had been only moments before. At last, he opened his eyes. For a second, he did not look at her. Instead, he looked through her, beyond her, to a place not of their world. Then his pupils dilated to focus on her before him.

Dominick's eyes radiated gold, and instead of casting light, they made the shadows on his face even darker. Lishka still held his wrists, though the blood she drew had dried and his skin had healed to smoothness.

"I heard your voice in the gray," Dominick whispered. He blinked at last and Lishka let go of his arms to sit back.

"You must be careful at all times," Lishka warned. "One small slip, one instant where you lose the grip on your body, and the connection will be severed. The power will catch and carry you away. I won't be able to help you then." Her voice sounded even, the cold instruction of a teacher, while inside she suppressed the fear that had arisen. Dominick had almost succumbed to the mist. Had she not been able to bring him back, he would have been lost to it forever. Lishka did not let herself dwell on that thought. Dominick had brought himself back, and now he knew what the currents truly felt like.

"Are you ready to try again?" She disliked having to push, but Dominick must learn. He had been exposed to the power beyond the Veil now, had tasted it, and it had tasted him. The currents would carry him away if he did not learn the proper control, how to protect himself without the use of the mage's mark.

Dominick nodded.

"This time, you must hold a part of yourself back. Let the current test you, but do not give in entirely. You must—" Lishka paused, thinking how best to describe it, "you must define the boundaries of yourself. Let the current flow around you, lift you, but not consume you. Does that make sense?"

"I think so," Dominick said, frowning again. He held out his hand.

"What?" She looked from his hand to his face.

"I felt your touch before when I heard your voice. I think it will help anchor me, as you call it," Dominick explained.

Lishka had heard of this type of magik before, a physical bond to help anchor the spirit. It was a poor substitute for the mage's mark, but the bond of the Maker would help to ground Dominick to the physical world. She slid closer to him and reached out to grasp his wrist.

"Now try again," she instructed.

ONCE DOMINICK HAD satisfactorily shown that he had enough control to enter beyond the Veil and draw himself back again, Lishka decided they'd had enough training for that night. The sun had lightened the sky, though the ridge of their basin meant dawn would arrive later than in the rest of the mountain range. They found shelter in a cave halfway up the slope and, from the stale scent inside, confirmed no bears had used it for a long time.

The following night, Lishka stopped them early once more. The nook of an uprooted tree would provide adequate shelter during the day, and they rolled a few larger boulders closer around it for additional protection. Again, Lishka gritted her teeth and clamped down on the inner pull. Not for the first time, she entertained the thought that she would be much farther along if she traveled alone.

"I'm going to teach you how to control the power," she explained at Dominick's questioning look. They still had several hours before dawn.

"Isn't that what you showed me last night?" Dominick asked. He hopped up to sit on a large boulder he had just placed beside their tree. His hair hung limp around his ears, still damp from the rain that had come and gone the hour prior.

"No. I taught you how to tap into the power, to draw it into you. But we can do more than just consume it. You can harness it, use magik to make things happen. Not a lot, though, not without the mage's mark." Dominick's eyes flicked to Lishka's own forehead, and she felt the stab of loss. She had not gotten used to the dead mark upon her forehead. "But I can teach you how to construct the symbols to give the magik purpose. It may come into use, later."

*When the mark is unbound.* Her sentence hung unfinished. Lishka did not know if Dominick's mark would be unbound, as hers had been promised. He had not earned the right to bear it, but perhaps if she taught him now, she could help him to do so.

"What can you do with the power?" Dominick asked.

"Many things," Lishka answered. "Make fire, cast wards of protection, create spells to lock people out. Cast defensive spells, of course. Take out your sword."

Dominick drew his blade from the scabbard on his back. Lishka stepped in closer so that she stood before him. The boulder he sat upon put their heads almost at equal height. He held the blade out between them and with her thumb and forefinger she pinched the steel to twist it toward him, being careful to avoid the sharp edge.

"Do you see the symbols etched upon the surface?" she asked.

"Yes."

"These symbols are for undoing." Even as she showed the marks to Dominick, Lishka couldn't help admiring Kiaban's craftsmanship.

"Undoing?" Dominick questioned.

"Our kind heals relatively quickly. The symbols prevent the healing, help to cause more damage that makes it much harder for our natural abilities to recover from. If you were to stab me with that blade, it might take hours for me to heal, thus weakening me and increasing your opportunity to kill me."

Dominick pulled his gaze from the sword to her, alarmed at her directness. He had not come from a world of death.

"You'd have to reach me, first," Lishka reassured him. "Which reminds me, I need to teach you how to fight."

Dominick made to slide down from the boulder, but Lishka pressed her hand against his shoulder to stop him.

"Not yet. Magik first."

"How will I learn all the symbols?" Dominick asked. He lifted the sword back over his head to sheath it.

"I will teach you," Lishka said. "There are many, but you'll find that your memory is much clearer than before. I need only show them to you once, and you will remember. There are some Master Mages who dedicate their lives to the craft. These mages create new symbols, new castings. From what we can tell, the creation of symbols and castings is infinite." As she spoke, Lishka thought of Kiaban. She saw the same eagerness in Dominick to learn, his mind curious and open.

"Reach out for the Veil," she directed, even as Dominick opened his mouth to ask more questions. "Can you still feel the power beyond it?"

Dominick closed his eyes. His fingers twitched. "Yes."

"Don't go through," Lishka warned. "You will need only a small amount drawn from beyond."

Dominick opened his eyes. "It's odd. It's like a hum at the back of my mind. I think it was always there, I just didn't know what it was."

"In some places, it will be stronger," Lishka acknowledged. "In Seattle, it was somewhat quieter, but here, closer to the North, you will feel it more. The Veil grows weaker here, so far from civilization."

"Who else can go beyond the Veil and use the power?" Dominick asked, momentarily distracted from their lesson.

"Our kind of course, and witches, those with a special affinity. You have to know the power is there to access it. Except for witches, humans usually cannot sense it, and so they do not know how to use it."

"But I could," Dominick said. "What does that mean?"

"I don't know," Lishka answered honestly. Dominick asked the very question that had plagued her before she'd turned him. "You are not a witch, I could tell that much from your energy. I don't know why you have an affinity, though there are a few other bloodlines that could carry the ability."

"What are the other bloodlines?" Their lesson had been completely discarded.

"Fey blood could enhance a mortal's sensitivity," Lishka explained. She gestured to her own violet eyes, almost out of habit.

"You said Zaral sensed the fey in you," Dominick said, remembering their conversation from several nights ago. Lishka tried not to flinch at her Maker's name. "You are part fey?" Dominick slid off the boulder to stand before her, as though to make a better study of her.

"Could you feel the Veil too, when you were human?" His voice grew eager at the possibility of discovering the reason for his difference. Lishka remembered her own need to understand, before she'd lost her humanity.

"Yes, I could access it and use the magik," Lishka said. "But I do not think you have fey blood," she added. "It's hard to explain, but fey, from what I can tell, has a violet haze about it. Your core feels different. Golden."

"Like a small sun." Dominick's unexpected whisper of Lishka's words weeks ago, before she'd turned him, sent a shiver up her spine. *He remembers.* They stood close, locked in each other's gaze, violet against brown. The moment stretched between them, until the soft hoot of an owl in the lower forest drew their senses back to their surroundings.

"Okay," Dominick said, focusing once more on the facts before him. "That aside for the minute, you can use symbols to make the energy do things, almost like instructions or a code." Lishka nodded. He had snapped into his familiar pattern of scientific investigation.

"And the energy comes from another place held back by a barrier, by the Veil," Dominick continued. "But it's also in the stones. The same energy that flows beyond the Veil is also contained in the Boreal Stones."

Lishka had not bothered to think of the stones, not since Dominick had been turned and everything had changed. But here they were, again before her and tied to Dominick.

"How did the power get into the stones?" he asked. "A witch? The Coven?"

Lishka shook her head. "No, the rocks are not the result of any spell." She recalled Kiaban's explanation. "It's more like the power somehow was drawn to the stone and the force of it fused the rock around it, trapping the energy inside."

"So it occurred naturally. And the Boreameter can detect it, show it to those who would not know it existed otherwise. You said most humans don't know about the power beyond the Veil. You wouldn't need to be able to sense it on your own, not with Professor Boreal's instrument."

Lishka began to shake her head.

"If it could be harnessed, imagine what that would mean," Dominick insisted, disregarding her reaction. "Sustainable energy."

Dominick's voice had taken on the fervor he exhibited when he had first told her about the study. A dangerous passion, which Dominick should know now more than anyone.

"Stop." Lishka's voice cut through Dominick's excitement. Even in the mountains, she felt as though Zaral listened. "You mustn't speak of the study, not ever again. It is lost now."

"But think of it, Lishka," Dominick said, ignoring her as his thoughts swirled with new revelation. "A new power. One that does not deplete the world, like fossil fuel. One that isn't poison. A self-sustaining, self-regenerating fuel that could power technology."

"It would never work," Lishka said, unable to help herself be drawn into Dominick's argument.

"Why not?" Dominick's voice held a note of defensiveness.

"The power does not meld well with technology. They are two utterly different elements. One is natural, of the earth, and one is unnatural, man-made, built from violating the natural world. Only a handful of skilled mages possess the ability to meld the two, and they will not allow humans to wield such power."

"The Boreameter works," Dominick countered. "And not all technology is evil. Not all of it is made to destroy."

Lishka did not want to argue with him; she had seen enough of humanity in her lifetime to demonstrate otherwise. Regardless of Dominick's desires, he would not be allowed to pursue the study further.

"The Coven will never allow you to continue the study," she said. "You are bound by our laws now. If you try, you will only put the humans you worked with in danger."

A shadow fell across Dominick's face and though he didn't move, Lishka sensed him draw back from her. She regretted that she must again remind him of the danger of their world. But Dominick had to know there was no going back.

Somewhere nearby, something small shuffled under the boulders, most likely a pika. The elusive creatures would be foraging for food during the day, though ready to dart back into their holes beneath the rocks the second they sensed danger.

"What do you think they'll do with it? With the study?" Dominick asked after a moment.

"I'm not sure," Lishka answered. "It depends on the humans still conducting the experiments. You will have been reported missing, or Kristoph may have spread the story that you've left, moved elsewhere, or had a family emergency. If the remaining professors carry on the study, Sieth may pursue them as well."

Dominick crossed his arms as though preparing to argue. He tilted his body away from Lishka and leaned against the boulder behind him, staring at the ground while he thought. Despite Lishka's warning, she could see she had not defeated his will to pursue the research.

"I am surprised the university allowed the study to

continue," Lishka admitted, before Dominick could speak. She had been uneasy with the university's persistence ever since Dominick had told her of the Boreal Stones. It didn't make sense, that the university had carried on the work while those affiliated died and disappeared.

Dominick looked up. "Why?"

"The Dean knows of the Coven," Lishka confessed. Dominick would learn the truth sooner or later, now that he belonged to the Coven. "He conducts business with us, as we are both leading organizations within Seattle. I'm surprised he allowed the study to move forward."

"The Dean knows?" Dominick asked, shocked. "Who else knows that vampires exist?"

"Most of human leadership," Lishka said. "They have to. We cannot exist solely in the shadows. Zaral and Zachriel have cultivated mankind over the centuries. But long ago, they decided that the public should remain oblivious to our kind. We must feed on their blood, you see. One human in leadership can be persuaded to work with us. Humans en masse are little more than any other kind of prey, quick to fear, quick to react—and usually in the worst way possible.

"Some humans do find out on their own," she conceded, envisioning those who visited *Midnight* to be fed upon. "Those born with an affinity for magik, who already have one step in the other world. Others are lured in by the fantasy of death, through drugs potent with magik."

"I never knew," Dominick murmured.

"But you felt the power beyond the Veil," Lishka said, to make him feel better.

"Maybe that's why the Dean stalled our funding. He was trying to kill the study without drawing too much attention." Dominick flinched at the word *kill* even as he said it, no doubt thinking of the professors and possibly himself.

"Maybe," Lishka granted. "Although there remains the fact that the Coven had begun to dispose of those involved in order to stop it. Why didn't the Dean halt the study then? He could have disallowed use of the labs and destroyed the Boreameter. It would have been university property."

*And then Zaral had come.*

"What are you thinking?" Dominick studied her as though he could uncover further truths she kept hidden.

"If the Coven had instructed the Dean to shut down the study, it never would have reached the stage you were at. The Boreameter should never have been built, unless…" She trailed off.

"Unless someone else told them to continue," Dominick finished. "Who?"

Lishka hesitated. Zachriel's Council had heard of the study. Lord Dorwan had admitted knowledge, just after her trial, when they'd invited her into their confidence.

"Dominick, the less you know, the better," she said instead. "When we return, it is better that you remain neutral, ignorant of the Council's manipulation. You will be able to integrate into the Coven and find a place for yourself, away from the politics of our kind." As Lishka had tried to do.

"I want to know," Dominick insisted. "I died for this, Lishka. I deserve to know what made that happen. And besides, I will be with you when we return, right?"

"Yes," Lishka said, before she could stop herself. She had never considered keeping Dominick with her, as she had stayed with Mordan. Yet he spoke to her with openness, obviously trusting her with his life. She could not abandon him to the rest of them.

Dominick crossed his arms and waited for her to explain.

"Zachriel's Council knew of the study," Lishka said. "They told me in secret, right before we left the Coven."

"You think Zachriel wants the study to continue?" Dominick asked. He tried to hide it, but Lishka heard the hope in his voice.

Lishka shrugged.

"It is possible. It would explain why the study continued, though it was not publicized or fully funded. It matters little, now."

"What side are you on?" Dominick asked. Any heat from his voice had dissipated. He did not accuse; instead, he sounded genuinely curious.

"What do you mean?"

"You said before that Zaral did not want the study to continue and would do what he could to stop it."

"Yes," Lishka confirmed. "He does not want to see humans discover the power beyond the Veil."

"What does Zachriel want?"

"I don't know." Lishka had never spoken so freely about Coven politics before. She always had to be on guard, watching for hidden motives. It had been smarter to say little, to keep her own thoughts close. But alone with Dominick, who had yet to be corrupted by their kind, she found herself wanting to speak freely. "Zachriel has always led alongside his brother before now. Zaral seeks power, to control mankind as well as the Covens. The Council Members loyal to Zachriel say he has another plan. They did not tell me what it is, only that there is a war coming."

"And where do you stand?" Dominick asked. Lishka did not answer right away. Even in the wilderness, where none but Dominick could hold her to her words, she did not want to commit to a side. Yet she knew her resistance was futile. She had accepted Zachriel's mission, and the fact that she had not been given much choice did not matter.

"Lishka?" Dominick prompted. She must answer. She had dragged him into this mess, and he deserved to know who they followed.

"Should it come to it, I will fight for Zachriel," Lishka answered finally.

"Then I supposed you'd better teach me magik, and how to use the sword," Dominick said. "So I can be ready to fight alongside you, when the time comes."

LISHKA SPENT THE NEXT few days teaching Dominick how to draw the symbols, though she dared not let him release them into full castings. The tracker had found them too easily before, and though they had traveled deep into the mountains and far from any settlements, any magik cast would leave a noticeable footprint. Then she taught him how to use his sword. Dominick took to the blade more than naturally, though he assured her he had never trained in swordplay. The steel formed a seamless extension of his arm, and more than once he came close to piercing Lishka's defense, though she never admitted it to him.

With Dominick learning both magik and the sword, Lishka pushed them on at a quicker pace. Somehow, training him had brought the danger closer. She worried he might have to use his new skills soon.

The snow began to drift from the sky in tiny round flakes to freeze on the ground. The patches of snow glittered under the moonlight when it broke through the cloud, and the few scraggly fir trees that dotted the mountainside cast long shadows to reach like bony fingers. The little streams that trickled off the mountain soon froze into shining droplets that wouldn't melt until springtime.

Low temperatures meant more than snow. The big game they had taken to hunting had also become scarce. Now and then they spotted the white mountain goat, who clipped along the narrowest ledges with impossible acrobatics, and kept clear of Lishka and Dominick. They would have to rely on the energy beyond the Veil for sustenance.

The mountainside gradually grew narrow, with the cliffside rising to either side of them. In fact, it began to form a corridor of sorts. Lishka stopped for Dominick, who walked several paces behind her.

"What do you think?"

Dominick looked up from his feet. Several snowflakes clung to his eyelashes and speckled his hair white. He sniffed the air.

"Feels okay." He had understood her meaning, and checked to be sure they remained alone. Lishka could sense no other presence nearby, but she disliked the narrow path before them. It had been placed a little too conveniently and would be the perfect location for an ambush. She reached out with other senses to once more check for any disturbances along the Veil, any marks to indicate that it had been tapped into recently. All remained undisturbed.

Hoofprints on the lightly worn path indicated that it had become an animal run, likely goat, this high up. The passage narrowed as they climbed so that Lishka could stretch out her arms to either side and barely graze the stone walls with her fingertips. The cliffs soared overhead, with notches and ledges carved into their weathered bulks. A faint glisten showed moisture in the cracks, and exposed veins of crystal high above sparkled in starlight.

After a while, clouds moved in to cover the moon and the path became quite dark, although not to Lishka and Dominick. The incline increased as it wound its way up the mountain. Occasionally a granite boulder blocked the way, a chunk that had dropped off from the cliff above, forcing them to either leap over or squeeze around.

Lishka found her thoughts drifting toward Seattle. Dominick had asked her of her loyalty, and now she found herself bound to Zachriel. Yet, Zaral had been in Seattle. *Had he sensed Lady Raseska's and Mordan's plan? Did he know of Mordan's betrayal?* Even just thinking the word *betrayal* caused her to freeze, to shrink away from the thought. Not for the first time, she pondered when Mordan's loyalty had shifted and how she had not noticed until it was too late.

Before she could help herself, she wondered if Mordan would be pleased or disappointed in her training of Dominick. He had proven himself an easy student, and, Lishka had to admit if only to herself, not horrible company. Suddenly, she remembered Mordan's words: *I think you might be glad to have him with you in the end.*

The snow had begun to fall more heavily and with it came a strange smell that hung in the air. Metallic and old, it clung to their clothes and hair, the residue of some ancient magik long past.

Lishka quickened her pace and Dominick fell into step beside her.

"What is that?" he asked, his voice hushed in the silent snow. They had not spoken for hours.

"I'm not sure," Lishka answered. The odor smelled oddly familiar, as if from a half-dream. If she had encountered it in the past, it had been a long time ago and she could not remember where.

At once light shined from ahead. The cliffs opened to reveal the edge of a platform carved into the mountainside, large enough to hold the Coven mansion and its outbuildings. To the east, the edge of the platform ended in rubble and open air, dropping many miles down to the forested valleys. Beside them, the mountain continued to rise, broken by narrow ledges and the odd withered fir, whose roots gripped what little purchase they could find. The smell that had risen in the mountain pass began to fade, dispersed in the open space. Yet Lishka still sensed the ancient magik deep below her feet. She walked forward toward the cliffside, allowing instinct to guide her. The snow had blown in drifts where the platform met the cliff.

The pressure built. Somewhere a strong source of energy pulsed, a point where the Veil thinned and power oozed through. Such a place would be ideal for her and Dominick to tap into the power, to recharge from their climb. At the back of her mind, an alarm rang. The smell still lingered, like an old perfume. She did not think it merited concern, though she wished she could place it.

Dominick saw it first.

"Look." He pointed ahead of them.

A gaping hole yawned before them. All around the opening, thousands of small cuts had been notched into the rock. Lishka recognized the etchings with a small thrill: symbols. Despite the natural elements, the symbols shone clear. Most of them she didn't recognize, their meanings lost long before her time. Those she did understand spoke two words: *Power. Containment.* She approached the entrance with caution, Dominick close behind.

"It's a tunnel," Dominick said unnecessarily. His words echoed into the mountain. Lishka peered inside. The hole plummeted to disappear into the depths of the rock. The air emanated that whiff of power, strong but also stale, as if whatever left it had been here long ago, and not come back since.

"I think it's safe," she said. "It might lead us through the mountain. It could save us days."

"I don't like that smell. I don't know why, but something about it feels wrong," Dominick said.

Lishka listened again but still she detected no recent activity, nor any other alarming signs.

"I think we should go in," she decided. "Whatever it is, it's old and likely gone." The pull inside her had grown stronger, and she had to fight to keep her feet still. She breathed a deep breath and finally recognized the scent. "Dragon."

Dominick's eyes widened.

"They exist?"

"They did. They're extinct now, more or less. The one that lived here is long gone, I can tell." Lishka inhaled again to be sure. On closer inspection, the marks, once strong with power, had also faded. They had no doubt been placed several millennia ago. She walked forward and her boots made no noise on the smooth rock floor. Without hesitation, Dominick followed her into the cold silence of the cave.

# CHAPTER 17

# THE ANCIENTS' GLYPHS

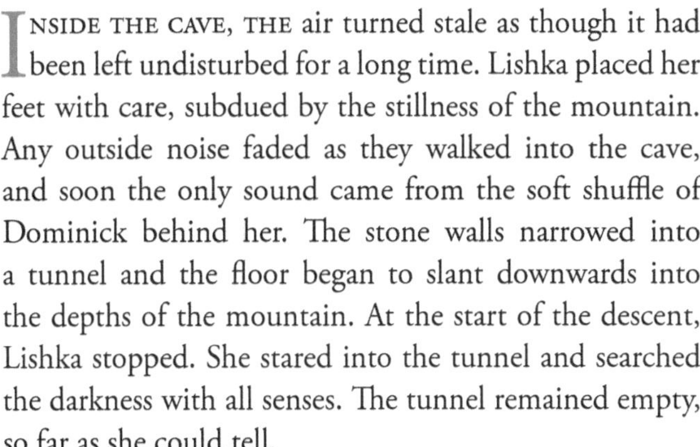

INSIDE THE CAVE, THE air turned stale as though it had been left undisturbed for a long time. Lishka placed her feet with care, subdued by the stillness of the mountain. Any outside noise faded as they walked into the cave, and soon the only sound came from the soft shuffle of Dominick behind her. The stone walls narrowed into a tunnel and the floor began to slant downwards into the depths of the mountain. At the start of the descent, Lishka stopped. She stared into the tunnel and searched the darkness with all senses. The tunnel remained empty, so far as she could tell.

Dominick made a soft exclamation behind her.

"There are pictures on the walls."

Lishka turned back. Dominick faced the wall with his nose only inches from the stone. He lifted his hand to trace the lines etched into the surface. Lishka retreated several steps to stand beside him, despite the urge to continue forward.

A mix of painted and carved images sprawled across the tunnel wall. Three crude drawings of people had been etched into the first scene. They stood in a semicircle around what appeared to be a bundle of wheat.

"Harvest," Lishka whispered.

"That's what this means?" Dominick's fingertips danced across the wheat, as though he channeled the artist's hand.

"Yes," Lishka answered. "And this one." She took several steps down the wall to the next scene. "This is the celebration of the fertility cycle that comes with the harvest time."

Dominick leaned over her to study the images of people dancing around campfires beneath a full moon.

"How do you know?" He kept his voice low to match Lishka's, as though they both did not want to disturb the air.

"Some of the symbols are similar to the ones used by my clan, when I was human," Lishka explained. "And if you look above, the carvings of the sun and moon help show the passage of time."

Dominick lifted his gaze to where she pointed. Moon and sun circles denoted the cyclical nature of years passing, marked by symbols that Lishka assumed represented the seasons. Together, she and Dominick inched along the timeline to study each scene. The more elaborate carvings had been enhanced with colors now faded. These appeared to represent important ceremonies, and Lishka said as much to Dominick. Lishka recognized the symbols for elemental magik—earth, fire, water, and air—but many of the others she could not decipher.

Further into the tunnel there appeared the first, rough

images of dragons, drawn in fiery reds that too had faded over time. In some of the pictures, small figures fought the dragons. The marks that encircled them matched those at the cave's entrance. *Power. Containment.* Despite their age, they still possessed some of the original magik. Lishka suppressed a shiver. The magik must have been strong, to have survived this long.

"Who were they?" Dominick asked.

"Ancients." Lishka stared at the small figures upon the stone, a race that had become myth long before she'd entered the world. "They lived many thousands of years ago, before the Veil had really developed. Then even humans still felt the power contained in the Earth." She traced the drawings, mimicking Dominick's study. "They're long gone. There's no place in this world for the ancient things anymore." A surprising wistfulness threaded through her words.

Dominick inched along the carvings, examining each.

"Is this one of the Ancients'?" He knelt to the floor in one fluid motion.

Lishka leaned down to see the image he spoke of. It had been carved only a foot from the ground against a cracked section of rock. Dust shifted at the base of the wall with their movement.

"It feels like the power beyond the Veil," Dominick murmured. Lishka brought her face closer so that the two of them crouched side by side, their heads almost touching as they studied the picture. A white column only three inches high twisted into a vaguely humanoid figure. Instinctively Lishka felt that it was feminine, although she couldn't explain why. With a start, she realized what made this image different. It had not been carved by hand, but instead placed there by magik. Unlike the other drawings with symbols that contained the energy, this drawing *was* the magik, though the remnants of the power had faded over time and now barely clung to the wall. Lishka frowned. She hadn't heard of anything like it before. Even more worrying, the surrounding depictions showed figures running away, and some lay flat as if stricken.

"Lishka?"

She shook herself. "I don't know. I don't think so. It's more likely some old being, one that went out of the world long ago." The air had become heavier with their talk of the ancient world. Dominick stared at the image, silent. She broke her gaze. "Come on."

Reluctantly, Dominick stood to follow her down into the heart of the mountain. As they descended, the air steadily cooled to well below freezing. Surprisingly, the walls stayed dry, even though they had to be far below the surface. Lishka supposed that the dragon once living in the tunnels had dried up any underground springs with its breath and body heat.

About a mile in, they came to an intersection, where the main tunnel diverged into three others leading off in different directions. Judging from their angles, Lishka guessed that they should continue straight into the slightly narrower middle tunnel. Her inner compass guiding her toward the fey agreed.

The middle tunnel, though smaller, still yawned wide enough to fit six people abreast, and the ceiling rose to at least twelve feet high. Either a small dragon had lived here or else had not used this particular tunnel to pass through the mountain. Once again, carvings decorated the stone, and the walls became unnaturally smooth. *This tunnel must have been created by the Ancients in the pictures.*

Lishka wondered when the last people had come through this way. She couldn't sense anything even semi-recent, besides a vague metallic undercurrent in the air different from that of the dragon; instead, it was reminiscent of the power beyond the Veil. She reached out to test the Veil, and it felt the same as before, thinner yet still present.

The pictures along this tunnel were rougher than those closer to the cave entrance, and older. A larger drawing on the wall portrayed a great winged shape, the medium used to create it such a pure black that it dulled even the dark of the tunnel.

"Are there any of them left?" Dominick said, interrupting the silence. "Dragons, I mean."

"Maybe," Lishka replied. "It's hard to tell. None have been seen for ages. If any still live, they slumber now, deep within the Earth." She sniffed: the metallic scent had grown stronger. A buzzing grated against her temples.

"What is that?" Dominick asked.

The air pressed in on them. Lishka's supernatural abilities meant she did not have a fear of confined spaces. If she had to, she could likely use her own strength combined with magik to blast her way to the surface, though it would deplete her energy. Dominick also did not appear to possess any squeamishness at being so deep underground. Yet the air had thickened to make the dark even more oppressive. An urge to stand once more beneath the open sky began to tug at her feet.

Lishka shook her head. "I'm not sure." A dry, musty smell permeated the tunnel, charged with particles of magik. She followed the scent forward to find a smaller side tunnel that opened crudely in the stone to their right.

Dominick stepped up beside her to face the entrance together, his solid presence reassuring. They stared into the muffled dark and a breeze washed over them. No wind blew this far under the mountain, but still the air moved, pushed by an invisible force.

The air tasted of something old.

"Maybe we should turn back." Lishka disliked the hesitation in her voice, but the scent triggered some primal fear inside her.

"What do you think it is?"

Lishka barely heard him though he stood close to her. Neither of them wanted to make any noise before this tunnel. Lishka restrained herself from drawing her sword and shook her head instead.

"I don't know." They stood a moment longer and the scent neither increased nor faded.

"We'll keep moving," Lishka decided. "We must be close to the center now, and from there, the incline back to the surface."

Dominick followed her with several glances back to the tunnel. Like Lishka, he too couldn't shake the sense that something had detected them in the bowels of the mountain. Their pace quickened, both eager to leave the side tunnel behind. They covered at least another mile of ground. No matter how carefully they placed their feet, each step seemed to echo behind them. The air still hung with heaviness and sparks of energy periodically tickled the napes of their necks.

A scraping whisper echoed out from the depths of the tunnel back the way they'd come, loud in the silent dark. Lishka whirled about. Dominick danced out of her way just in time, narrowly avoiding slamming into her. A jagged outcrop of rock at the bend in the tunnel prevented her from seeing back through the passage. The noise grew louder. The energy in the air pressed against her temples. Lishka planted her feet, sliding into a fighter's stance on instinct. Dominick shifted into a crouch, his hands curved, and teeth bared.

A wave of disorienting power plummeted into them. At once Lishka experienced the sensation of being submerged beyond the Veil. She no longer had physical form; instead, she bounced around buffeted by the currents of the gray mist. Lishka swayed and suddenly she had a hold of herself. The rock pushed solidly against her boots. Without thinking, she reached out to grip Dominick's forearm, his flesh firm and real beneath her fingers. Above his head, the pictures stood out stark against the wall, and Lishka found her gaze drawn to them.

The pictures were moving.

"We shouldn't have come here. We have to leave, now." Her voice grew louder against the rushing static pouring from the tunnel. Dominick stayed frozen, fixated on the passage. Lishka faced the noise and a blast of heat hit her face. From around the outcrop blazed a white light, blinding in the dark, the kind of light that obliterated all other shapes.

Lishka blinked several times in quick succession, trying to adjust to the brilliance after the dark. The light grew brighter, coalescing in the middle, seeming to become more solid. Shapes like legs appeared, then a torso, arms, and finally the vague outline of a head. Light billowing outward took on the appearance of hair. As they watched, the column of light pulled together until it was all contained in the figure of a woman. Lishka's mind flashed back to the drawing on the cave wall. Unwillingly the images of the figures laying stricken on the ground popped into her head. Instinct told her running would be foolish and so she stood absolutely still, willing Dominick to do the same. He straightened from his crouch, his bared teeth still gleaming in the light's brightness.

The woman glided toward them. Her light crackled around her, sparking off the stone. Lishka gathered her own power up within her, ready to pull a spell for destruction. She doubted even Kiaban's sword would do anything against this creature.

The woman paused a few feet before them, head tilted ever so slightly as if in study. The light lessened in brightness to reveal glowing eyes, a nose, and a mouth that twisted into a small smile.

"Interesting." Her voice crackled and a wave of heat shrank the air between them. "Two little children, wandering through my mountain."

Lishka held perfectly still. Beside her, Dominick couldn't help flinching at the power in the woman's voice. The woman snickered.

"So young and fresh." She clapped her hands together, delighted. White flames flew up from the contact, then flickered back down to her fingers. "What a treat." She reached for Dominick.

A quick, vibrant energy rose inside Lishka and, before she registered what happened, erupted from her to meet the light's hand. With a surprised hiss, the creature pulled back and focused on Lishka. The light recoiled into the woman, creating one blinding spot in the middle of the tunnel, then flared out to drown Lishka's energy in an instant.

"Fey," she spat. "It's been a long time since I've felt fey."

Lishka set her shoulders and willed her strange power to boil up again. Yet now it dulled, pale in comparison to the white light.

The woman inched closer to Lishka. "You seem different," she mused. "Familiar. Who are you?" Her question snapped the air, sharp against their ears.

"I am Lishka, of the Coven of Zachriel."

"Your blood smells familiar." The woman seemed to inhale. "Oh, yes. I remember now. My memory stretches back farther than you, little one, and I remember." She smiled. "He probably forgets me, hidden deep in the mountain caves. It is wrong to forget the ancient powers." Her eyes brightened. "It is wrong to forget Alaisadaille. I will make him remember." The light slunk forward again to close the gap between them. Lishka's senses unanimously screamed at her to run, but instead she stood transfixed by the power in the light.

Dominick shifted suddenly to put himself in front of Lishka. The woman's attention flew back to him. Long tendrils of white reached out to graze Dominick's face and shoulders. His muscle corded out from his neck down through his shoulders and arms, but he held his ground.

The woman hesitated.

"Oh!" Her smile widened to gape across her face. "Oh, I see." Laughter burst out of her in a harsh, grating noise that clawed at their skin. "Oh Zaral, you don't know what moves against you," she cackled gleefully. "I may be hidden in the depths of the world, but you are the one who is blind." She stilled her laughter.

"You may be the key," she said to Dominick, "but I am the gatekeeper. And none can pass here without my blessing." She drew her light up to raise herself to greater heights. Her head reached the stone of the ceiling, and her flames took up the width of the tunnel. She towered over them, and the air around her shimmered as the walls began to turn to molten rock. She would dissolve the tunnel around them. The light shone brighter—and disappeared. Lishka and Dominick stood still, connected by Lishka's grasp. No shapes of rock appeared. The light had left behind a void not even they could see through.

Lishka flicked her left hand to trace the symbols for light. She fumbled to find the symbols but the power beyond the Veil eluded her. She could sense neither the Veil nor the energy behind it. The void had removed everything. Lishka fought down the rising panic. She'd never not been able to sense the energy, even when human. She turned inward instead to search for that violet source, her fey magik. It too had disappeared, snuffed out by the white light.

Sudden warmth flooded up her arm. Lishka still held onto Dominick. Without fully realizing what he did, he transferred his own power into her. At once, Lishka felt the Veil again, though at a distance. She forced herself through the resistance to sluggishly pull some of the energy through her, forming the magik into a sloppy casting.

A small light reluctantly trickled from her hand to dangle in the air. With its release the blackness retreated. The tunnel appeared before them once more and beside her, Dominick's face came into focus. He stared into the space where the woman of light had disappeared. Above his head, the pictures had stilled. Lishka released his arm.

"Who was she?" Dominick rasped, his voice singed by the heat.

"I'm not sure." Lishka stepped away from Dominick, reluctant to turn her back to where the woman had disappeared, but wanting to escape the dark tunnels. Dominick stayed frozen in place.

"Dominick?" Lishka followed his stare. Blackness oozed out of the tunnel, and as they watched, flecks of light flickered within the void once more. Electricity popped in the air. Lishka's hair rose in response. There would be no talking this time, whatever the woman had said before. She grabbed Dominick's arm.

"Run!"

Faster than the eye could follow, Lishka whipped Dominick around and together they raced away from the light.

The pressure in the tunnel piled up behind them, a wall of competing dark and light, malicious intent laced within its core. As she ran, Lishka formed symbols in her head, holding them together while readying the words on her lips. The Veil contracted to almost nonexistence, and she reached out for the unleashed energy.

The tunnel sloped upward. Suddenly the power fell farther behind them. They had not outrun it; rather, it had slowed its pursuit. Lishka and Dominick kept running, their footfalls light against the hard rock. The tunnel narrowed ahead. A bright light shone, not behind them but in front, and Lishka drew heavily on what power she could reach, preparing herself to unleash the symbols. Yet this light felt different, softer. She hesitated. The symbols and magik dissolved unspent. The ground gave one last upheaval, before Dominick and Lishka burst out onto a clear white mountainside.

# CHAPTER 18

# TWIN PEAKS

LISHKA CAUGHT HERSELF BEFORE tumbling into the snow. Pink tinged the clear night sky. She blinked—*is it sunrise?* Night blanketed the eastern ridgeline, while in the west, streams of fading light highlighted the horizon. A full day had passed, at minimum. Time must run differently under the mountain. Alaisadaille surely had something to do with this. Time slipped away beyond the Veil, and Alaisadaille seemed to blur that barrier between the physical world and the power behind it.

Lishka glanced over at Dominick. "Did she hurt you?"

He stared back at her, his eyes wide. "No. I'm fine." His voice sounded surprisingly calm, though he unclenched his fists. "What was that thing?"

"Alaisadaille…" Lishka whispered the name as if to better understand. "I'm not sure. I've never encountered anything like it before." She faced the cave to search the depths with all senses. The tunnel appeared to be empty.

Alaisadaille had not followed them to the surface.

"It—She—felt like the power beyond the Veil," Dominick said. "Only different somehow, smaller I guess, though just as potent." He peered back at the tunnel mouth.

"I think maybe that's what she was," Lishka said, developing her theory based on her understanding of their world. "Some remnant of that power."

"How do you mean?" Dominick asked, his attention still flicking between Lishka and the gaping tunnel.

"The weak spots in the Veil," she theorized, trying to clarify even as she attempted to figure it out herself. "Every once in a while, when a wider rift occurs, a stronger entity gets through." She followed the thought, thinking back over the centuries to past conversations, teachings about magik. "I've heard that sometimes, when exposed to the input of human energy and emotion, that entity develops its own consciousness."

"A consciousness?" Dominick echoed.

"Do you remember how I told you that the power is likened to the essence of the Earth?"

Dominick nodded.

"It's alive, in a way, like plants are alive, animals, humans, ecosystems even," she elaborated. "Over a long time, a part might break off through the Veil and develop its own sense of self. That one we met is very, very old."

"That makes sense. Though I thought you said you've never seen anything like it. How do you know that's what it was?"

"I haven't," Lishka repeated. "And really, it's all theory. But some things Mordan has said in the past, the way he's described the power, almost like it's a consciousness in and of itself. He told me once that the power beyond the Veil can create more creatures from itself, although it's rare. It's the only thing that makes sense." She looked into the cave and shivered. "Come on. We'd better make the most of the night." She didn't need to voice her desire to get away from the tunnel. Dominick kept an eye on the entrance even as he followed her up the mountainside.

A tightness lifted from her chest at being once more in the open. Lishka raised her face to the cold air blowing down from the peak above them. The snow lay soft and took no effort to move across, though the drifts had piled many feet deep. This snow would not melt until high summer, and maybe not even then. They walked for a while in silence, taking turns kicking the trail. Every so often, the wind would whip through gullies and make a noise like flowing water. The first time, Dominick's head snapped around to stare behind them. The noise sounded suspiciously like Alaisadaille.

Lishka kept returning to the woman of light, her mind churning on her theory. As if thinking along the same lines, Dominick spoke.

"She said something to you, about Zaral. She said he doesn't know what moves against him. I wonder what she meant by that."

Lishka shook her head. "I don't know." This had also been bothering her. "Zaral is very powerful. With so much power there are always some who plot to overthrow that. Of course, the only one with any chance of that is Zachriel. She could have referred to the divide between the brothers."

"How would she know of that?" Dominick asked.

Again, Lishka had no answer.

"I've never heard anyone at the Coven speak of her, or anything like her, beyond only magik theory that Mordan told me," Lishka said. "And the Council Members did not warn me of her existence. I doubt they know she is there."

"She knew Zaral," Dominick repeated. "Is Zaral as powerful as she is?" Lishka could almost hear his thoughts, that the woman could be an ally against Zaral. But Alaisadaille had not seemed to Lishka like a being who would ally herself with anyone.

"Yes." Lishka tried not to think of Zaral's power. "Zaral and Zachriel are the first of our kind, but they were never human. Some legends even say that they are fallen angels, cursed by God, or whatever people choose to call that power, to wander the Earth forever, thirsting for life. That is likely a story, created by humans when the new religion developed. Divine or not, they are both very old and very powerful."

"And now they are against each other. Zaral does not want humans to have the power beyond the Veil, and Zachriel might?" Dominick deduced. He had clearly been thinking about their conversation from days ago. "Why now, though?"

Lishka thought on where to start. "There are nine major Covens belonging to either Zaral or Zachriel. They are located near points of power, most often in places where the Veil has grown thinner and the power beyond the Veil is more accessible."

"Like Seattle," Dominick said.

Lishka nodded. Being farther north and close to the undeveloped wilderness, Seattle had been an ideal location for a Coven.

"Further South, the Covens are strategically positioned to affect human politics, rather than utilize the weak points in the Veil," she added. "Many political leaders are heavily influenced. Decisions regarding international and foreign policy, trade, even the choice to go to war is fueled or extinguished by the Coven leaders, directed by Zaral and Zachriel. Zaral in particular has invested much in manipulating human leadership." She stopped, unsure of how much to tell him. She had told him before that she wanted him to have the chance to live outside their politics.

*And Dominick had said he wanted the truth.*

"In the past Zaral and Zachriel managed the humans together. However, in the last centuries, the balance between the two has become muddled, tense. Zaral wants chaos—from chaos he can have power and control. Zachriel, well, who knows. From what I've heard, his faction pursues enlightenment, free will, the power that comes when learned people make choices for themselves, choices based on knowledge."

"And what about you?" Dominick stopped to face her, and instinctively Lishka stopped with him. "What do you want?"

Lishka paused. She wanted the one thing she would never have, the one thing so many took for granted. "To be free."

"Aren't you?"

She glanced upward to find they had come mere steps away from another narrow ledge. Above, the mountain turned to a rock face coated in thin sheets of ice. Already the light grew bright in the east. The tunnel they had left what seemed only minutes ago lay miles below them.

She turned back to where Dominick waited for an answer.

"I have never been free." She faced away from him

and reached up to pull her long hair forward. On her exposed flesh a dark sign marked the nape of her neck: Zaral's symbol, given by him the moment before she lost her humanity, so that it would remain embedded in her skin forever, a constant reminder of who owned her.

A light touch sent a jolt through her veins. Dominick brushed his fingertips against the brand. Lishka shivered as his touch sent tingles across her skin. His presence warmed her back despite the fact that their bodies emitted little heat, and at once she became hyperaware of his closeness. Dominick's fingers lingered a second longer before he dropped his hand. Lishka took a half step forward and let her hair fall to cover the brand. Without looking back to him, she faced forward and began the steep climb up the rock face.

THEY REACHED THE top of the cliff by sunrise. Directly before them, more rock rose on either side to form a ravine. A natural path twisted in between to disappear around a sharp point. Presumably, it led upward to carry them higher into the mountains. It looked eerily similar to the one that had led them to the Ancients' tunnels, and to Alaisadaille.

Despite her misgivings, the ravine presented at a near-perfect time. Lishka had pushed them dangerously close to daylight. The clear sky and altitude would make the sun more painful, only worsening as it rose higher in the sky. Lishka pulled her hood close around her face and fought off the grogginess that had begun to weigh down her limbs.

As they entered the ravine, Lishka realized that they hadn't fed before the alpine peaks as she had planned. They wouldn't find much game this high up, especially with heavy snow. Not even a bird had come close for miles. They would have to rely on the power beyond the Veil to sustain them now.

The barrier had thinned since the tunnels. The power beyond now felt more in reach than it had since the binding of her mark, with the exception of Alaisadaille's influence. Lishka wondered if the accessibility had to do with the fey and the fact that they drew closer. What she thought of as her violet core buzzed with excitement, and somewhere up ahead, something of the same nature drew her forward. She glanced up.

In the splinter of exposed sky over their ravine, double peaks reared ahead of them. Their snowy caps broke through the clouds that had gathered around only their heads, leaving the rest of the sky empty. They beckoned to Lishka. At last, she saw the end of their journey.

"Look," she said.

Dominick followed her gaze.

"The Twin Peaks." She almost smiled. *Nearly there.*

"Is that where they are? The fey?"

Lishka nodded, still staring at the peaks. She found it difficult to believe that soon she would find herself in the presence of the folk, her ancestors.

"Should we keep going?" Dominick asked, gauging the distance. The peaks remained a way off yet, but they would reach them by the next sunrise. Lishka assessed the risk. At the sight of the peaks, her desire to be there intensified, pushing her forward. She studied the walls of rock to either side of them, which rose high enough to shield them from the most direct rays.

Even as she considered continuing during the day, a wave of drowsiness swept over her. If she wanted to travel through the day, she would need the power beyond the Veil.

"We'll rest for a bit," she decided. "We both need to go beyond the Veil and absorb the power as I showed you. We'll need the energy to fight against the day." *And to enter the realm of the fey.* A mixture of anticipation and uneasiness swirled in her chest. Lishka compartmentalized the sensation. She would need all her focus entering the Veil. Depleted and without her mark to tether her, she would be even more susceptible to the willful currents.

She and Dominick settled into a niche along the rock wall. Daylight hit the rock near the top of the cliffs, while the base remained shadowed. Snow filtered down like powder from the ledges above, shimmering in the early morning sun. Lishka closed her eyes and reached out to test the barrier. Energy grabbed hold of her, luring her through the Veil with little resistance. She withdrew and opened her eyes.

"What is it?" Dominick asked.

"The barrier is weak here, much weaker than I've felt before," she said. "Do you remember how to push through?"

Dominick nodded. "Yes."

"Try it again but be careful. The currents will try to suck you under and will be stronger with the Veil not as securely in place." This time, Lishka took his hand without being prompted.

Dominick sat straight against the rock. He placed his free hand on his knee and closed his eyes. An absolute stillness overtook his body. Lishka felt the moment he pushed past the Veil. Ripples of energy seemed to flow through his body, drifting off him like steam in the cold. It had been so much easier for him this time, and not only because of the weakened Veil. He didn't even have to use his hands to channel his focus. Dominick's strength grew much faster than she'd anticipated.

She watched him to ensure the force would not overpower him as it had the first time, and waited for him to come back to himself. The golden undertone in Dominick's hair and skin reminded her of the end of summer, when the low-setting sun made everything soft. With a start, she realized she'd drawn the image from her human memory.

Half an hour passed before Dominick stirred. Lishka snapped herself out of the trance-like state she'd entered. He shifted, rolling his shoulders as he drifted back into his body, adjusting to the feel of the physical. His hand flexed in Lishka's. Then he opened his eyes and they glowed with internal fire. A slow smile crept across his face as he relished the new strength the energy had given him. The air around him practically snapped.

"Alright," he said, his voice husky. Lishka released his hand. He moved his shoulders again and stretched out his back. "Let's keep going. I know it's day, but these rocks will keep most of the sunlight off us. We could make it there by nightfall, if not earlier."

"We should wait," Lishka argued. Her own energy lagged. "You haven't fed. Don't let the energy fool you into thinking you have more strength than you do."

"I feel great." Dominick grinned and rose to his feet to face the path. His eagerness gave away his inexperience.

He didn't yet understand the boundaries of the power to sustain him.

"The energy will give you strength, but only for so long," Lishka cautioned. "Your body will consume it much faster than blood. We'll stay here, rest for a little. We'll move on when the sun is lower in the sky. Besides, I must go beyond the Veil." Lishka suppressed the irritation that with his surge of energy, Dominick had forgotten that she too must recharge.

Dominick looked up at the sky, seemingly ignoring her. The air buzzed around him. Lishka closed her eyes and slid easily through the Veil. Soon the currents swept her up, and the energy twined around and through her. It pulled her further into the mist, until the boundaries of her spirit became tenuous. The last physical sensation she felt was Dominick's fingers sliding in between hers. Even beyond the Veil, his presence grounded her, tied her to her physical body, and kept her safe.

LISHKA WOKE AN hour after the sun had passed its zenith. She leaned against Dominick, her head on his shoulder. Their fingers remained interlaced, the anchor that had helped to draw her back. She gently extracted her hand and sat up.

Dominick stirred. He'd adopted the same trance-like state, a condition in between sleep and wakefulness. Lishka stood and her blade jostled loose from its position on her back so that the pommel knocked against her elbow. She pulled the belt and scabbard off to replace it correctly against her back. As she did so, one buckle twisted and dropped, and her blade knocked against the rock behind her. Dominick rose to his feet and before she could grab the belt, he lifted the scabbard into position and tightened the belt across her chest in perfect placement. His hair brushed against her face. He smelled like the forests in the lower mountains, sweet and sharp at the same time.

"Thank you." Lishka shifted the belt one more time to ensure it had settled properly.

"Happy to help." Dominick lifted his face to the sky and inhaled the cold mountain air, searching for smells of other creatures on the mountaintop. Lishka did the same, and finding nothing nearby, led the way to the mountain path.

They hiked for hours, past snow-covered rock that all looked the same. The shadows lengthened overhead, the light never reaching the bottom of their ravine, and day turned to dusk. What had started out as a clear sky soon became thickly overcast from a northern wind that blew in the clouds. Flecks of snow began to fall, and swirled down around their feet.

Night wore on and the snow fell more heavily, until it seemed the whole world was white. Even their coats became covered in a dusting that refused to melt. Lishka shook ice from her hair. Gradually, she became aware that stepping through the snow had become easier. She glanced down at her feet for the first time in hours.

Beneath the layer of snow, the ground lay uneven. She paused and kicked some of the snow aside to expose stone with a crisscross pattern carved deep for traction. *Steps. Old steps.* Someone long ago had gone to a lot of trouble to build a stairway up the mountain.

The steps made the going easier. For some reason, the snow wasn't sticking to them as much, so Lishka and Dominick increased their pace exponentially. A hint of magik lingered in the air and on the stone. It held warmth, like the touch of sunshine she could no longer feel without pain. If Dominick sensed it also, he kept the sensation to himself. The softness of the snow and the night invoked silence.

Moonlight lit up the clouds and made the snow glow. The snow muffled any wind, which added to the quiet, ethereal beauty of the landscape. The air had turned utterly cold. Even Lishka's skin tingled.

The path twisted around and abruptly the right wall dropped away, to leave them exposed on the mountainside. White surrounded them; one rise of rock grew almost indistinguishable from the next.

The air around them had been growing thicker since they'd first started climbing the stairs. The fog condensed and drifted around their feet. The higher they climbed, the more the fog moved in until it completely obscured the mountains and everything else around them. Now the whiteness really did enclose them. Not even the break of dawn could penetrate the thick mist. Lishka only knew the hour by instinct.

With the white blanketing them, it felt like they had been climbing forever. The fog made Lishka uneasy. It didn't feel entirely natural. She glanced back at Dominick and found reassurance at the sight of his form easily breaking through the mist.

Yet she couldn't shake her unease despite his presence. The nape of her neck tingled with the sensation that they were being followed. That they were being watched.

In her peripheral vision, a flurry of fog tightened. It almost appeared to be a figure. Lishka turned to see, and it swirled away to vanish in the mist. She focused back on the path, keeping a wary eye on the mist. Again, the fog shifted. This time she did not turn her head, instead, watching it from the corner of her eye. The fog condensed even more into a tall humanoid form. It hovered for a moment, as though studying her, then once again broke away into vapors.

Lishka stopped and stared at the place it had been.

"Do you see them too?" Dominick's low voice cut through their white cocoon.

Lishka looked back to him and nodded. She raised a finger to her lips and faced forward.

They continued climbing the stairs, shadowed by the figures in the mist. The higher they went, the more figures seemed to appear and, just as quickly, vanish. Lishka watched them as best she could, but she didn't sense any malice, only a faint warning. As the dawn wore on, she began to have an idea of what they were.

# CHAPTER 19

# THE WHITE LAKE

LISHKA KEPT HER HEAD bent to focus on the steps before her and the swirling figures that followed alongside, so she didn't know at first that they had reached their destination. She made to place her foot upon the next step, when she realized only smooth snow lay underfoot. She looked up.

A great, flat expanse of snow greeted her, white for at least a mile in every direction. At the far edge of the circle, trees rose in a unified stand. The mass of rich evergreens provided an unexpected reprieve from the rock that had surrounded them for days. The closest cliff slid into large boulders deposited from the steeper slope. Two peaks loomed high on either side, one to the southwest and the other more directly before her due north, to nestle them in a sheltered valley. With a start, Lishka realized that they must be at the intersection of the Twin Peaks. They had finally arrived.

Momentarily forgetting the figures of mist, she strode out into the flat expanse. On her first ten strides she kicked through powder. On the eleventh, her foot hit a harder surface only a few inches below the snow. She knelt and brushed the snow away to expose opaque ice. She re-examined the white landscape and the drifts that piled up along the edges of the otherwise smooth disc.

"The White Lake," she murmured.

"Is this it?" Dominick stopped alongside her. "This is where the fey live?

Lishka stood and dusted the unmelted snow from her hands.

"Yes."

"There's nothing here." Surprise and disappointment rang loud in his words.

Lishka surveyed the rock surrounding them and the trees on the far side of the frozen lake. Dominick was right. Except for the trees, she sensed nothing living in the vicinity. The figures that had been so numerous during their ascent had seemingly vanished into the fog from which they'd come.

Lishka walked several paces along the shore, unsure what else to do. Mordan and the others had shown the way on the map; they had told her that here she would find the fey. Even if she hadn't been sure, her fey blood inside her had quieted and no longer urged her on. They had found the place of the fey. *So where are they?*

Lishka realized that Dominick did not follow. She glanced back. He stood where she'd left him, staring at the ice with a strange expression on his face. Lishka walked back to him, not wanting to raise her voice even though they remained alone.

"What is it?" She followed Dominick's stare and saw only the snow-covered lake. Dominick visibly shook himself as though he had not realized she'd gone and come back.

"I don't know. There is a weird smell—no, not a smell. I'm not sure. I think there is something in the water."

Lishka snapped her attention back to the lake with alarm. She had not even considered that they might encounter another creature here. She focused on the lake and realized what Dominick must be sensing.

"The water contains magik," she said. "It possesses some of the essence of the power beyond the Veil." Now that Dominick had called attention to it, Lishka could detect the difference as well. She had attributed the metallic tingle in the air to the weaker Veil this far north. Yet as she reached out with her senses, she found that everything in this place held some of the power, no longer so contained behind the barrier.

"It's like the stones, but not," Dominick said. Lishka nodded.

"Yes. Unlike the stones, traces of the power flow uninhibited through the water, the trees, the rock. It's diluted but consistent. I've never felt anything like this before. I imagine this is how the world would be if—"

"If the Veil didn't exist," Dominick finished. They stared at each other.

"This place is Mirna Sorne," Lishka said after a moment, remembering the map. "The origin of the great Tiern River."

"The Tiern doesn't have this power, does it?" Dominick asked.

"No. The magik must disperse the farther south it

runs," Lishka answered. "Come, let's follow the shore. Maybe we'll find something of the fey on the far side."

Dominick narrowed his eyes as if he might be able to see through the snow and ice, and the creases in his brow deepened.

"Dominick?"

He pulled his attention from the water to Lishka. She tipped her head in the direction of the opposite bank and, with reluctance, he backed away from the ice to follow.

They circled the lake once, then twice. Lishka didn't know what to look for. She thought that once they arrived, there would be some sort of entrance to the fey realm, or that she would instinctively know how to reach it. But other than power flowing readily around them and the earlier figures in the fog, nothing appeared to give any indication that the fey existed. If the fey watched, they kept themselves well hidden.

On the third rotation, Lishka veered away from the shore to the mountainside, not far from where they had first stepped off the staircase. She pressed her hand against the rock. Dominick stood close behind, watching.

Lishka pushed on the rock. Either the ice or the mountain must hold the key to the realm, and so far the ice had been unyielding. *Open*, she thought at the rock, willing the entrance to reveal itself. She closed her eyes to turn inward and attempted to draw on her strange fey energy, but even it remained quiet, subdued here. She opened her eyes. Dull gray rock mocked her.

"The sun's breaking through," Dominick observed. Lishka dropped her hands and faced him. Behind him, light had begun to penetrate the cloud and mist.

"We can take shelter in the trees," she replied, swallowing the taste of failure.

The evergreens marked a stark divide between the vast emptiness of the frozen lake and the rest of the forested valley. Lishka and Dominick edged their way around the shore toward the tree line. Despite recognizing the power beyond the Veil, Lishka did not want to cross the lake itself. There was something unnatural about that water.

There was something unnatural about this entire place.

The trees had grown surprisingly large for the altitude. Their limbs stretched far and full of lush needles, so unlike their scraggly cousins on the lower, exposed slopes of the mountain. They would offer adequate shelter from daylight. Even as sunlight burned its way through the clouds, a mist began to form over the snow, inching its way across the lake to undulate through the firs. Lishka and Dominick navigated their way to a thick stand of trees still within sight of the lake and settled in to wait out the day. They leaned side by side against the same trunk, both wanting to stay close, yet not quite touching.

Lishka did not sleep well. Vivid dreams plagued her, of figures just out of reach, hazy shadows in the mist. She thought they whispered her name, but she couldn't be sure and instead they seemed to whisper *death*. She would wake often in the weak light and glance over to check on Dominick. He had entered the deep daysleep and didn't so much as twitch. Only the slight furrow between his brows betrayed that he did not sleep peacefully either.

Lishka rested her head against the rough bark of the tree. The sharp edges pressed into her scalp. *This is real.* Not half-imagined beings in the fog. Her shoulder brushed Dominick's and she leaned against him to help anchor herself in reality. Despite remaining deep in sleep, he shifted his weight in response to push back, letting his arm press against the length of hers. Lishka didn't move away.

Darkness inched over the peaks, and the last of the daylight turned the clouds golden and then pink. Lishka drifted in and out of consciousness while she waited for the night to return. She did not remember falling back asleep but knew that she dreamed again. The fog thickened in her dream and swirled about her, so that for a moment she thought that she had gone beyond the Veil. The sense of Dominick still pulsed beside her, and so she was not afraid.

A man, tall and lean, with wild golden hair, emerged from the mist to stand before her. *Or was he a man?* A pair of deer antlers grew from his forehead, but when she looked again, she saw only smooth skin. *A trick of the fog.* Behind him, the lake glimmered below moonlight, free of ice. The water whispered in delicate ripples that kissed the pebbled shore.

Lishka tore her eyes from the lake back to the man as he walked closer. He knelt to draw level with her gaze. She tensed at his proximity to Dominick just beside her, but he ignored Dominick and raised his hand to her cheek.

Lishka leaned forward, forgetting that he was a stranger, and that he had her face in his hand. *His eyes.* They mirrored her own, only they glowed a richer, vivid violet that made hers pale in comparison. If one considered Lishka's eyes to be somewhat strange in the mortal world, his would be unforgettable.

He whispered something under his breath, in a language that Lishka did not recognize. *But you do,* a part of her whispered. The words were half-remembered, even though she did not know the meaning. They evoked familiarity, like the echo of a childhood memory or long-forgotten dream.

He dropped his hand from her cheek to her left breast, where his palm rested over her still heart. Lishka stared at him. She did not even think to reach for her blade. He whispered something again and his palm pulsed with hot light.

And for a split second, Lishka's heart beat.

Her body trembled. Alarm began to penetrate her calm, but then she reassured herself: this was only a dream, after all, and strange things happened in dreams.

The man stood. He glanced at Dominick and frowned, as though he noticed him for the first time. He leaned down as though he might touch him. Lishka's fingers twitched for her sword. The man glanced at her and straightened away from Dominick. Lishka relaxed, and exhaustion entered her bones. Her head dropped to rest heavily against Dominick's shoulder. The man spoke then, quite clearly in the common tongue.

"You will know how to find us." Then he turned and disappeared into the mist.

LISHKA WOKE TO darkness. All light from the higher peaks had gone and clouds obscured any moonlight. She must have slept heavily, to not have instinct trigger her as soon as dusk fell. A dream pressed at the edge of her consciousness, and she tried to grasp at the memory but couldn't quite bring it to the forefront of her mind.

The dream faded as she became fully awake. She nudged Dominick, who was still sleeping, then stood to take stock of their surroundings. They had work to do. They must find a way to contact the fey.

A layer of ice had settled over the snow on the lake and the crystals shone despite the clouds. The ice reassured her, though she couldn't say why.

"What is it?" Dominick rose to stand beside her and followed her gaze through the trees to the lake.

"Nothing," Lishka answered. "I think. I don't know, something feels different. Perhaps it's the power in this place. I think I dreamt about the lake, but I can't remember."

"I had strange dreams too," Dominick said. "I don't remember them, either."

They exchanged a disturbed glance.

Without a word, they walked through the trees and back to the lake and open sky. Lishka drifted to the cliff face that lined the southwestern shore. The air still hung damp with mist, but instead of feeling like an oppressive weight, it now drifted through her hair and tickled her skin. Dominick walked beside her with confidence as well, and he studied the rock with renewed curiosity, rather than the disappointment and doubt that had filled them both the night before.

Lishka didn't exactly have hope or any reason to believe that today they would achieve success and find the entrance. But somehow, she moved with direction. Her uncertainty had turned to determination and a sense that they would find the way through to the realm of the fey.

Dominick paused halfway down the lake. Lishka stopped with him. He put his hand out to the rock to trace a line of white that splintered the gray.

"I think this is a breccia zone," he said suddenly.

"What?" Lishka examined where he had put his hand and saw only crystal in the rock.

"A breccia zone," Dominick repeated, excited. "Look, see that red, rusty color in the stone?"

Lishka had not taken the time to study the rock beyond looking for any sign of the fey. Yet now she noticed that the cliffside had taken on a reddish hue different from that of the mountainside lower below.

"These mountains are granodiorite, meaning they're made of rock that becomes crystalline under the ground," Dominick explained. "Granodiorite cooled underground and pushed up to the surface, so the grain size is larger, see? Versus if it had cooled quicker near the surface." Dominick gained confidence as he briefly returned to a familiar world. "They have less quartz and more mafic minerals, meaning they are darker colored and contain more iron and magnesium."

Lishka again studied the rock but could not see the change in grain that Dominick described.

"So what is a breccia zone?" she asked, unable to help her curiosity.

"Basically, as volatiles, like gasses and fluids, push up closer to the surface, rock forms and the pressure from the hot fluids left has to vent somewhere. So it blows out and fractures the rock to create a breccia zone, which contains quartz and pyrite crystals. They weather differently so they're left standing, like this cliff. And see, they have these interlocked quartz seams." Dominick traced a line of white crystals embedded in the rock. The seam ran up the cliff, splitting off in a web of white. Dominick smiled as he studied the veins. "If we had the tools, we could break apart a seam and extract the quartz." His voice grew wistful, no doubt recalling his human memories of collecting and studying minerals at the university.

They walked on several more paces before Dominick paused again.

"That's odd." Dominick put both hands against the cliff.

"What?" Lishka asked. Only a bare rock face appeared before her, this section free of even the quartz.

"Here." He grabbed her hand and pressed her palm to the rock. "Do you feel that?"

An invigorating energy flowed into Lishka's hand, and then through to Dominick. The power beyond the Veil did not just leak here, but rather, poured through a break much larger than Lishka had ever encountered.

"It's a fracture in the Veil," she said. She could barely feel the rock now, as the energy encompassed her hand. "Normally the power leaks through, but here it's flowing at a much higher rate."

Dominick released her and they both took a step back to assess the fracture. The wall appeared as normal rock, yet Lishka's senses rang with awareness. The power should have been a beacon to anyone with an affinity, yet it had escaped her detection the day prior.

*Unless it had not been there.* Some understanding lingered just beyond the edge of her memory.

"It's coming through the rock," Dominick stated. "Almost like the break is within, and the rock is acting like a conduit to help draw it out much faster. I wonder if that's what created the Boreal Stones. Look here." He moved his hand along the cliff, sensing something else that Lishka couldn't quite yet see. At once, Dominick jolted to a halt.

"What's wrong?" Lishka began to trace the symbols for a defensive spell when Dominick grinned. He didn't answer and instead grabbed her hand once more.

"Feel this." He guided her fingers to another spot on the wall. Expecting to touch solid rock, Lishka reached her hand through the stone to grasp at only air. An electric sensation buzzed about her flesh, mixed with the caress of the power beyond the Veil.

She withdrew her hand and met Dominick's excited gaze.

"It's an illusion," he explained. "Look, the energy must somehow reflect what's around it to disguise the break. There may be more. There could be bigger fractures, like an opening that you could walk through."

Lishka stared at him, suddenly full of understanding. "A doorway."

Dominic nodded. "Exactly."

Eagerly she pressed her other hand against the wall, feeling along the surface. Dominick followed, and their fingers traced the veins in the rock that suddenly seemed to glow violet. At once, Lishka could see them, as clearly as she could see Dominick. The veins spidered out to reach into the quartz seams, turning them to a sparkling violet that refracted starlight against the rock. In a rush of understanding, Lishka knew that she could have seen them all along, if she'd only known how to look.

*Dominick knew how to find them.* His scientific mind had led them to the key.

The veins grew brighter and spread faster and faster, to light up the cliff. Dominick and Lishka ran, following the path that ran on the wall alongside them, where lines twisted and crossed to form patterns and swirls in an illegible, yet familiar, script. Lishka sprinted alongside the words, and she could swear she heard whispering in the air.

The lines stopped abruptly three-quarters of the way down the lake. Lishka stopped with them, and Dominick skidded to a halt just behind her. They had come to the cliff that rose into the northernmost peak. Before them, etched into the rock, shone the outline of an arched entrance. It glowed, a warm inviting light emanating from its depths. Lishka could almost make out the silhouettes of trees beyond the light; she seemed to hear the sound of burbling water complemented by distant music. She ached to enter. Without realizing, she took several steps forward.

Dominick placed his hand on her shoulder.

"Are you sure it's safe?" His voice grounded her and Lishka broke her gaze from the light, though she found it difficult to do so. The desire to enter grew almost stronger than her lust for blood.

"No," she answered. She had only legend to hint at what lay beyond the doorway. The light drew her as a moth to a flame. Yet this light did not seem to be harmful. "But this is what we came here to do."

"I can't go with you," Dominick said suddenly, voicing the true reason for his hesitation. As soon as he spoke the words, Lishka realized that the same energy that drew her closer to the fey also rejected Dominick. Only her fey blood allowed her passage into their realm.

"I'll be fine."

Dominick didn't remove his hand.

"Do you remember the protection spells I taught you?" Lishka asked. Dominick nodded.

"Yes."

"Cast them. Just in case." Though she found it increasingly difficult to resist the light, she was held back by reluctance at the thought of leaving Dominick alone. She would not be able to protect him and, while strong, he had only just begun to learn how to defend himself. Yet they couldn't have been followed. They had not sensed anyone for weeks. Besides, anyone who slipped their notice would have had Alaisadaille to contend with, if they'd followed the same path.

"I'll be back soon," she said, making a promise that she had no way of knowing if she could keep.

Dominick gave her shoulder a small squeeze before letting her go. "Be careful."

"I will." She tried to give him reassurance even as she turned to face the doorway.

In hundreds of years, Lishka had never seen a hint of the fey, beyond what the color of her own eyes showed her. Now she would enter their realm. She braced herself, and with Dominick watching behind her, took a step forward into the light, and through to the realm of the fey.

C H A P T E R   2 0

# REALM OF THE FEY

DOMINICK WATCHED LISHKA WALK into the sunlight. The warm glow blurred the edges of her figure and set fire to her dark hair. Then she was gone. The light in the doorway flashed, and then dimmed. He took an anxious step forward. If the doorway closed, he couldn't be sure that it would reopen. All his instincts screamed at him to stay back, while the light burned where it touched his skin. He flinched and stopped in place, the toes of his boots frozen in the snow just before the entrance. The glow flickered once more and stabilized, several degrees duller.

Dominick didn't dare try again in case he caused the doorway to shut, trapping Lishka beyond. He rubbed his arm where the burns had already healed, still reacting to the echo of pain, and retreated several yards to sit in the snow with his back to the lake. Eyes fixed on the place where Lishka had disappeared, he flicked his hands up in the motions that would begin the casting of their protection spell. His attention split between door and spell, he settled in to wait.

LISHKA BLINKED IN the sudden brightness, much fiercer than it had appeared from outside the door. Instinctively, she threw her arm up over her face. But there was no pain. Instead, a soft warmth soaked into her flesh and down to her core. She lowered her arm to review her surroundings.

She stood at the edge of a clearing surrounded by a dense mix of evergreen and deciduous forest: fir, maple, ash, and hemlock. The leaves rustled, and their voices whispered music and laughter that wafted through her hair. Thick, spongy moss created a luxurious carpet beneath her feet. Behind her, the forest canopy cast lacy shadows across a plethora of ferns and nurse logs. The snow, the lake, and Dominick too had disappeared. Lishka shoved down concern that the way through had closed. She would have to address that problem later, when the time came to return.

Before her, tall prairie grass waved in a gentle breeze, their golden heads beginning to seed atop brown and green spindles. A man waited in the clearing. Lishka had not seen him in her first survey of the landscape, yet she couldn't shake the uneasy sense that he had been there the entire time, as though he waited for her. He stood taller than Dominick, though he had a narrower torso and shoulders. Wild bright hair that matched the low sunlight flowed to the middle of his chest. His eyes shone brilliant violet.

He gestured for her to come to him. Not sensing any

hostility from him, she complied.

"Who are you?" she asked when she drew close enough.

"I am Phoenix." His smooth voice lilted with musical undertones. "Come."

"Where are we going?"

He turned and pointed across the clearing to a small, overgrown road weaving between the trees. The path had not been there a moment ago.

"Do you know why I'm here?" Lishka asked. *Better to find out his motives now.*

Phoenix turned back to study her.

"Do *you*?" His voice had an underlying tone that she disliked. Before she could ask any further questions, he put his back to her to walk toward the path. Lishka had no choice but to follow.

The sunlight dappled her forearms as they passed beneath bright leaves, whose own veins glowed from the light shining through. Lishka twisted her hands in the light, unable to keep from being distracted by the miracle of it. Her mind couldn't quite wrap itself around the fact that there she stood, in direct sun, for the first time in a millennium.

Phoenix glanced back at her.

"How is this possible?" Lishka asked him.

He watched her, and for a moment, she thought he wouldn't answer.

"The fey in you protects you," he said finally. "The energy that runs through your blood allows you to exist here, under the light, without harm. You have had it buried deep within," he gestured to her heart, "but it was still there, waiting to be awakened."

Lishka put her hand over her still heart. Phoenix gave her a knowing look and turned to keep walking. Lishka felt at once that they'd met before, but she couldn't remember when.

"What do you mean, waiting to be awakened?"

Phoenix ignored the question.

"We are here."

The forest path had ended in a gathering, where long, narrow tables appeared to grow directly from the mossy earth, with roots for legs that sprouted newborn ferns. All sorts of fruit and drinks and other natural things lay strewn across the wooden surfaces in no particular order. Around them, the trees rose like grand pillars and their leaves interlocked into a delicate ceiling, which let in streams of sunlight to bathe all in gold.

Mixed about the trees and tables, eating, drinking, singing, and dancing, were the fey.

They wore light, airy clothing that flowed with every movement. Many went barefoot. They twirled beneath the shadows of the trees to music that seeped from the branches. Some glanced at Lishka, but they did not seem alarmed, only curious, and soon that curiosity diminished in favor of their carefree celebration.

A boy skipped up to her, his dark brown curls cascading from a delicate circlet of posies that rested above his brow. He held a wooden goblet between his hands, and from it emanated a sweet, thick smell. Lishka examined the boy. On a second look, she found that despite his youthful features, he was in fact quite old; even older, perhaps, than her. His eyes glowed a brighter violet and he winked at her impishly. He held up the goblet in offering.

Lishka stared at him. She remembered the myths that warned against eating or drinking anything from the folk. Those who made such a mistake became trapped in their realm, unable to leave. The few who managed escape did so only at the whim of the folk, and often found on their return that many years had passed since they first found the fey.

Phoenix took a step past the boy, who nudged the goblet closer to Lishka. She hesitated. The very essence reeked of the fey and of their unique magik. It was not unlike the power beyond the Veil, though she thought it unwise to take that essence into herself, in this place.

"Where is the Fey Queen?" Lishka asked instead, ignoring the boy. Phoenix watched her.

"If you wish to speak with her," the boy responded, "you must accept the hospitality of the fey."

Lishka looked back at the goblet now quite close to her face. A part of her desired the liquid, and a part of her shied away from it. She knew that if she accepted the fey's drink, she might not be able to easily leave their realm. The image of Dominick flitted across her mind. Lishka shoved her concern away; like the doorway, that would have to be a problem for later. She must be allowed to speak to the Queen and complete her mission.

She steeled herself, grasped the goblet from the fey's long fingers, and drank.

The liquid ran hot down her throat, spreading warmth into her body like sunlight. It both burned and soothed at the same time. Lishka gasped. Her skin began to glow violet, the energy giving her a new pulse beneath her veins. The warmth reached her core, then bubbled up, and she burst out laughing, unable to contain the joy that spread through her.

Around her, the muted voices crescendoed into full volume. Music poured from the trees, the grass, the very sky. All sang a different note, yet somehow, they became a part of the same song. Lishka sensed a hum deep within her that responded to the voices all around. Never before had she felt so connected. All concern melted away, dissipating beneath the sunlight.

The folk danced up to her and their nimble fingers reached out to stroke her skin, their touch no more than the kiss of a butterfly. Lishka allowed them to draw her into their midst. They led her through the celebration and deeper into the forest, to where the cool scent of water permeated the woods. A deep pool separated the trees ahead of them, the rocks at its banks cushioned by thick ferns and small white flowers. The fey helped her shuck her grimy clothing.

One of the fey took her sword and at this, alarm pricked at her happy haze. Even as she started to reach for the blade, she forgot what she had wanted and instead smiled. The fey smiled back, his wide eyes glowing a beautiful violet. Lishka eased herself into the pool and the water caressed her skin in welcome.

The days passed one into another seamlessly, one long stream of song, and dance, and the enjoyment of the earth around them. Lishka reclined with the others on soft dappled moss to soak in the sun's rays. No matter how long she lay in the sun, her skin remained pale, in contrast to the rose-colored fey so full of life. When she began to notice her difference, something else drew her attention—one of the fey pulling her to dance, a lazy butterfly drifting before her to land on a dandelion.

She swam with others in the forest pool. Like Lishka, they did not need to breathe, or they could hold their breath for a very long time, for they plunged down deep into the depths. Yet as far as she swam, Lishka could not find the bottom, and the water never became truly dark.

Other creatures lived there as well—birds, rabbits, deer, and elk. The great antlers of a stag reminded her of something, but she couldn't quite remember, and the thought soon drifted from her consciousness. The fey became a pleasurable constant. After centuries of isolation, Lishka was surprised to find that she enjoyed their company.

On rare occasions, Lishka's thoughts would return to the time before the fey and find only hazy half-memories, glimpses of dark eyes in the fog that made her afraid. Lishka did not want to feel afraid, so she focused on only the present around her. She couldn't tell how long she'd been with the fey; it might have been days, weeks, or even years. The thought should have bothered her but didn't. If and when she decided to leave, she would be unchanged, despite the long years that might have passed.

At that notion, unease squirmed its way through her golden happiness. She had forgotten something important, but the feeling of urgency faded as she drank from another offered goblet. Her attention became quickly consumed by the song of the earth and the harmony of those around her.

Like the power beyond the Veil, the energy of the fey sustained her and she didn't need to feed. Lishka gazed at her arms as she lay against a moss-cushioned rock. Where once her skin had been deathly white, it now glowed with its own rosy hue. Lishka frowned. She couldn't remember if her skin had always looked so warm. A delicate frock, woven from spider silk, draped over her legs. Lishka sat up straighter, noting at once the absent heaviness of her sword.

She surveyed the clearing. Instead of green grass and lush summer forest, she saw snow and ice over a vast sleeping lake. Lishka blinked and once more the golden forest sprawled before her, but this time the vision of the lake lingered in her mind. She must have been there before but couldn't remember when or why.

That night she slept fitfully beneath a starry velvet sky. At first it had been strange to her, to sleep at night and wake during the day. She had embarked on long walks in the nighttime forest, unable to shake the feeling that she should be awake and moving. Sometimes fey folk joined her. On other nights, she found company in the quiet nocturnal beasts that inhabited the woods. They would walk alongside her, or follow hidden in the trees, and Lishka could always tell when they were there, even if she couldn't always see them.

Now she slept and dreamt of snow. Nestled between two craggy peaks an immense lake spread out, its surface covered in glittering ice. A forest spanned the far shore, sharp pines stabbing like spears into an overcast sky. Lishka knew without looking that behind her a path had been carved through the rock in a steep staircase. Lishka frowned; she could not remember climbing, yet somehow, she knew exactly how many steps led from the bottom of the mountains to the lake. The hand-carved etchings on the stone had helped her maintain traction in the ice.

Fog crept in at the edge of her vision. It pulled her to

sleep and forgetfulness. Lishka fought against it. She did not want to sleep. A deep urgency filled her—she had to remember something. *Or someone.* She tried to hold on to that suspicion before it flitted away again. A high cliff rose to her left, and seams of white glistened. *Quartz. This is a breccia zone.* Lishka had no idea where that thought came from. A doorway shone gold from within the rock, almost at the opposite end of the lake. The light glowed almost unbearably bright against the dark gray of the rock and the muted haze that surrounded the lake. The door pulled her to it. Lishka couldn't resist the urge to pass through, so she let herself drift toward it, her toes barely skimming the snow, if they touched it at all.

But several yards from the doorway, she resisted the pull. A mound lay in the snow, shrouded in mist. Lishka bent to examine it. It was a sleeping man. Snow had fallen over his face and the fog lay over the ground, further obscuring his features. Lishka tried to blow at the fog and wave her hands to waft it away. She had to see his face. But her hands were insubstantial, no more than air, and she couldn't shift the mist or snow.

*"Wake up,"* she commanded. *"Wake up!"* She had no voice. Silence echoed around her. A desperation grew in her, and she willed him to wake. He stirred. The door tugged her toward it and she began to slide. The heat from the entrance warmed her side. Lishka couldn't help herself; she began to turn from the man to the light.

He shifted again and began to rise. Suddenly, the fog cleared from his face and their eyes met.

Lishka awoke.

Sunlight warmed her face. Around her, the fey folk

stretched and rose from their nested beds beneath the trees. Some did not sleep in the forest, for more always appeared during the day. She didn't know where they went, but she knew that there was more to this place than the forest glade. A woman approached her and held out a goblet, but Lishka ignored her. She no longer cared for the pleasure of forgetfulness, or the song in the earth.

She remembered Dominick.

Her memory returned: the Coven, Mordan, her mission. And Dominick. Dominick, who even now waited for her outside the entrance. A chill crept in, despite the sun. *How many years have passed? Does he still wait beyond the doorway, or has the dream also spanned time?*

Lishka stood. Her bare feet sank into the soft moss.

"Where is Phoenix?" she asked the fey woman. The fey did not answer and instead smiled while she held out the cup. Lishka pushed it away.

"I must speak with Phoenix," she insisted. The fey turned and pointed.

Across the glade, Phoenix lounged with several others against the knobby trunk of a wide ash tree. He held his own goblet and surveyed the clearing while a fey piped several musical notes beside him. His long tawny mane of hair circled his face like a halo.

Lishka strode across the glade, her steps focused and determined. The fey who danced hopped out of her way, unhappy that Lishka disrupted their peaceful joy. Phoenix watched her approach. She stopped at his feet to stare down at him.

"Take me to the Queen," she demanded.

"Have another drink of Elar," Phoenix replied, and he lifted his goblet. Lishka saw how she'd been tricked.

A thin sword strapped to his side belied his relaxed pose. Lishka felt at once that he'd appeared in the glade to watch her and wondered how many days he had been there that she'd not noticed. She knew he could bring her to the Queen. The others deferred to him; he had power here.

"Take me to her," she insisted. A dark energy rose from within her. It felt all wrong here and it grated at her nerves and pulled at her skin. It was harsh and real, and for the first time in many days, Lishka felt like herself again. The fey nearby withdrew from her, all laughter gone.

*Dominick has never been afraid.* She kept her eyes on Phoenix. He stared back at her, and no emotion passed over his face.

"Very well," he said at last. "Come this way."

Phoenix rose to lead her past the tables and through the fey folk. The glade had quieted as they all stood still to watch her leave. Several steps into the deeper woods, laughter and music resumed behind them. Lishka had already been forgotten. A part of her wanted to return, to dance and laugh with them, and so she faced forward to fixate on Phoenix's back, and they left the glade.

He led her deep into the forest, where the shadows fell longer, and rustling resounded in the thick of the surrounding ferns. The creatures of the woods oversaw their passing. After a while, the trees began to thin. The ground sloped downward and soon gave way to tall grass sprinkled with red poppies, then to the white pebbles of another lakeshore. The water stretched before them, shrouded in thick mist. A familiar scent wafted from the lake and Lishka knelt at the edge to dabble her fingers in the water. She looked up at Phoenix in surprise.

"Yes," he said. "This lake feeds the one between the

mountain peaks. Though diluted from that world, I think it still retains some of its power."

Lishka shivered. The water was very old and powerful. Even now, it tugged at her fingertips, inviting her to enter.

They stood at the lakeshore for several minutes. Phoenix stared forward expectantly and Lishka followed his gaze. Finally, the light splashing of a paddle hitting water broke the stillness and a small boat emerged from the mist. The bow and the stern both tapered to narrow points; its sides had been pieced together delicately with tree bark. Phoenix approached the boat, clearly intending to take it across the lake. Lishka followed, all the while eyeing the boat with trepidation. She had no desire to enter these waters.

The boat proved sturdier than it looked, and the craftsmen who made it were skilled, for her feet remained firmly above the water. The boatman stood at the bow while Lishka and Phoenix sat on the narrow benches. Strange purple tattoos marked the boatman's forearms, symbols that seemed to change every time she looked at them. He paddled them out into the middle of the lake, and the shore receded behind until water surrounded them as far as the eye could see. Lishka peered over the boat's side. Light lit the first few yards of water and a shoal of small fish darted beneath the surface. Beyond the fish, the water turned opaque.

Phoenix shuffled in the seat behind her, drawing her attention. Before them, parting the lake haze, a great island rose up from the water. Sandy shores gave way to bright green grass and lush forest, and a mountain that rose high into the sky, bringing many of the trees with it. At its highest point stood pillars of rock, set in a circle under the clear blue sky.

"It is called Avalon, for our Queen is the Lady of the Lake," Phoenix said. Lishka gazed upon the fabled isle, entranced. Though the Followers had spoken of this place, Lishka had doubted its existence even then. A myth to the rest of the world, the island had disappeared long before she'd been born. It was said to be a place of learning and worship, where one could commune with the Goddess. A place of power and of harmony.

"There was a time when a human vessel existed in the world of man," Phoenix intoned. "She was the Lady of the Lake, the one who communed with our Fey Queen, and so through her to the Goddess, the Earth Spirit. But that was many ages ago. There has not been a human vessel in many lifetimes. So our Queen took up the title. Even now she hopes that, one day, humans will believe again."

"I thought Avalon existed in the human world," Lishka said, recalling the Followers' belief. "Though none could ever find it."

"Once it did. Over time, as humans lost faith, it receded back beyond the Veil. It is little more than legend to them now."

As they drew nearer, the rock loomed above them, overwhelming in its beauty and majesty. *This would have meant something once, long ago.* When she had been human.

"You might have found it then," Phoenix said, as if he could read her mind. "If you had thought to look."

Lishka glanced at him, surprised, but his gaze stayed on Avalon.

The boatman navigated their canoe up to the island shore, where a jutting rock provided a boat launch. Phoenix slid out of the boat and walked up the natural jetty to the shore, not checking to see whether Lishka followed. She stepped out of the boat, avoiding touching the water, and strode after him. After a moment, she thought to look behind them at the boatman, but he and the boat had disappeared.

They followed a worn path up through the trees. Leaves and boughs reached toward her, almost as if in welcome. The air tickled her ears and stroked her face, bringing with it the smell of crushed grass and cool sleeping water deep within the earth.

The path continued to twist uphill. At the break between forest and mountain rock, the steps transitioned from dirt to stone. At their backs, the lake stretched sparkling to the hazy horizon. The island could have been the only piece of land in the world.

Phoenix led her up toward the stone circle, but instead of taking her to the mountain's peak, he led her around it. They passed rock caverns that had been carved out of the mountainside, the entrances supported by wide pillars. Behind the mountain lay not the shore, as Lishka expected, but sprawling, forested hills that rolled far into the distance, appearing as endless as the waters they drifted on. Lishka had the distinct feeling that this island was not anchored down to any lake bed, but instead had the tendency to move wherever it liked.

Phoenix took them down into the forest shade. It felt as if they walked for hours, days, deep within the woods, although Lishka knew not much time had passed since they had arrived on the white shore.

When the dust motes that drifted along the filtered sun rays began to glow, and the breeze started to whisper strange words in her ear, she knew they were drawing close. The trees aligned on either side of them to form a corridor. The light turned to gold once more and yellow leaves drifted in a steady curtain from the canopy, although the foliage remained full.

Ahead stood a grand natural archway. Two fey guarded the entrance, adorned in the same light tunics as those in the glade. Unlike those folk, thin blades gleamed at their sides, more for show since nothing would harm their Fey Queen here. A breath brushed over Lishka's hair and down along her sides. She glanced about to find the source, but no fey stood near her. The touch reminded her of entering Kiaban's lab—not hostile, but not welcoming either.

Phoenix led the way into the forest hall. An invisible force pressed against Lishka as she made to follow him, a resistance akin to the Veil. Only this barrier bent before her like something pliable, unwilling to release and let her pass. Lishka tried to force one foot before the other, keeping her focus on Phoenix's back. The guards watched her, unmoving.

The fey did not want her to enter their hall. Lishka's foot inched forward. She raised her other foot, meeting the same struggle. Phoenix now walked many steps before her, not slowing his pace. Lishka gritted her teeth. Her dark vampirism rose from within, and the barrier hardened. Now she could not even take a step. She willed herself calm in the face of their challenge and focused on the violet fey within her. At this, the barrier weakened. As she took the last step past the entry trees, the pressure released. The path became like the rest of the realm, the air once more yielding. Lishka lengthened her stride to catch up to Phoenix.

Trees lined the hall like pillars, rising hundreds of feet

high into the air. They grew so dense that no fey could fit between them, nor could any of the forest creatures so fond of scurrying up bark and bough. Their branches arched overhead and wove in amongst themselves, forming a leafy ceiling. Despite being tightly interwoven, light still somehow made its way through to illuminate the leaves, revealing the tiny veins that darkened the translucent green.

Before the trees stood fey, lean and lithe, dressed in flowing gowns and tunics. They whispered amongst themselves, then quieted as Phoenix and Lishka passed. *The fey court.* Lishka's keen ears picked up a whisper, which became more of a hiss the farther she progressed: *What is one of* them *doing here?*

At the end of the hall, a throne made of branches grew straight from the ground. From the branches sprouted white and yellow flowers with tiny purple centers. Residing on the throne was the Fey Queen.

Her hair flowed long and wild to form a gleaming halo about her slender face. One moment her hair shone the vivid red of the forest fox. Then the light caught her tresses and turned them amber brown, the hue matching that of the chestnut tree. Her lime-green dress drifted about her bare feet, so that she appeared to float upon the throne. Her almond-shaped eyes, large for her narrow face, shone so bright that Lishka found it hard to look directly into them. She settled instead for the edge of the throne's back, just beyond the Queen's left ear where a tiny bud had barely begun to blossom.

The silence deepened and the trees towered above them, showering them with tiny leaves cast in a late summer light.

Phoenix stepped to the right of the throne to stand

alongside his Queen, a united front that left Lishka alone before them.

She straightened her shoulders and lifted her chin. She might have been in their realm, but she came with the weight of Zachriel's Coven.

"Greetings, Queen of the Fey." Her voice resounded throughout the hall. "I come to your realm bearing a message from Lord Mordan and Lady Raseska, both servants and emissaries to Zachriel." Zachriel's name needed no title. He demanded no such extravagance from his followers; his name carried a grace and power all its own. To place a title before it would only lessen the meaning.

The Queen smiled a small half smile. "I know why you've come," she interrupted in a light, silky voice. Her eyes twinkled.

"Then what is your answer?" Lishka asked, shedding all formal ritual. The Queen rose fluidly from her chair and gazed down at Lishka solemnly.

"Zachriel calls on us to aid him in a war not of our concern, over a race of humanity that has long forgotten us." Her large eyes blinked, wide and deceptively childlike. "What business do we have in the human world? I will not send my folk to die for a cause not of our making. Many of them have long forgotten the feeling of the mortal world and have no desire to remember it."

A cold anger began to rise in Lishka. The fey had played with her since she had entered this place, and she had accommodated them to no avail. The Queen had never intended to align herself to a war outside the safety of her realm. In her growing anger, Lishka found that she could meet the Queen's luminous eyes after all.

"How can you say that?" she asked. "You belong to the forests, the trees, the grass, the earth, and sky. How can you stand back and watch Zaral destroy it?"

A chill passed through the Court and the golden light dimmed. Lishka had never admitted to herself that, deep down, she still held the Follower's belief in Avalon. She had not dared to acknowledge the hope that had begun to blossom when she entered the fey realm and saw the legendary home of the Goddess. Now that hope lay broken, and Lishka could not stop the rage that came with the wreckage, bearing with it the centuries endured under Zaral's rule.

The Queen watched Lishka, her expression unchanging, slender hands folded before her.

"We have not belonged to that world for ages upon ages." She swept her arm around the room, gesturing toward the high trees. "Look. We are hidden, deep within the mists. If it is indeed our time, perhaps we should stay here, lost and forgotten. The world does not belong to beings like us, not anymore."

"But you can help change that," Lishka argued. "You can take it back."

The Queen considered her for a moment.

"Why do you care, *Ula*?" she asked, her voice low and yet still strong in the quiet of the shade. Lishka recognized the name; she had heard it in the forest glade, when the fey folk talked to their young. *Child.* She bristled at the term, but the Queen merely studied her with thoughtfulness, meaning no insult. At once, Lishka realized how young she must look to the Queen, who had existed long before Lishka and most of her kind, perhaps even since the beginning of the world itself. The Fey Queen dropped any feign of childlike innocence and in her eyes, Lishka saw Time, and also, the absence of it.

"What is this war, this game between brothers, to garner your concern and passion?" The Queen's voice lowered to carry authoritative weight throughout the hall. "You, who have stayed hidden for so long in the world, ignoring all around you. You were a Follower once, but we both know you have not followed the Old Ways in centuries. Why is it important to you that I aid Zachriel?"

Lishka stood silent. Her fervor had also surprised her, bringing with it an onslaught of repressed emotion, and she did not know how to answer. She thought for a moment, and realized only the truth stood a chance of gaining the Fey Queen's favor.

"The world is dying," Lishka answered. "Every day, more of it is destroyed, trees burned, land poisoned. Every day the Veil grows stronger and stronger, and the spirit slips away." She knew this. She felt it in her soul, or whatever it was that now passed for a soul. She had seen it in the eyes of those who knew it also: Kiaban, Lady Raseska. *Mordan.*

The Queen shook her head and relaxed once more into a delighted smile.

"She cannot die," she laughed. "She only changes. All beings have a time to move on to the next state of existence, or nonexistence, even immortal ones. Perhaps it is our time now, to fade with her."

Lishka took one step forward, sensing her chance slipping away. "But if there is no magik in the world, what is worth fighting for?"

The Queen's eyes hardened. "Humans will always find something to fight for."

*Wrong choice of words.* Lishka thought fast. "Then what is worth living for?" Dominick appeared in her mind, and a warm tenderness tingled in her chest.

The Queen leaned forward, and malice sharpened the angles in her face.

"But you are not alive, are you, Lishka?"

The hall went cold. Lishka's eyes dilated in an uncontrolled response and her fangs cut the soft sides of her mouth. The Queen pressed against her vampirism and now the air thickened, seeking to push her out.

"I am still here."

The Queen gave her an odd, calculating look. She seemed to come to a decision, for she held her hand out to Phoenix and descended to the forest floor.

Lishka did not move as the Queen approached, until she stood face to face with the ancient being.

"Come," the Queen said, her gaze now even with Lishka's. "Walk with me." She turned and led the way across the hall to exit through a small opening in the trees that had not been there before. Lishka hurried after her, startled by the rapid change in the Queen's demeanor, with Phoenix close at her heels.

# CHAPTER 21

# THE RING OF STONES

TREES PARTED TO BRIGHT daylight. Lishka blinked against the sudden light and surveyed the landscape. They were no longer deep in the forest, as her instincts insisted they had to be. Instead, they stood at the edge of a large garden. She turned back to see the wide tree trunks slide close, so that the hall of the Queen disappeared behind their sturdy forms.

The Fey Queen led the way into the garden, which bore the semblance of a maze. Hedges at least twice Lishka's height grew in surprisingly organized squares to create open-ceilinged rooms. Not the typical manicured greenery, these hedges grew wild and unkempt, with sharp thorns that looked all too willing to draw blood if one got too close.

The first room couldn't have been more than twelve feet wide and had only one slender tree standing in the corner. Its delicate yellow leaves trembled and danced, though no breeze blew through the garden. The tree mimicked the sort that might belong in an ornamental orchard, decorative and not fruit-bearing. Tiny red flowers blossomed from a vine that curled up the trunk into the upper branches. A tiny figure of a woman lay at the base of the trunk, the bare minimum of straw twisted into a skirt, arms, and head. Despite its delicate appearance, the tree felt old, and the innocent-enough-looking doll evoked a sense of honor and respect to a greater entity. Lishka bowed her head as they passed.

They continued through an opening that could almost be a doorway, were the hedge branches not so wild and outstretched. A stone fountain sat in the center of the next larger room, crowned by a full-sized statue of a buck borne up from a bed of carved stone brambles. He reared back on his hind legs and his front hooves pawed the air defiantly. The water glistened as it pooled around his feet, and the dark lily pads partially obscured the surprisingly deep depths, for Lishka couldn't see the bottom.

An arch at the far side of the hedge led deeper into the maze, but instead of walking toward it, the Queen stopped at the fountain. She leaned over the pool and dipped her fingertips into the water. Lishka inched closer. She did not want to go too near the water, though it appeared ordinary enough.

The Fey Queen lifted her fingers to her lips to taste the droplets that lingered there.

"Come here," she said, her voice low and beckoning. Something rang in her words that Lishka did not quite like. Behind Lishka, Phoenix shuffled his feet with impatience. Lishka took several steps forward, her eyes drawn above the Queen's head to the buck statue. Now it seemed he stood on human legs, and his front hooves could almost be hands instead. She wondered if he really was a buck, after all.

Lishka shook herself and looked back to the edge of the fountain to where the Queen perched, examining her.

"You are lucky," the Queen said, "to have been made by Zaral." Her voice lingered over the word *made*, drawing it out longer than necessary.

"How can you say that?" Lishka questioned. "He goes against everything you stand for."

"Yes," agreed the Queen. "It is true I despise him. For he is destruction, or at least, that is what he chooses." She dropped her voice and leaned toward Lishka, turning up a small smile at the corner of her mouth as if about to share a secret. "But the bloodline is still powerful, undiluted. You are connected through him to something so much greater, young one."

"What do you mean?" Lishka asked. "He is not fey."

Phoenix snorted behind her, but the Queen ignored him.

"No," said the Queen. "Not fey." But her tone made it seem that he wasn't so very far from. "Energy binds us all together, creating everything that lives and dies." The Queen gestured around her as she spoke, to the sky, the earth, and the deep pool in the fountain. "It is both life and death, and also neither life nor death, and everything in between. It is the great crash of the waters of the sea, the silent peace of the forest glade, and the delicate step of a newborn moth. It is everything, and nothing."

"You mean the first spirit. The energy beyond the Veil," Lishka clarified. "The soul of the Earth."

"Long ago," the Queen continued as though Lishka had not spoken, "there existed only the few derived purely from this energy. They were the first to separate from the Source, to become individual conscious beings that lived in this world. Your darker side and the fey folk share a common ancestor." She smiled at Lishka's surprise. "Yes, despite our differences, we are kin in a strange sort of way. We are, after all, two halves of the same whole. Life and death. You cannot have one without the other."

The Queen leaned far over the pool to study her reflection. Her long hair, now turned golden in the direct sunlight, trailed down to dip in the cold water.

Lishka considered this new information. Their kinship made a strange sort of sense. After all, both species had the ability to connect to the energy beyond the Veil. Lishka had known the core of her vampirism came from the power itself, though now she wondered at how that core came to be. *Was Zaral one of the original beings?*

"You are even more so our kin." The Queen cocked her head to the side, her focus still on her reflection, or on the depths beyond it. "But then, you know that already. He might be too, I think," she mused, pursing her lips.

Lishka frowned. "Who?" She began to feel the sharp edge of impatience. She feared she'd spent too much time here already, and the Queen seemed no more inclined to provide her allegiance than she had in the Hall. The Queen looked up, a not altogether friendly smile playing about her lips.

"The one you left behind," she said.

"Dominick?"

The Queen remained silent as she held Lishka's eyes.

"He could have come through?" Lishka persisted. She took a step closer, ignoring her hesitation to be near the water.

"Perhaps," answered the Queen. "His true spirit is not unlike yours."

"Because I turned him."

The Queen shook her head and stood, her gaze now level with Lishka's. "You only passed the energy of your vampiric self to him in the Making. Fey spirit cannot be passed in such a way." Despite her talk of kinship, Lishka heard the scorn in her voice.

"Then why could he have come through?" Lishka asked. "How does he have fey in him?"

"His lineage is similar to yours, though somewhat further removed," the Queen said vaguely. "In any case, to enter our realm, you must be stripped of your vampiric self. Dominick is your tether. He anchors you to the mortal world, that you may more easily find the way back." She looked at Lishka sideways, an evil glint in her eye. Phoenix, who had remained mostly silent thus far, positioned himself to stand closer behind Lishka. Inside her, alarm bells began to resound. With the Fey Queen in front and Phoenix behind, she had the distinct feeling of being trapped between them.

"Are you willing to give up that tether?" The Fey Queen commanded her attention once again. "To be free from that part of you? To be fully here, where your deeper, true self belongs?"

Lishka instinctively reached for her sword, then remembered they had stripped her of her weapon when she'd drunk the Elar.

"No." She refused to give up Dominick, to disappear

once more into the fey realm. Without the tether, it was not likely she would be able to go back.

The Queen grinned and her teeth were sharp. "Then this will be very painful for you."

With that, Phoenix grasped the nape of Lishka's neck to fling her up over the rim of the fountain and down deep beneath the water.

Lishka gasped. She did not need air, but this water punched against her being with the force of a power that did not want her there. It permeated through her body and soul, until the smallest molecules of herself had separated and she herself became part of the water. A dreadful ache spread through her nonexistent chest. The water reached her core and the violet force flared, vibrant and strong, and the pain lessened. Yet as the fey rose inside her, that special feeling of earth, of security, of a different sort of warmth, began to disappear.

*NO!* Lishka screamed and at once she reached out for the link and grasped it tightly to her. She convulsed with the sharp, satisfying pain that meant the tether held. The water parted.

Light struck her eyelids. Firm ground held her, and a cool breeze wafted across her face that imparted the sense of a vast openness. Lishka opened her eyes.

She lay upon fresh green grass on the top of a mountain peak. The forest stretched out below her, and beyond, the lake glistened in the warm afternoon light.

She sat up, her clothes and body completely dry. Tall stone pillars rose from the earth in a circle around her. To her left at the center of the stone ring stood a matching stone basin, mounted on a waist-high pedestal. Lishka didn't need to see inside to know that water even more powerful than the fountain's filled the basin.

"That's interesting."

Lishka jumped to her feet and spun about. The creature that watched her from the circle's edge had the voice of the Fey Queen but was altogether wild. From the Queen's head curved delicate branches in place of hair, which sprouted smaller twigs, and a leaf or two twisted in the breeze. Graceful butterflies and even a hummingbird flitted about the limbs. From the creature's back grew a pair of translucent wings, the edges jagged and pierced with tiny holes. Her eyes remained the same and through the branches and the wings, Lishka saw the face of the Fey Queen and knew this to be her true form.

Next to the Queen, Phoenix appeared largely unchanged, aside from the two great antlers rising from his mane of golden tangles. He watched Lishka, his expression unreadable.

"Where am I?" Lishka's voice sounded strange to her, deeper and with a musical resonance that had not been there before.

The Queen smiled. "We are in the heart of Avalon."

Lishka took another sweep of the landscape and realized that they stood on top of the same peak they had encircled to reach the Queen's Hall.

"Why have you brought me here?"

"Look in the water." The Queen gestured toward the basin.

Lishka walked into the center of the stones, slowing her pace as she neared the basin's edge. She glanced back, but Phoenix and the Queen did not move closer. Lishka looked down at the thin layer of water covering the stone.

A strange face stared back at her. Her hair twisted into black leaves that framed her face and trailed down her shoulders. Delicate deep-red roses bloomed between the leaves, and sharp thorns edged the vines that bore them. Her eyes had darkened to almost appear black, aside from the bright violet flame in the center of her irises. Her face shone chalk-pale, and her teeth remained white and sharp. She stared at the foreign image. The water shifted and softened her reflection, making it hard to see. At once Lishka realized that the water did not shift, but rather, only her reflection did. The edges of her face blurred in an ongoing transition from a violet shine to a black haze, and back again.

"Your true self," said the Queen. While Lishka had been staring at her reflection, the Queen had moved to stand beside her.

Lishka couldn't take her eyes away from the image. "Why is it hazy?"

"You are split between two selves. You have not yet chosen who you will be."

"Two selves?"

"Yes, of course," the Queen said, as if Lishka should know already. "The one half, fey; the other half, your humanity turned vampiric. Two equal parts, at war with each other."

In an instant, Lishka forgot about her image. She turned to the Queen. "Equal parts? I am *half* fey?"

The Queen calmly met her stare. "Yes. How else would you be able to enter here, to walk freely and resist the lure of the drink? Only your fey blood, and myself of course, allows you to be in our realm."

*Half fey.* Never had Lishka suspected her fey bloodline to be so strong. She had assumed her fey inheritance came from some long-distant ancestor, as it had only ever manifested in her violet eyes and a small amount of power quickly subdued by her vampiric nature. Then again, Lishka had been only nineteen when Zaral took away her humanity. She could barely remember how it felt to be human and had only been at the start of discovering her magikal abilities when she had been made into an immortal creature. She studied her reflection with this new knowledge, trying to reconcile what she now saw with her understanding of herself.

"This is what I really look like?"

"Yes and no," said the Queen. "Just as this place is here and is not here. For if this place is not here, you cannot be here to look like this, you see?"

The image in the water glowered back at her, exasperated. The Queen smiled and looked over Lishka's head at Phoenix.

"Mordan was clever to send her to me," she said. "I think next time, I shall meet the other one as well. It is not every day one can witness the fulfillment of prophecy."

"What do you mean?" This time, Lishka faced her body toward the Queen, who now stood unsettlingly close.

The Queen examined Lishka's strange new face.

"I think it's time you returned to your world," she said after a moment. "Unless you wish to remain here forever, of course. The limit is fast approaching as to how long you can stay separated from that part of you."

Lishka spotted the diversion, but the prospect of never returning to Dominick loomed strongly enough to distract her for the moment.

"Will you let me move you?"

Lishka looked at her warily.

"It will not hurt," the Queen said. "I will merely return you to the gate. You are not breaking through any barriers to get there. Phoenix will accompany you."

Not reassured, Lishka nodded her acquiescence, nonetheless. She filed away the mention of prophecy for later consideration. The Fey Queen had shown herself to be untrustworthy, and Lishka knew she must take her opportunity to leave this realm before the Queen decided to keep her trapped within it. The Queen placed her palm against Lishka's forehead, just as Lishka closed her eyes.

When she opened them, Lishka found herself standing at the edge of the clearing where she had first entered the realm of the fey. Phoenix leaned against a nearby tree as though he had been there a great deal longer. The antlers had once more disappeared. Catching Lishka's attention, he pointed in front of them.

"Just walk through the barrier. You will be able to pass right through."

Lishka followed his arm to see where the air twisted. The fresh, clean sharpness of snow wafted toward them, at odds with this warm, earthy place. She took a step forward, then stopped.

"The Queen did not give me an answer," she said.

Phoenix crossed his arms before him and steadily returned her gaze.

"I ask once more for her assistance in the fight against Zaral." The name streamed off her tongue more easily than before, and Lishka found that she did not feel quite the same fear she once had at the mere mention of him.

"In her own time," Phoenix replied.

The air around Lishka shifted. Phoenix was forcing her through. She tried for a second to resist, to press for the fey's allegiance, but found that she just didn't want to stay badly enough. The golden light and green leaves faded, and she let go to walk toward the cold air, the soft moonlight, and Dominick.

DOMINICK NESTLED INTO the snowdrift, trying to get comfortable, while the deep hibernation of day sleep still eluded him. The snow that had first felt so soft to rest against had, after several days, started to seep through the supposedly waterproof cloth of his jacket and pants. He did not feel the cold, not really, but that didn't stop the dampness from being uncomfortable. He could have summoned a small spell to reinforce the material. Yet Lishka had warned him of using unnecessary energy, with so little life around them to replenish it. Besides, the tracker was still on his mind.

*Where is she?* He looked to the stone entrance for perhaps the hundredth time, where its bleak, cold exterior remained unchanged. Yet again, Dominick recalled the image of Lishka walking through the doorway, the light illuminating her dark hair before swallowing her. Then, a day after she'd left, the doorway closed.

Doubt crept into his mind. Lishka had fey in her. The niggling thought persisted that Lishka might choose to stay with them, where she could be free of Zaral, or so Dominick assumed. He pushed the doubt down once more, for perhaps the hundredth time as well. Lishka would come back.

Dominick tried to think back to the stories his sister read when they were little, remembering her with a small pang. That time now seemed like another life, much longer than the fifteen or so years that had passed. Jenn had loved the stories about fairies, and mermaids, and all wild things. Dominick had much preferred books grounded in science.

*What would she think of her brother now?*

Self-consciously, he traced his long canines with the edge of his tongue. He shouldn't think of her, not even in private. He had to keep her as far away from this life, as far away from himself, Lishka, and all that surrounded them, as possible. He really had left his old life behind.

Dominick shook off the sadness mixed with some regret. The fairies, he slowly remembered, had their own dimension, where time ran differently from the real world. If that held true outside of myth, then it could be weeks, maybe even years before Lishka returned.

He spared a glance at the surface of the wide lake, still smooth with ice and fallen snow. *What if she doesn't come back?* They were immortal, but still Dominick could not imagine waiting years for her return. Even the few weeks that had passed felt too long.

Lishka had to return. They had a task to complete, even if that was the only thing that brought her back to him. Dominick sighed and forced his mind and body still, to resume staring at the rock.

Hours or possibly days later, for time seemed to pause on top of the mountain, Dominick felt a stirring. The lake remained frozen, the trees still, with only the faintest breeze blowing through the valley between the peaks. Outwardly nothing had changed, and yet something had shifted, had shaken Dominick out of the trance-like state.

He stood from his snow nest and shook the flurries off his shoulders. The weak sun had not yet risen over the mountains, and the lake remained cast in shadow from the cliffs. Clouds consistently gathered over the peaks, stuck against them on their way to the western coast, and so Dominick's hood had been sufficient protection even in daylight. Now he pushed the hood off to expose his head to the freezing air, better to take stock of what had triggered him to wake.

A vibration resounded through the ground and through the air. Dominick took several steps forward to where the doorway had previously opened and placed his hands against the humming rock. An electric charge hit his palms and he jerked back. Light shone through the rock, and markings began to glow once more in an archway. The markings brightened and then the rock in the center of the door shimmered and turned translucent. Through the door, a path extended into the beyond. Sunlight obscured the surrounding landscape. Unused to the brightness, Dominick's eyes began to water, but he peered through the doorway nonetheless, trying to see further.

A shape appeared in the distance. *Lishka.* Dominick knew her at once from her silhouette. He couldn't help the excitement that rushed through him. He wanted to go through, to reunite with her before the door closed once more, but he held himself back, just out of the light's reach. His skin remembered the burning sensation.

Lishka came closer, clearer as Dominick grew used to

the light. She wore peculiar clothes; a loose gown flowed about her legs and arms, tied only at the waist by some green material. Her hair fluttered about her like leaves. *Are those leaves?* Dominick blinked, trying to see.

Lishka slowed and turned to look behind her. Dominick frowned and raised his hand to the sword at his back. Now that she stood closer, he saw the outline of someone standing behind her. The silhouette was tall and masculine, with what looked like antlers jutting from the figure's head. The being looked past Lishka to meet Dominick's stare. Dominick gripped the hilt of his blade and made to pull the steel free. At once, Lishka turned and resumed walking toward Dominick, more quickly now. As she did, the figure behind her faded. Dominick blinked again, wondering if he had imagined him.

The light lessened as Lishka drew closer and now Dominick saw her clearly. Emerging through the doorway, she appeared the same as when she had left him in her hooded coat, hair tumbling loosely down her shoulders. Dominick released the hold on his sword to drop his hands to his sides, ready to grab her should the doorway falter. The second her foot left the edge of the arch, the entrance solidified into mountain rock, with no hint that it had ever been anything else.

Lishka stood right before him as though she had never left. Dominick noted the smooth white skin and high cheekbones. He suddenly realized that her eyes glowed a stronger violet than before. He raised his arms to hug her and stopped himself, awkwardly patting her shoulder instead. Unexpectedly, she smiled up at him, a weary sort of smile, and the glow in her eyes faded, leaving her to be, once again, Lishka.

# CHAPTER 22

# THE BLADE

LISHKA EMERGED ONCE MORE into the cool early morning of the mountain valley. The shadows lay long against fresh mounds of snow and the air bit her cheeks, in sharp contrast to the golden warmth she had left behind. She ignored the cold and the snow. Before her stood Dominick. He watched her walk toward him, the same as when she'd left, as if he had stood there waiting the entire time. Lishka realized she must look strange now. She felt different, the violet core within her pulsing, having strengthened in her time with the folk. The warmth behind her vanished as the doorway closed, and the sense of the fey faded to only a whiff in the air of the summer forest.

Lishka met Dominick's worried gaze and smiled to reassure him. He lifted his hand to her shoulder in an action mirroring one at their parting, and relief softened his face. She must have been gone for some time.

His hand lingered on her shoulder and then dropped back to his side.

"How long?" Lishka asked, breaking the spell that tied the two realms together. Now only mountain stone and snow filled her nose.

"Two weeks?" Dominick guessed, his voice rough from lack of use. "Maybe give or take a few days."

"That's all?" It had felt much longer in the realm of the fey.

A slight frown knitted Dominick's brow, though he nodded.

"What was it like?" he asked. Lishka glanced behind her with the smallest amount of regret at the barren rock face. The realm of the fey had been safe, far from Zachriel, Zaral, and all the worries of this world. The memory lingered at the edge of her mind, of serene forgetfulness in the forest glade. But Dominick was in this world, and she could not have abandoned him.

*He might be able to go through.* She remembered the Fey Queen's words: *His true spirit is not unlike yours.* Yet the doorway had shut. Lishka knew it would not open to her again.

"Lishka? Did you find the fey?"

"Yes," Lishka answered, facing Dominick once more. "The Fey Queen will not aid Zachriel."

"She won't help?" Dominick pressed, his voice gaining strength. "She has to."

At once, the energy drained from Lishka. Traversing realms had sapped much of her strength, despite what power she'd gained through fully realizing her fey lineage.

"Come. Let's take shelter in the trees." She let her gaze slide from Dominick to where the sky brightened in the east. "And I will tell you all that transpired."

"WE COULD TRY again," Dominick suggested, though he sounded doubtful. The day had passed into dusk once more and they sat perched on boulders at the edge of the lakeshore. A clear starry sky stretched overhead, contained only by the outlines of the Twin Peaks to either side. Lishka shook her head; they had been through this before.

"No. The fey will not help us. They are too far gone behind the mists of the Veil to be concerned with this world. The people of this world abandoned them long ago, and now in return they themselves are being abandoned." Lishka sighed. "I wonder now what made Mordan think otherwise."

Lishka knew they had to return to the Coven, and soon. She would have to tell Mordan that they had been unsuccessful. She did not know what that would mean for Zachriel's cause, only that Mordan had trusted her, had shown such confidence in her, and she had failed him.

Beyond Mordan's disappointment, Lishka worried that the opportunity to regain the power of her mage's mark had also been lost. Lord Dorwan had told her that should she be successful, they would unbind her mark. She had indeed successfully entered the realm, but she carried no promise of fealty from the fey. Lishka cringed at the thought of returning to the Coven, of putting herself and Dominick in the middle of civil war, without the use of her full powers to protect them.

Even as her thoughts churned over what action to take, another pressing matter began to rise: Dominick needed to feed. The heightened energy of the Veil had helped to sustain him, but being so newly transitioned, he still required consistent blood. He did not tell her of his cravings, but Lishka noted the way he twitched at every stimulus, whether it was the trees creaking or the soft whomp of snow falling from overladen branches to the forest floor. His instincts pressed him to hunt.

"You said the Fey Queen told you I had fey blood?" Dominick asked, his gaze drifting across the frozen lake. The moonlight shadowed his eyes, drawing out the bruised skin beneath. The lower valleys would produce the larger game he needed.

"I don't know," Lishka answered before the pause became too noticeable. "She said you had a similar kinship to mine, though she did not elaborate."

"But you said before, you didn't sense that I had any fey energy."

Lishka shook her head again. "Nothing in you as a human nor as you are now feels like fey. But I am not so familiar with the nuance of the folk. They have long kept themselves hidden from the world. It is possible they possess a magik I've not encountered, nor have any of those at the Coven. I cannot be sure."

"Perhaps," Dominick mused, "maybe they will change their minds. You've made the argument for assisting Zachriel. They may just need time to consider the request, to think on what Zaral's effect on this world will do to theirs. The realms must be connected, right? What happens to one must impact the other if they are both linked to the power beyond the Veil."

Lishka shrugged. She appreciated Dominick's optimism, but she rather doubted the Fey Queen would change her mind. The Queen had not impressed her as one who would quickly act on a whim. She had known why Lishka entered their realm well before Lishka made her case, and she'd clearly had time to consider the request.

Dominick tipped his head back to stare at the bright stars above them. Lishka found herself following his gaze. She used to watch the sky often, in the early years. When she was human, she had been taught the constellations, including how to use them to find water, and the correct route when traveling. The stars could lead you places, help you survive, and teach you wisdom, if one knew how to read them. The Followers had shown her.

Her eyes drifted across the familiar patterns, recognizing the major constellations. She still remembered them, after all those centuries, even if she no longer needed them for what her heightened senses could tell her now.

"I can always find the Big Dipper," Dominick said, as though he read her mind. "Not much to brag about, most people can find that one. That, and Orion."

Lishka pointed and he followed the line of her arm to a grouping of stars in the northeast corner of the sky, just beside the northern peak.

"That one, there." She gestured to the bright cluster of stars. "That's Kirzan the Warrior." As she spoke the name, the stars seemed to form the outline of a fierce man, complete with a sword brandished against an unseen enemy. "And there." Lishka pointed to a place in the sky south of Kirzan. "There is Dymeth the huntress, and Syrze, the man who loved her and died for her, and followed her to the stars." She spoke the words softly, unconsciously reciting them in the lilting way she had been taught, those long years ago. Another lifetime.

Dominick kept his gaze on the heavens and a peaceful stillness fell between them. For a moment, they stopped worrying about their failed task and sat comfortably with their own thoughts.

"I think we need to go back," Lishka said at last, disrupting the welcome moment. "There is nothing more we can do here. The fey will not let me in again and our kind do not belong in their realm. Even one born of their blood is less than welcome." Lishka recalled the hostile stares and the angry whispers, even after she had danced and drunk with them. She could never be one of them. That chance had been stolen a long time ago, when Zaral first set eyes on her.

Dominick half smiled. "I guess we can't stay here forever," he said, speaking the wish that had been on both their minds. Lishka sighed.

"Tomorrow," she agreed. "Tomorrow we'll journey back south to the Coven."

DESPITE THEIR RESOLVE to leave the mountain the following night, they took their time circumventing the lake. Lishka couldn't help her gaze drifting to where the doorway had opened, in a vain hope that the fey would change their minds. But the rock remained gray, and the only glimmer within the stone was the white sparkle of the quartz. No violet gleamed in crystal seams, nor was there any to highlight hidden symbols of the fey language.

As they made their way along the shore, Dominick began to fall further behind. Lishka glanced back and caught him standing at the edge of the lake, staring out at the ice. A deep frown furrowed his brow. He visibly shook himself and turned away to continue walking, taking long strides to close the gap between them. Lishka continued forward. She remembered that when they had first arrived, Dominick had sensed the power in the water. Though ice contained the waters, the ancient magik still flowed sluggishly beneath, in the currents. Lishka shivered, even as her fey blood thrummed with excitement at the proximity to the waters of Avalon.

She walked on, her pace comfortable but not rushed. She had told Dominick they must leave, but still, reluctance dragged at her heels. *What will Mordan say?*

Lost in her thoughts, it took her longer to realize that Dominick had once more fallen behind. She stopped again, this time irritation itching under her skin. They had passed the midway point of the lake and moonlight reflected against the ice, the white in stark contrast to the far tree line. Dominick stood on the very edge of the ice. He tilted his head as though he listened to something, and this time, he did not resume following her. Lishka hurried back to his side, concern overriding irritation. After all, Dominick had found the doorway. Maybe he sensed something else that could aid them with the fey.

"What is it?"

"I don't know." Dominick peered across the lake. "I think there is something in the lake. Something is pulling…" His words petered off and he stepped away from the bank to stride purposefully out across the frozen water. Lishka gritted her teeth and forced herself to step onto the ice, the soles of her boots sliding against the ice and snow. Beneath her feet, the power churned in response.

Dominick led them farther out into the center of the lake, until the bank grew small behind them. Suddenly he stopped and looked straight down. Lishka followed his gaze. Hovering several feet below them, silver glinted. Lishka leaned over the spot, trying to make out the shape suspended in the ice.

Dominick knelt and brushed away the crystallized patches of snow.

"It's a sword," Dominick said with surprise. Now they could clearly see the graceful lines of the crossed pommel and the long smooth shine of the metal. "What is a sword doing in the ice?"

"How did you know it was here?" Lishka asked, unable to answer his question. A hum vibrated the soles of her boots.

"I don't know," Dominick answered. His eyes had not left the sword. "I just felt something pulling me. I guess it was like the compulsion to find you. How do you think we should get it out?"

A shiver ran through Lishka at the comparison Dominick made to the sword calling to him, as he once professed she had done in his dream. Dominick didn't notice, his attention fixed solely on the blade.

"Break the ice, I suppose. Use your sword? But be careful. The ice is thick, but the water is tricksome." Uneasiness lifted her voice, which Lishka did not like but couldn't help. The sword, combined with the power in the water, worried her. She suspected the waters would not be so forgiving to them here, outside the fey realm.

Dominick shook his head. "I don't think…" and he trailed off. Suddenly he smashed his hand into the ice.

It shattered in an instant and hairline cracks snaked out from the hole. Lishka jumped back to keep her toes on solid ice. The smell of the ancient water filled the air, invoking Avalon. It called to her, both drawing and repulsing her as the fey realm had. Dominick balled his hand into a fist and punched the edges of the ice to make the hole wider. The sword looked a long way down; he would have to swim for it.

Even as she thought this, the ice around the hole began to glow in the same light that had emanated from the entrance to the realm of the fey. Dominick didn't hesitate. He plunged his arm into the hole up to his shoulder. Lishka reached out to grasp the back of his coat, in case he should fall all the way in. Dominick grunted, frowning with concentration. At once he swung up and back, rising to his feet. Droplets showered them both in a cascade of golden light that formed an arch over Dominick's head, and then the silver blade shone bright in moonlight, firmly gripped in Dominick's hand.

LISHKA DID NOT allow them to linger on the ice once the sword had been pulled. There was no time to discuss what the blade signified. The hairline cracks from the hole Dominick created began to widen and spread, and so they both ran to the shore, chased by water bubbling through the breakage in the ice.

At the shore they paused to look back to where water seeped over the ice, already beginning to refreeze. Lishka turned her attention to Dominick at her side. He did not stare at the ice as she did, but instead he held the blade before him. He smiled at the steel, almost laughing, and his wind-blown hair lay boyishly tousled.

Lishka shifted her gaze to the sword. At a first glance, it appeared like any well-made sword, a finely crafted weapon set into a worn leather-bound hilt. But as the moonlight caught the steel, symbols flashed up the edge and the air hummed with its energy. A sense of urgency flooded her. They had to leave the White Lake, and the entrance to the fey.

"Dominick."

Dominick ignored her, enamored with the weapon in his hands.

"Dominick," Lishka said more forcefully. He jolted and pried his eyes from the sword to her with surprise, as though he had forgotten she stood beside him. "Are you alright?"

Dominick slowly nodded, a little more of himself returning.

"I think so," he replied. "The water didn't hurt me." That wasn't quite what Lishka had meant, but she let it go for the moment.

"We should leave. Here." She held out her hand.

Dominick took a step back, thinking she meant to take the sword from him.

"Turn around," Lishka commanded. He obeyed, and she unbuckled the scabbard from around his back, then unsheathed the sword Kiaban had given him. A master-crafted weapon, it paled in comparison to the blade from the ice. Lishka re-strapped the scabbard, wrapping her arms around Dominick to buckle it again at his front. She had to press her chest against his back to reach, and his hair brushed against her cheek.

Next, she wedged in the unsheathed Coven sword

alongside the scabbard, using leather cord pulled from her own coat to help secure it, so that it would not cut Dominick's clothes or flesh.

"Okay." She stepped back to assess her work. Dominick reached up to feel where the scabbard rested, then lifted the sword overhead and sheathed it. The blade stuck out about an inch from the scabbard, being a little longer than his original sword. Dominick turned to face her.

"If we make haste, we can traverse most of the stairs before dawn," she said. He glanced up to the night sky. They still had many hours of night left, despite their delay.

Lishka led them along the shore and back to the narrow stair at the southern end of the lake. Dominick kept close behind this time, the source of his distraction now on his back. Lishka couldn't shake the uneasy feeling that they had lingered at the lake in order for Dominick to find the sword.

The whole scene made her nervous. The sword had been pulled, and even though it had come not from stone, but water and ice, the parallel was too strong to ignore. The blade had power, that much Lishka could feel—a different sort of power than the swords Kiaban crafted. Then there was the fact that the blade had manifested just outside the portal to the realm of the fey, keepers of such creations.

Lishka knew the stories, the legend. It had become a popular, oft-told myth, reenacted in plays, novels, and more recently the cinema. Lishka had never really considered that the origins of the story might be fact. She tried to recall the whispered rumors that had drifted to the Followers, during a time when the legend could have been closer to truth. Lishka could not remember much. She had been young, and news did not travel then as it did now.

*Avalon existed. Why not the legendary sword?*

Lishka shook herself. Even to think it made her feel silly, like a young foolish girl who believed that because she prayed to the Goddess, she would be kept safe.

In much less time than it took to ascend, they reached a fork in the staircase that they had missed before. Dominick paused only a step behind her, and the air hummed about them, tingling against the back of Lishka's neck.

Lishka forced herself to ignore the sword for the moment, to instead examine the paths.

"Alaisadaille," Dominick whispered.

Lishka judged the angle of the other path that led southeast instead of due south. Dominick was right; that path had been the one they'd taken when they emerged from Alaisadaille's tunnel. In their haste, they had not seen the secondary route that must provide a safer road through the mountain.

"This way, then," she said, leading them to the southern stairs.

When the sky began to lighten, they took shelter beneath an outcrop along the stair. Clouds had moved in once more and snow began to drift in constricted flurries. Dominick withdrew the sword to study it, his fingers absentmindedly stroking the pommel. Lishka turned her back to him and drew her hood up close to try to sleep.

The following night, the stairway widened and gradually wore down to unaltered mountainside once more. They found themselves in a sparse forest and the scent of deer drifted in between the evergreen. Finally, something pulled Dominick's attention from the sword.

He stopped and lifted his head to sniff the light breeze that periodically wafted through the forest. His eyes dilated, shadowed in the faint moonlight. Lishka watched him, allowing him to take the lead in the hunt. Deep inside, she also felt the cravings stirring, hungering for the nearby life. The deer's heartbeat pounded loudly in her ears, each thump a promise of rich blood. She knew the craving would be stronger for Dominick.

He tilted his head and at once leapt into the forest. Lishka sprinted after him. They veered apart in perfect sync, to encircle the deer who bounded ahead of them through the forest. The animal's sweat and fear sharpened the scent and Lishka allowed her predator instincts to take over. Her focus narrowed to only the deer. She could almost see the blood flowing through its veins.

The animal didn't stand a chance. Dominick launched himself forward to wrap his arms about its back and sink his teeth into its neck. The beast stumbled a few steps and then fell to the ground. Lishka slowed to watch, holding onto her control despite the coppery scent that thickened the air.

Blood dripping from his lips, Dominick raised his head. The deer rolled a wide eye back toward him, its side heaving up and down in shallow bursts. Dominick laid a comforting hand on its neck, even as he withdrew the dagger from his boot and plunged it into the deer's heart.

Lishka took a few steps forward to kneel beside Dominick. Through the bloodlust in his eyes, she saw sadness. She put a hand on his shoulder and together, they bent over the fallen animal and fed.

Despite their newfound energy that would have allowed them to continue into the early hours of morning, Lishka stopped them just before dawn. Her sense of urgency to return to the Coven had begun to dissipate, as her concern about the blade's nature increased. She knelt in a ring of blue spruce and, though it felt foolish, conjured a small fire with symbols made easier using the energy she had gained from the deer. The fire softened the shadows in the trees, evoking a false sense of security that creatures of night should not need. But Lishka could not shake her unease. Dominick sat down on a fallen log across from her and balanced the sword over his knees. Shifting patterns of red and orange, the fire's reflection, undulated in the steel.

"Where do you think it came from?" Dominick's voice startled Lishka from her study of the blade. She glanced up to find his gaze still fixated on the steel.

"From the lake," she answered.

Finally, Dominick tore his eyes from the blade. "I mean, who do you think made it?"

"I'm not sure," Lishka answered. "Possibly the fey, though they said no word of it to me." This too had bothered her. The blade could have only come from the Queen, though she had not made any mention of a weapon that would aid them. Lishka did not trust the Queen, or her intentions.

"There are no signs of wear or use anywhere on it," Dominick observed, once more studying the steel. "But it must be old. It feels old. Look, there are symbols."

Lishka leaned in closer. Made brighter by the fire, marks now shone along the blade's edge. She thought of Kiaban, but these looked different from those he inscribed on the Coven's weapons.

"They look like the symbols in Alaisadaille's cave," Lishka said. "Do you remember?" Dominick nodded, his eyes wide.

"You're right. The line usage is similar to the patterns from the cave. Do you know what they mean?"

Lishka shook her head. "No. It must be a similar language, or if it's the same, they use symbols not written in the tunnels. They must be related to the Old Ways."

"The Old Ways?" Again, Dominick pulled his attention from the blade to focus on Lishka, and she felt a small sense of relief.

"The old beliefs in the Goddess," Lishka elaborated. "According to the Followers, long ago, when more magikal things still walked the earth, humans and creatures alike followed religion rooted in the belief of the earth and the Goddess. I saw similar symbols in the pagan temples of the Goddess, centuries ago."

"The sword feels old," Dominick repeated. "I know that your sword, and mine, are spelled, but this one feels different. It's more than the carrier of magik. It feels—" He stopped.

"Alive," Lishka finished. "It feels alive."

Dominick held her gaze, not-quite fear coloring his eyes a darker brown.

"Kiaban will know," Lishka said without thinking. Dominick's fingers tightened around the pommel.

"What do you mean?"

"Kiaban will know what the sword is," Lishka

repeated with confidence. If anyone could ascertain the sword's origins, it would be Kiaban. Dominick glanced down at the sword once more, then back up at Lishka.

"I don't think we should bring it to the Coven," he said at last.

"What do you mean? We must return to the Coven, to tell Mordan of the fey's refusal to assist Zachriel. And if this is a weapon that can aid him, we must give it to the Council Members."

Dominick stood, gripping the blade. He would not release it to anyone, Lishka saw clearly. She stood as well and carefully kept her hand from straying to her own sword. Dominick would not harm her and yet she worried what the blade might be doing to him. At once Dominick sighed and lessened his hold on the hilt. Lishka watched him cautiously.

"I didn't want to say, back on the stairs. But I don't think we should return to the Coven."

"Why do you say this?" Lishka did not quite relax, her fingers still ready to cast a spell of restraint should she need it, despite the energy it would consume. The power beyond the Veil did not flow as readily in the lower mountains as it had in the White Lake, and the magik felt sluggish.

"I don't think we should take this sword there," Dominick repeated. "You said Zaral has strong followers there, right? What happens if they see it, feel it there? What happens if Zaral tries to take it?"

Dominick was right. Lishka had not wanted to think beyond getting the sword before Mordan, and Kiaban. Zachriel's Council Members would know what to do, or so she had told herself. She opened her mouth to answer when a familiar pressure nudged against her mind. Dominick experienced the sensation at the same moment. In an instant, he brought the blade up before him in an offensive stance. Lishka snuffed the fire with a flick of her hand, casting them into sudden darkness. She drew her own sword and closed the gap between them to put her back to Dominick's.

Someone approached them, not even bothering to hide their footsteps. Lishka searched the trees. The person drew closer now, and she remembered the tracker and the black thread tethering him to an insidious Master. She recoiled from touching the intruder's mind, worried at what she might find. Behind her, Dominick stood ready to fight and his strength surged through her, empowering her to stand before their would-be attacker. She pressed forward once more with both her vampiric influence and her fey intuition, to touch the presence approaching them.

At once, she relaxed into the familiarity and smiled.

"What is it?" Dominick sensed her change, though he kept the blade before him. Lishka stepped away from him to face the same direction into the woods. She drew the symbol that would bring the fire embers to a soft glow before them. Mere minutes later a worn figure emerged from the tree line, and the fire cast light onto the familiar features of Mordan.

# CHAPTER 23

# PROPHECY AND LEGEND

"WHAT ARE YOU DOING here?" The words slipped out of her mouth before she had time to censor them. Regardless of their relationship, Mordan's status as a Council Member demanded respect, especially in the presence of Dominick. "My Lord," Lishka added with a slight dip of her head.

Mordan took several more steps to bring him to the smoldering embers of their fire.

"Lishka, Dominick." Mordan nodded to one, then the other, in greeting. "Well met." He smiled, a small, worn smile as though he had been traveling nonstop for quite some time. Something inside Lishka unclenched at the sight of him.

*Mordan would know what to do.*

"I am on my own mission of sorts. Although now, coming upon the two of you, I'm struck with an idea. But more on that later. That fire you had going, the one that

I could see from over a mile off…"

Lishka flinched. She had known the fire was a foolish idea and allowed emotion to guide her hand regardless.

"Maybe we'll have that going again." Mordan flicked his hand to Lishka's surprise, and the embers sparked to flame, casting an orange glow on the ring of spruce about them. "I detect nothing close by to cause concern, and fire is always a good companion to storytelling. I have a feeling there are some stories to be told." Mordan eyed the sword in Dominick's hand.

*Of course, he must have sensed it.*

Mordan settled himself on the log Dominick had occupied previously and gestured to Dominick and Lishka to do the same. Dominick sheathed the blade and walked back into the trees without a word. Lishka debated whether she should follow him, but he did not seem upset. She glanced back to assess Mordan's reaction. Mordan watched where Dominick had disappeared into the shadows, and Lishka took the opportunity to observe her mentor. Mordan's hair fell a little sloppily across his brow and his unchanging face looked drawn in the flickering light. His gray eyes remained as sharp as ever.

The sound of branches breaking just within the tree line interrupted the softer crackling of fire. Dominick emerged once more, carrying a second log. He dropped it across from Mordan and plunked himself down, adjusting the swords at his back so that they did not hit the wood. Lishka sat beside him.

"First things first," Mordan said once they were settled. "I take it you reached the doorway to the realm of the fey?"

Lishka nodded.

"And they let you enter."

Dominick and Lishka nodded in unison.

"Were you successful?"

Lishka grimaced. She had planned on having more time to prepare to face Mordan and admit her failure. "No. I was not."

Mordan looked from Lishka to Dominick, judging their reactions. He leaned forward and clasped his hands between his knees.

"I think you had better start from the beginning. Tell me everything that has happened since you left the Coven."

PERHAPS AN HOUR remained until dawn. Already the sky lay not quite so dark, the shadows not quite so long, when Lishka finished their story. She stopped at the point when she had returned from the fey realm. The rest, the pulling of the sword, belonged to Dominick.

"So the Fey Queen refused," Mordan repeated. "I thought she might. She is fierce and stubborn, though passionate for those she protects. Or at least, she was once. But I'm afraid she has spent too long in the mist to feel much attachment to this world and the people in it." Mordan sighed. "And Alaisadaille has awoken. We had a little chat, you might say, as I was traveling through. She was not pleased at how easily you passed below the mountains."

"Easily?" Dominick broke his thoughtful silence. He had not spoken for the duration of Lishka's story. Lishka recalled the sensation of the tunnel falling away from them, and the unending current of the power beyond the Veil.

"Yes. Alaisadaille is a being of great power," Mordan explained. "She likes young things, and she enjoys causing mischief, not unlike her fey kin, I suppose. She sensed what was hidden, deep within. She would have kept you there, if she could have, if only out of spite for those more powerful than she."

"Riddles, Mordan?" Lishka asked gently, half amused and half annoyed.

"Alaisadaille and I have a long history. I'll tell you about it, someday. Besides, you have yet to tell me the most interesting part," Mordan said, bringing them all back to the point of the conversation. "What drew me here, to you both."

"What do you mean?" Lishka asked. "Couldn't you sense us if you were close?"

"Perhaps, though my run-in with Alaisadaille left me more worn-out than I would have thought," Mordan admitted. The tiredness in his eyes and the hunch in his shoulders underscored his statement. Mordan had always been solid, powerful and confident, and it disturbed Lishka to see the cracks in his armor.

"And I had already passed through these parts to crest the mountain range beyond Mirna Sorne," Mordan continued. "It is unlikely that we would have sensed each other except for the surge of power that lit up the mountains about four days ago."

The unease that had been sitting with Lishka since Dominick pulled the sword began to grow. Lishka did not look at Dominick, nor the sword at his back, keeping her gaze on Mordan instead.

"The energy shone like a beacon, signaling your

location to all for many miles around." Mordan studied them both, though he did not sound accusatory. "I'm glad I caught the scent, for I was able to track you and cover your trail somewhat, in case anyone else happened to be in the vicinity. I did not sense any others, but I cannot be sure that you were not detected. The forest has its own eyes and ears, and not all of them align with Zachriel."

Lishka focused on the woods past Mordan, as though any minute some creature of Zaral's might appear. Her senses met with nothing malicious. Only the nocturnal forest dwellers disrupted the night as they went about their business of finding food.

"May I see the blade?" Mordan asked Dominick. Lishka noted that Mordan did not command him, though it was well within his rights to do so.

Dominick did not move or otherwise acknowledge the request. Instead, he considered Mordan for a long moment. Lishka bit her tongue from encouraging Dominick, knowing that he must make this decision. She checked to see whether Mordan grew angry at the disrespect, but Mordan merely waited patiently as though he sensed the inner turmoil.

At once, Dominick stood and reached behind him for the blade. As he drew the sword, the firelight raced along the silver edge. Mordan followed the flare but remained seated, his hands clasped loosely before him. Finally, Dominick held the blade across the fire, the hilt and his hand above the flames. As Mordan reached out to take it, he dipped his head in an almost imperceptible gesture. Dominick released the blade and sat down closer to Lishka, his eyes not leaving the steel.

Mordan held the blade out straight before him to test

its balance.

"Beautiful," he murmured. "Not too heavy, yet with a grace and heft that may be easily handled by the right wielder." He brought the sword in front of him, and careful fingers explored the fine edge as he examined the symbols in the metal. He twisted the sword at different angles and as it caught the fire, additional flashes of light flickered in their circle.

After several minutes of inspection, he stood and handed the blade back to Dominick. Dominick could not quite hide his eagerness to reclaim it. This time he did not sheath the sword but instead sat with it balanced across his knees.

"Now," Mordan said, "how did you come to pull the sword?"

Dominick raised his eyebrows in surprise.

"It is not so hard to guess," Mordan elaborated. "A sword like that leaves a clear mark, and there are rules concerning how such a weapon may be obtained."

"Rules?" Dominick asked.

"It is a sword of great power, greater even than those forged by Kiaban. But you know this of course."

Lishka found herself nodding along with Mordan's words.

"Such weapons are offered through earth materials, such as ice, water, sometimes fire, or even stone. I can make a guess, but I'd rather hear it from you—how the sword came to be in your possession."

"I noticed it the second we arrived at the lake," Dominick answered obediently. "The best way I can describe it is like the force of a magnet being pulled together, only half of the magnet was inside me, the other in the water. It was almost similar to—" He stopped himself and cast a quick side glance at Lishka.

"It's okay. You can trust Mordan," Lishka reassured him. At once, she remembered that Dominick had met Mordan briefly when he had awoken from being turned.

"Similar to what I felt when I first met Lishka," Dominick finished. "At first, it was more like an itch, under my skin. The lake kept pulling my attention, but I didn't know why. I assumed it was just a byproduct of the energy that flowed much more freely through the air, electrifying it."

Lishka remembered when they had first arrived, how Dominick had paused at the lakeshore. She had assumed he'd been sensing the power in the waters. She should have paid closer attention.

"Then we found the doorway and Lishka went through. When the door opened, the feeling of the light and energy overcame any other sensation. I wasn't drawn to the ice then. I was too distracted, too worried about Lishka."

"But this pull increased when Lishka returned and the doorway closed," Mordan surmised. Dominick nodded.

"Yes. After the doorway closed, the pull started to grow at the back of my mind. It didn't happen all at once. The longer we stayed, the stronger it became and when we tried to leave, the feeling became overpowering. I didn't have a choice, I had to go out onto the ice. It felt like—" Dominick's eyes flicked to Lishka, "like the sword was waiting for me to claim it. Even now, I can feel it calling to me. It feels right to hold it."

"And it felt wrong to hand it to me," Mordan asserted. Dominick nodded again. Lishka had not realized how strong the bond between Dominick and the blade had become, and she liked the weapon even less.

"What is it?" Lishka asked Mordan.

"That sword," Mordan said, "is the reason you were sent here. Oh, we needed to reach out to the fey, sure enough," he continued, silencing Lishka's unvoiced protests. "But that is the real reason you had to come. Zachriel had long suspected the fey had it. He almost came to retrieve it himself, except to do so would mean revealing the sword to Zaral."

"But why does the sword call to Dominick?" Lishka asked, momentarily setting aside the question of why Zachriel desired the blade. Beside her, Dominick shifted forward, also eager to hear Mordan's answer.

"That's the heart of it," Mordan replied. "I wasn't even sure until now, but the sword proves it."

"Proves what?" Dominick asked, and he gripped the sword a little tighter.

Mordan turned to him. "Your blood. Or rather, your bloodline. I believe you are born from one of the greatest bloodlines of ancient Britain."

Uneasiness twisted in the pit of Lishka's stomach as Mordan's words tugged at half-memories of rumors and myth.

"That," she said, "is the legendary sword?"

Mordan nodded. "If such legends are to be believed, then yes. This is the sword wielded by the High King, in a time when pagans and Christians worshipped alike, before the great Saxon invasion."

Dominick stared at the sword and loosened his grip as if it had suddenly grown hot. The blade lay still across his knees while the color drained from his face.

"But everyone knows that Arthur is just a legend,"

Lishka persisted. Even in her time, the story had been just that—a story. Though, there had always been whispers.

"There is usually some truth to legends, and some more than others," Mordan said.

Lishka did not want to voice the sword's true name. *Excalibur.*

Mordan turned to catch Dominick's eyes. "If the legend is to be believed, then you are the descendant of Morgyne le Fey and Arthur Pendragon."

Dominick's face went even whiter, the shadows under his eyes almost turning dark as bruises.

"What?" His voice sounded thick with confusion and dread.

"Mordred," Lishka whispered.

"But they were brother and sister," Dominick protested. *So he knows of the fable.*

Mordan brushed Dominick's horror away with a wave of his hand. "Only if we are believing that part of the legend. Besides, their union occurred centuries upon centuries ago, and the line has since greatly diminished, though it brings you now the ability to draw that sword." Mordan tipped his head in the direction of the blade. "And several other gifts, I'm sure."

"Wait." Lishka remembered the legends, trying to somehow discredit Mordan's revelation for Dominick's sake. "Mordred was killed. Arthur killed him."

"Mordred had already grown to manhood by the time he faced Arthur," Mordan said with gentleness, as he observed their reactions. "He had plenty of time to father a child."

Dominick stared at the sword, silent and thinking.

"The blood does not lie." Mordan once more directed

his words to Dominick, who kept his gaze lowered. "Their magik runs strong in your veins. Which means that you have some fey in your blood as well.

"Dominick."

Dominick twitched at the mention of his name.

"Only you can bear the blade to the Wielder. It is in your blood and it is your duty, and yours alone. You must bear the blade to Zachriel."

"What will Zachriel do with it?" asked Dominick, finally tearing his eyes from Excalibur to meet Mordan's.

"Zaral wants power; it is all he thinks about," Mordan said, providing a blunt summary. "Zachriel, on the other hand, seeks to restore balance to the world, between nature and humanity."

"What does that mean, to restore the balance?" Dominick asked.

"Did Lishka explain to you what the Veil is?" Mordan asked.

"She said it was a barrier caused by human disbelief in the power beyond the Veil. Or at least, that is one theory," Dominick corrected himself.

Mordan pressed his palms together as if in prayer, though Lishka could tell he was choosing his words carefully.

"When humans stopped believing in the Earth as its own living thing, as something to live with rather than simply on, they began using up its resources to satiate their deep hunger. They consumed beyond need and forsook the natural balance. In doing so, they inadvertently created the barrier that separated the Earth's energy from this world, like a soul split from its flesh.

"Regardless of whether you believe that theory, it is

proven that where human populations are denser, the Veil is much stronger. And in the wilderness scarce of humans, the Veil is thinner."

"In the North," Dominick said.

Mordan nodded.

"Zachriel wants to restore balance by returning the energy, the Source, to this world and all the creatures that inhabit it."

"By breaking the Veil," Lishka interrupted. *Zachriel means to break the Veil.* The idea seemed unthinkable; the Veil had existed since long before Lishka's birth. *What might that world look like?*

"Yes," Mordan confirmed. "He believes this is the only way to stop humans from consuming the Earth. Some agree and will go to great lengths to support him, even to war. Then there are those who have yet to choose a side. The fey," Mordan nodded to Lishka, "and the wolves among them."

"What choice is there?" Lishka's question echoed the one she had asked the Fey Queen. "Humans are destroying the world. Why shouldn't the fey and the wolves also seek to stop them, as Zachriel's followers do?" Lishka understood why both Zaral's followers and Zaral himself chose to ignore the impact human greed had on the Earth. They wanted power and would do anything to keep it, even if that meant destroying all else in the process. But the Fey Queen's ambivalence still stung.

"It is not so simple," Mordan sighed. Lishka again noted the shadows under his eyes, intensified by firelight, and she wondered when he had last fed. "There are those who wish to stay hidden. Some remember a time when humans knew they existed and hunted them. They are afraid that breaking the Veil will bring not only the Source back into the world but also the knowledge of all magikal beings with it. Humans will no longer be able to deny that they share their world. And while humans are weak as individuals, they are dangerous as a species."

"But there are people who want to see things change," Dominick argued. "There are many in the scientific community who wish to find sustainable ways of living."

"You mean the Boreal Stones."

"What do you know of them?" Dominick studied Mordan with a hunger for information.

"The Council is aware of the stones, to an extent," Mordan admitted. "Rumors entered the Coven a few years ago, of an arctic expedition set out to explore geologic landforms, but instead uncovered something shrouded in mystery. The explorers found a stone that emitted an unknown energy. At first the Covens found it easy to dismiss the rumor as exaggerated human imagination, one of their dramatic tales of the North. Even their own scientific community had largely written off the stones as another of Professor Boreal's unorthodox theories. He had quite a reputation in the community, as an eccentric explorer, and not necessarily in a respected sense.

"This may have helped Boreal," Mordan added at the defensive expression on Dominick's face. "It was easier for him to keep his study hidden, if others did not believe his theories valid."

"What changed?" Dominick asked. "What made the research suddenly draw interest?"

Lishka knew Dominick's real question: *why were he and the others murdered?* She waited for Mordan's answer, curious herself. Dominick needed to know why he had been killed, and her explanation had only partially satisfied him.

"The university published a short article on recent discoveries," Mordan explained. "It contained only a brief mention of the stones and omitted both the purpose of the study and Boreal's name altogether. Yet that was enough. A publication meant that the stones were indeed real and that the research had the possibility to be funded, to be taken seriously. Zaral could not allow humans to investigate the power in the stones, or worse, to find a way to harness the energy they contained. He could not allow humans to rediscover the Source."

"It was Professor Miller," Dominick said, his voice low. "Boreal's research partner. He was excited by the findings and wanted to solicit funding to conduct further tests. Boreal kept refusing, but Miller found a way to circumvent him."

"And he paid the price," Mordan said. They sat silent for a moment, all contemplating the fate of the professors. The fire crackled and Dominick grabbed a log close by his feet to toss onto the embers. While born of magik, the flames had become true fire and lapped eagerly at the wood.

"What happened to the study?" Dominick asked suddenly, pulling his gaze from the fire back to Mordan. Lishka had not considered how hard it must be for Dominick, to be so violently pulled from a study he had such passion for and have no news of the others involved.

"Do you mean the Boreameter?" Mordan asked, a glint in his eye.

Dominick whipped his head around to stare at Lishka. She almost flinched at the hurt on his face.

"Do not be upset with Lishka," Mordan said kindly.

"Lord Dorwan already knew of its existence, though he neglected to share this information with myself, Lady Raseska, or Lord Cutler. Something that caused a bit of tension, to be sure."

Lishka remembered the lack of reaction from Lord Dorwan when she'd told Zachriel's Council of the Boreameter.

"Lord Cutler went to the lab in secret to find it, to protect it, but it was no longer there," Mordan continued.

"What do you mean, not there?" Dominick asked, his voice sharp.

"Neither the instrument nor any of the diagrams or findings could be found. It was as if it never existed."

"Zaral?" Lishka's voice barely rose above a whisper. She did not want to look at Dominick.

Mordan shook his head. "I think not. We have not heard of any rumors that Zaral knew of the instrument, or that he now possesses it. Have you heard of the Conservatory?"

Lishka shook her head while Dominick nodded.

"The secret coalition of scientists," Dominick explained to Lishka, shifting his weight slightly toward her. At the mention of the Conservatory, he had relaxed a small amount. "It's only a rumor. Supposedly they are a private organization made up of the best minds in the scientific community. At North Pacific, they are referred to like the Freemasons and other secret historic societies. Most people don't actually believe they exist. Some do, though." The way he said this made Lishka think Dominick was in the latter camp. He turned back to Mordan. "You're saying the Conservatory took the Boreameter?"

This time Mordan nodded. "Only they could be

discreet enough to have concealed it without Lord Cutler's knowledge. Even he grudgingly respects their skill at gathering information—and their ability to keep their actions concealed from the Covens."

Lishka could only imagine Lord Cutler's reaction at being bested by humans, but then again, he did not seem the type of man who would be made angry by that. Instead, she pictured him rather impressed.

"I still don't understand why Zaral hates the study so much," Dominick said. "Doesn't he use the power too? At the White Lake, I felt so much more powerful. I could scarcely sense the Veil and the energy flowed freely, easily accessible. Even just proximity to it made me stronger, heightened my senses. Wouldn't Zaral benefit from more of it in the world?"

Mordan shook his head. "Zaral has his own power, innate to what he is. While the power beyond the Veil does give him strength, it also limits him. The Source reinforces a precise balance of life and death."

"Like any ecosystem," Dominick interjected.

"Yes," Mordan agreed. "The Source may provide you with additional power to draw from, but you'll find over time you are much more weakened during the day. While it enhances your natural strengths, so too will it intensify your weaknesses."

Lishka had not noticed any increase in her sensitivity to daylight. Instead, ever since she left the realm of the fey, she had found it easier to endure both the pain and lethargy that daylight brought. She made a mental note to mention this to Mordan later.

"The Veil mostly prevents the power beyond it from

entering this world," Mordan was saying. "Without the Source energy, Zaral can upset the balance and become even more powerful. He has nothing to temper him. He has chosen to gain additional power through dominion over mankind, whose expanding numbers have become a problem. Humans desire to possess things and because they are short-lived and thus short-sighted, they will destroy their planet to do so."

"So why would Zaral want that?" Dominick asked again. "Wouldn't he be destroyed too?"

"Zaral believes he can control them," Mordan said, and he sounded unconvinced, despite knowing Zaral's power. "He draws on the life of his followers. He does not just consume blood; his is a stronger, deeper pull on the soul, which gives him more power. Lishka has felt it."

Lishka could not help but shudder at the sudden memory Mordan's words evoked. Dominick glanced at her with concern.

"Look at the last century alone," Mordan pressed. "The creation of the atomic bomb, oil spills, massive deforestation, nuclear weapons. Human capacity for destruction has jumped exponentially in the last century. Zachriel has witnessed this change and fears for the future, as do we all. Humans will not change their course, not under Zaral's influence. Zachriel believes the Source is the only way to stop them.

"That sword was made, among many reasons, to draw those in opposition together." Mordan gestured to the blade, where Dominick rested his palms possessively against the steel, being mindful of the edge. "Arthur used it to unite the Christians and the pagans under one banner, albeit only for a short time. Zachriel will use it for something much bigger. He will use the sword to tear through the fabric of the Veil and reunite soul with flesh."

"But wouldn't such a release of energy be dangerous?" Lishka asked. She recalled the sensation of the currents beyond the Veil. They had a will of their own.

"Zaral will not allow for a slow introduction," Mordan said, and Lishka noticed he did not answer her question. "The only way is to force the restoration, before Zaral has time to prevent it."

"You said you knew of the sword," Lishka said accusingly, frustrated at Mordan's partial release of information. He had not revealed to her the true nature of their quest. "You knew that the weapon was here and that's why you sent us."

"I couldn't be sure," Mordan said. "But yes, I suspected the fey might hold it, ever since I learned of its existence, and Zachriel's plan to wield it."

Lishka reconsidered her perception of her mentor. She knew Mordan must have valid reasons for his secrecy, and yet she somehow still felt used. Had Mordan known all along that they would fail in recruiting the fey?

"How did you know the Queen would release it?" she asked instead.

"Zaral goes against everything the fey stand for. The Queen may not risk her fey in direct confrontation, but the sword is another matter." Mordan looked at Dominick. "You are the Bearer." He shifted to catch Lishka's eyes, and her anger subsided in the steady gaze of the man who had protected her for a millennium.

"The Finder will find the way. The Bearer will draw the blade. The Wielder will wield it and break the world."

Mordan's words rang like the echo of a dream, and

yet Lishka couldn't think where she would have heard them before. They carried the weight of prophecy.

"What does that mean?" she asked. The fire snapped, loud in the sudden hushed stillness of their circle.

"It is an ancient prophecy that foretold the way to return the Source," Mordan answered. "I learned of it when I learned of the sword's existence. Those of us loyal to Zachriel have been watching for the signs."

*Zachriel, Wielder. Dominick, Bearer.* And Lishka was the Finder. She had led Dominick to the fey and so to the sword. At once Lishka understood the connection that had brought her and Dominick together. They had been locked by fate, each to perform their role in bearing the sword to Zachriel and restoring the balance. Dominick's words echoed in her memory: *Where will you lead me?*

"Dominick."

At her command, he shifted to meet her eyes.

"The sword must go to Zachriel," she said, her words soft so that he knew the decision was his to make. She could almost see his thoughts churning with all that had been revealed. At last, they had the answer as to what had drawn him to Lishka in the beginning. He was the Bearer.

"I know," he said. Lishka noted the tension in his jaw and the determination in his eyes, once more driven by purpose. Dominick had thought to help humanity using the Boreal Stones. Instead, he would deliver the blade that would break the Veil.

She turned back to Mordan as a thought occurred to her.

"Mordan, how long have you known of the prophecy? Of the sword?"

"Only recently did I learn of it, in the past few decades," Mordan said, understanding her true question.

"I did not know when Zaral turned you."

His tone held something more, what almost sounded like guilt, though Lishka couldn't guess why.

"Why didn't you tell me at the Coven? Why the secret?" He'd had ample opportunity in Lady Raseska's quarters when they had assigned her to seek the fey. *Unless the other Council Members did not know of the prophecy.*

"If I had interfered, you might not have led Dominick to the sword," Mordan answered.

Lishka shook her head. "That's not good enough. You suspected the sword resided with the fey. I would have found them, knowledge of the truth or not."

Mordan sighed and it was as if the weight of the worlds pressed upon him.

"I could not be certain that regardless of your hatred, you would not betray us to Zaral."

Lishka recoiled. She had not expected such an answer. She had never considered that Mordan might not trust her.

"It's not so unbelievable," Mordan said. "Zaral has ways of compelling those to do his will other than simply through loyalty. He had just sought you out, attempting to subjugate you to his command."

Lishka tried not to react to the invoking of Zaral's violation of her in the alley. Next to her, Dominick watched them intently, trying to understand what lay unspoken between them.

"So," Lishka said at once, before Dominick could ask for an explanation. "Dominick has the blade. What do we do now?"

"Now you must take the sword to Zachriel." Mordan spoke as if it were a thing easily done.

"Where is he?" Lishka asked. For one foolish moment,

she imagined the first of their kind simply waiting at the Coven for them, back in Seattle.

"I believe he journeys North," Mordan said.

"You believe?" Lishka couldn't conceal the doubt in her voice. A weariness had begun to settle deep in her immortal bones.

"When I left the Coven over two weeks ago, the last word we had was that Zachriel made his way North, into Glacies Tellus, with many of his followers both before him and in his wake."

At once Sieth's words resurfaced. *There are rumors that members of the Coven are traveling North. Members loyal to Zachriel.*

"Wouldn't it be easier for him to meet us instead? Safer?" Dominick asked.

Mordan shook his head. "The two of you were able to mostly sneak out of the Coven unnoticed. But Zaral watches his brother's movements much more closely. He may even suspect Zachriel's intent, but he does not know of the method in which Zachriel hopes to restore the balance; he does not yet know of the blade's existence. So, you must continue in stealth to deliver it to Zachriel."

"North then," Lishka confirmed. She had never traveled so far from the Coven, not since she'd first arrived from the Old Country. What lay in the land of ice and snow had only been brought to her in rumors and stories. The thrill that had first awakened in her at the mention of the journey east, what felt much longer ago in Lady Raseska's quarters, tingled once more.

"We might make a little stop along the way." A scheming glint shone in Mordan's eyes. "How do you feel about wolves?"

# CHAPTER 24

# AN ACT OF WAR

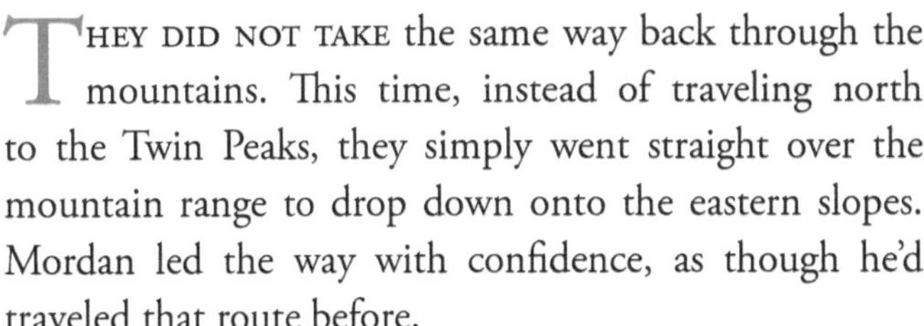

THEY DID NOT TAKE the same way back through the mountains. This time, instead of traveling north to the Twin Peaks, they simply went straight over the mountain range to drop down onto the eastern slopes. Mordan led the way with confidence, as though he'd traveled that route before.

The urgency that had pressed Lishka and Dominick to reach the fey once more nipped their heels at the discovery of the blade's true purpose. Lishka couldn't shake the sense that at any minute another tracker could appear and send word of the blade to Zaral.

As they descended, the thin snow cover dwindled even further to reveal shabby stale patches on grassy slopes; it turned to a mere dusting under the increasingly thick stands of evergreen now mixed with maple, poplar, and alder. There in the lower foothills, winter had yet to show her icy face, though the red and gold that consumed the broad, once-green leaves signaled impending frost.

On the third night of travel, they entered a valley where the musky scent of elk lingered beneath the trees. Circles of flattened grass further signaled that a herd must be passing nearby. Catching the enticing scent on the wind, Dominick tensed, and he slowed, pulled by the urge to hunt. He had fed recently enough to stave off the worst cravings, but his new body still urged him to pursue the fresh blood. Better to hunt when the opportunity for large game arose. Lishka did not know when they might return to the Coven and human civilization.

Lishka opted not to feed so that she might have a moment alone with Mordan. Dominick paused when he saw that they did not intend to join him.

"Are you okay alone with him?" Dominick ducked his head down close to Lishka, while Mordan politely wandered toward a creek that bounced its way down sloped rock, the water shimmering in filtered moonlight.

"Yes. Mordan is my mentor. While I don't like that he kept so many secrets, I trust him. He may tell me more, alone."

Dominick glanced at Mordan, who had knelt to put his hand in the cool water, and watched him for a moment.

"Go. Feed and gain strength," Lishka urged. "We'll continue east but will move slowly. Find us when you've finished."

Dominick nodded and turned to dart off into the forest. The exposed steel of Excalibur shone at the top of the ill-fitting scabbard.

Lishka walked to Mordan. The earth had turned soft underfoot with composted leaves, and each step emitted the damp, wet smell of rotted wood and soil. Her boots made little to no sound, though the ferns brushed against her calves with gentle strokes. It had rained earlier, and the droplets had become gleaming pearls on the delicate fiddleheads.

Mordan stood at her approach.

"Dominick is coming along well," he commented. "He shows satisfactory control of his bloodlust."

"Yes," Lishka agreed. "Even around the mountain men, he did not succumb to the craving."

"And his training?"

"He knows the basic spells, and then some of the more complex symbols. He has adapted to the sword quite quickly."

"Likely due to his heritage as the Bearer," Mordan surmised. "That is good. He will be an asset in the fight to come."

Lishka flinched. She had known that at some point Dominick would have to use his new skills to fight for his life, but hearing Mordan say it aloud made this all the more real. The image flickered in her memory of a human Dominick watching her leave his apartment after just learning that his world was not as he thought. She mentally shook it away.

"Why have you really come? You said you had your own mission?" Lishka half expected him not to answer her.

"As we sent you to the fey folk, so I am sent to gain the allegiance of the wolves," Mordan said.

"The wolves? They would ally with Zachriel? I thought you said they were undecided."

"As of now, they have not committed to one side or the other," Mordan confirmed. "The brothers are not openly in conflict, so the wolves have been able to wait and watch to see the outcome. But the time for open war is soon at hand. Once Zachriel has the sword, Zaral will do all that he can to stop the breaking. We will need our allies, then."

They stood silent for a minute, each in their own thoughts.

"Why you?" Lishka asked. "Why did Zachriel's Coven send you to gain the wolves' allegiance?"

"Many years ago, Zaral sent me as emissary between the wolves and the Covens. I lived with them for a time. Wolves have long lifetimes; for the most part, those that knew me are still alive, and in positions of power."

Mordan turned from her to start walking east, and Lishka followed, matching his pace.

"Why did you leave them?" She asked the question carefully; having found Mordan surprisingly open, she did not want to push too hard lest he decide to stop answering her questions.

"The Coven called me back, to serve as Zaral's Council Member."

Lishka sensed there was more to the reason, but Mordan offered no additional explanation.

"On my way back, I discovered Alaisadaille," he continued after a moment. "She told me the route to Mirna Sorne, among other things. I took the stairs and the Fey Queen made herself known to me, on the ice. She saw my allegiance had turned and so she revealed the prophecy."

"She trusted you?" Mordan's description did not sound like the Fey Queen Lishka had met, direct instead of secretive and tricksome.

"She has a unique ability to see one's true nature. I believe she had told Alaisadaille to send me to her, though neither ever confirmed it."

Lishka again remembered her own shifting reflection in the water, and the Queen's penetrating stare.

"When I returned to the Coven, I watched for who I could trust. I knew that Lady Raseska would never turn from Zachriel and so I confided in her the prophecy from the Fey Queen. It was she who suspected that the Fey Queen, clever as she is, must possess the very weapon Zachriel needed. Then we only had to watch and wait to see if a likely candidate for the Finder made themself known."

"And I was that candidate," Lishka finished. Of course, the fey blood inside her made her an obvious choice. If the fey possessed the sword, and she had the means to find them, it made sense that she would be the Finder. They had only to watch her to see if the Bearer would make himself known to her.

"I would have kept you from this, if I could," Mordan said, and Lishka knew he spoke the truth.

"I wanted to stay," Lishka confessed to him, because she had to admit it to someone, and she could not tell Dominick. "I wanted to stay with the fey. I almost did, before I remembered why I had been sent there."

"The lure of the fey is strong," Mordan acknowledged with understanding. "They can choose to be carefree, to lose themselves in their forests. For all that they are mischievous, they are also simple folk who want only to cultivate the green spaces."

As he spoke, Lishka's mind conjured golden sunlight that forever shined on green leaves and blue waters. Her skin tingled with the memory of Avalon.

"Mordan," she said, disrupting the quiet that had fallen between them. Somewhere in the distance, footsteps vibrated the earth. Dominick had fed and was now returning to them. She did not have much longer with Mordan alone. "What made you turn from Zaral?"

This was the question that had pressed upon her since she first saw Mordan in Lady Raseska's chambers.

Mordan thought for a moment, as though weighing how much to tell her.

"Zaral has always craved power and worked to gain it through control of mankind. I helped him to do so. I turned countries against one another to serve Zaral's agenda. I sowed fear-based rumors to ensure the common folk followed those whom Zaral put in power. I did not only do this for Zaral. I enjoyed manipulating the thoughts and actions of humans. I had done this as a man and gained power from it, and then Zaral turned me and unleashed me on them tenfold.

"But as the centuries passed, humans flourished. Their population increased, their civilization evolved. It is as I said, the last century has seen exponential technological advances and with it, the potential to do great damage. I began to notice what Zachriel did: that left unchecked, humans would cause untold harm to this world and all living creatures in it."

Mordan's stated motives were indeed admirable, but Lishka sensed he had left a part of the story out. He had turned against his Maker, one-half of the creator of their species. Zaral had given him power. Lishka wasn't sure that Mordan would put himself so at-risk simply because he was concerned by human ambition.

"Does Zaral suspect you?" she asked. Mordan's

motives, while intriguing, were not the most pressing concern. Though if Zaral knew Mordan's allegiances had changed, Mordan would not be standing with her now.

"It is possible," Mordan said with some unease. "He has taken me into his confidence less. He did not inform me that he intended to visit Seattle. If he told the others, they kept it secret from me, though I doubt Lord Aragnus knew. Lord Sootha, now… Ah, I think I hear Dominick."

They stopped and listened, and less than a moment later, Dominick emerged from a dense stand of spruce. His cheeks held the faintest rosy tint, and the musty smell of elk increased as he drew closer.

Mordan glanced up to the sky. A few hours of night remained, though the very edges of the sky had just begun to lighten.

"I must contact Lady Raseska. She should know that I have found you, and that we travel together to the wolves. I require someplace high to cast the spell."

"Won't that help Zaral to sense you?" Lishka asked. To make contact over such a distance would require a large amount of energy, which would attract anyone or anything magikal within miles around.

"There is that risk," Mordan acknowledged. "But I have not sensed anyone close enough, and I think this time, the risk is worth taking. If I am wrong, anyone who senses my magik will be too far away to catch up to us before we enter wolf territory. To enter their territory uninvited would be an act of war."

Before Lishka could utter another word of protest, Mordan leapt from her side to disappear into the forest. Unlike Dominick, his boots made no sound and soon she could not detect where he had gone.

"One would never know his age," Dominick observed. Lishka glanced at him in surprise, and he smiled. "Did he tell you anything useful?

"He has betrayed Zaral," Lishka said, returning her gaze to where Mordan had vanished. She felt odd saying it out loud, as though she herself betrayed Mordan. "He knew of the prophecy long before I met you, had suspected I was the Finder due to my fey blood. I wonder, if Sieth had not found you so quickly, would Mordan have intervened to keep you safe?"

Dominick shrugged as if to say it didn't matter now. They stood in silence for several minutes, listening to the night forest about them and waiting for Mordan to return.

"How do you feel?" Lishka asked after a short time, and she faced Dominick to assess him. She realized she had not checked on him since they'd learned of his heritage and of his role as the Bearer. Dominick's left fingers twitched and Lishka knew he wanted to draw the blade, to hold it in his hand.

"It's weird. When you're a kid, you dream about one day doing great things. Who wouldn't want to be Arthur, the one who pulls the sword? But those are just myths, legends." Dominick frowned. "I know I should feel different, but I don't. Not really. I guess it's a relief to know why I was drawn to you, why this happened." He gestured to his body. "Though I would be lying if I said I was thrilled at descending from incest."

"Morgyne was a strong and powerful woman. She fought hard for those she loved, and for what she believed in. You should be honored." Lishka said this to comfort Dominick, but even as the words left her lips, she sensed the truth behind them. Her learnings from the Followers had not been as forgotten as she'd thought.

"Did you know her?" Dominick asked, at once surprised.

"No," Lishka shook her head. "She was a legend in my time as well. But that legend carried more truth then, and the women of my clan held great respect for her. She was revered as the most powerful High Priestess who had ever lived."

"I keep forgetting how old you really are," Dominick commented, and at once the distance between them felt vast.

The sounds of rustling ferns drew their attention. Mordan appeared, almost a blur as he ran between the trees.

"We must hurry," he called to them. In half a second, he stood before them, then ran past before Lishka had time to react. Both she and Dominick leapt after him, soon catching his pace as he slowed minutely for them.

"What's wrong?" Lishka asked.

"It has begun." Mordan's voice was grim. "Zaral has openly moved against Zachriel. He has attacked the Seattle Coven."

Lishka almost stopped in surprise, then caught herself.

"What happened? Who survived?" She began to mentally catalog those she cared about enough to want to see them live. *Kristoph. Kiaban. Lady Raseska.*

"Many died, Darrak among them. Syral will no doubt be out for blood. They had sided with Zaral, so when the attack came, it was led by those within the Coven. But we triumphed and drove those surviving from the city.

Kiaban made the armory safe and so the attackers do not have the advantage of those weapons and spellwork, at least. I do not know how the other Covens fared, though I suspect they endured their own civil wars."

"Sieth?" Lishka couldn't help asking. Dominick stiffened beside her, though he kept pace.

"He managed to slither off, no doubt to join his Master."

Lishka allowed herself a brief moment of disappointment.

"It gets worse." Mordan slowed. "Lord Barik has betrayed us. He has sided with Zaral."

Lord Barik, made by Zachriel and sworn to him.

"But how can that be possible?" Lishka asked. "He is bound to Zachriel through blood."

"As you are to Zaral?" Mordan challenged. "As am I? Oh it is possible, though I am remiss for not suspecting him."

A thought stopped Lishka in her tracks, and Mordan and Dominick halted with her.

"Did Lord Barik know?" Lishka asked. "Did he know that Dominick and I headed east, to the fey?"

"While I did not think to question Lord Barik's loyalty, it seems Lady Raseska was much more perceptive. She excluded him from our plans around both your mission and the sword, which is fortunate for us."

"Why now?" Dominick interjected. "Everything you've said alludes to Zaral working in the shadows. Why would he attack Zachriel now and risk defeat?"

"It is a *challenge*," Lishka said quietly, at once understanding.

"Yes," Mordan said. "It is a challenge to Zachriel

to face him. Zaral must see Zachriel's movement to the North as a sign that Zachriel has discovered a way to return the Source. He is trying to distract him by forcing a war. Also, and I do not say this to frighten you but rather to warn you—"

Lishka and Dominick spared a quick glance for each other.

"The blade is made of the Source direct, as are the Fey Queen, Zachriel, and Zaral. They are linked. When Dominick pulled the sword and brought it into this world, so too would there have been an effect on Zachriel and Zaral."

"Why did you not say this before?" Lishka asked, her voice now heated with anger and fear. "You said Zaral does not know of the blade."

"He cannot know of it, for if he did, he would have found us in an instant. He must not know what the pull meant. But he may suspect that it is a part of Zachriel's plan, which would spur him to action. Zaral has long been plotting his move. It is no coincidence that he appeared in Seattle when he did. Lady Raseska reports the massing of an army, in the upper boundaries of Glacies Tellus, and they do not belong only to Zachriel. She told me of a rumor from the North, of a great dark presence. Zaral prepares to strike, before Zachriel can make his move, and I can only assume that the dark presence is the evil of this army. Or—" Mordan shook his head. "But no, it cannot be. It is impossible."

"What?" Lishka asked. "What is it?"

Mordan shook his head again. "Rumors are not always truth. I may yet be mistaken. Now we must go. We must deliver that to Zachriel." He gestured to the blade. "And the Goddess willing, we go with the wolves as well."

They took off once more, traveling down into the lower foothills of the mountains where thick forest unfurled like a blanket over the rolling wild of what would soon become Uru. They ran well into dawn, though it pained Mordan the most to do so. They stopped only as the light began to reach through the canopy, before resuming their journey once more at dusk. Lishka and Dominick kept close together, the weight of the sword pressing upon them. Lishka did not want to see him again come to harm, not if she could help it.

The following night, the dark forests of Uru came into view. As if in ominous prediction, angry gray thunderclouds growled in the distance, moving steadily closer even as the travelers entered the very edge of the wolf kingdom.

PART III

# WIELDER

# CHAPTER 25

# URU

THE AIR SHIFTED PERCEPTIBLY the moment they neared Uru's borders. The forest vibrated with primal energy and beneath the looming trees, bushes crouched in the shape of great beasts to play tricks on skittish minds. Lishka's instincts hummed, and she could tell by the shift in Dominick's step that he felt the change as well. Mordan did not allow them to enter and instead led the way north, parallel to the boundary of wolf country.

"The wolves have their own set of rules," Mordan explained. "We must show the proper respect." He inhaled the forest scent, tensing as he caught something else. Briefly, but not so quick that Lishka missed it, the echo of a smile flashed across Mordan's face. "I smell wolves nearby, likely patrolling the border. I am known to this pack's Alpha; I will go and present myself to them. Wait here for my return."

With a rustle of fern, he disappeared into the underbrush.

Dominick and Lishka surveyed the forest around them. Lishka had not sensed the wolves, beyond an edginess that gnawed at her and made her want to run, to hunt, to move, to do anything but wait. Dominick seemed less affected. He walked several paces to sit down on an old, twisted nurse log, rub his face with his hands, and smooth back his hair. The waves quickly bounced back to flop over his forehead.

Anxiety pushed Lishka to take some sort of action. Unlike Dominick, she couldn't bring herself to stay still. She paced a small circle around Dominick, constantly examining the surrounding landscape. A mouse's skittering footsteps through the dried leaves, the rustle of an owl's wings, the burrowing of an earthworm, each caught her ears, drew her attention. This territory belonged to another predator, and she didn't know yet if they were welcome in it.

"How long do you think he'll be gone?" Dominick asked. Though his words were softly spoken, his voice sounded loud in the subdued forest.

"I can't say."

Lishka thought she heard something in the woods, the crack of branches beneath a heavy paw.

Dominick followed her gaze for a moment and then leaned his head back to observe the moon that had just begun to peek out from behind the thunderclouds. The storm they'd seen earlier had dissipated, though the clouds still hung heavy, the threat of rain filling the air with moisture.

"Where do they come from?" Dominick asked.

"The wolves?" Lishka strained to hear past the ordinary night noises, to sense something of the creatures she knew lived out in the deeper parts of the forest.

"Yeah. How did they become wolves? Were they people first? Or wolves that became human?"

Lishka refocused on Dominick, having found nothing to cause alarm.

"I don't know. I'm not sure they do either, or if they do, they keep their origins close. Wolves can be very secretive. They're pack animals, and they keep close to the pack. There are stories, myths, if you will," she added, remembering rumors that traveled through the Coven on the infrequent occasions the wolves drew attention and became a topic of interest. "Who knows if they bear any kernels of truth."

Temporarily reassured that they remained alone, Lishka sat down against a tree close to Dominick's nurse log. Her sword she unstrapped from her back to place within easy reach at her side. Dominick leaned back on his elbows against a thick branch of vine maple that paralleled his log, waiting for her to go on. His double swords lay crossed at his back to extend their pommels behind each ear, Excalibur rising a few inches higher than Kiaban's blade, almost like his own set of uneven antlers.

"In Greek mythology, they tell the story of Lycaon," Lishka continued once settled. "Lycaon was a great king, yet he was a tyrant. As in many of the Grecian myths, he mocked the gods, and they struck back. And so he fled in terror. As he ran, he howled and tried to speak, but only foam dripped from his mouth. He was gripped by blood thirst. He attacked the herders' sheep, and his arms, legs, and clothing became shaggy hair. He turned into a wolf. Lycanthrope."

"I remember that one," Dominick interjected. "In

my freshman year at North Pacific, I took a class on Greek literature." He trailed off, no doubt remembering a time when the subjects of such stories remained safely fictional.

"Another legend tells of an ancient people who celebrated the Moon, sister to the Earth Goddess," Lishka said, drawing Dominick's attention away from his past. "They worshipped her, dutifully, loyally, never faulting in their devotion. And so she granted them a second form, the powerful and graceful wolf. The wolves can change at will, except during the full moon, when the Goddess holds her sway, reminding them that it was she who gave them their gift. They continue to worship her to this day, lifting their heads and howling their praise when she is at her fullest and most beautiful."

Dominick had been watching Lishka as she spoke and at her last word he raised his head back to the moon, wholly revealed now, almost full and surrounded by a ring of glowing clouds.

"I like the second one best. Even if it is only a story."

"I do too." Lishka rested her head against the rough trunk. Moonlight shone between the wide maple leaves, turning them into black silhouettes. Under the wolves' forest canopy, the air grew heavy. In the open spaces, rock and moss lay exposed, doused in cool light, while shadows gathered thick beneath the trees. The wind that pushed the clouds doggedly across the sky diluted to only a soft breeze closer to the earth.

As if in prediction of the pending rain, a mist began to fall. Frogs in a nearby pond added their own calls to the night, raising their voices in a final farewell before winter hibernation.

Despite their peaceful surroundings, Lishka's thoughts raced in circles, always returning to the news of the Coven. She had assumed they would return there, and that Dominick might find his own place in the hierarchy where she could help keep him relatively safe from Zaral's followers.

*What does the Coven look like now? Mordan said Zachriel's followers secured it, but at what cost?*

Lishka snuck a glance at Dominick and felt the familiar guilt, the heavy burden of responsibility. He had lost his place too, although he might not yet realize it. They had become adrift, with only each other for tethers in the coming war.

Near sunrise, a long, solitary howl marked the end of the night. It sounded many miles away, fading as it drew even further back into the recesses of Uru's forests.

A noise slithered through the underbrush. It could have been the step of a deer, or the shuffle of a little mouse hunting earthworms. Lishka tensed nonetheless. She strained her senses, and the sound came again, same as before, the slow press of a boot into mulched earth. Lishka leapt to her feet, drawn sword in hand.

*Mordan would not approach with such stealth.*

Dominick's head snapped up, his thoughts pulled back from wherever they had wandered. Lishka caught his eyes, and she didn't need to tell him to be on guard. He rose to a half-crouch, and with silent care, drew Excalibur up from the scabbard on his back to bring it before him. The silver flashed in light.

*Light?*

Lishka spared a second of her attention to glance at the quickly changing sky. They had waited too long for

Mordan, and now daybreak's fingers stroked the forest canopy, lighting up the treetops.

Instinctively, she and Dominick drew close together, their backs against one another. A wisp of brown flitted between the trees to the left, neither wolf nor human, for not even a mage could move at that speed. Lishka fixated on the assumed path of the creature, and her fingers traced the symbols of an offensive spell while the words formed in her throat.

The footsteps retreated and only the vibrations in the earth revealed the creature's location. Lishka focused her attention on the dense undergrowth to their left. Whoever it was, they did not want to attack outright, or else they would have done so already. With Dominick on guard, Lishka reached out once more with her other sense.

A coldness snapped back at her touch: a newly made vampire, strong but unskilled and unable to defend against Lishka's influence. Disbelief sought to crowd out what she knew to be fact—this vampire had been made as recently as Dominick. Until that moment, she had understood Dominick to be the only vampire created in at least half a century. This new vampire was proof, even more so than Mordan's announcement of the attack on the Seattle Coven, that the rule of law governing both Great Covens had dissolved. Lishka pressed harder against the new vampire's mind, ignoring the sharp taste of Zaral's bloodline that infused their aura.

The vampiric presence vanished as quickly as it had come. A primal musk filled the still space beneath the trees and Lishka and Dominick pressed together, eyes watchful for the new threat. Around them the underbrush rippled, and several large wolves stepped out from the waist-high ferns, lips pulled back to reveal long, glistening teeth.

Lishka did not move, though neither did she lower her sword. The wolves encircled them. Suddenly, the wolf closest threw its head back and let loose a long, keening howl. Barely disturbing the ferns, the wolves retreated to disappear back into the forest, the thudding footsteps of their great paws indicating a southwestern direction.

Lishka stared into the brush after them, unsure what to make of both their rapid arrival and departure. A hooded figure materialized from the space they had gone, the shadows pulling back to reveal Mordan.

Lishka lowered her sword though she did not sheath it, for beside Mordan strode a lean sandy-haired man with the shadow of the wolf on his face.

"This is Luka," Mordan said by way of introduction. "His patrol is gathered just five miles from here. We will convene with them and travel to the rest of the pack, about a three-days' journey north."

Lishka sheathed her sword warily. "What about the vampire?"

Dominick followed her lead, hiding Excalibur's gleam once more in dull leather.

"We'll take care of him," Luka growled, and then ruined the threat with a wide smile. His sharp teeth shone against the tree shadows.

Beside Lishka, Dominick's attention flickered between Luka and the forest beyond. His back and shoulders tensed as he fought the instinct to follow the wolves in the hunt for their would-be attacker. Lishka pushed down her own need to pursue. She did not like the idea of allowing the wolves to dispatch the vampire before she had a chance at interrogation.

"This land belongs to the wolves, as does the right to protect its boundaries," Mordan said, reading their body language. "The wolves will want the honor of doing so."

Lishka nodded in acknowledgement, though she couldn't shake her unease. She had sensed something all too familiar in the vampire's aura, more distinct than the taste of Zaral's blood. She wondered if Dominick had felt it, too.

Sieth's gift as both a mage and a vampire involved the binding of those he turned. Beyond the normal Maker influence, the attachment crossed over into something that bordered unquestioning obedience. For this reason, Zachriel's Coven had barred him from creating new vampires many centuries ago.

Yet Lishka had caught the smell of Sieth in this vampire's blood. The bond would supersede any sense of self-preservation. Lishka had heard rumors that Sieth could enter the minds of those he turned, see through their eyes, even somewhat control their actions.

She recalled Mordan's words: *He managed to slither off, no doubt to join his Master.*

Lishka once more probed the area around them. Only the whiff of wolf lingered beneath the trees. Not reassured, she moved to follow Mordan and Luka as they turned back the way they had come, to lead deeper into the forest. Dominick grabbed her arm to draw her back.

"He's seen the sword," he whispered, leaning close. "The vampire. I saw his face, just before he ran off. I think he knew it was different."

Dread weighted her stomach.

"Then we had better hope the wolves catch him," she responded. If the vampire got a message to Sieth before the wolves caught him, or worse, if Sieth had been watching them through those eyes, he would know the sword was different. He would go directly to Zaral.

Lishka fought the irrational impulse to put her hand to the brand on her neck, as if covering Zaral's mark could somehow break her own bond.

"Come. We're running out of night." She broke from Dominick's hold and darted after Mordan, Dominick close behind, to cross together over the boundary into Uru.

LUKA BROUGHT THEM to a protected place, a shallow valley in the Uruan hills and the rendezvous of his patrol pack. Forest flowed from the hillside into the valley, interrupted by hovel-sized boulders that had rolled down to rest and provide homes for lush green mosses. At the southern side, a jumble of boulders formed a rock outcrop and several wolves perched there to oversee the rest of the valley.

The camp appeared to contain at least five dozen male and female wolves, though the number constantly changed as more appeared, silent yet unsurprising to those near them. At the arrival of wolves, those who lay about in the underbrush rose to their feet, yawned, and then disappeared into the trees and did not return.

Not all wolves wore their fur. Some walked about on two feet, lightly clothed in woven tunics and pants of various greens and browns to match the forest. As Luka led them into the camp, both wolf and human eyes stared at Mordan, Lishka, and Dominick. Luka, who had remained in human form as a courtesy, glanced back at them in reassurance.

"Don't worry," Luka said, keeping close to show his pack that they presented no threat. "My wolves were expecting you, though many will not have seen your kind before."

"Are the wolves really that private?" Lishka asked. It seemed strange that in such a rapidly shrinking world, the wolves could remain so isolated.

"The world is changing. By keeping close to the territory, we keep Uru safe." Luka led them through the trees to the hillside, where rock rose from the earth. Ferns grew from its crevices over a narrow opening. Luka gestured to the fissure.

"It's small, but large enough to fit the three of you."

Lishka peered inside and the smell of wolf assaulted her nose, pungent in the confined space.

"Thank you, Luka," Mordan said, and Luka flashed him another bright smile.

A trio of fallen trees lay balanced beside the rock, having toppled in a recent windstorm. Luka perched on one and invited them to do the same, his high energy subdued for the moment by a captive audience.

"There is a restlessness spreading among wolfkind, one that even Urith is finding hard to control." Luka focused on Dominick, as though he sensed Dominick's lack of knowledge. "King Urith rules over Uru as the High Alpha," Luka explained. "There are thirteen packs, thirteen territories across Uru, and Urith leads them all. He is descended from a long line of Alphas who have helped Uru to prosper, despite the alarming spread of mankind."

"Of course, he has had some help," Mordan interjected, his words light but not without underlying meaning.

"Yes," Luka conceded with a dip of his head. "Though it is the strength of his Alphas, and the strength of the land, that gives him the power to protect Uru and keep it strong." Luka shared a meaningful look with Mordan, and Lishka couldn't help but sense their familiarity.

*Mordan already knew Luka.* The realization came to her with a jolt, and she studied Luka with newly appraising eyes.

"The spread of mankind, and their technology, has not escaped the wolves' notice. Urith is not convinced of Zachriel's plans to return the knowledge of magik to humankind, as this will bring Uru back into the world of man," Luka said bluntly. Lishka shared a surprised glance with Dominick.

"I apprised Luka of our mission," Mordan said, correctly judging their reactions. "He is to be trusted."

"Uru is not so isolated that we don't take notice of the events that will affect the wolves." Luka smiled slightly. "We have lived alongside the Covens since we first took our wolfskins and know well how to read when change is coming. Besides, our Queen has her own way of getting information." He seemed to direct this last statement to Mordan, though Mordan did not react. Luka continued.

"So far, Uru remains far enough north of human development to avoid their attention. Their technology does not work well here, and many are too scared, too worried of hardship, to come this far, save for the northern settlers at the edge of the ice land."

"Do those people know about the wolves?" Dominick asked. He leaned toward Luka, all anxiety about their attacker now forgotten, clearly excited to hear more about wolfkind. Lishka noted at once that any bloodlust Dominick had felt around humans seemed to have disappeared. Of course, she reminded herself, the wolves had more than human blood in them, their own magik a natural deterrent against vampire hunger.

Luka nodded in response to Dominick's question.

"They follow the Old Ways and respect the wolf territory. In turn, the wolves mostly leave them alone, except when we allow them to trade at our borders. Yet if Zachriel breaks the Veil, Uru will be exposed to the greater world. Those who live in the North are more tolerant, shall we say, to living alongside stronger kin. Urith cannot be sure how humans will react to the knowledge that they share their world with beings more powerful than they." Almost as an afterthought, he added, "They are weak, but they are many."

"But that is not the thinking of all wolves," Mordan said.

"No, it's not," agreed Luka. "Some of us know it's only a matter of time before humans reach our borders, despite their ignorance. With the return of the balance, Uru could once again gain its foothold in the world, grow even stronger."

Luka spoke of Uru as one entity, his pride showing as he described Uru's strength.

"Queen Vissa strongly considers what Zachriel proposes. She is the Alpha of my pack," Luka explained to Lishka and Dominick. Luka shifted his attention back to Mordan. "Others will listen to her, if you can convince her to speak in Uruden on Zachriel's behalf. She leans but is still undecided. You must present your case to her first. She is your best chance of convincing Urith to follow Zachriel into battle. He will listen to her, as will the others." Luka smiled. "Our Queen is fierce and cunning. She won her right to her throne with skill, the first of her kind."

Curiosity pricked Lishka at the notion of meeting the first Wolf Queen. She had heard her spoken of offhandedly at the Coven, though at the time she didn't pay much attention to the happenings of the wolves. Vissa had earned her throne to become the only female Alpha in all of wolf history.

"How is she?" Mordan asked the question carefully—a little too carefully, in a way that insinuated some intimacy with the subject.

"She is well." Luka's smile broadened. "She will be interested to see you." His words did not give away whether the Queen would be pleased or not. Luka rose to his feet, signaling the end of their conversation. "Wait here for now. As long as you travel with my patrol, you'll be safe. I'll round up the rest. We leave at dusk."

With that, he sprang away into the forest. Lishka heard the popping of bone and the cracking of the spine elongated as Luka mutated from man to wolf. Dominick stood and peered through the underbrush to catch a glimpse of the change, but Luka moved too quickly and had already disappeared.

Mordan rose as well and drew his hood up to cover his face. He turned his back to them to enter the narrow cave. Lishka burned to ask him questions about his time with the wolves, but sensed he did not wish to talk. The daylight pulled at her, made her groggy, and Mordan with his greater age would only feel it all the more.

Under the thick canopy of fir, hemlock, maple, and cedar, the only sun that managed to penetrate in narrow patches turned a faint green, losing its potency. The green reminded Lishka of another forest, a place of eternal summer. Nearby, wolves prowled the valley or lay resting on beds of moss. Despite her awareness of the predators, for the moment Lishka felt comforted by their presence. Luka had assured them of their safety as guests of the wolves, and Mordan certainly seemed to trust him. Lishka wanted to think on all that Luka had told them, but the daylight weighed too heavily. Instead, she followed Dominick into the cave, which was not quite so snug as it had appeared from the outside. There she allowed herself to slip into the comatose daysleep, with Mordan and Dominick reassuringly beside her.

With the end of autumn, night fell more swiftly upon the forest. Lishka rose at dusk to discover that more wolves had joined the hunting pack, filling the narrow valley. The wolves jostled for attention, nipping at each other in a continual play for dominance. Their blood ran hot in their veins and warmed the air around them.

Luka had spoken of the wolves' restlessness, and it showed in the way they paced the valley, unable to stay still. The urgency crept under Lishka's skin as well and drove her to her feet.

Despite the chill in the air, the wolves who took on their human form wore minimal clothing and kept their feet bare. Like Lishka's kind, they did not seem to feel cold the way humans did. In an absurd thought quite separate from the severity of their mission, Lishka wondered where their clothes went when they changed.

A man approached her, wearing no shirt at all, a wide expanse of tawny chest. When Lishka thought he might stop, he took several paces closer past a socially acceptable distance to peer intently into her eyes. Lishka remained still and studied him in return. Where his body emitted heat, she emanated a deep chill and so even the air between them became combative.

The silence dragged out. Behind her, Dominick had risen as well and observed them, as did several of the nearby wolves. Mordan had disappeared.

"I've never seen a vampire before," the wolf said abruptly. Lishka did not respond, as the statement did not merit it.

"You're very pale," he added. He leaned an inch closer, his breath warm against her cheeks. "Do all vampires have purple eyes?" His own eyes glinted mischievously.

"Do all wolves have blue ones?" Lishka countered. The wolf winked one of his bright blue eyes at her.

"Nah, I'm just a lucky one." He slapped her heavily on the shoulder and his eyes widened to find her solid and unmoving. He appraised her once more. "You're alright. I am Nolan."

Lishka sensed she had passed some sort of test. The wolves around them relaxed, losing interest in the interaction. Wolves respected power, and she had not retreated from his aggression.

"I am Lishka. This is Dominick." She nodded behind her to Dominick, who took a step closer to join them.

Dominick outstretched his hand in a very human gesture. Nolan looked at it and then at Dominick in surprise. When the moment might have gotten awkward, he reached out and took Dominick's hand in a firm shake.

"Welcome to Morvane," Nolan said.

"Morvane?" Dominick asked. "I thought this was Uru."

Nolan grinned.

"Morvane is one of Uru's packs and of course is the best of them all." He turned to retreat to his companions, who had watched the entire altercation from a stand of maple trees. Dominick departed from Lishka's side to follow him.

"Does it hurt to change into wolf?" Dominick asked boldly, seizing the invitation to join them. Nolan shook his head.

"No. Well, a little at first," Nolan conceded. "But soon it becomes a welcome pain, to take on our strongest form."

Dominick nodded as though he understood.

"And you can change at any time?" he asked. Nolan glanced at him, a curious smile on his weathered face.

"Of course. Wolf pups change when they enter their thirteenth year, and then change until they die."

Arriving at Nolan's group, Dominick interrupted his questioning to shake hands and introduce himself; the group reciprocated with clear delight. Lishka, confident Dominick would come to no harm, turned her attention back to their surroundings and spotted Mordan further away, deep in conversation with Luka. Mordan glanced over, feeling her eyes on him, and interrupted his conversation to walk toward her.

"Luka is awaiting his runners," Mordan said once he'd reached her, answering her unasked question. "His pack split into smaller groups to better patrol the boundary, so he sent runners to either bring them back or give them instruction. Some will remain at the border to guard, while the rest will escort us to their den, to meet with Queen Vissa. They caught the vampire."

Relief helped her to relax just the slightest. There was still a chance their mission remained secret.

"I sensed Sieth in his blood," Lishka said, keeping her voice low; the wolves possessed incredible hearing.

"I know. But I think Luka's wolves managed to dispatch him before any message got out. Though we cannot know for sure," Mordan added, dispelling any reassurance. "Use of our magik on wolf soil is forbidden, so I cannot warn Lady Raseska. We must proceed on our path with haste."

They stood silent for a moment, watching the wolves' activity.

"Is it normal for this many to guard the border?" Lishka asked, noting how large the pack had grown. Mordan shook his head.

"This is an unusual size. The wolves frequently check their borders, but only in times of unrest do they send so many to keep vigilant."

Mordan's assessment further underscored what Luka had told them. Times were changing.

Still with his newfound wolf friends, Dominick remained oblivious for the moment to their conversation. He tested his strength and skill against the wolves in play-fighting. One wolf had changed to wolfskin and prowled sneakily around Dominick, who was occupied with wrestling a wolf still in human flesh. Lishka narrowed her eyes, thinking Dominick hadn't noticed the second challenger. The wolf pulled back his lips to reveal long, sharp teeth, crouched, and then sprang up. At the last moment, Dominick spun around, caught him by his shoulders to avoid the teeth, and hurled him back. The wolf flew several yards through the air to hit the ground with a thud.

While the others jeered, letting fly childish taunts and insults, the wolf got up and shook himself, head hung sheepishly, his mouth now turned up in a toothy wolf grin.

Dominick's laugh peeled out from him uninhibited, contagious to the group who couldn't help but join him. The man he had wrestled with clapped his hands on Dominick's back, then threw a brotherly arm about his shoulders.

*How easily Dominick integrated into the pack.*

"It is hard not to like them," Mordan commented. "They remind us of what it was like to be human."

Lishka caught a wistfulness in his voice, though he kept his words light.

"They live intensely, their emotions running high, and they like to play and enjoy their time," Mordan continued. "Don't let that deceive you; they also like a good fight. You would not want to be on the other end of that in a battle."

The wolf Dominick had thrown sauntered back to the group, muscles hard and taut beneath thick fur.

"No," Lishka agreed. Again, she wondered at Mordan's time spent with the wolves. She opened her mouth to ask him, when Dominick peeled away from the wolves to rejoin them. He couldn't help the smile that stretched across his face, nor the delight in his eyes. Lishka had not seen him so lighthearted before, not even as a human.

"What's the plan?" he asked. Mordan reiterated what he had told Lishka. Just as he finished, a long low howl split the forest noises, seeping through the shadow and bramble. They turned to the source.

A long-legged, sandy-colored wolf stood on a rocky outcrop to the south of where the pack had gathered. *Luka.* Around them, wolves rose to their feet and Dominick received his wish, for those that had not yet transitioned bent low to the ground. Joints popped and reversed, spines lengthened, jaws broke and protruded to grow into strong, bone-crushing muzzles. Fur spread along bare spines to coat the wolves in a variety of thick hides, in varying browns, mottled gray, black, and a flash here and there of red.

Energy thrummed through the air. Clouds amassed overhead and, in the distance, thunder rumbled against the horizon. Yet the moon's pull remained strong. It hung almost full behind its blanket and the blood of the wolves ran hot.

Lishka glanced at Dominick. He grinned and excitement made his eyes flash red. A thrill rushed through her body, flooded with adrenaline. They could not resist the power of the wolves in their true form, the bond of the pack, and the urge to run fast across the unbroken forests of Uru.

At once, Luka leapt off the outcrop, a shining flash against the shadow, before his paws hit the ground in an explosion of moss and dirt. Another leap and he flew into the trees, the rest of the pack hot on his heels. Lishka momentarily let go of all worry, and together with Mordan and Dominick, embraced the energy of the wolves to dive after them into the thick Uruan forest.

# THE GOLDEN EYE PACK

S WORD FERNS, VINE MAPLES, and decaying nurse logs pervaded the space beneath Uru's trees, so that barely any light penetrated down to the forest floor. The darkness did not matter to the wolves, who had sharp eyes, and even stronger smell and hearing. They knew this land, from the rugged evergreen at the edge of the mountains, to the thick deciduous groves in the center of the rolling valleys, to the windswept rocky tundra that bordered the northern territory of Glacies Tellus, the ice land.

Lishka, Dominick, and Mordan did not need to know the forest. They could see clearly as if in daylight, with hearing to match the wolves, and smell almost as fine. They swept through the undergrowth effortlessly, keeping close together as a trio. On either side of them, the sinuous forms of wolves bounded over logs and wound about the trees. Lishka relished their unbound energy, their simple joy of the run. Overhead, thunder rolled closer, muffled by the thudding of wolf paws. The wolves had no need for stealth. This territory belonged to them, and all who lived there knew it.

At last, the clouds released, and a steady curtain of rain fell through the upper canopy to run in rivulets through Lishka's hair. Ferns brushed against her calves, testing the waterproof leather of her boots. Where her feet hit the ground, the rich smell of dirt mixed with decomposing leaves filled the air.

They ran for hours without break or change in pace. Beneath the excitement and thrill of the night lurked the ever-present sense of urgency. *Zachriel must have the blade.* Dominick ran beside her, the sword strapped tightly to his back.

Even the joy of the run could not silence the thoughts that swirled in her head. For now, they had the protection of the pack. *But has the vampire managed to get a message to Sieth?* Not even the power of the wolves could stand against Zaral if he knew they sheltered the blade, the weapon that could undo his plans.

Lishka shoved down dark imaginings of worst-case scenarios. Uru's forest left no room for doubt, no forgiveness of weakness. She must follow Mordan's lead and move forward with their mission. Only the wolves' allegiance mattered. The rest would have to wait until they passed out of Uru's borders.

*Or until the danger finds us.*

The rainfall turned into a steady drizzle, which in turn created a damp mist that hung caught below the trees. When day arrived, they barely noticed but for the tugging that pulled them to sleep. The dense layer of cloud blocked the strongest rays, while the lush canopy further diluted what light managed to trickle through. For the moment, the sky stood with them, helping them along.

At midday, the wolves stopped beneath the trees. They were strong but still mortal and their bodies needed both water and rest. Lishka itched to continue, but no wolf would allow a vampire to traverse their territory unescorted. They resumed their run at dusk, continuing in this way for the next two days.

On the third day, a change in the wolves' stride alerted Lishka to the end of their run. Wolf eyes looked not to the now-brightening sky, but instead eagerly ahead to their packmates who awaited their return.

Leading the run, Luka let out a welcoming howl to announce their arrival. A long high-pitched call answered him from somewhere up ahead of them, the voice distinctly female. She let her howl taper off in several playful yips, drawing the wolves onward. Her notes lingered in the air, clinging to the raindrops. Ahead but still near enough to Mordan, Lishka, and Dominick, Luka's ears pricked forward and Lishka detected an eager bounce in his step.

Trees and underbrush began to thin, revealing well-trod paths twisting through the woods. Through the trunks, Lishka caught a glimpse of humble wooden structures, what must be the wolves' more permanent homes. The wolves' loping run turned to a steady trot and Mordan slowed with them. Lishka and Dominick kept close, not knowing what sort of welcome they might expect from the greater part of the pack.

A nimble brown wolf, streaks of copper highlighting her thick fur, sprang toward the wolves to slam into Luka. Being quite a bit smaller, she barely moved him.

He stopped in his tracks as she poked at his sides with her nose and nipped at his chin. His mouth turned up in a wide toothy smile as he absorbed her increasingly rough blows. Finally, her playful assault subsided, and she tossed a curious glance at his guests before joining his side to lead them deeper into the wolf settlement. She was the first of many wolves who arrived to greet them, and they witnessed several playful interactions as pack members welcomed the patrol home.

As they progressed, the narrow forest path turned into a wider main thoroughfare lined with roughly constructed wooden homes. Bushels of dried plants and animal hides hung from many doorways, and a symbol of what looked like the three moon cycles—waxing crescent, full moon, and waning crescent—had been carved into doors and window frames. Curious eyes peered out from the doorways and trees. Blue eyes like Nolan's appeared to be in the minority; Lishka observed most of the wolves possessed amber irises, many bright enough they could be considered gold. They would have trouble blending in outside Uru, as their eyes rivaled her own in their oddity.

Ahead, the remaining trees parted to reveal a large building of wood and stone that loomed above the others, surrounded by a crowd of interested wolves both in human and wolf form.

"Morvane Den," Mordan said. Lishka appraised the main holding of this pack. Grander than the little houses surrounding it, the Den was perhaps a fifth the size of the Coven mansion and nowhere near its extravagance. Still, the structure appeared soundly built. Rows of thick stone blocks made up its sides, carved from the surrounding mountain granite. Five deep stairs led up to the wide entryway platform, where two heavy wooden pillars supported the overhanging roof. Surprisingly intricate carvings of the trees, wolves, and the moon in various stages wove about the pillars to frame the high arched doors of the Den, which had been thrown open to reveal a dark interior.

"What does that mean, Den?" Dominick asked, also studying the building with open interest.

"It is the center of the pack Morvane, more commonly known as the Golden Eye pack," Mordan explained. "Here Queen Vissa, Alpha of Morvane, holds her station."

Luka returned to them then, having transitioned back to his human form. He wore only a pair of soft leather trousers, and a fine blond fur still dusted his chest.

"Our Queen is not here," Luka said, before Mordan could ask. "She is on the hunt, though she should be back by dusk."

If the news disappointed Mordan, he did not show it.

"Wait here, I will see if there are open rooms in the Den." As quickly as he had checked in, Luka bounded off again, scaling the Den's stairs in long strides.

The clouds overhead glowed with early morning sunlight attempting to pierce through. Mordan drew his hood up a little further around his face and tucked his hands into the folds of his long coat.

"More waiting," Lishka murmured. Mordan did not reply. Beside her, Dominick shuffled his feet and watched the wolves about them. The energetic activity had only slightly diminished since they'd arrived. Much of Luka's party had dispersed into the settlement and now the early morning duties resumed. A few wolves meandered about in wolfskins, but most performed their chores as humans. An older woman, her graying hair braided with small animal bones, bustled by them with only raised eyebrows to indicate her notice. She carried in her arms a large woven basket and the scent of mountain huckleberry wafted over them as she passed. She followed Luka's path up the steps to disappear into the Den. Several other men and women trailed in her wake, each carrying a large basket that contained either plants, berries, or nuts.

Nearby, Nolan and his friends lingered close enough that Lishka suspected they had been instructed to watch them in Luka's absence. One of the wolves, now in man-form, had wrapped his arms around a curvy woman with wild chestnut tresses. He kissed her neck profusely and her squealing laughter cut through the air. He pulled back and gestured toward Dominick as he spoke, his voice low.

"Well, he could have thrown you farther if you spent a little more time hunting, and a little less time lounging 'bout the fire." Her higher pitch carried the words to them, and she reached out to pinch his side. He yelped and ducked away from her, amidst his friends' delighted heckling. This only encouraged her more and she chased him through the group, her seeking fingers grasping at wads of bare flesh, until he fled amongst great howls of laughter.

Mordan glanced back to the Den, and Lishka followed his gaze. A young woman had emerged from the recesses of the Den to stand upon the platform, surveying those before her. For a foolish moment, Lishka wondered if this was the fabled Queen of Wolves, before she remembered that the Queen hunted.

Thick hair the color of walnuts had been tied back

from the wolf's face in a series of braids. Her cheeks bore a youthful fullness and her loose tunic engulfed her slight frame. Her gaze landed on Mordan, and she smiled. She stepped off the platform and her woven skirt swirled about her legs, a slit in the fabric opening to reveal lean muscle and worn leather boots.

"Mordan." She stopped before them, her eyes flitting to Dominick and Lishka before resting on Mordan.

"Baya." Mordan inclined his head in a small, respectful greeting.

"The Queen will be pleased to see you." A wry smile played across her lips. Despite her smooth skin and soft cheeks, the mark of long years held steady in her gentle brown eyes.

"I hope so," Mordan replied. The thread of doubt in his voice unsettled Lishka.

Baya's eyes twinkled knowingly. "She is the Queen."

Mordan's gaze drifted over Baya's head to the trees and beyond, where mottled gray and brown fur mixed with the green fern and moss.

"Come," Baya said at once. "I've had a couple of rooms prepared for you, to wait in safety from the sun at Luka's request."

"But the sky," Lishka gestured to the thick clouds amassed above them. "We could wait out here, in the forest." She disliked the idea of being trapped indoors in another's territory.

Baya shook her head. "Don't let those fool you. In Uru, the sky is a trickster. Come afternoon, it will be clear and free of clouds. The moon will be bright tonight." She smiled and despite her delicate features and soft voice, her teeth were sharp.

They followed her into the Den. A wide hall spread out before them. Fifty or so rectangular wood tables sat in rows up to the great stone hearth on the far wall. Several wolves knelt before the hearth, stacking the firebox with thick rounds of wood. Pillars that matched those at the entrance lined the walls and supported a high ceiling that made the space look much larger than it appeared from outside. Between the pillars, arched doors led deeper into the Den.

Baya led them through one such door into a narrower hallway. They passed several more wolves who stared at Lishka, Dominick, and Mordan, but did not address them. Finally, Baya paused before a set of wooden doors spaced perhaps five feet apart, which were anchored to the stone wall with heavy iron hinges. She pushed one open and gestured to Mordan, who followed her invitation to enter.

Lishka hesitated, not liking that Baya separated them.

"We are safe here," Mordan said gently, while Baya stood discreetly to the side and averted her eyes, though she could still hear them. "Rest and regain your strength. I will come for you both at dusk."

Lishka wanted to protest, but the weariness in Mordan's eyes stopped her. She had sensed no hostility from the wolves, only curiosity. If anything, Luka and Baya had been friendly. She allowed herself to be ushered into her own private chamber, with Dominick comfortably in the room beside hers.

Thick stone enclosed the small space. Mounted sconces had been lit with natural flame and gave the room a warm, cozy glow. Tapestries woven in intricate forest scenes decorated the walls, depicting golden images of summer that once more evoked the realm of the fey. Lishka wondered if the wolves had taken note of her own strange eyes and knew what the color meant.

A four-poster bed with its head against the left wall took up much of the room. Green curtains hung draped from the frame to provide additional privacy. Lishka sat on the bed and found the mattress firm yet pliant. In the peaceful quiet of the room, she released some of the tension she carried, and the pull of day seeped in, urging her to rest. She unstrapped her sword from her back to hold on her chest as she lay down. Not even the reassurances of Mordan or the apparent civility of the wolves could convince her to let her weapon out of arm's reach.

Before she allowed the daysleep to consume her, she reached out to sense Dominick. His golden warmth responded, that comfort dispelling any last resistance to sleep.

THE COOL DUSK air held the bite of impending frost, while the trees that lined the edges of Morvane center rose like pikes to pierce the darkening sky. As Baya predicted, the clouds had dispersed and several stars already twinkled overhead, though the moon had yet to reveal herself.

Lishka and Dominick followed Mordan down the Den's stone steps. From the forest, a baying announced the return of the hunting party. The wolves around them paused and heads lifted to focus on the location of the howl.

Red flashed near where the main path joined the forest. A brilliant sleek wolf burst through the trees in a wild firestorm of energy and radiance. The thundering of paws announced the hunters' return and a mix of brown, gray, and black wolves spewed out of the forest. They numbered at least thirty, all in their prime. At the rear of the pack, ten more of the wolves had changed and carried three massive elk across their broad shoulders.

The red wolf ran to the Den where Mordan, Lishka, and Dominick stood at the base of the stairs, keeping to the left to allow her room to pass. She loped up the steps without pausing to acknowledge them. Baya and another female wolf greeted her from the doorway and dropped their fingers to trail comfortably across her back as she slowed to walk between them. The three disappeared into the inner hall.

At the leaving of their Queen, the hunting party dispersed to greet the other wolves and to return to their homes. Several turned to Lishka, Mordan, and Dominick and openly stared, the fur raising along several backs. The hunt had stoked their desire to fight.

Mordan did not acknowledge them, doing nothing that might either encourage or discourage their hostility. Instead, he stepped away from the Den to approach the hunters' kill. Lishka followed his lead, keeping her eye on the wolves. Dominick watched with clear longing, his muscles tense beneath cloth and leather. The wolves, finding no satisfaction in their guests, turned to snap at each other, and mini fights broke out that turned to more play than aggression.

Up close, the elk were massive. Great brown bodies lay heavily on the ground, once-majestic beings now just sacks of meat. Blood seeped from deep neck wounds, and one bore claw gouges in its hindquarters.

"A good kill," Mordan said to one of the wolves focused on skinning the animal. "Clean and honorable."

The wolfman squatting in the dirt before them nodded, taking up a wicked blade in dexterous fingers that ended in sharp, black claws. His other hand lay on the elk's neck. "None surpass Morvane wolves in the hunt." He grinned wickedly up at Mordan and red stained his sharp canines. "You should know that best of all, Mordan."

"I did wonder if you'd recognize me, Amond." Mordan smiled with fondness. "You were scarcely a pup."

"The wolves don't forget," Amond said, tapping his temple with the wooden knife hilt. "We hear disturbing news from the Northern traders. Your kind is moving North and with them, trouble comes close to Uru's borders."

Mordan knelt to bring himself to Amond's level. "That is why we are here, to gain an audience with the High Alpha. We hope to go with Morvane's support."

Amond sighed. "I thought as much. Here's your chance." He nodded to the space behind Mordan and then ducked his head down to focus on his work.

The hair rose at the nape of Lishka's neck. She turned around to face the source of Amond's abrupt silence.

Queen Vissa was not a large woman, but she had *power*. Vitality crackled around her fiery hair, and her sharp eyes blazed pure gold. She approached them with long, purposeful strides and her soft brown boots made no sound against the packed earth. Baya and two others trailed comfortably in her wake, ready to serve their

Alpha's every command.

The Queen stopped before them. Mordan stood and bowed his head. At Mordan's side, Lishka and Dominick followed his example.

"My Queen," Mordan murmured, and he raised his head to gaze upon her.

"Mordan," she replied with warmth in her husky voice. "It's been a while."

Lishka looked upon the face of the Alpha…and froze. Upon the Queen's forehead blazed the mage's mark. At once, Lishka remembered Lord Aragnus' words from her Council hearing.

*Is this to be allowed, Mordan?*

The words had been targeted. Lishka studied both Mordan and Queen Vissa. Mordan had been to Uru before and clearly cared about the Wolf Queen. He must have been the one to gift the wolf with the weapon of their kind. Any anger she felt at the Queen bearing the mark while her own lay bound dissipated at the thought that quickly followed. *What must Zaral have done to him, once he learned of this betrayal?*

The Queen nodded toward Amond behind them. "That looks well done," she said. "A clean cut for a fine kill."

Amond responded to the compliment with a wide grin.

"Aye, my Queen, it will make a good feast for our guests." He cocked an eyebrow, a mischievous glint in his eye. He knew what they really fed on.

"Queen Vissa, we come to ask your favor as emissary to Uru's High King," Mordan said, disrupting the wolves' shared teasing.

Queen Vissa brushed aside Mordan's words with a wave of her hand.

"I know why you've come, what has caused you to drag yourself back here in the call of duty. Though I must say, I had thought you'd return sooner." Her words sounded light, but Lishka heard the edge to them.

Mordan ignored the bait. "We must have your help," he insisted. "You know what Zaral will do if not stopped; you knew this time was coming." He took a step closer, then stopped at the glint in Vissa's eye. "You have always known it," he said in a low voice.

Queen Vissa crossed her arms, her face impassive. "We'll discuss this tonight," she said decisively, leaving no room for argument. "Drinking and feasting first, then politics. Or have you forgotten all the ways of the wolves?" She turned to bark out orders to her pack members. "Let us show the nightwalkers how the wolves live in Uru."

The wolves yipped and howled around them, fierce and challenging, all under the sway of this woman. She would be a strong ally—if she could be swayed to Zachriel.

THE FIRE HAD been lit in the great hearth and now burned dark red within the stone. The Den's solid cedar doors remained open to the night forest and moon beyond the threshold. Wolves gathered in the hall, reclining on the wooden benches, their elbows and mugs resting on the now cleared tables, bellies full from an evening of feasting on venison, berries, and nuts. There remained a general sense of restlessness as wolves came and went from the hall, some unable to resist the call of the forest despite their Queen holding her own sort of court. Yet the mood had quieted in the comfort of the pack gathering as one. Golden eyes gazed unabashedly at the visitors, and gossip filled Lishka's ears as the wolves speculated on the purpose of their visit. Lishka ignored the attention, fixing her own focus upon the quiet conversation between Queen Vissa and Mordan.

The Queen had invited Mordan to join the table at the end of the hall, which faced her wolves with the fire behind them. Luka reclined at her right side; Mordan she had sat at her left as a sign of honor. Dominick and Lishka sat at the table just to their right, with several other of the high-ranking wolves.

Mordan leaned toward the wolf to speak low against her ear and Lishka noted the Queen's response. Her flesh ran hot and whether she meant to or not, she shifted her body toward Mordan in return. They sat comfortably, and it occurred to Lishka that they had once been intimate. She pushed the thought away for later consideration, to focus on their words.

"You were powerful rulers once," Mordan was saying in a quiet voice. Vissa laughed a little too sharply.

"We still are." She tossed back a mane of red hair that caught the smoldering firelight and shone like fire itself.

Mordan shook his head, sadness and affection in his eyes for the Wolf Queen.

"Uru is not as great as it once was," he said. "Your wolfkind are strong and you still hold the territory. But day by day, that territory shrinks. Humans chip away at the outer edges, logging and stripping the land at your borders. They do not believe. You do not have the numbers to risk making them believe. And since they do not believe, they have no fear to hold them in check. Humans are dangerous, self-destructive without a check."

Queen Vissa narrowed her eyes and tilted her head, reminding Lishka of a wolf with ears perked. She tucked her face against Mordan's ear and whispered something to him, words intended for only him that not even Lishka could hear. Mordan tensed, just the barest amount, as if whatever she said had struck him.

"What do you think there is between them?" Dominick whispered, disrupting Lishka's thoughts. She glanced at him, and he smiled at her. The wolves had drained some of the elk blood to feed their guests, and the blood had once more brought a slight color back to Dominick's face. His eyes held a teasing warmth.

Before she could answer, a shift in the wolves' energy drew her attention to the hall. From their high table, Vissa and Mordan stopped in their conversation and also looked outward. At the far edge of the hall, nearest to the door, a low growl turned into song, deep and warm with moonspirits, a drink made from fermented berries. One by one, wolves joined in, until the ballad of Uru ran strong through the hall. They sang in the words of Luna, the old tongue of the moon worshippers, and loosely translated, it went as follows:

*Below dark boughs*
*'Neath swords of pine*
*Through fern and rock*
*Past curling vine*

*The blessed light*

*Brings bones to bend*
*Paws tread the earth*
*Where daylight ends*

*Howl to the sky*
*Fur tipped with stars*
*Breath knows no strain*
*Run fast and far*

*The lands of wolves*
*Are far and wide*
*The night is young*
*The moon is wild*

The song tapered off into a quiet rumble. Lishka imagined she saw the shadows of fang and fur behind the shapes of men and women. A slight breeze blew through the open door to caress faces, and carried with it the smells of the forest and the bite of snow from the western mountains.

The night beckoned. Around them, wolves shifted, and teeth lengthened while eyes glowed yellow. Their attention turned to their Queen, whose own gaze now fixed upon Dominick. Lishka tensed but Dominick merely looked back at the wolves. He admired them, and had found some friendship there.

"You know what you carry." Queen Vissa's voice traveled across the hall, though she sat not far from them. The sword remained at Dominick's side; he had not let it from his body since they arrived and now his hand strayed protectively to the hilt. Vissa's eyes flashed.

"Yes." Dominick's voice held steady.

"And how did you come by this weapon?" Queen Vissa asked, too casually. Lishka saw the dangerous interest in the Queen's eyes and at once became acutely aware that the wolves surrounded them. A moment ago, the room had been filled with relaxed languor. Now the energy rose to a heightened pitch, as though the room held its breath, ready to spring to violence.

"It called me," Dominick said, his voice low yet loud enough to carry through the now silent hall. Lishka heard the disbelief in his voice, as though he still couldn't believe the sword had chosen him. "From the lake of the fey. I can't explain how, I just felt…drawn. I looked down and it was there, so I pulled it from the ice. It felt right. It felt like—" He paused, as if unsure of how to express the calling, the desire in the sword itself that spoke to inexplicable consciousness. "Like it *wanted* to be pulled."

Lishka looked from him to Queen Vissa. *She already knows, or at least suspects. She just wanted to see if he'd answer honestly.* At Vissa's side, Mordan gave her the faintest hint of a smile at the corner of his mouth. Lishka allowed herself to relax the smallest amount.

"The fair folk are tricky," Queen Vissa conceded. She smiled, her teeth long and razor sharp. "But we are honored to have the Bearer in our presence."

Dominick stared at the Wolf Queen. "You know what it really is?"

Vissa laughed. "Of course. The wolves are not so quick to forget what humans disappear into legend and fairy tales."

She rose from her table and strode around it to come to Dominick. Lishka forced herself to remain still as the Queen stood over him and reached down to cup his face in her strong hands. Golden eyes bore into brown, calling upon his lingering humanity.

"You have a flame in you," she all but whispered. "It burns bright as the sun."

Lishka started at the intimacy. The Queen's words echoed Lishka's, spoken many months ago to a human Dominick.

Dominick matched the Queen's gaze, and at once she smiled again, only this time emitting a bright genuine warmth.

"I have a fire in my belly, too." She sighed then. "It's a pity that they got to you. If only the Bearer had been born wolf…but no matter. You are here now." She patted his cheek, not so softly. "Now, we hunt."

Queen Vissa stepped away from them into the center of the hall. At a wave of her hand, at least twenty young wolfmen stepped quickly forward. Thin loose clothing covered their bodies, and they flexed their muscles, the moon reflecting in their eyes. Already, the change had begun in several of them.

Dominick rose as well, and Lishka with him. Queen Vissa turned back to Dominick and gestured him to her side. As he reached her, she held out her hand, palm upwards. He slowly drew the sword from its scabbard and the light made its symbols flash. Vissa's eyes lingered on the steel, before again meeting Dominick's. With great care, he sheathed the sword and relinquished it to her firm grip.

*He trusts her. Dominick would not have so freely given Excalibur to one he didn't trust.* He had shown more resistance even to Mordan. Deep in Lishka's stomach, something twisted.

Queen Vissa handed the sword to Baya, who had appeared at her side as though willed there. She turned back to Dominick and her golden eyes had taken on the shape of the wolf.

"Your arrival means one thing."

The wolves had stilled, all eyes on their Queen with eager anticipation.

"The hour has come for the Hunt of the King Stag."

C H A P T E R  2 7

# THE QUEEN'S HUNT

**"T**HESE ARE YOUR OPPONENTS."

Queen Vissa swept her hand before the young wolfmen, who looked less and less like men, and more like their alter wolves.

"Opponents in what?" Dominick asked. The muscles in his back clenched with anticipation, though of what, he didn't know.

"We felt his presence the moment you pulled the sword," Queen Vissa said in lieu of a more direct explanation. "The trees stilled to listen, and the creatures grew distracted from their gathering and hunting, their attention drawn elsewhere. It was as though all the woods held a bated breath. *He* has returned from the heart of the forest. The time has arrived." Her eyes bored into Dominick's, and he didn't dare blink first.

"Your drawing of the blade has set a great many ancient ways in motion," Vissa continued, her voice heavy with premonition. "The memories of the wolves are long. Though we ourselves were not present, the wolves remember the signs. This has happened before, centuries and centuries ago. It is the Way." She faced outward to the hall.

"Kill the King Stag, and you are wolfkind forever." She spoke now to all the competitors. "Kill the King Stag and earn Uru's highest honor. Kill the King Stag," she turned to Dominick and her voice dropped to just above a whisper, "and prove you are worthy to bear it."

Dominick licked his lips. He would be allowed to hunt with the wolves as one of them. He barely registered the Wolf Queen's gesture to someone behind him, scarcely noticed the soft touch of nimble fingers peeling his coat from his shoulders. He now stood in only his thin tunic, dirty from weeks of mountain weather, though unspoiled by sweat. Dominick no longer sweated.

"So that you will not be encumbered by it," the gentle voice whispered in his ear, and Dominick recognized Baya. His focus narrowed on the wolfmen before him, whose jaws had elongated past speech. As he stared, one of them bent double and then dropped to the floor when the transitioning curve of his spine meant he could no longer stand erect.

A surprising heat rose from somewhere deep inside Dominick's core and his veins thrummed not with blood, but with whatever energy fueled this immortal body. Dominick could not turn to beast to become truly one with the forest, but the darkness beyond beckoned him just the same. His muscles coiled and his feet gripped the stone floor, ready to leap into the night. At once he saw the King Stag in his mind's eye. The creature's great antlers pierced the sky, his breath created dense clouds in his wake, and his heavy hooves made the earth tremble. Dominick felt the vibrations in his feet. It would require great cunning and skill, as well as strength, to bring down such an unnaturally quick and strong animal.

Now only wolves stood in his path. The urge to run, to howl, and to hunt thrummed in them all. The moon called them to change, while the Stag's beating heart drew them to the forest.

From the doorway, a sandy-colored wolf appeared. *Luka.* The pack leader lifted his head to howl into the night and the song cut through the stone walls, reaching down into the core of all who heard it. The notes sank into Dominick's bones and as it reached its crescendo, something inside the wolves seemed to snap and they sprang forward to the forest, Dominick deep in their midst.

A RUSH POUNDED in Lishka's ears. Luka's lingering howl still permeated her being, calling her to hunt. Firm hands gripped her shoulders. She glanced back at Mordan. He shook his head, just the barest motion, and a stab of longing mixed with bitter resentment filled her.

"Only the chosen may hunt," Mordan said, his voice tight with understanding. Lishka returned her gaze to the forest.

With Luka's call, the wolves had leapt from the doorway to land on the earth below, Dominick with them. In a flash he drew even with the leaders and before he disappeared into the trees, Lishka espied the moonlight glinting off the golden brown in his hair. Feeling his footsteps surpass the wolves—a different vibration than that of paws—she almost smiled.

Mordan didn't have to tell her that Dominick would have to be the one to kill the King Stag.

Only a few feet away in the Hall, Queen Vissa's golden eyes glowed but she made no move to change her form. Whatever the rules of the Hunt, it was clear that she too had been excluded from the chase.

The Wolf Queen pulled her eyes from the night to shift her attention instead to Baya, who, having predicted her Queen's desires, approached with Excalibur held before her in both hands. Lishka tensed. Queen Vissa gripped the hilt, and in a practiced motion, drew the blade an additional several inches out of the scabbard to admire its fine edge.

Lishka took a step forward before she checked herself, even as a surge of protectiveness rose within her. Vissa sighed and then pushed the sword back into the scabbard, as far as the leather would allow it. Behind her, Mordan had yet to move. His attention flitted between the Wolf Queen and the activity in the forest beyond the Den. Desire made his eyes flare momentarily red and Lishka wondered whether he longed for the Queen or the Hunt. *Or both.* Perhaps he would share the Queen's bed tonight. The silence of the Hall was deafening, despite the night noises that made their way to sensitive hearing. Again, Lishka considered what had been between this queen of wolves and Mordan.

As if sensing her thoughts, Vissa tilted her head and her golden eyes captured Lishka's. She studied Lishka for a drawn-out moment.

"Come. I want to show you something." Without

waiting for Lishka's agreement, Vissa swiveled on her heel to stride through the Den's doors and down the stone steps. Lishka paused for only a second before succumbing to both her curiosity and a desire to be free from the walls of the Den. This time, she did not spare a glance back for Mordan, and the silence behind told her that he did not follow.

Vissa's hair gleamed various shades of red beneath the full moon, mimicking the smoldering embers of the fire they had just left. She led Lishka down the stairs and to the dirt path, then through the dark dwellings of Morvane. The homes' inhabitants now wore fur and fang and would not return until the early hours of morning. Lishka lengthened her stride to keep pace, while behind her several more female wolves joined their procession, until they numbered at least thirty filing through the forest. The trees closed around them, before once more thinning to end in exposed hillside. The moon hung heavy above to cast a silvery light on the dewed grass.

Lishka found her gaze drawn uphill to the crest. Nine white stones rose from the ground to stand in a crescent at the top of the hill. During the waxing and waning moons, the stones would be a mirror reflection of the moon on earth. At once, the image of Avalon came on so clearly that, for a second, Lishka thought the Fey Queen had once again transported her back to the realm of the fey. She didn't know whether to be comforted or afraid of this stone circle so reminiscent of the folk and her own lost heritage. Even at the distance, the power that flowed within the stones pulsed against her senses. Unlike the fey folk, this was a primal power, full of heat and hunger.

Lishka forced her attention from the stones to assess

her surroundings. More pack members now dotted the hillside, mostly females in various stages of their transition to wolf. At least twenty more stood within the stone crescent, and those that had yet to change wore translucent white robes. They raised their hands and their faces to the sky and howled from human and wolf vocal cords.

The hair rose on the back of Lishka's neck. Vissa continued up the hill toward the crescent and Lishka had no choice but to follow. Their strongest males might hunt the King Stag in the forest, but the power of their females gathered on this hill. Lishka's human memory rose to consciousness; she remembered linen robes belted with willow and elder in a circle around a bonfire at dusk. The Followers had gathered during solstice to draw energy from the earth, much as the wolves drew energy from their moon.

At the crescent, Vissa stopped. She pressed a palm upon the first stone and whispered a phrase in Luna that Lishka could not decipher, though the warmth in her voice indicated a greeting. Instinctively, Lishka knew that the stones recognized and welcomed Vissa in return. This wolf belonged to the land as naturally as the stones themselves.

Vissa did not step inside the crescent. Instead, she led Lishka around the outside. Within the arrangement of the stones, the wolfwomen began to dance, swirling in circles that seemed to mimic the phases of the moon. Lishka let her gaze linger on their beauty for a single moment. Their robes reflected the moon's light and drew the radiance into the fabric, as well as into their hair and skin. Together, they moved as one in perfect harmony. Along the stones, symbols glowed as the wolves came close; they matched neither those of the Coven nor the Ancients, though perhaps they came closer to the Ancients' symbols in their construction.

*Dominick would want to see this.*

The thought crossed Lishka's mind before she could register it, and she wondered whether Dominick had killed the King Stag. But the wolves still danced, and Vissa marched on. The Hunt must yet continue.

Beyond the crest of the hill and the stones, dark rock loomed up from the surrounding trees. Yawning mouths marked the entrance of caves into the Krebarvitch foothills. Vissa led Lishka to the largest opening and at last stopped and turned to face Lishka.

"These caves are our sacred place," Vissa said, her voice low. "Like the stones, they hold the strength of the Morvanian wolves."

Lishka sensed Vissa did not require acknowledgement and so she waited, lingering in the gravitas of the moment.

"None but wolves have entered these caves for thousands of years. But these are not normal times, and we cannot choose who fulfills prophecy. As the Finder, we gift you with the right to enter." The Wolf Queen stepped to the side and swept her arm forward. Lishka remembered the last time she had traveled below the mountain. Yet unlike Alaisadaille's tunnel, these caves felt warm and lived-in. Something deep within her stirred, responding to the pack energy that lingered in the rock. With the cold night air at her back and the hum of the stones in her ears, Lishka took a step forward to enter.

The mulch of the forest floor pressed upon Dominick's bare feet, intertwined with thorns that threatened to poke through skin. He had shed his boots several miles back, the better to connect to the forest as his wolf companions did with their paw pads. Vibrations against the soles of his feet guided him through the forest. The pounding hooves of the King Stag drew closer.

Only a few wolves stayed close on Dominick's heels. The rest had fanned out, seeking to drive the Stag toward known parts of their forest where he would be easy to corner, where they could take him down as a pack. Yet the Stag proved to be no common quarry. He refused to be herded and at the last second, when the wolves drew in, he would find a gap in their offense and dart through to disappear into the trees.

No wind stirred the leaves or ferns, and no night calls from owls or other nocturnal creatures broke the silence. It was as though the forest held its breath, all awaiting the outcome of the hunt. Dominick slipped through the ferns, and their gentle rustle at his passing gave him away, despite his supernatural abilities to shroud his movement in silence. He stopped for a moment, having lost the sense of the hooves against the Earth and his feet. He stretched his face up to the night sky instead, where bright stars shone, cupped in the silhouettes of leaves.

The King Stag called him to come. Dominick could see it in his mind's eye, as clearly as though it stood before him. The Stag's heartbeat shook the leaves about him; his heaving lungs pushed gusts of wind against Dominick's face. His hooves, strong enough to bash the skull of a wolf, pawed at the forest floor and laid it open. Razor antlers sliced through the air, flaying the night sky. Through the gaping hole poured stars and moonlight.

It would tire soon. The creature was mortal; the wolves were mortal.

Dominick was not.

THE DARK ROCK of the cave encased Lishka, in a gloaming broken only by glimmers of silver nearer to the ceiling that caught the moonlight from the entrance, and then the fire from mounted torches further inside. As in Alaisadaille's cave, images had been carved into the rock. This time, Lishka recognized the symbols of the wolf language, accompanied by intricate carvings of wolves, the forest, and the cycles of the moon. While the Ancients' drawings had been simplistic, using simple lines to illustrate scenes, the murals of the wolves boasted such intricate drawings that they almost jumped off the wall.

Lishka walked slowly deeper into the cave, studying the images. They wove together to form a story, a map of wolf life and wolf history. The farther she went, the denser the images became, until they filled the high walls. When the entrance to the cave could no longer be seen, Lishka paused to study the scene at her right. It showed the hillside with the crescent stones and a full moon overhead repeated in four quadrants. In the top left quadrant, two wolves faced each other in the ring, one clearly larger than the other. Between the stones hulked a great black wolf, watching them. The top right showed the wolves fighting, their long teeth glimmering with inlaid silver, and it seemed like the larger wolf had the advantage. The lower left showed the two wolves rolled so tightly together that Lishka could not tell where one ended and the other began. In the final scene, the smaller wolf stood victorious over its slain opponent.

Soft footsteps announced Queen Vissa's presence. Lishka continued to study the two wolves locked in eternal combat until Vissa drew even with her. Vissa did not speak and suddenly, Lishka realized that she was witnessing Vissa's own rise to Queenhood. The hint of red glimmered in the grooves of the smaller wolf carving.

"This way," Vissa commanded  after a moment, not revealing her thoughts as she looked upon the death she had caused.

Lishka followed her still deeper into the caves. They wound their way down into what had to be the heart of the mountain, past centuries of wolf history, past the same depiction of the treaty between the Coven and the wolves, and then further where the carvings became more worn, though no less detailed.

Despite the depth the caves remained mostly dry and were supplied with well-maintained torches that Vissa lit with the one she carried. Holes in the cave walls interrupted the murals to spider off into additional tunnels, forming a vast network beneath the hills. Some led into shallower caves filled with furs, and several boasted obvious fertility images carved into the rock.

Finally, Vissa stopped at a smaller, rougher cave. Unlike the yawning mouths of those previous, this entrance was little more than a narrow crevice that Lishka and Vissa had to duck through to enter. Before them, a small room glowed with a shaft of moonlight let in through a hole drilled in the ceiling. Lishka frowned; were her senses off, she wondered, for she thought Vissa had led them downward, not up. Even if the hole had been drilled directly down from the surface, moonlight could not have penetrated the distance through to the cave.

This floor remained bare, with flowers, small bowls of liquids, and strings of bones and small gemstones piled against the far wall. The offerings evoked the same ancient reverence as the tree in the Fey Queen's garden that had the little straw figure at its base. Lishka shivered.

On the wall, the King Stag had been carved life-sized to face them, and his soft eyes stared down at them. From his head rose magnificent antlers, their prongs cupping the moon in her various cycles. Red ran down the lines of the carving, weeping into the dirt at their feet.

Vissa turned to the right wall and placed her torch within a stone notch to hold it. Then she knelt to the floor and dipped her head in respect. After a moment, she stood holding a knife that, unknown to Lishka, had lain at the Stag's hooves. Before Lishka could ask, Vissa whipped the knife across her palm to cut a deep slash. The iron scent of fresh blood filled the small cave, tinged with the metallic smell of magik. Lishka's body tightened at the scent, but already Vissa raised her dripping palm to streak her hand down the Stag's chest—her offering to the protector of their forest.

Wordlessly, she handed the knife to Lishka. Lishka mirrored her actions, taking her left hand down the left side of the Stag, filling his chest with red.

The snap of a branch in the dark alerted Dominick. The Stag did not bother to hide his footsteps; where the wolves had more stealth, he had the better hearing and speed. Dominick pivoted left, slowing to creep through the ferns. He knew the Stag rested nearby. He had changed his tactic to follow at a distance, waiting for the Stag to tire. He knew he must make the kill soon. The King Stag played his own waiting game, and the eastern treetops had already begun to lighten. No wolves prowled nearby, not yet. Dominick had maybe minutes before the strongest arrived.

Dominick quickened his steps and sensed the Stag's hesitation. The Stag's wide ears meant he could detect the smallest noise. He had heard Dominick.

Dominick burst into a sprint, a blur to any human eye. He bounded up an exposed slope and froze. There, in the clearing before him, stood the King of the forest. Moonlight shone through his fine white coat, and but for his dark alert eyes he could have been a statue of marble. He faced Dominick head on and did not move. Dominick paused, taking in the magnificence of the creature. The beast held his eyes and in him, Dominick saw a deep, profound knowledge. He knew he must kill the Stag and complete the wolves' ritual and yet, in that moment, he hated that he was required to bring death to such a being.

The Stag's hindquarters tensed, the massive muscles preparing to carry him deep into the forest in a single bound. If Dominick did not strike, he would lose the Stag to the forest, and without a doubt, would lose the wolves' allegiance. Yet still he hesitated.

The Stag ducked his head and pawed the ground in a challenge. Dominick crouched lower, and instead of meeting the King's gaze, he studied the Stag's legs. The Stag lunged right, and Dominick lunged left, so that when the Stag shifted mid-leap, Dominick met him in the air. His distribution of weight had given him away. Dominick wrapped his arms around the beast's shoulders and sank his teeth deep into the fleshy part where the head joined to the neck, severing the Stag's main artery. Blood splashed out hot to cover his face and instead of iron, he tasted the forest.

"IT IS DONE. The King Stag is dead."

Vissa's voice interrupted their thoughts. Lishka dropped her gaze from the Stag to Vissa, who still regarded him with loving reverence. She couldn't help a sadness that trickled its way through her veins.

"Don't grieve for him," Vissa said, and she gifted Lishka with a small, knowing smile. "He is not truly gone. Only this version of him has died. There will always be a protector of the forest. Your Dominick truly is the Bearer."

Relief replaced any sorrow. Dominick had passed the wolves' second test.

"What now?" Lishka asked.

"He will come for you," Vissa said. "He cannot help it. He will be drawn to the Finder."

"What does that mean?" Lishka did not like the implication behind Vissa's words, that both she and

Dominick were simply pawns in a prophecy that moved them on an already determined path.

Vissa ignored her question and turned to exit the cave. At the mouth, she paused, her already healed hand gripping the rock.

"You will see. You will see what *She* asks of you to give. Wait for him here." She disappeared into the tunnel.

Lishka looked back up at the Stag. Now the blood on his chest represented not an offering, but his death. At once, she wanted to be free of the wolf ritual and beneath the clear night sky.

Her eyes drifted above the antlers and moons to symbols she had not noticed upon first inspecting the carving. Three of them in an arc: prey on the left, predator on the right, and in the middle the symbol for the balance that held both in check. The balance that was everything, that Zachriel sought to restore.

Lishka sensed Dominick long before she heard him. A deep thrumming in her bones told her he drew close, the calling of the Maker's bond. More than just prophecy, Lishka had bound them together when she took Dominick's mortal life and gave him her immortality. She did not have to be controlled by prophecy. She had agency over their future, as did Dominick. They had brought themselves to this place, whatever fate may have helped guide them.

Dominick slipped through the crevice and stepped up beside her. Lishka turned to him. She almost hesitated, for Dominick's eyes did not hold the soft brown she had grown used to. Instead, they looked darker, deeper, and seemed to contain all the forest within them. The scent of the Stag filled her nose.

Lishka ignored the magik that wove itself through Dominick's veins. She had claimed him first.

*You will see what* She *asks of you to give.*

She reached up and drew back the collar of her coat and shirt to expose her pale neck.

"Take it." Her voice was low. "Take what has been stolen."

Dominick blinked and, in an instant, his eyes became his own. He was Dominick again. His eyes flicked from her face down to her exposed neck and back again. A confused crease marred the smooth skin on his forehead.

Lishka realized she still gripped the knife. She raised the point to pierce her skin, drawing a single bead of blood at her collarbone.

"Take it."

Hunger and the flickering of desire passed across Dominick's face. With agonizing slowness, he reached his hand out to cup Lishka's waist, the other wrapping around the back of her neck, warming the place marred by the brand. He bent his head down and put his teeth to her skin, widening the puncture with sharp pain. Then he drew on her blood.

For one moment, Lishka wanted to pull back. She remembered the night of Dominick's Making, the loss of control that emptied them both into the power beyond the Veil. Then strength rolled up from within her. This was her choice, hers and Dominick's. On instinct, she twisted her head and sank her teeth into Dominick's shoulder. Copper flooded her mouth, tinged with an odd taste of the forest and earth. She, too, drank deep, each of them taking and replenishing the other. Then they stood in an embrace, simply feeling the form of the other, long after they'd taken enough to seal the bond.

# CHAPTER 28

# INTO THE NORTH

THE HUNT SUCCESSFUL, THE rites completed, the time had come to take their leave of Uru.

"You have done all you could, more than I hoped," Mordan said. They stood at the bottom of the steps to the Den. Around them bustled many wolves mostly in human form, while overhead, the sky had once more turned to a gradient blue with the coming night. Ten hours prior, Lishka and Dominick had emerged from the cave to dawn and had just enough time to seek shelter at the Den. The sun had been unusually bright for the time of year, bursting with radiance in a mackerel sky.

"You have served your purpose," Mordan stated rather formally. He had not been allowed to attend the rites, being neither chosen nor wolfkind. "I alone will travel with Queen Vissa and a selection of her pack to Uruden, the center of Uru and where High King Urith holds his court."

Lishka opened her mouth to protest but Mordan held up his hand before she could speak.

"No," he said, his voice gentle yet firm. "You must take a different path. There must be no more delay in getting the sword to Zachriel. His plan hinges upon the wielding of that weapon."

Lishka stifled her words, unable to argue with Mordan's reasoning. Several yards before them, Dominick stood in a small circle of wolves exchanging words of friendship and goodbyes. Lishka recognized Nolan and a few others who had participated in the ritual. One man clapped Dominick on his back, avoiding the two blades once more in a cross. Dominick laughed.

Lishka couldn't help the feeling of guilt at having to lead Dominick away from the pack. She had not seen him so comfortable and at ease.

"It was a good thing, bringing Dominick with you," Mordan observed. Lishka wanted to refute his words out of pride but knew them to be true.

"We cannot stand alone," Mordan added. His eyes drifted beyond Dominick to where Queen Vissa strode through her pack, barking out orders instructing who was to accompany her to Uruden.

"Is that why you gave her the mage's mark?" Lishka kept her voice low, so that those around them could not overhear.

"She was a strong mage already. Our fates are all bound together, and we must strengthen each other if we are to survive."

Lishka knew that was the closest to an answer she would get. She didn't dare ask the price Mordan had paid for the mark.

"I have a gift for you," Mordan said, turning to fully face her.

He placed his two forefingers upon her forehead, over her own deadened mage's mark. A fierce hope blossomed. At once, the mark seared hot beneath Mordan's fingers. The shackle around Lishka's power twisted and writhed, stretching like iron bars becoming malleable. Lishka froze, not wanting to interrupt the spell. The binding flexed…and held. Mordan dropped his hand.

"It took all of us to bind it. It will take at least the equivalent of that power to break it. But," his eyes gleamed, "I think you will find the binding weakened, just a little."

Lishka took a moment to assess the mark. Before, she could only sense a dead space where once she had been able to direct and funnel energy. Now, she felt the barest awakening within the cage of the binding. Not recovered enough to control the power beyond the Veil, the mark might yet assist her once more in pulling the magik through the barrier.

A shift in energy told them that the wolves neared the end of their farewells. Vissa's accompanying wolves would travel light to Uruden, though they would be trailed by a caravan bringing Morvanian goods to the High Alpha, to show the proper respect. Mordan had revealed to Lishka that the wolves kept hunting camps strategically placed throughout their territory, stocked with clothing and furs should they decide to spend the cold nights in human form. Lishka didn't understand why the wolves would change to human when in the wild, but Mordan had explained that the wolves enjoyed experiencing their forests in both their forms equally.

Across the organized chaos, Vissa made eye contact with Mordan and nodded. Mordan placed his hands on Lishka's shoulders. The time had come for their parting.

Before she could say anything, Mordan spoke.

"Lishka, there is another reason Zaral turned you."

"What?" She had not expected those words.

"I told you he found you because of your fey. That is true. Your fey both blessed and cursed you, for the strength of it in your veins drew his attention. Zaral did not want fey blood infiltrating humans, where they could be turned from his influence. But there is more." He spoke urgently, as though to prevent Lishka's interruption. "Do you remember your learnings about Avalon?"

Lishka nodded, not yet understanding the connection.

"Avalon was always meant to be the center of the Goddess here on Earth," Mordan continued. "More accurately, it is a vessel to commune with the power beyond the Veil into this realm, to help maintain the balance. Because it is for humanity, only a human may hold the seat, to keep Avalon anchored to this world. In the past, that human has always been female."

A slow, horrible realization began to dawn on her. She found she could not look away from Mordan, could not even blink. His eyes bore into hers, willing her to understand.

"The Fey Queen will only relinquish such power to one worthy to hold it. Such a power in the wrong hands would be terrible. There has been only one deemed worthy enough to replace her as the High Priestess in the last several millennia."

The truth came upon Lishka with the weight of a distant loss. The wolves dissolved around her so that only

Mordan and his revelation consumed her attention.

"Me."

Her voice was flat.

Mordan nodded.

"There was a time when the Fey Queen thought you might be the one to hold Avalon, to draw it back from the mists and help maintain the balance on earth."

"How would that be possible?" Already the sense of loss faded. Lishka had not been human for a long time and could scarcely remember the feel of her humanity.

"You were an anointed Follower, both mortal and fey, mortal enough to tie Avalon to humanity and fey enough to bind the power of Avalon back across the Veil. You were the perfect vessel, the perfect bridge that the Fey Queen wanted to hold the throne. She never forgave Zaral for taking you."

"Zaral did not want Avalon returned," Lishka said, pulling the pieces together. *Of course, he did not.* More than any other place, Avalon represented the power beyond the Veil. "And you knew this too, when you sent me to ask for their allegiance?"

Mordan sighed. "I thought you would serve as a reminder to the Fey Queen of what Zaral had taken and what he is prepared to do. He will never let the balance be restored, not willingly. He craves only his own power, his ascension to total dominance."

Mordan's hands tightened against Lishka's shoulders. "He may have turned you into one of us, but he could not consume your fey. That remains within you, buried over these past centuries. Have you felt it awaken?"

Lishka nodded. That vibrant core that led her to the fey had grown stronger ever since she left the Coven, since she entered the realm of the fey. And, though she had not yet had the time to examine what it meant, this power had strengthened even more since she had shared blood with Dominick in the wolf caves. A warmth seeped into her bones—life, after centuries spent cold.

"Good." Mordan smiled, though the expression of feeling did not quite reach his tired eyes. "The bond with Zaral weakens."

Lishka lifted her hands to rest over Mordan's and he leaned forward to place his forehead against hers in a silent farewell. She knew the next time she saw Mordan might be on the battlefield, if she saw him at all.

Dominick drifted over to them as they parted, having taken his time with his own goodbyes to give them privacy. Behind him, Vissa also now approached.

"Bearer," she called out and Dominick turned to face her. "I have something for you."

She held out her hands that grasped a long scabbard. The leather gleamed with hints of red and its surface had been skillfully engraved. The moon trinity repeated at the edge, along with etchings of the forest. At the top of the scabbard, the face of the King Stag watched them with benevolence.

"Not that the Coven's skill is not impressive," Vissa said, nodding in respect to Mordan. "But such a sword as this should be borne by the skill of the wolves."

Dominick reached over his shoulder to grip Excalibur's hilt and draw it from the Coven scabbard. The steel shone and he took the wolves' scabbard from Vissa and slid the blade effortlessly into the leather. The hilt came just to the edge in a perfect fit. Dominick smoothed his hands over the leather, tracing the symbols.

"It was made in Falar by the best of our kind," Vissa said.

"Falar?"

"The unofficial fourteenth pack of Uru and home to the strongest of our wolf witches. They reside just outside Uru's boundaries," Vissa added, seeing the question in Dominick's expression. "Farther in the northeast."

"How did you know?" Dominick asked, understanding that the scabbard must have been made long before they arrived at Uru. Vissa smiled.

"Vissa is a rare wolf," Mordan said with clear affection.

"I see things, sometimes," Vissa confided in a low voice, more for effect, for anyone could easily see she kept few secrets from her pack. "Possible futures, hints of things to come. I sensed the blade had been drawn, though I did not know by one of the Coven." Again, the hint of wistfulness threaded her words. "Come now. Night is upon us. Luka and Wren will show you the quickest way to the North."

LUKA AND WREN led them by the secret paths, where the trees grew so thick that they could scarcely move between them. Lishka kept her sword strapped at her back to ensure unhindered movement. Dominick had to take extra care that the two hilts did not slip past his shoulders and snag on the massive tree trunks.

On the fourth day of travel, the sound of rushing water harmonized with the wind and gradually grew to a dull roar. They had reached the Sook River. This water ran down from the heart of Glacies Tellus to flow south along Morvane's eastern border, where it eventually fed into the Tiern.

Here, the wolves did not leave the river but instead continued along the bank to lead them all due north. When they stopped to rest during the day, Luka transitioned to man in order to speak with them.

"It is the easier route," he explained. "The other way is more direct, but it traverses some deep ravines that would slow down myself and Wren."

At the mention of her name, Wren glanced over from where she had been drinking at the water's edge. She had not taken on her human form for the duration of their journey.

"Wren and I must hunt," Luka said. "Once the day peaks and you are able, follow the river north. We'll meet you at nightfall."

Beside her, Dominick perked up at the mention of hunting, though he knew he could not join. The rites had been an exception. Lishka and Dominick would not be allowed to hunt on wolf lands.

Luka crouched low to the ground and began his change. Lishka recognized this as a sign of trust, for the wolves were most vulnerable when between their two forms. Lishka felt she should avert her eyes, but for wolves, the transition was akin to putting on a change of clothes. And wolves had no shame of nudity.

The change happened both in parallel and in stages. Luka's spine arched to push him forward to all fours. At the same time, his jaw popped and jutted out into the slender wolf muzzle while his ears grew longer and shifted to the top of his head. His arms and legs inverted to reverse the joints of his elbows and knees. Fur swept in silky waves across his back, face, and down his legs.

It might have been alarming or even abhorrent, but it wasn't. The wolf change had beauty.

The moment the last of Luka's fur swept down his tail, he and Wren dove into the thick undergrowth, their excitement to hunt together almost tangible in the cool damp air. The bond between them couldn't help but inspire joy. Dominick shifted his weight to stand closer to Lishka, their shoulders almost touching, as they gazed into the forest after Luka and Wren. The wolves' pawsteps faded into only the sounds of birds calling their morning songs.

"Are you okay?" Dominick asked, his voice hushed against the singing birds and rush of the river.

Lishka glanced at him and saw concern.

"What do you mean?"

"I heard what Mordan said," Dominick answered with the smallest bit of guilt. "Sorry. I tried not to." He shrugged.

"I don't mind." In truth, Lishka did not like having secrets from Dominick. They had been charged to keep each other safe, to partner on this mission. Secrets brought risk.

Lishka returned to her watch of the forest. Despite the wolves' reassurances of safety on their lands, Sieth's vampire had approached them alarmingly close to Uru's borders. Dominick remained by her side, following her gaze to the trees. The memory of the caves came upon her in a rush and with it, the feel of Dominick against her and the taste of his blood willingly given.

"What Mordan spoke of happened long ago," Lishka said quickly, to cover the flush of that memory. "It doesn't change anything."

"But it's a part of who you are," Dominick pressed. "Just like learning of my heritage, and that I'm the Bearer. It does change things."

Lishka considered the comparison. For Dominick, discovering his heritage had been a revelation. He learned how much he fit into the world beyond what he had known. For Lishka, the truth meant only another loss.

"Maybe," she said to pacify him. "But the Fey Queen did not react to me as her intended successor. Mordan's plan did not work, though she did release the blade. Come. We should keep moving while the wolves hunt and before the sun breaks through."

She started forward to stop any more conversation.

They continued upriver, kept company by the churning white rapids of the Sook. The cartographers in the more developed South considered the northern river merely a minor tributary of the greater Tiern. However, those who dwelled at the edge of Glacies Tellus affectionately called it the Gifter and relied on the waters to bring the fishing villages their way of life.

Settlements grew scarce in the North, though Luka had assured them there remained a steady enough trade route up and down the river. Those willing to live a rough life ferried wares to the people in the North. They also traded with the wolves in exchange for easier passage along Uru's border and, sometimes, through Uru on the river itself.

A trade route boded well and ill for them. It meant Lishka could get news of Seattle without using any magik that might draw attention. It also meant more opportunity for Lishka and Dominick to be observed and reported on. Even in the sparse North, Sieth might have spies planted along the route.

At the height of day, Lishka and Dominick stopped to seek shelter beneath the thick tree canopy along the river. Clouds steadily drifted in, amassing to cover the sky in gray fluff so that not even sunlight could pierce them. After only a few hours, Lishka deemed it safe enough to travel again beneath the trees.

The shadows lengthened in the forest. With the retreat of day, the sluggishness that pulled at them faded and their steps quickened. Dominick's head lifted and he smiled.

"What is it?"

"I hear them." Dominick's smile widened at the sound of their wolf companions. Lishka frowned and listened. She had allowed her thoughts to wander and had not sensed their return. The faint musk of wolf drifted in the air.

"Ahead, at the river," she said. Dominick nodded. They made their way through the trees, and the rush of the river grew louder as they emerged.

The sandy-colored wolf and the smaller brown wolf raised their heads from the bank, where they had been drinking. Luka yipped in greeting. Lishka and Dominick walked across the pebbled bank to join them. Luka lifted his nose and pointed north to indicate they should continue along their path. Without waiting for any sign from Lishka and Dominick, he turned to bound off along the shore, Wren at his side before she took the lead. Luka yipped again, this time in indignation, and pushed to catch her but she was too quick.

"We must be close to the borderlands," Lishka said, following the wolves with Dominick, though at a slightly slower pace in order to explain.

"Why do you say that?"

"Luka didn't change. He wouldn't, close to the border. They will keep their strongest form, in case—"

"In case anyone waits for us," Dominick finished darkly. This time, Lishka nodded.

"What are the borderlands?" Dominick asked.

"It's the unclaimed land between the wolves and the North," Lishka answered. "It's not very wide, only a few miles, but it marks a buffer. It's where those of the North and the wolves can go to trade. There will be game there, too," she offered. At the mention of hunting, Dominick's step picked up.

"We can hunt?"

"Yes, the borderlands are not considered part of Uru. Wolves do not hunt there, but neither do humans as it is so close to Uru. We should find something."

Luka and Wren had now drawn so far ahead that they disappeared beyond the next river bend. Lishka increased her speed, fairly flying over the river rock, and Dominick matched her so that they covered several miles in only a short amount of time. Soon they reached the wolves, who, while fast, could not outpace them.

As she ran, Lishka kept all her senses on alert. The overcast sky stayed free of rain, though a mist dampened the air around them. In the river, the flash of silver indicated a healthy number of fish. Lishka kept a close eye on the waterway, waiting to see signs of human life that would indicate they had left Uru and entered the North.

A dark shape shot out from around the bend to smash against a boulder that rose from the middle of the river. In unison, the group stopped moving to cluster together against attack. Bared wolf teeth glistened, and steel shone in the vestiges of gray daylight.

The shape raced toward them. Shards of wood splintered off to fly into the river spray. *A boat.*

Lishka relaxed her defensive posture, though she kept her sword ready. She stopped herself from flicking her fingers in the shape of a spell. They still stood on wolf land, which forbade use of their kind of magik.

In silence, they watched the dinghy approach. It rode too high in the water to be occupied. With another *thunk* against a submerged rock, the boat shot past them and disappeared down the currents.

Dominick and Lishka shared a worried look. Luka whined at their side to indicate his unease. A breeze stirred his fur.

The wolves froze, their noses in the air. The fur along their spines lifted to alarming heights and Wren issued a low, guttural growl. A second later, the smell hit Dominick and Lishka.

The wind had shifted to blow directly from the North. It brought with it the rancid smell of death.

C H A P T E R   2 9

# VILLAGE OF THE DEAD

THE WOLVES LOWERED THEIR heads close to the ground and crept forward. Lishka stayed by Dominick, searching the surrounding forest for any signs of what had produced the smell. The wind blew intermittently, wafting the heavy scent across their faces as they picked their way north parallel to the river.

The river turned several tight bends, and the water, forced into the narrow passageway, continued to churn in deep, violent waves. This section would require a skilled boatman to navigate the currents and boulders successfully. No more boats came crashing down from upriver, though the group did not relax their guard.

The temperature had dropped in the early hours of twilight. A solemn disquiet fell over the group, and they progressed at a much slower pace in order to detect any hint of threat well in advance. The landscape did not change; the same wind blew across their faces, stinking of carrion, and yet something had shifted when they left Uru. They had entered the borderlands, and the North.

The wolves continued forward, not parting at the border as originally planned. They could not ignore a potential threat at Uru's borders, and they had yet to discover the source of the fetid air. A horrible sinking sensation had settled like a weight in Lishka's stomach the further they traveled without finding the dead game that would explain the smell.

Several miles passed in silence. The thick trees along the shore cast long shadows across the banks and river. The far bank turned from forest to high rock, the perfect vantage point from which to mount an attack. Lishka scanned the trees at the top of the rock face uneasily, searching for any signs of life. None appeared, not even birds to sing their final evening calls. Aside from the rush of the river and the whistling of the wind, the forest had become eerily silent.

Wren's nose shot once more into the air and again she froze. Luka stopped only a foot behind her and stared at her, awaiting her signal. She sniffed, then growled, her warning barely discernible against the rapids. She launched forward into a loping gait, Luka close on her tail.

The scent on the wind had thickened. Something else threaded through the death, something that pulled at memory. Lishka and Dominick hurried their pace to follow the wolves. The rock face opposite them loomed, then sloped down back to level shore. Here the river widened, and the rapids smoothed to a flat expanse of water.

"Look," Dominick whispered. Ahead, the wolves had stopped to face the far shore.

A series of rough wooden yurts stood along the shore. Docks jutted into the river, with several boats still tied to the posts and drifting sluggishly in place as the current tried to push them onward. All but two were partially submerged, their narrow bows sticking up from the water like ominous rocks.

"Someone tried to stop them escaping," Dominick observed quietly. Lishka looked beyond the boats, up the docks and to the dark yurts. Behind them, a single thread of smoke drifted up toward the clouds.

"We can jump the distance," Dominick said.

"We should continue." Lishka could not sense any activity in the village. "Whoever destroyed the boats could still be nearby."

Dominick didn't move. They stood staring at the village, searching for any signs of life or threat.

"Very well," Lishka said after a minute. She did not like that scent still lingering on the air, which teased her memory. But Dominick was right; there could be survivors, and better to know what they might face.

She remembered Mordan's message from Lady Raseska, when they'd learned of the attack on the Seattle Coven. Lady Raseska had reported the amassing of a great army. Who knew what creatures Zaral called to fight for him, what even now might be lurking in the shadows, waiting for full dark. She scanned the shore more carefully, straining with her senses both physical and supernatural to detect any sign of danger.

"We won't jump the river," she said, discovering nothing other than the heavy pall of death. "We should take a slower route, to be on alert in case of ambush. They should have boats on this side, if those have not also been destroyed. Search the tree line."

In the end, Luka found the hidden dinghy tucked in an inlet a quarter-mile upriver.

"Trust a wolf's nose," Dominick said as he pushed the small boat into the river. Immediately, the current grabbed the bow and pulled the boat at an angle. "Quick!"

Luka and Wren leapt into the boat. Wren darted to the helm to position herself in the direction of the village. Her long ears perked forward. Luka stayed in the middle, leaving space for Dominick and Lishka to jump into the back. Dominick thrust a small wooden paddle into Lishka's hands and then took up the second to begin paddling frantically on the right. Lishka followed his lead and soon they redirected the boat to point downstream across the river.

Despite the current, Dominick and Lishka's strong paddling carried them quickly across. The metallic sense of magik rose from the water and stroked Lishka's skin, reminiscent of the waters of Avalon. This river carried some of that essence.

Dominick slowed his paddling as they approached the docks. Along the shore, the current lessened by a degree. Lishka's attention wavered between the shore and Wren. Wren's superior nose and hearing would sense any danger before they could, unless the attack that came was magikal. Wren did not move, still poised with her attention on the village. Dominick steered them to the nearest dock. With several feet remaining between the boat and the dock, Wren launched herself off the bow and hit the planks with a light thud. She paused to sniff, then took off toward the shore.

"Wait," Lishka started to say, but to no avail.

Luka could not allow Wren to be unprotected. He leapt from the boat to follow suit. The dinghy rocked dangerously and water sloshed over the edge. Dominick wrenched his paddle through the water to carry them the remaining distance and they slammed into the dock unceremoniously. He reached out to grip the end post and stabilize the boat.

"So much for stealth," he grumbled, though without any real annoyance. They had yet to sense anything living or undead that would pose a threat.

Dominick held the boat stable while Lishka stood and climbed out; she knelt and did the same for him. He took a thick rope left draped over one of the posts to tie off the boat, in case anyone had been left alive.

An honorable gesture, but unlikely to be needed. Without the water to act as a barrier, the stench of rotting flesh hit them with fury. They entered the village, while up ahead the wolves padded through, inspecting each yurt.

"They left in a hurry," Dominick said. Stomped-on baskets, clothes, and broken clay pots lay scattered along the shore, evidence of a hasty mass exodus.

"But why?" Lishka asked.

"Maybe some of them made it out," Dominick said, trying to ignore the smell that told them most had not. In front of the yurts, fishing nets had been strung up for safekeeping; drying fish still hung from the entryways. Smoke wafted from several of the blackened doorways and many of the roofs had gaping holes, though the fire had since burned out.

"Why would anyone be interested in a fishing village?" Dominick asked.

Lishka shook her head. "I don't know."

At the last yurt closest to the forest, Luka stood in the doorway. A growl rumbled from his belly. Lishka and Dominick picked their way through the village to join him.

The smell intensified. This yurt still retained its roof and structure, being the farthest from the rest.

"Wait here," Lishka said, addressing both Dominick and Luka. As she crossed the threshold, a wave of rot washed over her. Lishka steadied herself and continued forward.

The villagers they had been searching for lay piled in the center of the hut. The edges of their clothes were singed, and their bodies had begun to show the signs of decay. That and the smell told her they had died a week, maybe two, prior. Beneath them blood congealed, staining the floor. Not being fresh, it did nothing to quicken Lishka's predator instinct. She felt only disgust and regret that they had not arrived in time to save them. The scent that disturbed her lingered in the air and she retreated to think.

Dominick had drawn Excalibur to guard the entrance, facing away from the yurt. He shifted toward her as she exited.

"Don't go in there," she instructed. Dominick peered past her into the gloomy interior.

"You found them." He could already tell by the smell befouling the air and the sense of the dead. Lishka nodded.

"They've been there for at least a week, maybe longer. We could not have arrived in time to help them." She said this to assuage her own guilt, as much as Dominick's.

Dominick frowned.

"That doesn't make sense."

"What do you mean?"

"Look at the houses." He gestured toward the rest of the buildings. "They're still smoldering. They can't have been burned more than a day ago. If you're saying these people died weeks ago…" He paused. "Where did they come from?"

He was right. Lishka studied the homes again, even as subconscious memory surfaced.

"Siernak."

Luka growled and the hair rose once more along his back and mane.

"What is that?" Dominick asked, watching Luka's reaction.

"Eaters of the dead," Lishka explained grimly. "They feed on the dead and dying, quickening decay."

"So that explains the bodies," Dominick said.

"Yes." Lishka searched the doorway for the telltale marks she knew she would find. The soot had hidden at a glance the three claw gashes that marked the house as Taken. *We should leave this place.*

"I've never heard of them," Dominick said. "Not in any myth or lore."

"No, you wouldn't have. They usually don't kill or otherwise show themselves to humans. They linger at the edges of war zones, masking themselves in the shadows until they can slip in and feed. They're scavengers, members of the ghoul family, though much harder to kill. Something has summoned them from hiding."

"Or someone," Dominick added. They exchanged a knowing look.

*What other manner of creatures has Zaral pulled from the depths of this world, to answer his call to war?*

Wren yipped to draw their attention. Her nose once more to the wind, she took a few steps toward the trees, urging them to follow. Lishka glanced back at the wolves and then to the sky. Night had almost fallen and only a thin streak on the horizon bore the last of the daylight.

"We can't leave them like this," Dominick said.

"Dominick, we must go. We cannot let them see the blade. The magik in Excalibur will call them."

Dominick sheathed the sword, as if that could hide it from greedy eyes. He planted his feet in the doorway and crossed his arms. Lishka sighed.

"I can set a fire," she said. "Though the magik may attract attention. We must move quickly once I cast the spell."

Dominick nodded and stepped aside.

"Thank you," he said softly.

Lishka ducked back into the yurt. Her first entry had disturbed the lingering smoke and let some air in, so the smell was not quite as overpowering as before. She flicked her fingers in the shapes of the fire symbols and at the same time, drew on her own inner reserves to call forth the energy that she would shape into the spell. She dared not draw on the power beyond the Veil, though her mage's mark twinged just the smallest amount within its binding, and the thinning of the Veil in the North tempted her to do so.

A spark alit at the corner of a woman's dress, then grew to a small flame. The fabric caught and the flames licked higher. Lishka retreated from the yurt to join Dominick and Luka.

"Hurry," she said. "If any of the Siernak linger, they will have caught the scent of my magik."

They ran for the trees, breathing in the cool forest air. Behind them, the wind picked up, swirling the fire that consumed the villagers and laid them to rest. Elsewhere in the village, ash shifted and settled. A chime hanging from one of the rafters tinkled in a cheery note. No one remained to hear it but the dead.

DESPITE THE THREAT, they decided to remain on the village's side of the river and not cross to the opposite shore. The river continued to widen with a strong current, making the water impassable for the wolves. Lishka thought Luka and Wren might turn back but they kept pushing north, their noses in the air, scouting.

The silence lay heavy beneath the trees. Overhead, clouds amassed to block any moonlight and the shadowed places between trunks and ferns turned to inky black. The broad maple and thick alder trees gradually receded, leaving them once more in a forest of evergreen.

Ahead, Wren stopped and stared into the space between the trees before them. Her head dropped low, and her mane rose high. A vibration resonated against Lishka's feet, and it took her a moment to realize the sound came from Luka, in a growl so low she could only feel it.

In unison, Lishka and Dominick withdrew their blades. Excalibur hummed in Dominick's grip, in an even lower vibration than Luka's that shook the molecules around it. Luka crouched and slowly approached Wren until he stood at her side.

The reek of rotting flesh seeped into the air around them. Lishka dropped her sword before her in a defensive posture, already drawing the symbols for Kiaban's fire in her mind, to be ready to call them forth. Dominick stepped forward to position himself just slightly before her, ready to protect her while she prepared the spell.

They stared into the area within the trees as Wren directed. The shadows shifted. A clawed hand grew from the blackness to rest against the trunk. Shadow clung to the shape, elongating the claws. With the movement, the dark swirled to reveal a long, thin arm protected by tarnished black armor. The creature pulled itself from the shadows that still lingered about its skeletal frame. It stood taller than Dominick, and achingly thin. What parched skin they could see stretched taut over its skull, with neither muscle nor fat to soften the edges. Dark hollowed sockets marked the places of eyes below its spiked helmet.

The Siernak hesitated. As Lishka had explained, they scavenged to sate their greedy appetites. They did not normally fight unless forced. Lishka stared at the thing and the brand at her neck twinged. Zaral's will clung to them. He had bound them. Even as she realized this, the Siernak's eyeless face shifted to Dominick, and it jerked. It sensed Excalibur.

The thing opened its mouth wide, wider still, wider to fill half its face in a gaping black hole—and wailed. The sounds of death assaulted their ears, the screams of battle and despair, and the last shuddering breath of the dying.

Beside her, Dominick did not falter. He set himself

firm against the ground and gripped Excalibur tighter, ready.

Behind the first, more Siernak emerged from the darkness to form a half-circle before them. Lishka quickly counted them, assessing the threat. Seven, against four.

The Siernak struck. Their long limbs carried them impossibly fast across the distance where they met the wolves. Luka evaded the scraping claws of the first and launched himself up to the creature's throat, finding purchase. The creature inhaled to scream and, meeting its quick end, only gurgled its own dying song.

Wren wove among their legs, her long teeth taking chunks from the skin and bone exposed through the joints of the armor. The Siernak swung their claws in a blur of movement, but still they could not catch Wren. She made it through the group, then swiveled to leap onto the back of the closest Siernak before it could pivot to face her.

Dominick raised his sword as the first Siernak bore down on him; despite needing to keep her focus on those before her, Lishka felt a stab of fear. While Dominick had shown skill in their training, he had never truly fought for his life. He had never used his sword against another creature. For one precious moment, she let herself be distracted. The Siernak raised its claws and Dominick wielded Excalibur to block the attack. Bone claw met steel, and Excalibur sliced through with ease. The Siernak howled. No normal blade could cut its bone so easily and it staggered back to reassess Dominick and the sword.

Lishka wrenched around to parry the blow of the Siernak that had come within her defensive circle. It smashed the full weight of its armored body against her, locking its claws and her sword between their bodies. She stared into its soulless eye sockets only an inch before her. The rancid smell of decayed meat oozed from its open mouth, which widened to emit another screeching wail. Lishka grimaced and shoved against it. The Siernak staggered back, surprisingly dense despite its frail-appearing frame. Before it could recover, Lishka swung her sword in a wide arc toward the narrow space between its helmet and armor and lopped off its head.

At her right, Dominick had killed the first Siernak with a strike through its grizzled heart. Now he fought a second, who had learned from its predecessor's mistake and kept clear of the swing of Excalibur. It looked for a moment when Dominick might drop his guard and it could dart in and strike. The wolves faced off against the remaining three Siernak, one of which limped from a savaged leg. Wren's handiwork.

Lishka checked around her for any she had missed. For the moment, she stood free and so she shifted her sword to one hand and drew the symbols for the fire with the other. This time, casting caution aside, she drew from the power beyond the Veil.

The energy came sluggishly, as though drawn through a partially frozen tap, but come it did. It seeped into her veins, her bones, her core to fill her with strength. She bound the magik into the symbols, bending them to purpose. The violet fire flared in her right palm, brighter even than it had been in the armory. This time, she let it grow to travel up her wrist and then her arm. The Siernak shifted their attention to this new threat. In that moment of distraction, Dominick swung Excalibur and cleaved his opponent in two.

The remaining three clustered together, unsure of this new power. They had long memories. They remembered a time when beings made of a similar energy roamed the earth freely, creating succulent life but also protecting it with a horrid brightness. The fire extinguished their beloved shadows and exposed them. They opened their mouths to wail, and their claws reached for the wolves before them.

"Stay back," Lishka commanded the wolves and Dominick. The three threw themselves away from the Siernak. She released the fire.

The flames fell upon the Siernak to engulf them in violet light. They clawed at themselves to be rid of it, and their claws shredded armor and then thin skin to expose white bone. Consumed, they howled their last horrible breaths. The fire swirled over their heads, and they disintegrated into a soft pile of black ash.

A stillness fell. The last of Lishka's fire flickered out. Shadows returned to the forest, but this time they merely softened the places where the trees stood, creating safety for nocturnal creatures to explore and hunt. In the distance, the low hoot of an owl penetrated the overhead branches.

Lishka sheathed her sword and Dominick followed her lead. The wolves trotted in a large circle around them, sniffing the trees to be sure the threat had been eliminated. Dominick peered into the trees beyond them.

"What is it?" Lishka asked. Dominick shook his head.

"I'm not sure. I felt something in the Siernak, something familiar. And wrong."

"Zaral," Lishka said in a low voice, reluctant to

utter his name despite having destroyed his attackers. Dominick shook his head again.

"No, it's something else, I think. Something familiar. I don't know." He shook his head as if to dismiss his worries. "It's probably nothing."

Ahead, Luka and Wren stopped in their scouting to look back at Lishka and Dominick, clearly wanting them to follow.

"We'd best leave this place," Lishka said. "Before anything else is called by the magik."

Lishka and Dominick strode ahead to meet the wolves, increasing their pace to run beneath the trees, adrenaline from their first battle pushing them faster. The attack had made the threat real. The war between the Great Covens had arrived in the North.

Behind them, unbeknownst to Lishka, a small seedling emerged from the remains of the Siernak. Tiny green leaves unfurled to reach toward the night sky, new growth from the ashes of death.

C H A P T E R   3 0

# RUNES ON THE STONES

LUKA AND WREN KEPT close until dawn streaked the sky with pink. At last, when the trees had thinned to only a sparse scattering and the undergrowth had succeeded to Arctic grass and lichen, the wolves stopped to face them and say goodbye. They had seen them safely into the North. Now, they must take the news of the attack back to Uru, where Lishka hoped it would aid Mordan's cause to gain the allegiance of the wolf king.

Dominick knelt before them and bowed his head in thanks. Luka, now standing a full head above Dominick, bent to nudge his forehead against Dominick's in gentle farewell. In a burst of unexpected warmth, Wren pressed forward alongside Luka to lick the side of Dominick's cheek.

Smiling, Dominick rose to stand by Lishka's side.

"Travel safely and swiftly," Lishka said. Golden eyes gazed up at her. "And thank you."

Luka smiled, showing his lower canines and a wide, pink tongue. With a yip, he and Wren took off. The muscles in their hindquarters rippled under thick fur and their claws dug into the earth to propel them forward. In less than a minute, they had disappeared.

Dominick watched after them with a longing that Lishka could understand. She would miss the wolves too. The surrounding land felt quieter, less alive somehow, without them.

A stand of clustered trees nearby provided refuge from the day that came to slow blossom. The days had grown short, with night lingering and then coming swiftly once more. While this aided Lishka and Dominick, it would benefit the enemy as well.

They hunkered down as best they could against the trees to wait for twilight. Somewhere in the overhead branches, skittering told them a local resident had awakened to start its daily foraging.

"Where are we going?" Dominick asked, before the daysleep could pull them under. Both found themselves reluctant to submit to unconsciousness after the Siernak's attack.

"Dirn," Lishka answered after thinking for a moment. "It is the first true town in the North, and probably the last. I want to see what news they have of Seattle, if any. Mordan did not tell me exactly where Zachriel is, only that he is north."

"He didn't know?"

Lishka shook her head. "I don't think he knew an exact location, and we could not use magik to contact Lady Raseska. To be honest, I think he believes that the prophecy and the sword will guide us to Zachriel."

Her eyes drifted to the hilt behind Dominick's right ear.

"I don't feel it leading me," Dominick said bluntly. "It has an energy that draws me to it, makes it feel like mine. But it's not like how the fey called you. I don't feel pulled in any direction." Lishka could tell he was worried.

"We'll go to Dirn," she said with a confidence she didn't feel. "Then we can decide what to do next." She closed her eyes.

"Lishka."

She opened her eyes to look at Dominick across from her.

"I'm just supposed to give the sword to Zachriel, right? I'm not supposed to fight Zaral."

The weight of daysleep evaporated and Lishka sat up straight.

"No." She put as much weight into her answer as she could muster. "No, we must avoid Zaral at all costs."

Dominick shifted his head slightly to one side and evaluated her response. The worry he had expressed appeared to fall away in place of another emotion that Lishka could not quite be sure of.

"It was strange, fighting the Siernak," he said. "I've never been in a fight before, not really. Just the usual boyhood scuffles, things like that. But to use a weapon to defend myself, to protect you, Luka, Wren…" He trailed off but Lishka caught a gleam in his eye that she did not like.

"The Siernak are dangerous and strong." She could not deny the skill and strength it took to defeat them. "You did well. But Dominick, they are nothing to Zaral. He is sheer power. His will alone—" She stopped, and her brand ached with echo-pain drawn up from memory. She did not know how to convince him. Along with the power from his immortal body, Excalibur gave Dominick additional strength. Still, he would be no match for Zaral.

*None of us would.*

"Even Sieth has but a minor fraction of Zaral's power." Invoking Sieth's name had the desired effect. Dominick's jaw clenched and a shadow fell across his face. Lishka wanted to regret that she had used the memory of Dominick's death against him, but she could not, not if it conveyed to him the true threat of Zaral.

Dominick sat back against the tree trunk and tucked his head to his chest so that his hood draped down to cover his face. He crossed his arms tight over his torso, retreating into himself to think or sleep, or both. Lishka watched him for a moment and then did the same, closing her eyes to sink into welcome oblivion.

Lishka and Dominick continued to use the river as their path north. Several hundred miles ahead, Dirn sat along the Sook, which supplied the inhabitants with almost year-round fish and a route to travel to Uru for trading. Trees lined the shore so the banks continued to offer the best protection against the weakened daylight.

Half the night had gone by when they came upon another fishing village. Yurts stood along the opposite shore, a mirror image of the village downstream that they had first encountered. For one brief moment, Lishka's heart clenched at the sight of it. Thick smoke rose from several of the blackened roofs.

A person emerged from one of the yurts to walk toward an intact boat moored at the dock. Somewhere deeper in the village, a dog began to bark. Lishka's vision cleared. The roofs bore dark animal hides and the smoke wafted not from destruction, but from a cooking fire in the hearth. The Siernak had not reached this village.

Lishka and Dominick paused to study the yurts. Little activity stirred the village, the inhabitants of which had mostly taken to their homes for the evening.

"There," whispered Dominick. He stood shoulder to shoulder with Lishka within a thick grove of trees. Their shore rose a little higher than the far side of the river, giving them the better vantage point. She followed his gaze to the southern end of the village. Tucked into the denser bushes along the river, a person had hunkered down. The shape of a bow elongated their silhouette.

"A sentry," Lishka said. "They know what happened to the other village. Someone must have escaped." She exchanged a hopeful glance with Dominick.

"They're leaving," Dominick observed, voicing what she had already noticed. Indeed, the boats on the dock rode low in the water, laden with bundles of furs and other goods.

"They know war is coming." Lishka's words fell heavily on them both. They watched a moment longer. Farther downstream, a hint of movement indicated more sentries.

The villagers' precautions both reassured and worried Lishka. It pressed upon them the urgency of their mission. They had no time for delay. She shuddered to think what might have befallen the village if they had not destroyed the Siernak. Bows would have been little help against the dead eaters.

She gestured to Dominick, and they withdrew back into the shelter of the trees where they could not be spotted by the sentries, before speeding north away from the village. Lishka glanced to her right, where Dominick ran alongside her. He had worked to conceal the quickening of his hunger at the sight of the Northerners, yet Lishka knew the signs. The circles had returned to darken his eyes and his skin had tightened across his cheeks, further defining his cheekbones. He needed to feed before they arrived at Dirn. She listened and watched for any signs of nearby game that would feed them both.

They had only to wait one more day. In the lower lands, they had hunted elk. Here they found the caribou, elk's close cousins, and full of the sweet wildness of the North. The herd grazed several miles inland of the opposite shore, west of the river. The riverbed had narrowed since the village and so Lishka and Dominick easily jumped across to take down their prey.

Dominick's face flushed with the new blood and adrenaline of the hunt. He stroked the neck of the animal at their feet and murmured a soft thanks for its life. Lishka had taken her own fill and then some. They would need all the strength they could get.

"It feels wrong to leave it here," Dominick said, admiring the beast.

"Its life won't go to waste," Lishka reassured him. "There are single-shape wolves, and bears, and foxes. Many will appreciate the easy meal."

With one final caress, Dominick stood. The moon had risen in an unusually clear night and overhead, the sky filled with stars. He leaned his head back to absorb the brightness. The starlight illuminated his face and made his hair shine with golden-brown streaks, almost as though he stood bathed once more in sunlight.

The moment of calm after the hunt was short-lived. Dominick moved with an edginess that not even the fresh blood could subdue. He seemed distracted and constantly his gaze scanned the horizon, as though he knew something waited there for him. Lishka wondered if the blade called him onward, despite his saying that it didn't.

With half her mind on the surrounding terrain, always watching for danger, she spared a thought for Mordan. *Has he met with the Wolf King? Even now, does he follow with an army of wolves at his back?*

She had failed to secure the fey to fight with them. *If the wolves did not agree, will we have enough might to stand against Zaral?* Ahead, the two hilts at Dominick's ears shone in the starlight. They did not have to defeat Zaral. They had only to distract him long enough to bring Zachriel the sword.

For the first time, Lishka realized that they might not survive this fight. She had lived for a thousand years, but Dominick… Guilt threatened to flood her and she shoved away the thought.

Ahead, Dominick stopped and knelt. Lishka hurried to his side.

"What is it?"

He cupped something in his hand and stood.

"Look." He held out a smooth stone. "It's like the Boreal Stones, only it has markings I've never seen before."

The rock emitted a faint hum, akin to the Boreal Stones. The Veil grew thinner in the North, and more of its power leaked into the air. With the gentle hum around them, Lishka had failed to notice the power in the stones at their feet.

Smooth fine lines formed delicate symbols beneath the surface of the rock as though they had formed with the stone, not etched on the surface.

"They're runes," Lishka said.

"What are runes?"

"They are magikal symbols to represent concepts, to help direct energy into purpose. They are like the symbols I taught you to cast spells, only these I've not seen before."

"They look similar to the Ancients' drawings in the cave," Dominick observed, turning the stone over in his hands to study all the marks. "But not the same."

"If I had to guess, I would think they might mean containment, to trap the power within the stone," Lishka ventured. Dominick nodded.

"That makes sense. But why did the Boreal Stones not have them?"

"I don't know."

Dominick pocketed the rock and knelt to study the others.

"There are more."

Now that he had drawn her attention to the rocks, Lishka sensed the gentle hum radiating all around them. Not every rock bore the runes, but enough did that it did not appear to be a singular phenomenon. Dominick said as much.

He picked up another and held it to his ear. His eyes widened.

"What is it?" Lishka asked. Dominick shook his head and reached behind him to pull Excalibur from its scabbard. He held the sword alongside the runes, and both began to visibly vibrate.

"They're like magnets," Dominick murmured, lost in his scientific examination of the stones. "See the runes?"

Lishka focused on the rock. The runes shifted within, a visible energy rippling through them.

"It's like the power in the sword is drawn to the power within the stone. They must be made of the same energy."

He sheathed the sword to hum quietly in its leather scabbard.

"I wonder if the sword was made from metals in these stones."

"It's possible," Lishka said, trying to think of anything she had learned in Kiaban's lab to help explain the sword's reaction to the stones. "But whatever the technique, it's a method we lost long ago. I don't know of anyone making swords like that. Kiaban surely would have known of it."

"Well, this explains part of the legend at least," Dominick said. He smiled and Lishka couldn't help her curiosity.

"What do you mean?"

"It would have been very difficult to pull a sword from a stone of runes."

AT THEIR REST during the height of day, Dominick's excitement prevented him from daysleep. Instead, he withdrew the stone he had kept to experiment.

He held the blade in his hand and practiced moving the two objects closer and then farther apart.

"See, the power is reaching through the rock to connect to the sword," he explained. "It's contained, but not really trapped as it can still affect other objects and energy around it. When I move the blade farther away—" he demonstrated by pulling the blade an arm-width away, "the energy pulls back to the stone and stops affecting the sword." Indeed, Excalibur had quieted. "So, the energy in the stone has limitations."

"It is only a small amount," Lishka agreed. "Only so much power can be contained in such a small vessel."

"I don't think it's acting as a prison for the energy," Dominick continued as though he had not heard her. "It's a container, but also more than that. Obviously, it's attracted to itself, to like energy in other forms. I think you were right. The runes are anchoring it to the stone, so that even though it is drawn to other objects with the same energy, it won't leave the rock. Not without more force, anyway." He paused to consider his learnings.

"With the right amount of force, I bet you could draw the power out of the rock entirely," he said after a moment. "I wonder if you could contain it into a new vessel, a larger rock with these runes, and grow the power in a contained space."

Lishka knew that Dominick thought of the Boreal Study and the quest for a sustainable energy force. With the Boreameter, the rocks could be an accessible source of the power beyond the Veil to humans lacking any magikal affinity.

Dominick fixed his attention on the stone. The space between his brows narrowed and he stared with single-focused intensity at the runes. At once, Lishka sensed a small bolt of energy exit the stone and enter Dominick. He jerked.

"What did you do?" She scooped the stone from his hand and examined it. The stone had not physically changed, but had deadened to become standard rock. The runes remained but no power existed inside.

"I think I consumed it," Dominick said. "It's like I focused on the energy and whatever power I have inside me overpowered the runes to pull it out. It felt… satisfying." He grinned.

"Can you put it back?" Lishka asked.

"Let me see."

It turned out that he could. They practiced pulling the energy from the stone and then channeling it back in. Despite Dominick's infectious excitement, Lishka soon found the exercise tedious. Drawing energy from the stones only allowed for the transfer of a minute amount of energy and could not even approach replacing the elegance and yield of going beyond the Veil.

Several hours later, the clouds had rolled in, and the sky darkened. In the distance, intermittent flashes illuminated the far mountain range. The stones had been an interesting discovery, but there was a mission to complete.

The bank along the river began to increase in elevation. Below them, the river cut deeper and narrower into a ravine. No longer the calm river that supported fishing villages, it had become a rushing, foaming creature of the untamed ice land. True to the name, patches of snow had begun to appear alongside the banks.

Lishka ran with Dominick, leaping gracefully up large boulders that formed the top of the ravine. As she ran, a burning sensation began to pulse at the nape of her neck. She slowed and pressed her hand to the brand.

"Does it always hurt?" Dominick had stayed with her and now watched her with concern.

Lishka shook her head and dropped her hand. The brand twinged once more.

"Only sometimes. Sometimes I feel him, like an echo." Reluctant to say his name, she also did not want to tell Dominick that Zaral could call to the mark, that he could call to her. But Lishka did not think the burning came from Zaral beckoning her. With luck, he did not think to spare attention for her, whom he thought he had subjugated months ago in Seattle.

"I think we are getting closer," she whispered. "I think he is here, in the North."

Dominick clenched his jaw.

"We better move fast."

Lishka nodded and they set off once more, this time pushing themselves to speed along the top of the ravine. At dawn, the ground leveled off and the trees receded back from the river. Snow-covered ground turned to rock that extended over an impressive waterfall, which made up for its narrowness with steep height. On the opposite shore, the trees thickened around several large boulders that leaned against one another to allow a gap between them.

Lishka turned to tell Dominick they should take refuge there.

Dominick faced away from her to stare behind them at the tree line west of the river. His hands bunched at his sides and his eyes had dilated to almost completely black. Every muscle along his back had gone rigid so that his entire body became one coil.

Lishka froze and searched the tree line. A familiar presence snapped against her mind, cold and sinister. Her mark seared and she gasped at the intense pain.

Dominick whirled around and crossed the distance between them in less than a second. His body hit hers with enough force to carry them both forward, his arms wrapping around her back and waist. Over his right shoulder, a flash of pale blond caught her eye and then only air surrounded them. In a moment of illogical relief, they seemed to hover in the emptiness. Then they were falling through the air and Dominick's arms pressed her tight to his body, the only stable thing in the void.

He twisted them about, gripping her so tightly he broke skin, so that when they hit the hard, unyielding surface of the water, it was his back that absorbed the force of the fall to break on the sharp rocks beneath.

# CHAPTER 31

# DIRN

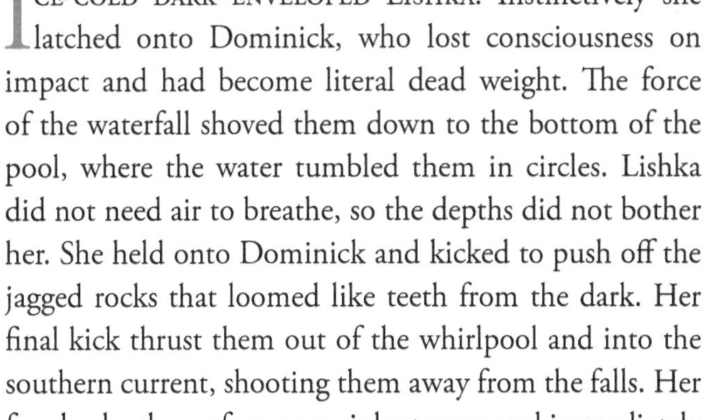

ICE-COLD DARK ENVELOPED LISHKA. Instinctively she latched onto Dominick, who lost consciousness on impact and had become literal dead weight. The force of the waterfall shoved them down to the bottom of the pool, where the water tumbled them in circles. Lishka did not need air to breathe, so the depths did not bother her. She held onto Dominick and kicked to push off the jagged rocks that loomed like teeth from the dark. Her final kick thrust them out of the whirlpool and into the southern current, shooting them away from the falls. Her face broke the surface on a violent wave and immediately she searched for the outcrop, which had already begun to recede into the distance.

No sign of Sieth. She reached out with her senses and still could not detect any trace of him, or his Master's power. The water heaved and roiled, crashing against the large boulders disrupting the riverbed. Luckily, the quickest part of the current had hold of them, and with some maneuvering, Lishka kept them in the swells and away from the rocks.

Downstream from the falls, the river flowed strong but contained fewer boulders to break legs. Lishka took a moment to wrestle her arms under Dominick's armpits and turn him so that he floated on his back, half across her torso, the hilts of his swords on either side of her face. She rested her chin on his sodden head and as they floated, she kept alert for any boulders.

Sieth had not followed them into the river, and she did not sense him on the bank. With luck, she thought, the water might have subdued her magikal aura and he would not have realized they had gone in. He had not challenged them directly. Perhaps he waited until they stood distracted, hoping to catch them off guard.

This thought comforted her. She took it as a sign that Sieth did not trust he could overpower the two of them together.

Yet Dominick was injured, and the jump into the river had drained her of energy. They were vulnerable. Lishka could only hope Sieth did not double back to follow them before she had a chance to heal Dominick and replenish her strength.

As she searched the shores for threat, her fingers did their own assessment of Dominick. Holding him with one arm, she withdrew the other to explore his back beneath the swords. Sharp bone pressed against her fingers, and she gave a firm push to reset his spine. He had not yet begun to mend. Something was preventing his own innate healing ability.

*The water.* Lishka had been distracted by Sieth and

by having to maintain hold of Dominick. Only now did she feel the magik in the water encouraging her fey and dampening her vampirism. The water contained the same, though diluted, power of Mirna Sorne. Dominick's ability to heal came from his immortal side. His injury had not worsened, but he would also not heal on his own in these waters.

The injury would have to wait. Lishka let the river carry them for several more hours to put a more comfortable distance between them and Sieth, until daylight arrived and threatened to reach them in the depths of the ravine. She eyed the shore, looking for a bank large enough with trees to shelter them for when the sun rose high enough overhead to reach the river. Finally, she spotted a place ahead that looked suitable for rest and healing. The current pushed them in gentle waves that lapped a sandy pebbled shore. Lishka pulled her body away from Dominick's to kick her legs and propel them out of the main current. Her boots hit the river floor and she let Dominick float for as long as she could, before lifting him across the shore and into the trees to lay him on a bed of moss.

She studied their surroundings. They rested in a grove of alders. She did not sense the wolves as she had in Uru. They'd been carried maybe thirty miles and remained in the North.

She turned her attention back to Dominick. His hair draped over his forehead and rivulets of water ran across his eyes and down his cheeks. She unbuckled the scabbards at his chest and carefully eased the swords out from under him, so that his back lay flat against the earth. She set Excalibur under his right hand.

Then she removed his heavy coat and her own as well to free her movement. She would use the coats to create a shelter to protect him once the healing spell had completed. Ready for the casting, she placed one hand on the center of his chest and slid the other underneath him to the point of the severest break.

She closed her eyes and reached for her power. A grinding sensation of wrongness overtook her. Lishka stopped to assess. The binding of the mage's mark should not limit her innate energy. She reached again, and again met with resistance. She frowned. Her kind possessed death magik, not the magik of life that could heal. Still, she had found success performing minor spells on herself in the past, to speed her own natural healing ability.

She gazed down at Dominick. His face smoothed in unconsciousness. He could almost be human again, but for the coolness of his body and the paleness of his skin. He looked vulnerable and the desire to protect him tightened her chest. A different energy expanded from her core, the same power that had drawn her to the fey. She allowed it to fill her veins and flow from her palms into Dominick. As she did so, Dominick's own energy flickered in his chest, responding to her.

A loud pop broke the silence. The bones had realigned. Beneath her fingers, the rough bumps of the break smoothed. Muscle and flesh knit together, and his skin became smooth once more beneath the cloth of his shirt.

Lishka opened her eyes. On Dominick's forehead, a gash had healed, the only remaining trace the pink stream running down the side of his forehead. She used her sleeve to wipe away the diluted blood, then tried to wipe the rest of his face despite her own clothing being soaked through. She smoothed the hair away from his forehead and eyes.

He remained unconscious. Lishka frowned. *He should have the strength to regain consciousness now that his flesh and bone have repaired itself.* But dawn had arrived, so he had likely slipped into daysleep. She should let him rest and yet an urge to look into his eyes overtook her. The fear of the attack, of seeing Dominick injured, rose from where she had suppressed it. She shook him slightly, trying to keep from being too rough. Still, he slept.

Lishka placed both hands on his firm shoulders and leaned over to put her face right before his. She pressed her influence against him, urging him to awaken. Behind his eyelids, Dominick's eyes twitched as though he dreamt. She didn't move. He opened his eyes.

Lishka felt with hyperintensity every point of their connection. Her palms pressed against his shoulders, her leg pushed against his thigh where she knelt beside him. She held perfectly still and so did Dominick. He stared into her eyes and she into his. Golden flecked the soft brown, which had not changed despite becoming immortal.

Slowly, as if to not drive her away, Dominick raised his hands to cup her waist. In a graceful movement, he lifted her onto him so that she lay along the full length of his body. Her face now only an inch before his, she had but to exhale to close the distance. They stayed there for a moment longer. Lishka reached her right hand from Dominick's shoulder to cushion his head and bury her fingers into the damp waves. She leaned down and pressed her lips to his.

Dominick yielded immediately. He wrapped his arms around her in a vise, returning her kiss with hunger. He tasted of the river; his cold, soft lips quickly warmed against hers. She gripped his hair to the point of pain, and he reached up and did the same, trapping her against him before flipping them around to press her into the soft moss. The scent of rich earth filled her nose, combining with the smell of Dominick.

A new urgency overtook them, a desperation for a connection beyond the sharing of blood. Lishka pulled at the waistline of his pants and Dominick buried his face against the curve of her neck as he gathered her to him. A sharp pain at her neck and he drew just the smallest amount of blood. She tucked her face to his shoulder and her teeth punctured the delicate flesh at his collarbone. A sweet copper taste filled her mouth, filling her with satisfaction until another pleasure took hold of her body.

Lishka gripped Dominick's shoulders and then his back, pressing herself to him. Worry, fear, all else disappeared but for Dominick and the delicious sensations he gave her. Heat circulated between them, the energy from him flowing through her and then back to him with their shared blood, entwining to become one entity.

For one jolting second, Lishka's heart beat. Then Dominick bit her harder, driving deeper, and she arched her back and forgot everything.

In the early light of dawn, they continued to hold each other tight, bound to one another, to find warm comfort amidst the cold, silent vastness of the wilderness.

A RESTLESS URGE deep inside awakened her. Lishka opened her eyes to black. She pushed the coat off the structure made of branches that Dominick had built, revealing a charcoal gray sky. Tiny snowflakes swirled down from the alders to catch in her eyelashes. She blinked to shake them loose, and they dropped to stick to her cheeks, where they didn't melt against her cold skin.

She lay still, staring into the flakes, letting her mind go blank. The snow twirled in circles, a never-ending stream of white dust. Her head rested on Dominick's shoulder, and he shifted, coming to consciousness at the impending night. He squeezed her arm to draw her closer, and then released her, allowing her to put some space between them. The cold air trickled into the gap and Lishka suppressed the sudden urge to push back into Dominick's arms.

Yet their moment of respite, of forgetfulness, had passed. They must continue north. With Sieth's attack they had lost at least a day of travel.

Lishka sat up and knocked the branches off to uncover them, shaking more snow into their laps. She stood and put on her coat, pulling up the hood to hang low over her face. Night had not fully fallen, though the last of the daylight lacked any potency and did nothing more than irritate her skin.

Dominick rose as well, following Lishka's lead to ready himself for travel. He donned his coat and grabbed the swords, strapping Kiaban's first across his back, buckling the scabbard over his chest. Then he hefted Excalibur to position it over the Coven blade. Lishka stepped behind him and he shifted at the same time to put his back to her, so that she could adjust the blades in an even cross.

He bent to pick up her sword and help her secure it to her back. When finished, he stood behind her for a moment, his hands on her shoulders. She held still, her entire body tingling from where he almost touched her with his thighs, hips, and chest. Desire rose within her, an ache to once more close the gap between them.

Slowly, she raised her hands to rest over the tops of his, seeking comfort in his touch. They stood there for a moment more. When she could no longer justify the delay to herself, she released him. Dominick dropped his hands from her shoulders and sighed so just the smallest exhale shifted the hair around her ear. Lishka shivered, and took a step forward to lead the way out of the grove.

They trekked back up the river, now on the opposite side from their original route. Away from the false safety of their grove, their attention turned to their surroundings with hyperfocus. Sieth had gotten too close before Dominick detected him. Lishka cursed herself under her breath for her negligence. She recognized now what Dominick had sensed after the Siernak, what she had felt in her brand. She did not have to give voice to the fear that plagued them both.

*Had Sieth seen the blade for what it was?*

Where before Dominick would occasionally stray from her side, he now stayed close. When day forced them to take shelter, they tucked themselves shoulder-to-shoulder in nooks between boulders or beneath thicker trees, and Dominick wrapped his arms around Lishka to let her rest comfortably against him.

On the second day, they passed the point of Sieth's ambush. Lishka drew her sword and Dominick drew Excalibur. They slowed their pace to creep through, reaching with all senses to search the land around them. Only the sounds of natural life resounded along the river. Still, they continued well past dawn until the light began to burn, to put as many miles between them and the waterfall as possible.

The following night, the banks leveled out. Flat tundra stretched as far as they could see, where it met with the Krebarvitch Mountains to the west. The river cut a shimmering swath through the land. The banks had been mostly covered by snow, but here and there, patches of brown grass broke through and in the near distance, the odd cluster of narrow evergreens disrupted the smooth landscape.

The scent of humans lingered in the air.

"Dirn," Lishka said.

"Where is it?" Dominick asked, not seeing the town before them.

"Close."

They sped along the river. Where the land had looked flat at a distance, they found it dipped and rose again. On one such rise, the town came into view below.

Where the fishing villages contained temporary yurts, the town of Dirn had permanent structures made of stone and wood. Pelts hung stretched on racks next to doorways, and smoking huts for fish and meat produced long streams of smoke into the night sky. The town sprawled for at least a mile along the eastern shore. Numerous boats of all sizes bobbed on the water, the largest being a barge that could carry several cars. The river had spread since the waterfall to its widest point yet.

"We should wait here," Lishka said, "and approach in daylight."

Dominick raised his eyebrows in question.

"The people of Dirn are not like those in the South, nor even in Seattle. They know of the wild things. They will have likely been warned by the fishing village of the Siernak's attack and may meet us with hostility. We will have better luck getting news in daylight."

"Can you withstand it?" Dominick asked. His own sensitivity had not increased past sluggishness and discomfort, both diminished by the overcast sky and weakened winter sun.

"Yes," Lishka said. "We'll approach late afternoon, when the sun is on the descent."

Several large boulders dotted the gentle hillside, and they took refuge behind one, staying in its shadow. Before dawn arrived, Lishka climbed up on the boulder to lie on her stomach and survey the land before them. To the west, a glimmering revealed a great marsh that had not quite frozen over. In the spring, the gnats would gather so thickly there that they blotted out the daylight, and the vast herds of caribou that roamed this place would have chewed coats from their encounters. Directly before them against the northern horizon, the bare rock of the lower foothills broke the plateau, and behind, the snow-covered Krebarvitch Mountains curved gently northwest to cup them in their shadow.

Lishka focused on the area just beyond the foothills. Her blood stirred. Her fey didn't call her forth. Instead, a darker part of her rose and drew her there. At once, a sharp pain lanced through her brand.

She pulled all her power into herself and slid from the boulder down to the ground, putting rock between her and the land beyond. Her entire body tightened, as though she could hide just by being small.

"What is it?" Dominick's firm hand gripped her shoulder, shaking her back to herself.

"I thought I felt him. Beyond, in the foothills."

Dominick made to rise and Lishka reached out her hand to his forearm.

"Don't."

Dominick hesitated, registering the look on her face. He knelt back down to sit beside her. On instinct, Lishka took his hand in her own. The warmth of his unique power flowed into her palm to dilute the ice in her veins from Zaral's touch. They sat with hands clasped, leaning into each other. At Dominick's back, Excalibur emitted a quiet hum.

For the size of the town, Dirn fairly bustled in the late afternoon hour. Lishka and Dominick approached the humans carefully. A low, rough fence had been erected around the town in clear haste and a sentry sat at the top of the entrance, bow in hand. Lishka prepared a spell to divert any arrows, yet he merely glanced at them and resumed his watch of the terrain.

They began to walk through the doorway, which had been built to account for two horses abreast, or a single-horse cart. Another sentry peeled away from the wall.

"Stop there."

Lishka and Dominick paused. Lishka detected an

odd tang about the sentry's person, what she had come to think of as Northern magik. It had a hint of wildness she did not encounter further south, not even in Seattle.

The sentry approached to face them. Despite their clear otherness, he displayed no fear. As Lishka had said, the Northerners were accustomed to wilder things.

"There will be no hunting in the town," he said bluntly, revealing yellow teeth behind a matted black beard. He stared into Lishka's eyes and recognition showed in his own.

"Those of the Folk are welcome in Dirn, as long as Dirn stays safe from their mischief."

Lishka dipped her head in acknowledgement.

"We won't hurt anyone," Dominick said, eager to reassure the man. "Do—"

The gatekeeper turned on his heel and retreated to his post, waving them through as he walked. Dominick stifled his question, glanced at Lishka, and shrugged.

They passed through into the main town. The buildings on the bank faced the water and seemed to be mostly for storing fishing equipment and processing the catch. There did not appear to be any general stores or other services. Dirn survived as a community, more clan-like than the transactional southern cities. Each inhabitant contributed to the overall health of the town by growing or catching food, building tools, and sewing clothes from plush animal hides that would keep them warm in the long winters.

Lishka had expected a certain wary interest from the townsfolk. Instead, they ignored Lishka and Dominick to rush by in a flurry of activity. The barges they had seen from the hill floated low in the river, laden with all manner of pelts, containers for food, and nets. On the shore, more goods sat scattered all down the bank, ready for loading.

Before she could stop him, Dominick intercepted a man rushing past with a crate full of fishing wire.

"What's going on?" Dominick asked.

The man stopped to assess Lishka and Dominick. Immediately, he looked to their foreheads where their deadened mage's marks rested, invisible to all but those who knew how to see them.

"I take it you're new to the North." His voice rumbled out gruff and strangely accented. He shrugged back his thick fur hood to get a better look at them.

Dominick nodded. "We've come from Seattle."

"What brings you 'ere?"

"Our own business," Lishka said, her voice sharp. The man stared at her.

"Well, I 'ope your business don't lead you north," he said at last. "Something happens there. Strange things been coming from the south. Some tried to come through Dirn, but others stopped them."

"Who stopped them? What were they?" Lishka thought of Mordan but given the distance to travel to Uruden and then north, he could not have arrived so soon.

The man leaned in as if to share a secret and Dominick did the same, though he could hear him just fine.

"Witches," the man whispered. "Witches fighting witches."

"Are you sure?" Lishka asked. Witches would not fight for Zaral, who had persecuted them for centuries.

The man shrugged. "They 'ad the power about them.

They breathed the air and melted the snow with warm bodies. They were not like you."

"Is that why everyone is leaving?" Dominick asked. The man switched his attention to Dominick.

"Aye. Too many attacks on surrounding villages. The witch fight was the last straw. Then there's the smell."

"Smell?" Dominick encouraged the man to continue talking by providing a rapt audience. The man shifted forward again.

"A strange smell, like fire and smoke. Never 'ad it this far north. The smell of molten rock." He emitted a strange guffaw-like noise, halfway between a cough and sneeze. Dominick twitched but did not pull back in case of offending their source of information.

"Take my advice, go south. Those things that come in the dark all seem to be goin' that-aways." He nodded his head in the direction of the foothills and spat into the frozen ground. "Evil is what's brewing there. Best to keep away." He shuffled off to the river's edge, where a small boat awaited him. His wide boots left deep footprints in the mud.

"What do you think that means?" Dominick asked.

"I don't know. The witches may have been fighting mages like the tracker. But the fire smell is disturbing. It could be a spell or…" Lishka stopped. She didn't want to think what else might create the scent of fire, and at such a distance if it truly came from the hills.

"Those boats won't make it over the falls," Dominick observed. Indeed, in places downstream, the river had narrowed enough that it would not hold the larger barges.

"They are river folk," Lishka said. "I'm sure they have a way through. Perhaps they will go in part by foot. Uru will let them pass if they are refugees from our war."

The words hung between them: *our war.*

"What now?" Dominick asked.

"We continue north. If those who have passed through head for the foothills, then that is where we must go."

She tried not to think of her brand's reaction the night before. They must find those who supported Zachriel. If witches fought for Dirn, that was encouraging. It meant somewhere out there in the wilderness, Zachriel's followers had arrived and now prepared for war.

In the distance beyond the town, the foothills rose in an ominous line across the horizon.

THEY DEPARTED DIRN with no resistance. The boats had begun to steadily push out into the river, long oars and poles directing them downstream. By the time they left, over half of the boats had launched. The remainder saw an increased rush to complete loading them, as no one wanted to be left behind when night fell.

The rush only underscored the sense of urgency that squeezed both Lishka's and Dominick's chests and drove them forward. The sense that time had run out hung over them. At Dominick's back, Excalibur continued to hum in a constant vibration.

The foothills sat deceptively close. Knowing they contained unknown danger made them seem to loom that much closer, as though they stood almost on Dirn's doorsteps. Lishka and Dominick found this not to be the case. The more ground they covered, the farther away the hills appeared to be. Stark white rocks dotted the landscape, barely discernible from the snow. Small at first, they grew to boulders more than double Lishka's height.

They might have used the rocks to seek shelter from daylight, but soon found they had no need. The sky turned to night and the following day brought angry storm clouds that blotted out almost all light. The reek of magik filled their noses.

Finally, on the third full day and night of travel, for they did not stop to rest, the ground began to rise in elevation. They had reached the start of the foothills. Bare rock rose from the dry grass in increasingly steep steps. Lishka almost crushed the nest of a grass-dwelling bird who had long since fled. She realized that they had not sensed any animals for days. The land had become all but barren, with only the hardiest plants and insects to give it life.

They scrambled over the stone, constantly on the alert for any threat. As they ran, something began to tug at Lishka's mind. She scanned the land around them, and Dominick did the same. The sense tickled her mind, like a frequency played just out of range. The hills dipped into a flat snow-covered plateau a mile wide, which sat encircled by steep, exposed rock. With the high ground around it, this would be the perfect place for an ambush. Lishka paused at the crest of the hill, searching once more. She shifted her hood away from her face, where the diluted late afternoon light did nothing more than tingle her skin. The quickest way forward lay across the plateau. She caught Dominick's eye and with her fingers made the gesture for running. Few things could catch them when they ran.

They leapt off the boulder to hit the ground, then sprang forward in twin blurs. Movement streaked on the edges of her peripheral vision and a wild musk filled her nose. At her side, Dominick slowed and grinned.

Wolves flowed from the hills, their collective paws shaking the earth. The fur across their backs rippled and they ran in a continuous stream, overtaking Lishka and Dominick to surround them. They numbered at least sixty to fill the plateau. Relief flooded Lishka, and she sped up once more to match the wolves' pace. Overhead, roiling charcoal clouds rumbled in harmony with the pawsteps of the wolves.

With their furred escort as their guide, they crossed into the foothills and entered Zachriel's camp.

C H A P T E R  3 2

# ZACHRIEL'S ARMY

ZACHRIEL'S ENCAMPMENT LAY TWENTY miles further in the depths of the hills, strategically placed in a shallow valley to hide his army. Lishka would not have known this section of foothills to be any different to the others, but as the clouds turned black with the coming of night, a wolf at the lead let out a long howl. Several others joined to amplify the call. On the nearest ridgeline, a narrow shape peeled away from the rock to stand alert.

The wolves slowed to flow through a narrow opening where two slopes met. Lishka searched the rock overhead for more sentries. Their skill hid them from even her eyes. As she passed, a delicate touch tickled her skin and senses. It intensified almost to pain against her brand. Then the sensation receded.

Before them, tents and other temporary structures stretched for miles across the valley. Scattered across the roofs flew the standard of the eagle on the scales of balance. Lishka had never seen Zachriel's crest unpaired from the hawk of his brother's. A chill crept underneath her skin to lodge there. There would be no turning back to a united Coven. She knew this already, but to see it made it real.

"Where are the rest of them?" Dominick asked. Lishka took in what Dominick had already observed. Most of the tents stood empty, with far too few soldiers remaining. The soldiers still there rushed either away from them or past them toward the center of the camp.

A firm nudge at the back of her knees pushed her forward. Their escort had dispersed and now only ten wolves remained with them, urging them along. Lishka allowed herself to be led. Ahead, a low flat rock stood surrounded; on the outside of the circle, a lean wolfwoman with narrow hips crossed her arms, and bit her lower lip until it bled. She stared at the rock and the circle, but as they approached, her nostrils flared, and her head snapped up to stare at Lishka and Dominick. She didn't smile, but her gaze softened in recognition, and she dipped her head in welcome.

*Wren.*

She turned to call over to someone, and Luka appeared. He bounded toward them, his steps light though his face had settled into a grim expression.

"The battle has started." His voice carried ahead of him. Seconds later, he stood before them. "Zaral's forces arrived and met with Zachriel maybe one hundred miles northeast of here."

"What is the status?" Lishka asked. The urgency that had pressed them onward tightened her chest to the point of suffocation. They had not traveled this far, come so close, only to fail.

"We hold them off, away from Zachriel. He waits for you now." Luka's eyes fell to Dominick. Dominick straightened his shoulders and nodded.

"Come. We will find the way through." Luka turned to lead them to the rock table.

"How did the wolves arrive so quickly?" Lishka asked as they followed him. Luka smiled, chasing away for a moment the severity of war.

"Wren and I hurried back from the borderlands to report the Siernak's attack. We headed for Uruden, to meet Queen Vissa there and bring the news to King Urith. A day after leaving you, we found King Urith and his army of wolves."

"That's not possible. Mordan said Uruden would take at least a week's travel," Lishka interjected.

"There's more," Luka said. "Queen Vissa and Mordan never arrived at Uruden. En route, they intercepted a messenger heading for Morvane. King Urith had already amassed an army, as many as he could call within the week, sending messengers to the farther territories. Queen Vissa took her wolves and rushed north with Mordan, while the messenger carried on to Morvane.

"She arrived just before the battle, and she and our King are there now. More wolves have been arriving every day, though many remain in Uru, to protect its borders… in case." Luka did not need to elaborate.

"How did King Urith know?" Lishka asked. Mordan could not have used magik to warn him. *Could Zachriel himself have called to the King?*

"There is an ancient tree in the center of Uruden." Wren had appeared at their side. Her voice carried a musical undertone. "Its leaves never change or die. They say that in a time of great need, a leaf will drop and with it, a tea can be brewed that will cure any illness or injury."

Dominick frowned, confused at the sudden direction in the tale. Lishka remembered the tree in the realm of the fey, with the small straw figure at its base, and the chill in her bones intensified.

"The leaves began to fall," Wren continued.

"A warning," Lishka said. Wren and Luka nodded in unison. *So, the Fey Queen had provided aid, after all. Just not quite as Mordan had hoped.*

They had arrived at the table. Not a table, Lishka realized. A shallow basin, in which spread a thin sheet of water. Around it stood men and women, with their palms rested flat upon the rim, the edges of their fingers barely touching. Humans and wolves, Lishka realized. Each wolf bore a crescent tattoo on their left inner wrist.

"We stayed to wait for you," Luka said quietly. "And to protect the witches."

"Witches?" Dominick asked, and he studied those in the circle more closely. He had only ever seen one witch, the woman they had rescued from the ghoul.

"They are scrying," Luka explained. "They watch the battle, to help identify points of weakness in the enemy and to connect our leaders on the field."

Several members of Zachriel's Covens stood sprinkled amongst the others in the circle. Lishka recognized Maeva, one of only two humans turned by Mordan himself. She must be connected to Mordan, using the Maker's bond to feed him information. Clearly, Maeva had followed her Maker to Zachriel's cause. Lishka wondered if Luseth had followed as well, or if he now fought for Zaral, turning against his Maker as she had turned against hers.

Maeva whispered something to an unchanged wolf near her. The wolf nodded and hurried over to Luka.

"We've found Mordan. He fights at the western point of the crescent ridge. He will know the way to Zachriel."

Luka nodded.

"We will lead you to Mordan," Luka said.

"Isn't it a mistake to bring the sword into the battle?" Lishka asked. She did not want Dominick in the fight. Their charge was only to deliver the sword.

"Zachriel and Zaral are not there. Mordan will know how you can find Zachriel," Luka answered.

"Can't the witches tell us where Zachriel is?" Dominick pushed. The wolf witch who had given the message shook his head.

"They dare not try to connect to Zachriel. He and Zaral are linked. We cannot reach one without the other. Now we must hurry. The sword is here. At any moment, Zaral may discover it, may see how Zachriel intends to break the Veil."

In a tremendous upheaval of flesh and bone, Luka hurried his change to stand before them in his strongest form. Dominick took the moment to grab Lishka's hand and squeezed. She held his hand tight for only a second before they released each other. Wren, now also a wolf, joined Luka and the wolf witch, to lead the way from the camp to the tundra beyond.

They followed the hills northeast for several hours, always on alert for any of Zaral's army who might have stayed behind to pick off stragglers. A few wolves who had joined their small group soon peeled off to disappear into the quickening darkness, likely to dispatch the enemy.

The day did not linger, and twilight faded quickly

into true night. The grass gave way to talus, the uneven terrain slowing their pace. A wind struck up from the north and brought with it the distant sounds of battle. Overhead, the heavy clouds parted to show a three-quarter waning moon rising over a jagged ridge a mile before them. Magik once more sharpened the air, and beneath it hung the smell of fire and sulfur.

The wolves led them to the northwestern point of the ridge, which curved like a crescent northeast to cup the turmoil at its base. They slowed to creep up the lesser southern slope, keeping the rock between them and the battle below. Steel rang against steel, cutting through screams of pain and rage. Every few minutes, a howl rose above the chaos to sound out the location of the wolves, before either fading or cutting out abruptly. A dull underlying roar wove the cries and snarls together into white noise that Lishka closed her ears to. They had a more immediate concern. Overhead, at the top of the ridge, shapes skittered along the rock. Beside her, Luka curled his lip.

The ghouls had been lured by Zaral's promise of magik. They would be no match for the wolves, nor for Lishka and Dominick. Yet they posed the threat of discovery.

*The ghouls will be drawn to the blade.*

Even as the thought skirted through Lishka's mind, a round shape rose from the sharp line of rock only a few feet above them. The ghoul's eyeless head tilted to the left, toward Dominick, and it opened its mouth to reveal rows of needle-like teeth. Inky shadows stretched above its head and reached to either side of its body; the bat-like wings swept forward once and the stink of decay, reminiscent of the Siernak, hit Lishka's face.

Before it could call to others, Dominick lunged up and forward. He had drawn Kiaban's blade and thrust the point through the ghoul's neck. The ghoul gurgled and fell, tumbling over the top of them down the side of the ridge to lie lifeless on the boulders at the base.

Dominick kept his blade drawn and pushed forward up the ridge. Lishka followed him, all the while searching for any more of the creatures.

They scaled the ridge and hid against several boulders to stare down at the chaos below. Moonlight shone on thousands of creatures engaged in a frantic, sprawling mass of horror and gore. The armies had merged so thoroughly that Lishka couldn't tell where Zachriel's army ended and Zaral's began. Pockets of wolves and witches distinguished themselves from the Covens as belonging to Zachriel, fighting in groups against an onslaught of mages. The wrongness around the humans told Lishka they possessed the inverted mage's mark, drawing on followers of Zaral to enhance their power.

Along the ridge, ghouls climbed down like spiders to descend upon the heads of those below. Magik drew them and so they sought out the witches, those who possessed the organic magik they desired most. Though Zaral had called them, they did not easily distinguish ally from foe. One dropped onto the head of a mage who had been backed too close to the rock. He screamed as the ghoul dug its claws into his shoulders and attempted to suction his energy. The ghoul had the upper hand before the mage reached up to grip its head. An angry electricity glimmered up from the mage's hands into the ghoul and the creature's veins lit up from within, a glowing network that mapped its blood. Then it twitched twice and flopped onto the ground. The mage straightened in victory and gasped his last breath as a sword ran him through the heart.

At the base of the ridge, shadows spread. The Siernak lingered within them, consuming any wolf or witch who crossed into the dark. Long clawed hands reached past the ink to rake across the back of a wolf and expose muscle. The wolf screamed in agony and shuddered to the earth. Its companion dove across its back to launch into the dark. Several more wolves attacked with increased frenzy at the enemy around them, keeping clear of the shadows' edges. Protected for the moment in their center, a human witch crouched over to prepare a spell. At once, she rose to her feet and charged the nearest cloud. Fire blazed from her hands, brighter than lightning. She flung it into the dark and the Siernak, exposed, screamed and howled, all their senses blinded. Several members of Zachriel's Coven rushed in to hack them to rotten pieces.

"There are so many," Dominick said. He stood at Lishka's side, hypnotized by the fighting below them. "I didn't think there would be so many."

"The Great Covens have been gathering their followers for centuries, possibly longer," Lishka said. She could not tell which way the battle turned. Dominick gripped Kiaban's blade even tighter, and Lishka knew he ached to draw Excalibur instead.

"We must find Mordan," she whispered. Still, they stood, watching. Lishka did not want to bring Dominick into that. The fear that had surged when Dominick fell into the river threatened to overtake her once more. She forced her mind to instead analyze the situation. To fear would be to invite weakness, and Dominick needed her strength. She had been in battles before.

*Though none like this.*

Yet Lishka took small comfort that she did not sense Zaral in the melee. As Luka had said, neither Zaral nor Zachriel fought alongside their followers.

Wren dropped her head to stare miles down at the base of the rock. She turned to lope along the ridge, assuming they would follow. Lishka drew her sword. She would not use magik unless forced, and certainly not Kiaban's fire. Her fey magik left an unmistakable footprint and would draw the ghouls and those who fought for Zaral.

They picked their way across the ridge, using the rock to shield them from those below. A ghoul scrambled up onto a boulder directly to Dominick's right and stared into the turmoil, searching for witches and the easiest path down the rock. Dominick began to lift his sword. The ghoul stiffened and then flopped over, a short arrow lodged in its neck.

A witch stood before them, her bow in hand. The remains of a spell for accuracy dissipated into the air. She reached for another arrow, then stopped her movement at the sight of the wolves. She dipped her head to them and then to Lishka and Dominick, hesitating for one moment to stare at Lishka's eyes. Her head snapped to the right, and she glared over Lishka's shoulder. In a smooth motion, she pulled another arrow into her bow and bounded forward back the way they had come, the words for a spell already forming on her lips.

The steep cliff meant that only skilled climbers could take that route into the battle; the climb would leave them vulnerable on the rock. The distance from ridge to ground was too great for even longbows wielded by the Covens, and so the ghouls alone used this as their vantage point. The nearby violence churned in Lishka's veins and she itched to put sword to flesh, but the witch had cleared their path of the ghouls and they made their way unhindered.

They ran for the last mile down the crescent point. The noise of the battle increased and Lishka gripped her sword tighter. Sporadic trees grew near the base of the ridge where rock met earth, and Lishka stayed close to Dominick as they wove their way through, the wolves now blurs just ahead.

A clash of steel rang at her left, and she whirled about. Two vampires stood pressed against each other with their blades locked in a cross. She focused on the larger of the two, who snapped at his smaller opponent with bared fangs. Zaral's blood called to Lishka's.

The other fighter, a woman, glowered up at her aggressor. Zachriel's eagle crest had been carved into the leather of her sleeve. With a snarl, she shoved the opposing vampire back several feet. Rather than destabilize him, he used the momentum to turn about and rush her. The woman pivoted on her back heel to dodge the edge of his swinging sword.

Dominick had already left Lishka's side and now slowed ahead with the wolves. Around them, more fights erupted. They had entered the battle. Lishka paused, torn between needing to be with Dominick and a desire to help Zachriel's warrior.

Almost too fast for even Lishka to track, the woman raised her sword and Zaral's vampire swept his blade across in a blur to penetrate the opening she had left. The steel point split flesh.

One of their kind could heal from that wound. Before the woman could clear the reach of his sword, he pushed past her last attempt to block his blow and cut off her head.

Lishka raced forward. Zaral's soldier twirled to face her head on, his eyes savage with the thrill of the kill. She knew the moment he caught the scent of their shared blood. His eyes darkened and he bared his teeth in a malicious smile. Lishka gathered her strength, already assessing the vampire's weakness. While her mage's mark was bound, his forehead remained bare. He would not be able to match her in battle. A grim joy rose inside her; finally, here was someone she could fight.

Before she could reach him, two figures cut across her path. The vampire raised his sword with glee to meet them in a whirlwind of steel.

Without breaking stride, Lishka veered away to let Zachriel's followers finish it, her excitement already subsiding. She had been foolish to hesitate and now she ran back to Dominick's side. The wolves kept him protected for the moment and Zaral's soldiers had not found him. Rather than engage in the fight around them, they ducked and wove through the trees, doing their best to avoid the skirmishes. Ahead, a churn of bodies blocked the path forward.

To her left, Dominick stiffened.

*"Sieth."*

His whisper roared in her ears, and she turned from where the main battle raged. Shadows spread through the trees from their left and the unmistakable decay thickened the air. Beneath that, the cold familiarity grated against her senses. The shadow roiled toward them unnaturally fast. They would be outmatched. Those nearby who belonged to Zachriel engaged in their own fights and could not help them. Lishka reached inside her to summon the symbols for the violet fire.

Beside her, Luka growled, then lifted his head to the sky. He let loose a long howl that pierced the sounds of war around them. From somewhere in the battle behind them, an answer rumbled, deep and full of power. Luka cut his howl off, lowered his head, and raised all the fur along his mane. He snarled and dove into the shadows, Wren with him.

Lishka could not let the wolves die for them. She rushed forward. The shapes of the Siernak appeared and she arched her blade forward to slice satisfyingly through armor and bone, severing an arm. The resounding screech scraped her nerves and she swung again.

*"Ready to die?"* The question slithered through the shadow.

Lishka spun to her right, to Dominick. Just past him, the shadows withdrew to reveal Sieth. Dominick raised his sword and barely blocked a strike. Kiaban's steel matched itself and so the sword held true against Sieth's blade. Sieth snarled with fury.

Anger flooded through Lishka, that Sieth dared to wield a weapon forged by Kiaban, whom he had no doubt attacked in the Seattle Coven insurrection. She lunged forward to distract him from Dominick, but Sieth's focus had fixed on the pommel above Dominick's ear. His eyes narrowed.

Lishka swung her sword and Sieth launched himself back out of reach. The whisper of movement at her side alerted her, and she dodged the scraping Siernak claw.

Sieth smiled. They could not long stand against both him and the Siernak.

A rumble of movement churned at her back. Sieth stopped his forward slashing and glared beyond her right shoulder. Before she could seize the opportunity, he whirled the shadows about him and disappeared into the dark. A second later, a great wolf the size of a small bear thundered past her. Not even the Siernak's shade could match the deep black of his coat. The sense of vast forests and primal strength swept over Lishka at his passing. Behind him, a river of wolves spread out to devour all in their path.

The Wolf King had answered Luka's call.

Luka emerged from the fray with Wren and slammed into Lishka, driving her back from the fighting. A shallow gash dripped blood from his side, already healing.

*"Lishka."*

For one second, her blood froze at the sound of her name called across the turmoil. Then, in a wave of relief, she recognized the warmth in the voice.

In less than a second, Mordan stood beside her. Behind him, Lady Raseska kept Zaral's minions at bay. Holding a curved blade in each hand, she swung them about to cleave her opponents into pieces. Two sharpened horns rose from an iron helmet that exposed her face. In a smooth movement, she bent backward at an angle no mortal spine could endure to slice both points across the abdomen of the closest vampire. He shuddered and dropped to his knees, where he met his end against her blades. She continued the circular movement to spin back to face them and she smiled, revealing red, sharp teeth.

"Well met on the field," she exclaimed.

Mordan grabbed Lishka's arm and drew her close, capturing her attention. Lady Raseska continued to fight with the wolves to give them a moment of reprieve.

"Zachriel waits for you," Mordan said. "You must bring him the sword."

"Where is he?" Lishka asked.

"Close. He holds Zaral at bay, or maybe Zaral holds him. He will do what he is able to prevent Zaral from joining this fight, to spare as many as he can. Follow—"

Mordan grunted and shoved against Lishka. She grabbed his shoulders to absorb his weight. The tip of a sword stuck through his right collarbone. Behind him, the vampire who had slipped past Lady Raseska wrenched the sword back and raised it high. Dominick pushed in front of them, ready to block the attack.

A blur of red slammed into the vampire to carry him to the ground. In a snarling mess of blood, the wolf tore into his flesh, ripping away huge chunks that not even his supernatural healing ability could endure.

Mordan straightened away from Lishka. The wound at his shoulder oozed blood. The sword had been spelled, and though the blow had not been fatal, the casting would delay the healing. Nonetheless, he hefted his sword in his right hand as though the wound had been a mere scratch. Now at his side, Queen Vissa studied him with concern, her muzzle stained with blood.

"Go now, quickly," Mordan instructed. "Follow the line of the crescent point northeast until you come to another ridge. You will know it. You will feel them."

He held Lishka's gaze and lowered his voice even further.

"Let nothing stop you."

Lishka nodded. Mordan stepped away and raised his sword once more.

"The wolves will see you away from here," Mordan called, already turning to meet the next onslaught.

Queen Vissa barked and at least twenty wolves gathered around them, encircling Lishka and Dominick. They pushed against Zaral's army to create space between the enemy and the blade. At the front, Queen Vissa let loose a growling howl and leapt forward to tear out a mage's throat, dissipating the spell he'd been about to cast on her wolves.

Beyond her, Lishka caught a glimpse of Lord Dorwan. He glowered through the battle before him. A mage stepped too close, and Lord Dorwan cut him down without a glance. Lishka followed his stare through the bodies to catch a glimpse of white hair before the fighting obstructed her view.

Lord Dorwan raised a sword over half as long as Lishka to bring it down. Lord Barik, in a fit of strength and grace in juxtaposition to his seemingly frail appearance, twisted away and the steel struck another of Zaral's lesser followers in his place.

Jostled and pushed forward, the battle consumed Lord Dorwan and Lishka could not see whether he emerged victorious. To her left, a glimpse of a familiar pale face told her Kristoph had survived Seattle. He directed a unit of Keepers to attack a cluster of Siernak who had dared to stray from the base of the ridge.

The wolves hacked and bit and clawed their way through the battle to the edge so successfully that no danger reached Lishka and Dominick. They kept running, even when the fighting diminished around them. Queen

Vissa's wolves peeled off until only she remained. Then, with a low howl, she stopped running, her fading notes encouraging them on. The echo of her war cry told them she rejoined the fight.

The wolves could not remain with them and draw attention to the blade. Dominick and Lishka would have to bear it alone.

They streaked across the terrain, which smoothed out once more to rock in the distance. Behind one of those ridges, Zachriel waited.

*With Zaral.*

Again the fear rose and again Lishka worked to subdue it. In all her long life, she had done her best to hide from her Maker. Now she ran willingly to him.

Shapes moved past them in the dark, either sprinting toward or away from the battle, though none headed in the direction of the far ridge. The light wind hummed with an electricity that dropped the already frigid air several degrees. Overhead, drifting clouds intermittently covered the moon and cast shadows on the ground, not caring about those who fought and died below them.

A shape to Lishka's right approached. She expected it to flee past them, as the rest had done. The shape drew closer. Lishka slowed to face it, waving Dominick on. He had to continue. Ignoring her, Dominick once more drew Kiaban's blade.

Moonlight shone on pale hair. Anger filled her. This time, she would protect Dominick.

The attacker's pale hair flowed long, as though its owner swam underwater. Syral's wide smile highlighted her fangs, and she threw herself toward Dominick. He swung the sword, and nimbly she danced out of his range, laughing.

Lishka reached for her blade. A hand gripped her arm and spun her about to come nose to nose with Darrak.

"Not this time," he whispered. Unlike Syral, he did not smile. Too fast for her to react, he whipped her around to face Dominick, trapping her arms at her sides and pressing her to him. Syral had drawn a wicked knife and now stalked Dominick, who kept his sword between them. Dominick turned in a slow, steady circle to follow her movement.

Darrak leaned down to whisper into her ear.

"See now. See how she draws him in. He is no match for her. She has trained for centuries."

Lishka jerked and Darrak squeezed her tighter, delighted at her reaction. She wanted to defend Dominick, but she could not argue. Syral needed to see only a second of weakness, a single misstep, and she would take him. A calculating hunger gleamed in Syral's sharp eyes as she stared at Dominick, moving with precision that forced him to pivot and keep her in his sight. Dominick had undeniable skill, but Darrak was right. He'd barely had time to train.

"I thought you were dead," Lishka said, trying to buy time to think. Darrak's cheek brushed hers as he smiled.

"Those who are loyal are rewarded."

Indeed, the power flowed from his unbound mage's mark. Lishka tasted the sharp tang of it in the air and her skin prickled against the rough magik. The violet fey magik within her churned in response. Darrak had been made stronger somehow, and within the magik she detected the spell that had masked his presence and softened his steps. Syral had been the distraction.

He tilted his head away from her, as though he listened. Dominick and Syral continued to circle each other.

"He is coming."

Darrak could not have meant Zaral, who remained locked with his brother in battle. He could only mean Sieth. Sieth's arrival would mean their defeat. They could not overcome all three, even with Excalibur.

At that moment, Dominick's movement brought Lishka into his line of sight, and his eyes flicked past Syral to Lishka. Syral lunged forward and moonlight caught the wicked edge of her blade.

A burst of violet energy exploded from Lishka and flung Darrak back. New electricity snapped in the air, combating the power that froze their veins. Syral twisted to protect herself from the outburst and Dominick did not hesitate. Lishka blinked and met Syral's gaze. Syral's eyes widened. She looked down at her chest, where the steel pierced her heart.

"No!" Darrak's voice cut through any power in the air, poisonous hatred mixed with shock and grief.

Syral crumpled.

Lishka whirled to look for Darrak, who would no doubt avenge his partner's death. He crouched where he had fallen over twenty yards to her left. For a long moment, they stared at each other. Then Darrak leapt to his feet and streaked back toward the battle.

Lishka knew he went for Sieth. Sheathing her blade, she turned to Dominick.

"Are you okay?" Her voice came out sharper than intended. Dominick nodded.

"You?"

"Yes. Quick now. He will bring Sieth, and more." She did not want to tell Dominick what else she had felt. In the moment that her fey magik exploded, something sinister stirred, and directed its attention to them. Somewhere beyond the rock, Zaral sensed their approach.

They ran. The ridge rose before them now, more ominous in its stillness than the crescent they had left behind. They had made it. Behind this last hurdle, Zachriel waited for the sword.

Dominick drew before her, about to reach the rocks at the base of the ridge. Lishka slowed.

"Wait."

Something about the ridge felt wrong.

Dominick stopped and glanced back at her in question. At his back, the blade hummed, urging him onward. It yearned for the hand of its true wielder, now so close.

Lishka shook her head.

"Something is wrong." She studied the jagged ridgeline. "Something is there." This time she whispered, and Dominick caught her words. He studied the incline before them. A hot wind gusted down from the ridge and sulfur filled the air. It burned in Lishka's nose and chest.

A crash echoed through the night. A boulder bounced down from the higher ridge. It soared into the air and then smashed against more rock, before flying up again on impact. Where it landed, it shifted more rocks loose, cascading them into a mini avalanche that rumbled down the slope to where Lishka and Dominick stood.

The ridge moved. It heaved and twisted, and a gigantic piece broke off to stretch along the sky.

*Not a mountain.*

A long, thick neck uncoiled from the crest, stretching out to a narrow head that ended in a pointed snout. Overlapping scales as wide as a person glinted in the moonlight, contracting and stretching with the movement of muscles beneath. Great curved horns rose from the head to scrape against the sky. Sharp talons gripped the rock to send more boulders tumbling down, and a tapered tail lashed out, splitting open the side of the ridge. Red embers flashed and the blistering eyes blinked once, twice, then turned to find them in the dark.

*"My Goddess."* Lishka uttered her prayer on instinct.

The dragon reared up and fixed them in its evil sight.

C H A P T E R  3 3

# The Enemy's Secret Weapon

"Katal Baruk," Lishka breathed.

"What?" Dominick asked. The dragon had begun to beat its wings, bat-like things of immense size that created a forceful downdraft off the ridge. Wind roared about their ears and drowned out any other noise. The heat intensified, combating the below-freezing temperature of the arctic night.

"Katal Baruk," Lishka repeated, this time much louder. "The great black dragon of the ancient world."

"Dragon!" Dominick yelled over the howl of the wind. "I thought you said they were all sleeping!"

"They were. Zaral must have awakened it."

The dragon shifted its stance. Its talons gripped the rock, shaking more of it loose to bounce down the slope.

"It's going to crush us," Dominick shouted. A boulder ricocheted off the rubble and splintered into smaller pieces that flew like bullets. Dominick ducked, narrowly

525

avoiding a hit to his right eye. The dragon's head swiveled left and then right, scanning the tundra before them. Its nostrils flared and it fixated on the point where the battle still raged.

"It's going to see us," Lishka said, and she leapt forward to close the gap between her and Dominick.

"There." She pointed to a place half a mile to their right. A wide slab of rock rested over two boulders to create a shelter the size of a small house, nestled into the mountainside. The structure would withstand most of the rubble that poured off the ridge. They ran toward the shelter, keeping an eye on the dragon. Just as they reached the opening, it turned its attention from the battle to survey the base of the ridge.

Lishka dove under the rock with Dominick behind her. They hunkered down and peered through the crack between the boulders, watching for the dragon's next move.

"What's it doing?" Dominick whispered.

"I'm not sure." Lishka didn't want to tell Dominick what she really thought. Dread wormed its way deep into her core. As if it sensed her thoughts, Excalibur began to emit a low hum.

The dragon whipped its head around to stare at their pile of rocks. Bright fires burned in its eyes like twin red stars rising above the ridge.

"Can you make it stop?" Lishka asked, knowing Dominick had little control over the sword.

"I think it wants to fight the dragon," Dominick said through gritted teeth. As they watched, the dragon lowered its head level with its front feet for closer inspection of the mountainside. It folded its wings back along its great body and the wind subsided.

"We have to find a way around it," Lishka said. "You have to find a way."

Dominick cut her a sharp look.

"You cannot fight that alone," he said bluntly.

"I don't see that I have a choice." Lishka could distract the beast, enough that Dominick could scale the ridge and find Zachriel. "It might be drawn to the blade. I cannot be sure, but I think…" Lishka paused.

"What? What is it?" Dominick turned his gaze to hers and despite their predicament, a welcome warmth flowed through her. Lishka drew courage.

"I think it's a familiar."

"What's a familiar?"

"An animal that is linked to a witch, usually. It is a bond that allows the witch to see through its eyes, and sometimes control it."

"Whose familiar?" Dominick asked, even as he began to understand Lishka's meaning. His voice dropped. "Zaral's?"

Lishka nodded.

"It is possible that Zaral has forced his will upon it. It has not yet left the ridge, despite the battle full of creatures to eat and burn to ash. It guards what lies beyond it."

"And prevents any help from reaching Zachriel," Dominick finished.

"It cannot be allowed to see the sword, to understand what it truly is. If it does, we are finished." Lishka peered up through the crack in their rock shelter. The dragon still searched the area around them. It did not know they lurked there; it only suspected.

"The sword is what matters," she whispered. Dominick

shifted beside her. He did not protest and instead slid his hand into hers. They interlocked fingers for a long moment. The dragon tilted its head and glanced up, back toward the battle.

Lishka turned in her crouch and reached up to grip Dominick's face. Before he could react, she pressed her lips to his, losing herself for just a second. He raised his hand to cup the nape of her neck, against her brand, and held her even closer to him.

Then he released her. Lishka did not look at Dominick. Instead, she spun around and propelled herself out of the rock shelter.

Her feet flew over the earth, barely skimming the rock and dirt and patches of snow. She zigzagged across the open land like a little rabbit. Overhead, she felt the great dragon fix its gaze upon her, saw in her mind's eye the vastness of its wingspan that blotted out the stars. She did not turn to look. At any moment, she expected the strike of talons or a blaze of fire to destroy her.

The resounding roar of the rock avalanche told her when the dragon took flight. Lishka pushed herself harder, ran even faster. Within herself, she drew on the violet core and the energy came much more easily now, to flow up through her veins where it set her skin aglow. Lishka encouraged the energy. *The dragon may be drawn to the light and power.*

She chanced to look up at the sky. It shone only with stars and glowing clouds. The dragon did not circle overhead. She slowed and whipped around, scanning the ridge for any sign of Dominick.

Heat sucked out all moisture from the air to her left, where she had been only a second before. Fire followed in a white flash, momentarily blinding her, and the edges of her hair were singed in the inferno. She threw herself away from the blast, even as the dragon swooped so low overhead that she could have reached up and touched it.

Lishka flung herself to the ground and rolled away from the fire. The dragon stopped its spit and swung up into the sky, screeching at the failure. This time, Lishka tracked it with her eyes. The dark shape flew high into the air and paused to find her, silhouetted against the moon. She reached down for the fey magik once more, drawing it up to protect herself against the next blast. She envisioned her energy reaching the dragon, the violet consuming the destructive fire instead.

At once her view expanded. The entire tundra rolled out below her, stretching to the rocky hills, to the far Krebarvitch Mountains.

*Below?*

An ache grew in her chest for cold mountain rock made warm again, for the flow of molten lava deep in the belly of the mountains. Her wings stretched strong and caught the updraft of the wind, holding her steady. Far below, a tiny figure shone violet against the white snow and rock of the earth, exposed on the frozen land.

Lishka moved her wings, no, not her wing but her arm, and blinked. She stood on the ground awash in violet light.

A roaring boom exploded in her head.

*I am Katal Baruk. The Great One, the Black Death. What insignificant creature seeks to speak with me in the Old Way?*

The dragon's voice undulated and hissed in the ancient tongue, and somehow Lishka understood it.

Instinct drove her, some old learning buried in her fey blood. She *thought* to it, projecting her own voice.

*I am Lishka, follower of Zachriel.*

*Zachriel?* Katal Baruk sneered. *You are not of Zachriel. I smell Zaral on you. You cannot hide what you are from the Black Dragon.*

*No*, she insisted. *I am a follower of Zachriel. I do not ally with Zaral, though I am made from him.*

The dragon sniffed, a billow of hot smoke.

*Zachriel or Zaral, it does not matter. Both are death. I smell your death to your core. See how many your kind has killed over the eons, so much delicious pain for pleasure and for greed. I see their deaths stretching far back, smears upon your soul. The bloodline contaminates you. Not even the fey you try to claim can wipe the stain from you.*

Katal Baruk's truth pierced Lishka. She swayed with the despair that trickled through her veins, dissipating the life of the fey magik. She had not truly admitted the tiny hope to herself, and now it sparked out under the weight of the dragon's words. She had been a fool to think that her fey blood might have saved her from Zaral's curse. She belonged to him, and would forever.

*And now Dominick does too.*

At the thought of Dominick, Lishka shook off the despair that Katal Baruk's words had inflicted upon her. She snapped her head back up to the sky. The dragon had drifted closer, silent on the updraft, and hung floating in the air like an ominous ship. Katal Baruk could open its jaws and set her ablaze in an instant. Despite its advantage, it made no move to attack. Lishka allowed herself a moment of distraction to look past it to the far ridge. She could not tell whether Dominick had crested the ridge yet.

The dragon dropped its head even lower to study her.

*I am Earth Destroyer, Bringer of Fire. The world is meant to burn, and I was born to burn it. It is the way of things.*

It still thought it held Lishka. It could have destroyed her by now, yet it seemed to enjoy weaving its own spell upon her. The dragon had slept for thousands of years. Perhaps it found her interesting. Lishka increased her sway, simulating entrancement. Tucked behind her, she flicked her hands in the symbol of Kiaban's fire.

At once, Excalibur's hum reverberated across the earth. It vibrated up through Lishka's feet and rang the molecules in the air. Katal Baruk screeched and snapped its head around to focus on the ridge. In a split second, its fiery eyes changed and Lishka froze. The ancient dragon no longer stared out from those eyes. Instead, the embers turned black. The tendons connecting the wings to the body strained as it pivoted to streak back to the ridge.

Lishka ran. Hope once more blossomed in her chest. *Had Dominick given the sword to Zachriel?*

Even as she thought it, her brand seared. Cutting pain spasmed up her neck, spreading through her shoulders and chest. She stumbled and lost ground to the dragon.

Lishka reached for her fey magik, the warmth that might quell Zaral's icy fire. Her fey magik flickered, sending one tiny tendril of soothing sensation through her body that was instantly extinguished under the onslaught. Lishka bowed under the pain, but she forced one foot before the other and dragged her head up to focus on the ridge. The stabbing knives receded up her nerve endings to pulse at the base of her neck. She pushed herself faster. Halfway up the slope, a flash of blond caught her eye and then the bright glint of steel.

*Sieth.*

If Lishka had distracted the dragon, then so too had it distracted her. Dominick had not reached Zachriel. Lishka forced herself to move forward. She had to find a way to keep Katal Baruk from Dominick.

She reached the ridge seconds after the dragon. Katal Baruk hovered over Sieth and Dominick too, who scattered beneath the flattening wind from its wings. The dragon positioned itself so that it hung in the air vertically. It arched its neck and opened its narrow jaw filled with rows of sharp teeth. A stream of white fire sprayed from its mouth to smash into the rock.

Lishka began to climb, the heat blazing against her cheeks. She blinked to clear the white light from her vision and searched the dark for any sign of Dominick.

In an instant, she found herself in the air. For one horrible moment, she wondered if Katal Baruk had plucked her from the earth. Then she hit rock, her shoulder and hip absorbing the landing. She rolled with the momentum of the fall and leapt to her feet.

Steel and bared teeth rushed her. Lishka threw herself out of the way in a vertical spin, landing this time on her feet. She drew her sword and held it before her.

Sieth spun to face her, snarling.

"Do you really think you can turn from your Master? He, who made you all that you are?"

Lishka studied him. He had no obvious wounds, though the smell of blood came from his being. The tip of his sword was red.

Sieth followed her gaze, dropping his blade to bring the point closer to her.

"Nothing on this earth will make *that* superior to

your Maker. You can train him, gift him with powerful weapons, and he will still be the weakling I found cowering in filth."

Anger raged through Lishka, yet she forced herself to be quiet, not rising to the bait. Sieth still did not understand the meaning of Excalibur. *But Katal Baruk does.*

Lishka kept her sword in position against Sieth. She began to move and Sieth followed her. Several more steps and she had put his back to the ridge. She spared one second to look beyond his left shoulder. Sieth lunged forward with impossible speed. Lishka raised her sword and on instinct envisioned the symbols for Kiaban's fire in her mind. Violet flames poured from her palms to run up the length of the blade. Sieth twisted to the right as she drove the sword toward him. Where steel failed to meet flesh, fire flicked out to strike the side of his face and take hold. He screamed and slapped his palm to his cheek to stop her magik from eating into his skin.

Lishka released her grip on her sword to free her left hand. In her palm she gathered more fire into a swirling ball. Sieth had put out the flames on his face and glared at her, his left cheek a mess of red muscle and charcoaled flesh. Even as she stared, the skin peeled away further, the magik continuing to eat into skin and then muscle.

A cold power froze the air and threatened to seep into her bones. Sieth drew on his own magik, on his Master's blood. The skin began to knit back together, and he raised his sword to Lishka.

The earth shook and a thundering boom resonated down the mountain. Sieth's eyes widened. The following rumbling gave only a few seconds' warning and Lishka twisted about to face the new threat. Katal Baruk had landed on the slope above them, and the impact had started a massive rockslide. Boulders tumbled toward them, riding on shifting scree. Lishka leapt to the right and began to climb to put distance between herself and Sieth. She kept her feet light as she ducked the larger rocks. She didn't have time to sheath her sword, and several smaller pebbles pinged off the steel, a tinny noise against the roar of the mountain. Below her, Sieth threw himself in the opposite direction to clear the rockslide and disappeared from her view.

The dragon was snaking its head about, seeking Excalibur. Its body undulated along the rock, surprisingly graceful for its massive size. Its eyes once more held fire; Zaral's hold had momentarily broken.

Below its chest, movement caught Lishka's attention. She focused on the shadows between the rocks.

A pale face turned to her, and Dominick captured her gaze. He met her eyes for a meaningful moment, then deliberately glanced up at the dragon towering over him. The plated armor of its neck shifted above his head. He looked back at Lishka and widened his eyes. With great caution, he adjusted his stance so that he crouched with Excalibur pointed directly upwards, only a foot between its tip and the dragon's armored skin.

Lishka shook her head. She had not come all this way only to watch Dominick die. He stared back at her, determined.

In unison, Lishka launched forward and Dominick sprang up. Katal Baruk's head snapped around to Lishka and its jaws opened to show rows of teeth as long as she was tall, even as its neck plates separated for a single second to expose vulnerable flesh.

Dominick drove Excalibur deep into the dragon's neck, wrenching the blade across in one smooth motion. Black steaming blood poured out from the gaping wound. Katal Baruk screamed and the screech of a thousand thousand deaths reverberated across the tundra, all the way to the boundaries of the North. Those on the battlefield bowed under the weight of the blast. None in Dirn remained to hear it.

Lishka knelt and dug her sword into the rock to brace herself. She raised her head to peer at the dragon, who shook itself, spraying blood. It beat its wings, attempting to take flight. The wings flapped sluggishly at first, then grew stronger. Lishka assessed the wound. Already it began to close and once more she saw the flicker of Zaral in the dragon's eyes. Its enslaver attempted to heal it.

She half scrambled, half ran up the slope. Katal Baruk's tail lashed the air, swiping toward her. She ducked and the thick spikes along the tail missed her head by inches. She kept climbing. The dragon continued to beat its wings but still held its head low to the ground, not daring to reopen the gash at its neck before it healed. Its front feet left the ground as it began to rear up to catch more air that would carry it aloft.

Lishka used her momentum to leap high into the air. Katal Baruk lifted its head and opened its jaws. Teeth approached her, glimmering in moonlight, and Lishka twisted midair. Her hip caught the narrow tip of its snout and she rolled to carry herself further down along its nose. She ripped the dagger from her boot and slammed it against the bridge of the dragon's nose to help hold herself in place.

The steel shattered. Lishka scrambled to hold onto the armored ridges with her left hand, her right still gripping her sword. Katal Baruk swung its head up and then down to dislodge her. Air whipped her hair across her face and her legs lifted into the air, to then slam down against the ridges. Even with her enhanced strength, she would not be able to hold on much longer.

On the down movement, she glimpsed Dominick darting between the talons, trying to find another gap in the armor. Katal Baruk threw up its head and flattened Lishka to its snout. Her right cheek dug into the sharp scales, and hot liquid trickled down the skin just below her right eye where the rough hide had drawn blood.

The head descended once more; the force sent her legs into the air yet again before she dropped back down as the dragon ceased its movement. Leaping to her feet, Lishka ran up the bridge of its snout. In two seconds, she reached its eye, just as the dragon began to raise its head, intending to toss her into the air from whence—she knew—it would catch her in its jaws. As her feet left its hide, she used all her strength to press downward. From the smoldering embers deep in its right eye, an ancient evil glared out at her. The heat seared against Lishka's mind even as she plunged the point of her sword into the dragon's pupil down to the hilt, to puncture the brain.

Katal Baruk's head jerked up, twitched, and then began to drop like a stone to the earth. Lishka hung onto the hilt as they fell, her arm slick with hot, black blood. The rocks approached alarmingly fast, and she threw herself free of the beast just before impact. The dragon's head landed against the rock and its body slumped to one side. The wings went slack, and the great creature shuddered once, twice, then stilled. The fire in its uninjured eye flared, then dulled to dark red.

The night went silent, the air cold. Lishka stared at the creature that had lived for more lifetimes than she could count, that might even have been older than the mountain they lay upon. Her hand gripped the sword she had taken with her, turned black now with blood. Katal Baruk had been perhaps as old as the earth itself. And she had killed it.

Fire pierced her body, sharp and all-consuming. Lishka convulsed. For one moment, she thought that Katal Baruk had reawakened, that she had not killed it, and that it now encased her in its white flame.

The dragon lay dark before her. The fire did not heat the air around her, but instead raced along every nerve ending. Her own blood turned against her, freezing to ice in her veins. Imposing his will, Zaral called on the blood he had given her. White burst behind her eyes and the violet at her core withered.

Firm hands gripped her shoulders and lifted her to her feet.

"Come on."

Dominick's voice penetrated the fog in her mind, and she tried to grasp onto his words. He flung her arm over his shoulders and began to run forward, half carrying her. From somewhere in her mind, she remembered his blood on Sieth's sword. She knew she had to help him and so she tried to get her feet under her control. But her limbs would not respond properly. Zaral tried to take control of her, as he had taken control of Katal Baruk.

*No!* The cold threatened to invade her mind and she gritted her teeth, forcing herself to look ahead. She could not let him have her body. She would not allow Zaral to use her as his weapon to destroy Dominick.

The violet flared, just a little. She made her legs move. The top of the ridge turned to rock and dirt, and they dug their fingers into the soil to pull themselves upward. Dominick kept one hand on Lishka and pushed her forward. She scrambled, maintaining partial control over her legs, and in a final surge of effort, crested the ridge.

A basin lay before them, cupped by the jagged ridgeline. The bare rock sloped steeply downward to become scree, which in turn flowed to meet the snow-dusted ground. Hardly any vegetation grew from the rocky base, and only the odd tuft of brown grass poked through rock and snow.

Two figures stood locked together, far below in the basin's center. Lishka blinked away the haze in her mind to focus on the creators of her kind. Zaral and Zachriel gripped each other, their heads almost touching. Their expressions were impossible to see at such a distance and yet Lishka shivered. She imagined those black eyes finding her on the ridgeline. Waves of power emanated from the brothers, rolling up the sides of the ridges and over. Lishka braced herself against the onslaught.

*Both are death.*

Katal Baruk's words echoed through Lishka's mind, drifting in the fog that threatened to overtake her. Death filled the basin below them, a darkness greater even than the one consuming her soul, a despair and hunger that could never be sated.

Her vision flickered. The figures separated and then joined once more together in a clash of energy.

*They are not both evil death.* Zachriel's power was the kiss of death that was welcomed, the slip into a painless, never-ending sleep. Cold yet not evil. Destruction that invited renewal.

A sharp pain pierced her side. Lishka jerked and her head dropped down. Bloodied steel protruded just below her ribs. She stood still, even as her side clenched around the foreign object. Then the white-hot agony ripped through her muscles, a different pain than the fire that encased her veins—the rendering of flesh and not of the soul. Lishka almost welcomed the distraction from the tearing deep at her core.

The steel wrenched back and released her. In a second, she dropped to her knees and Dominick turned to catch her, his eyes wide even as he yelled her name. She saw him rip his gaze from her to stare above her head, and the dark flickered at the edges of her vision.

Sieth stood behind her. His aura had been masked by Zaral's. She tried to grip her sword and turn to him, but her fingers wouldn't quite work, and any movement sent spasms through her torso. The magik in his steel had already begun to undo her flesh. On instinct, she put her left hand against the wound, as if she could hold in her organs and blood.

Sieth raised his sword and Dominick released her to slump the rest of the way to the ground. Coven steel once more met Excalibur. Sieth snarled and Dominick growled, and the two locked blade to blade over Lishka's head.

"She only postponed the inevitable the day she made you," Sieth hissed. "Now I will unmake you."

Lishka heard no response from Dominick. She strained and found herself able to raise her head just an inch to watch them. The symbols burrowed into her skin, preventing any healing. With her own fey power, she could initiate the healing, but she could not spare the attention away from Dominick. She could not let Sieth take the blade.

She could not let Sieth kill Dominick again.

Dominick gripped Excalibur tight and pushed against Sieth to force him back. The ridge curved several feet behind him and there the earth became softer, destabilized. Sieth resisted and dug his feet down into the earth. The side of his face had not fully healed from Lishka's magik. Burned flesh still hung from the remains of charred muscle at the corner of his mouth, drawing his lips into an extended, macabre grin.

They pushed themselves apart. Sieth whipped his sword overhead, a blurred arc bringing the steel down toward Dominick's left shoulder, where it would cleave him in two. Dominick stepped back and at the last second blocked the blow with Excalibur, though both blades came dangerously close to his head.

He wrenched Excalibur's edge down the Coven steel to force Sieth's sword back. The momentum carried the swords down and back up into defensive positions before their owners. Before Lishka could blink, she watched Sieth bring his sword up again and Dominick lean back so the point barely skimmed along his neck, drawing a thin trickle of blood.

Sieth's false grin turned to a real one as copper tinged the air.

Dominick could not win against him—not without help. Sieth had the benefit of thousands of years to craft his skill. Lishka shifted her weight and tried to ignore the pain that lanced through her body. Carefully, she reached down to her right boot to work her second, lesser knife out from the leather. The movement spurred on the flow of blood from her wound, which now dripped down her side and her leg to pool at her feet. Her energy waned. She gritted her teeth and freed the dagger to clutch it in her right hand.

Sieth swept his sword low to Dominick's legs and Dominick again leapt back to avoid the blow. Sieth moved too fast to allow him to take the offensive. He blocked the attack, moving in a blur. But Sieth needed only one opportunity and their mission would fail.

*Bring him closer.*

Lishka tried to will Dominick to push Sieth in her direction. Dominick forward-thrust the blade, forcing Sieth to reflexively step back. Lishka couldn't tell whether Dominick somehow felt her intention, or if pure luck nudged Sieth within her reach. Dominick brought Excalibur up to defend another blow and the sword hummed, reverberating up the Coven blade and into Sieth's arms. Sieth tensed to absorb the shock, shifting again in Lishka's direction to regain his balance.

Lishka lunged forward, her body screaming in pain, and stabbed her knife deep into Sieth's calf, just above his boot.

Sieth stared at Dominick, ignoring Lishka at his feet. But he buckled just an inch on his injured leg. In that moment, Dominick ducked the swing that had gone awry and he plunged Excalibur through Sieth's heart.

Sieth's face froze into a snarl, his pale eyes sharp with hatred. Dominick stared into the face of his murderer, his face set with determination but not malice.

Then Sieth's eyes began to cloud. Excalibur worked

its own magik, and the blow was fatal. Sieth's heart could not heal fast enough to save him. Dominick wrenched Excalibur out and shoved Sieth back. Sieth's sword dropped to his side and he staggered on his feet, the hilt of Lishka's knife still protruding from his leg. The loose rock shifted under him as he reached the edge of the ridge and toppled back out of sight.

A gale whipped up through the basin, churning with anger.

*I will break you.*

The voice crept along the wailing of the wind, soft yet more powerful than the gusts; each word slid through Lishka's mind as though they had always lived there, lurking in the deepest recesses of herself. The ice in her blood incapacitated her, even more than the damage to her torso. She could not move, could barely think. Zaral's presence filled her. He had sensed Sieth's death, and even worse, knew what had killed him.

Dominick bent over her to buffer the wind and her hair flew in streams around them both. He gripped Lishka's shoulders to keep her upright. The touch shocked her. She blinked, trying to focus on him instead.

"Dominick," she whispered, forcing her voice through the pain. He stared into her eyes, his nose almost touching hers. "The sword. Take the sword to Zachriel."

The wind swirled around them, bringing with it Zaral's malice. Yet for one moment it seemed that time stood still and there were only the two of them, alone on the ridge. Even the throbbing pain of her side dulled, the darkness inside making her numb.

"I'm not leaving you. You'll die."

"The sword must go to Zachriel. We have no time."

Dominick growled once more in frustration.

"We made it. He is waiting," Lishka said to urge him on. The blackness filled her vision so that only Dominick remained, and now his face grew hazy.

*Bring it to me.* The voice reverberated within them, firm and commanding, yet this time without malice.

Lishka immediately recognized the voice, both like and so unlike her Maker's. *Zachriel.*

Dominick's jaw clenched. Excalibur hummed beside him, yearning for Zachriel, and Lishka knew that Dominick also desired to bring it to him. Yet he did not move.

Lishka's head dropped, unable to hold herself upright with the last of her energy. She sagged even more so that only Dominick's hands kept her sitting.

"No!" The howl came in anguish on the wind, momentarily disrupting the fog in her mind. Dominick called out in frustration and despair, his emotion in stark contrast to the cold malevolence that surrounded them. He shook her shoulders, sending sharp knives up her side. Lishka almost gasped, but she had no more strength.

Her cheek fell to his chest, and he wrapped his arms around her.

Lishka tried to will him onward as the dark overtook her.

*Go.*

Warmth seeped into her side. It had to be her blood. The thought gave her pause. Yet her immortal blood no longer contained any warmth. The heat expanded from her side up into her chest, encircling her heart, where it flowed outward into her arms and legs, chasing away the ice. The darkness receded from her mind. Vibrant, nourishing energy flowed through her body. The pain dulled at her side as muscle and flesh knitted back together.

Lishka opened her eyes.

Her cheek still rested against Dominick's chest and his arms held her steady. Hundreds of rocks of all sizes hovered in the air around them. Symbols glowed within them. Lishka stared, entranced by their beauty. She could almost see the power flowing from the rocks into Dominick, and then into her, a steady stream akin to going beyond the Veil.

She sat up straighter and the rocks flared, then dimmed, and dropped back to the earth, their energy spent. Dominick opened his eyes and put his hands to her face, holding her for just a second.

"The sword," she said. He nodded and took her hands to pull her to her feet. Her side twinged, but this time it was the feeling of a wound several weeks old; healed but still delicate. The energy had warmed her core, helping to eradicate Zaral's influence although his power still flowed around them.

They ran down the side of the ridge toward the center of the basin. Every instinct screamed at Lishka to turn back, but she kept pace with Dominick. He needed no encouragement now. Excalibur pushed him on, and he could not stop even if he wanted to.

Ahead of them, mirror images of the other, Zachriel and Zaral held each other, fighting with their bodies and their power. Closer now, Lishka realized they did not stand on the ground. They hovered several feet above it and had begun to rise.

They had *wings*.

Great shadowy wings billowed about them, driving down to carry them upward. They gripped each other's arms and looked like one many-limbed beast.

Zaral turned and locked eyes with Lishka. She froze in her tracks. His black eyes seared deep into her core, extinguishing all that made her Lishka.

Dominick faltered ahead, torn between Zachriel and Lishka. She could not move to urge him onward. Zaral's eyes alighted on Dominick. Dominick slowed, though his muscles strained to move forward.

Zaral had exerted his influence over his bloodline— the same blood that flowed in Lishka also flowed in Dominick. She had cursed him.

The veins corded in Dominick's neck; his eyes went bloodshot from the effort to break Zaral's hold. He took one step forward and then another. Lishka felt Zaral within him, seeking to control every cell, just as he controlled her.

*Not every cell.*

The whisper of sunlight, of violets, and of green things tickled her mind. At once, both the fey and the power beyond the Veil surged through her. The link that anchored her to the earth, to the Source, solidified.

Zachriel had unbound her mage's mark.

Dominick jerked with the power that flowed suddenly into his body.

*Now.*

The voice of Zachriel boomed once more in their

minds. Dominick drew Excalibur and before Lishka could react, he arched it over his head and flung it like a spear.

The blade shot forward in a blur to streak toward Zachriel and Zaral. Zaral smiled; he was in front of his brother and would reach the blade first. Lishka's violet fey energy filled her, stronger than it had ever been before, and she stretched out her hands. The fey magik erupted from her like lightning, to gain control of the sword. Using a power Zaral never understood or respected, she guided the blade just past his reach and directed it into Zachriel's waiting, outstretched hand.

# CHAPTER 34

# AN AWAKENING

Zachriel launched into the sky. His right hand held Excalibur as an extension of himself, pointing directly upward as though it, and not the power of his wings, carried him higher. With his left hand, he gripped Zaral tight by his shoulder, and Zaral mutated into a swirling vortex of violence. He clawed at Zachriel, striking him with hands and wings. His efforts were in vain. The sword had fused to Zachriel as the true Wielder. They could not be parted.

Zachriel ignored Zaral's attack and carried his brother even higher. Then Lishka heard him once more in her mind, as clearly as if he stood beside her.

*Brother. The time has come. It is what we were meant to do.*

Zaral twisted in his grip.

*No!*

Zaral's voice contained only hate and hunger. The

sound encapsulated all of Lishka's darkest desires: the urge to feed, to hunt, maim, and kill.

*Remember.*

Zachriel's voice resounded with calm surety. He carried none of the raw power of his brother. His voice rang with the steadiness of a being who understood his purpose.

*Remember the Beginning. Remember why we were sent here. We must return the balance.*

*There is no balance.* Zaral's force shattered the calm. *There is Power.* At the last word, he struck hard against Zachriel, and for an instant Zachriel faltered.

*YOU ARE WRONG.*

Zachriel's words blazed out, pounding at Lishka's temple. His wings wrenched downward in a propulsive burst of power, and they soared to incredible heights. At the last moment when Zaral might have freed himself, Zachriel swept his wings once more and with one hand still holding his brother, he thrust Excalibur into the sky.

The night exploded into brilliant light. The basin lit up brighter than day and everything turned to white. Lishka ducked her head, not quick enough to avoid the flares bursting at the back of her eyes. Energy rippled out to envelop them in a blaze both harsh and comforting. Electricity snapped at each of her cells, threatening to rip her apart and at the same time, filling her with invigorating energy. A low hum pulsed in her ears. She bowed in the rush of the power beyond the Veil, which churned in magnificent currents. Her mage's mark anchored her to the earth and even still, her soul pushed against her flesh, wanting to break free and join its Source.

Then Dominick slid his hand into her own. She squeezed his palm, felt each of his fingers press into the back of her hand. Her soul quieted within her body. They fell to their knees to lean against each other, buffeted by howling wind and the flashes in the sky into which Zachriel and Zaral had disappeared.

At the crescent ridge behind them, those who still fought stopped. Their weapons dropped to their sides in the sudden vacuum left by their Masters. An older power rolled through the air, cool and earthy, and they turned their faces to the North.

The Siernak oozed into their dark shadows, to flee back into hiding. The wolves threw back their heads and howled to the moon, their harmony echoing across the tundra. Farther away, those who had left Dirn shuddered at the sudden energy in the air. They stopped navigating the southern-flowing rivers to stare up at the sky, which undulated in shifting patterns of bursting color.

*"How beautiful are the Northern lights tonight,"* those further down the river would say, all the while knowing in their hearts that this was different.

In the lowlands, the Southerners frowned as their technology died, assuming rolling blackouts to be the cause. All around the world, the people stepped outside to tilt their faces upwards. On the other side of the world, vibrant light streaked across the day sky, outshining even the sun. The people shielded their eyes from the ferocity and stared at each other, in fear and in awe. The air hummed with a power that their minds had forgotten, but their bodies instinctively yearned for. Many bent on their knees and prayed, and called the event the end of things.

Lishka opened her eyes and lifted her head, drawn to the sky. The initial brightness had faded to a beautiful painting of color and light. She rose to her feet, drawing Dominick with her. They entwined their fingers and searched the heavens. No sign of Zaral or Zachriel remained.

Instead, the sky had broken apart and rained down stars.

MORDAN FOUND THEM at the center of the basin. They held hands and stood with their faces lifted to the night sky. He let his footsteps fall more heavily to announce his approach. When he had come within several yards, Lishka turned around and smiled, a tired smile, but true.

She looked different. Mordan studied her familiar face. A leaf rustled in her hair, out of place in the arctic winter. The curve of a vine draped alongside her neck, and beside it, the crimson red of a rose contrasted against her pale skin. Her violet eyes glowed. Mordan blinked and the image disappeared. She became Lishka again.

"The battle is over," he told them. "Zaral's followers felt the loss of him, and fled when they no longer sensed his power. I sense it too, the emptiness."

Lishka frowned and Mordan wondered what she felt. She had forever been plagued with Zaral's influence, forced upon her. Dominick watched Mordan, impassive.

"The world is changed now," Lishka said.

"Yes," Mordan agreed. "For better or worse, the world has awakened to itself. There will be a reckoning."

Lishka glanced at Dominick and her face softened. They seemed as one, utterly connected in a way that even Mordan, in all the centuries he had existed, could not fully comprehend.

"What of the sword?" he asked.

Dominick released Lishka's hand to touch the pommel behind his right ear. The sword once more lay strapped across his back and it seemed to fit there.

"It is all that remains of them," Lishka said, her voice thoughtful. "Dominick found it embedded here." She gestured to a patch of flattened ground nearby.

Mordan cocked an eyebrow.

"It is dead," Dominick said, understanding the implied question. "Whatever power it had was spent on that." He nodded his head upward.

Mordan's eyes lingered on the sword for a moment longer. The sword did not call out to him and yet…

"I must go back to the Council and let them know what happened here," he said. "The world is new again. Rewritten. We must decide what kind of world we will have a hand in making. Humans will be in chaos. Their technology will not have survived the re-emergence of the power beyond the Veil. I expect I will see you both back at the Coven. There will be much to do, to set right."

"Of course," Lishka said.

They all knew she was lying. Mordan turned and walked away from them, back to the ridge and to those of Zachriel who waited at the crescent ridge to begin the journey south.

LISHKA AND DOMINICK watched the wilderness swallow the small figure of Mordan. Assessing herself, Lishka sensed the same absence Mordan had spoken of, like a hole inside her core. She still possessed the darkness of her kind, but somehow it contained less threatening malice. Around them, the energy that exploded into the world had diminished, and now the tingle of magik tickled her skin. The air held an electricity that had not been there before, a softer, diluted version of the currents that had been so long contained behind the Veil.

"What now?" Dominick asked.

Lishka thought about their next steps. She had always expected to return to the Coven, should they survive. Yet now, she could not imagine herself resuming her role as a Keeper, maintaining control over a destabilized city.

"We go north. Into the wild." She surprised herself, even as her blood stirred with the call to the unknown.

Dominick smiled and his brown eyes held hers for a long moment. They turned to the opposite ridge that surrounded the basin in a gentler slope. An hour later they scaled the ridge to survey the tundra sprawled before them, marked with more unexplored ridges and hills. Together they bounded north, away from the Coven, the Council, and the upheaval of civilization behind them. In the far distance, the sunrise glowed on sharp white peaks.

At Dominick's back, Excalibur stirred as if taking a quiet breath in hibernation, allowed to sleep in a world made anew.

I FIRST HAD the idea for *Lishka* when I was nineteen, the same age Lishka was when she became immortal. The journey from conception to the finished novel has been long and challenging, and would not have been possible without the support of many along the way.

The influence of my wonderful parents, John and Kristin, is especially present in *Lishka's* epic landscapes. Our many family camping and hiking trips throughout the North Cascades informed the geography in *Lishka*, and some of our special places can be found in Lishka's world. My dad, an avid mineral collector, inspired Dominick's love of geology, and in fact several of his explanations are used verbatim when Dominick describes geologic observations. My mom provided much-needed subject matter expertise when it came to flora and fauna, helping me to accurately capture our beloved Pacific Northwest.

My husband, Chris, was a constant source of encouragement and he shared in my joy as self-publishing milestones were completed. He remained supportive even when I had to close my office door and post a quippy do-not-disturb sign, and on the (rare) occasions I ignored his calls when the amazing dinners he cooked were ready.

Killian and Cami, those first friends and editors with whom I shared *Lishka* (outside of family), gave me the confidence to publicly celebrate being a writer, after having kept this private for so long. I still cannot find the words to express how impactful their support has been to *Lishka*, and to me as an author. Killian's passion for world-building encouraged me to explore *Lishka's* universe much more thoroughly and create layers of depth in the novel. Cami's magician-like skill with sentences pushed me to continually strive for stronger storytelling. She never let me settle for subpar writing despite my many negotiations, and even (reluctantly) agreed to my use of the Oxford comma.

I have so much appreciation for my fantastic friends and family who read the book and gave me honest feedback, and I also want to give a special shout-out to those who read *Lishka* in its earlier, rougher drafts. Their validation and excellent critical insights all contributed to making this novel the best it could be.

Finally, more than thank you to Kendra, my twin, my soulmate, my first and biggest fan. Her unwavering support and excitement both for this novel, and for sharing Lishka's world with others, motivated me to continue when I felt I had no more energy to give to this story. I have always thought that if Kendra was excited by *Lishka*, then it would be a success. *Lishka* would not exist if not for my other half.

This is our book.

Jaima Lindell was born in Seattle and raised in Ravensdale, Washington, a small town nestled in the foothills of the Cascade Mountains. She attended Western Washington University and earned her BA in English with an emphasis on creative writing. After embarking on an adventure to live in New Zealand, Australia, and Spain, Jaima settled back in her native Pacific Northwest with her husband, Chris, and their ginger cat, Paul.

A project manager by day, Jaima spends her personal time reading other authors' delicious words, writing about fantastical worlds, and exploring the many mountains, forests, and lakes of northern Washington. Jaima's excitement for discovering new books—and revisiting previously loved stories—means she can often be found at the local bookstore, no matter where in the world she is.

*Lishka* is Jaima's debut novel.

jaimalindell.com

@jaimalindell_author

www.ingramcontent.com/pod-product-compliance
Lightning Source LLC
Chambersburg PA
CBHW022009300726
48970CB00003B/815